ONCE UPON A LIE

REBECCA TAYLOR

OPHELIA HOUSE

www.rebeccataylorbooks.com

Sign up for Rebecca's Newsletter

For the girl I used to know

CHAPTER 1

*M*ia scanned the ten-foot hedge surrounding her yard. It was overgrown, with errant shoots of new branches breaking free from the trimmed straight edges on every side. It was thick, impenetrable—or so she'd been told. It would be impossible for someone to hide on the other side, watching her, staring at her. Alexander, her husband, had assured her and even led her by the hand to the other side to show her and prove it to her. She had looked for herself, and she believed him.

And still, she felt eyes all over her body.

Mia pushed the distressing thoughts from her mind and watched her twin girls, a month away from their sixth birthday, clasp hands and leap in unison into the deep end of their backyard pool. Their short brown hair was wet and plastered flat against their heads.

Their classmate and guest, Caleb, watched from his perch at the pool's edge. His thin arms threaded through the flotation pillows his mother had blown up and attached to him

1

earlier. For the last half-hour, Caleb had teetered on the brink of having fun. But no matter how much the girls harangued him, he continued to sit with only his feet dangling below the surface.

"Caleb!" His mother called from the rattan lounger beside Mia's. "Just jump in! The floaties!" She pointed to her own arms. "They'll keep you up!"

Caleb said nothing and gave his mother a skeptical look before ignoring her advice and settling for watching Sasha and Everly have all the fun.

With a sigh, his mother gave up. "He did the same thing at every single one of his swim lessons all summer. I swear, the minute I tell him it's time to leave, he'll decide he's ready to play."

Mia gave Dominique a sympathetic smile, picked up the half-empty bottle of chardonnay between them, and offered to refill Dominique's glass.

"I shouldn't," Dominique said as she held out her glass and smiled. "But I will anyway."

Mia poured, smiled, and hoped her hostess act was a good camouflage for the interior storm gathering inside her. The last thing she wanted was for Dominique Richards, PTA president and most influential parent at Beacon Hill Private Academy, to suspect something was wrong with Mia Strauss. She should say something, she realized. Something off-the-cuff, relaxed, witty—anything other than this incessant nodding and smiling. Instead, Mia reached for a lock of her waist-length, jet-black hair and drew it like a curtain over the eight-inch scar that ran down the right side of her face.

Her nervous, unshakable habit.

Dominique had obviously seen this broadcast of insecurity. But like most people, she was polite enough to pretend she never noticed Mia's facial disfigurement. Dominique turned away and centered her line of sight on their children laughing in the pool.

"Do you mind watching my girls for a minute?" Mia asked. "I'm just going to use the restroom."

Dominique faced Mia again with her very white, perfectly straight smile. "Of course." She swiped her hand through the air. It's *nothing.* "Maybe I'll slide into the pool myself and see if I can lure my son in."

"Thank you," Mia said, sounding too grateful. *God, she was terrible at socializing, speaking, and acting like a human.* Without another word—that could only make this situation even more awkward—Mia slipped her legs over the edge of her lounger, stood up, and forced herself to walk normally, not flee, to the backdoor of her house.

Once inside, with the door closed and protecting her from further scrutiny, Mia fell back against it and covered her face with her hands. Her original plan had been to get to know Dominique and establish some sort of normal, school-based relationships for Sasha and Everly. Then pull off a real birthday party, with friends from school, next month. And even though she dreaded doing any of this, Mia cared enough about her girls to make an effort and pull her shit together. But they were only an hour into the playdate, and Mia felt that she was already rattling apart from the effort. Inviting Dominique and her son here for the afternoon was a terrible idea. Mia now wished she'd never even considered it.

She dropped her hands, took a breath, and stood up straight. "Well, it's too late for that now," she whispered. It's not like she could hide in the house for the rest of the day while Dominique watched the kids alone.

Could she?

Mia shook her head at the stupidity of the thought. "Of course not," she muttered. Jesus, consider how much worse it would look—and what Dominique might tell the other parents—if Mia just didn't reappear.

She gave her arms a violent shake, squared her shoulders, and headed for the stairs. She could do this. She would do this. She just needed a little more help.

Mia realized one of the biggest problems was the shirt she had forced herself to wear. Which now, in hindsight, seemed obvious—the short sleeves exposed her arms. Earlier, before Dominique and Caleb had arrived, Mia had stood at the center of the walk-in closet she and Alexander shared and decided to forgo the safety of one of her typical long-sleeves— she feared Dominique would find it strange to see her covered from head to toe while they lounged by the pool in eighty-degree heat. She had paired her most drapey black linen pants with one of the few short sleeve blouses still remaining in her wardrobe.

But from the moment she had slipped it over her head, it had felt like a mistake. The loose sleeves stopped short right above her elbow, exposing her forearm and hands. Once she reached the safety of her bedroom, Mia pulled the shirt up over her head and dropped it into the trash can beside her dresser. She pulled one of her Anthony Thomas Melillo mock turtlenecks from her middle drawer. She threaded her arms into the extra-long sleeves before lifting it over her head and smoothing the familiar fabric into place along her long torso.

Mia held her neck between her two cupped hands, closed

her eyes, and waited for relief. She could feel every pulse of her rapid heartbeat course through the jugulars beneath her palms. But with every second that passed, and deep breath Mia took, the pressure and intensity thrumming through her body ebbed, and she was able to drop her hands.

Crisis averted.

She pulled the extra-long sleeves over each of her hands to the base of her long, delicate fingers, then turned and headed for the drawer in her bathroom where she kept her meds. When she pressed and twisted the safety cap off and into her palm, she saw only three pills at the bottom of the brown plastic bottle.

She checked the date on the label—it had only been a week since she'd had it refilled. This worried her for several reasons. For starters, if her husband, Alexander, found out how quickly she'd run through these, she would have a problem. Secondly, she dreaded having to try and convince her doctor to refill it again—because what if she refused? But by far, her biggest concern was that she'd need to ration these last pills while also knowing she would need all three of them before this day had finished.

Mia placed one pill on her tongue and swallowed it dry as she slipped the other two into the front pocket of her linen pants.

She'd left Dominique alone for too long, beyond what might be considered normal or polite for a guest she hardly knew. But before she headed back downstairs, she needed to ensure she looked okay. Mia hurried back into their walk-in closet and opened the bottom drawer of the center island, where she kept several of her essential accessories. She grabbed her selfie stick, mounted her cell phone into the holder, and extended the arm before snapping several full-length photos of herself from various angles.

After checking each photo and feeling satisfied her appearance was appropriate, she returned the stick to the drawer, tucked the hair on the left side of her face behind her ear, and deleted each photo from her phone as she headed for the stairs. Undoubtedly, Dominique would think Mia's behavior today was a little weird. Still, Mia felt sure she could turn the rest of the visit around and leave the PTA president with a more favorable overall impression before she and Caleb left for the day.

When she was halfway down the staircase, Mia heard Sasha and Everly's voices. She stopped, realized that everyone must now be inside, and hoped she would still have the opportunity to show Dominique that she was a good and normal mother. That her girls were good and normal girls. And that coming here along with their entire kindergarten class of kids and parents for Sasha and Everly's sixth birthday party was something Dominique would definitely want to do.

Mia picked up her pace and descended the stairs.

As she passed through the foyer at the bottom of the stairs, she remembered to smile as she passed under the archway and into the portrait room. "I'm so sorry about that, and I hope you don't think I'm incredibly rude for leaving you all alone with the kids while I changed," she kept her tone breezy and light. She could see all three kids sitting at the large kitchen island down the hall, each wrapped in a plush bath sheet and snacking on the bowl of cut fruit Mia had taken outside for them earlier.

Dominique stood in the portrait room, her back to Mia, her gaze fixed upward on the oil painting of Mia's father that hung above the fireplace. When Mia first spoke, Dominique glanced back to acknowledge her, but she didn't appear to register what had been said.

"This is really him?" Dominique asked.

Mia stopped short at the unexpected question. "Yes," she whispered and raised her eyes to meet those of her long-dead father, Raphael Renaud. "It's really him."

CHAPTER 2

"*A*mazing," Dominique said as she tilted her head left, then right. "It's um...a *unique* composition. Almost as if...well, he was such a handsome man in real life. And this.... It almost reminds me of a caricature. The way it exaggerates his most unflattering features. But they do that, don't they? These grotesque pictures of very famous people. It's so interesting because I feel like I'm looking at a different version of him. And yet, the work is so striking but also off-putting." Dominique leaned in to examine the artist's signature. "Who is the artist?" she asked as she turned back to face Mia.

Mia stared up at the portrait. "We don't know. I took this from my childhood home several years ago, and I didn't even think to ask who the artist was. We were trying to include it under our insurance policy earlier this summer, but without any history or even knowing who the artist was...." Mia shrugged. "They told us it was impossible to estimate a value without more information."

"You should take it to some of the dealers in the city," Dominique suggested. "I bet they could help you figure it out."

Mia nodded. "I've thought about it. It's just one of those things you never actually get around to taking care of, I guess."

"I can't even begin to imagine what it must have *been* like for you. Growing up? I mean, the stories you must have." Dominique smiled wide at this—an open invitation for Mia to tell her a story, any story about a childhood spent growing up as the daughter of arguably the most famous film director in the entire world, Raphael Renaud.

Mia opened her mouth to respond but realized that even after all these years, she still didn't have a straightforward and easy way to convey the inevitable information that must come next. Or if it was even something she wanted to share with this woman she barely knew.

Dominique watched her, her eyes wide with a hungry expectation, and waited for Mia's reply.

Maybe this was why she avoided getting to know new people, this need to constantly explain her past. Because there wasn't any way to have relationships with other people without them learning, almost immediately, about the singularly most tragic event of her life.

It was all because of him. Raphael Renaud. If her father had been nobody special to anyone else, she would likely avoid these questions for as long as she pleased.

No one would ever have to know unless she chose to tell them.

But her father wasn't a nobody; he was one of the biggest somebodies of his generation. And the public's continuing love and admiration of him and his extensive body of work meant that Mia never got to avoid her past.

Because her past was always the one topic everyone most wanted to hear her talk about.

"The truth is," Mia said. "I don't remember a thing about him."

Dominique furrowed her brow and pulled her head back in surprise. "What do you mean?"

Mia glanced over her shoulder and checked that the kids were still too occupied with their own chatter and snacks to pay attention to her and Dominique. When she turned back, she could see that Dominique looked confused.

Mia inhaled once, then reached for the sheet of her jet-black hair on the right side of her head and swept it back and over her shoulder to keep it out of the way. With her slender index finger, Mia pointed to the place on her forehead where her scar began and traced its path down her face. "You already know how my father died?" Mia asked, knowing the answer was *yes*. The entire planet knew about Raphael Renaud's tragic and untimely death.

Dominique nodded.

Mia drew in another breath and continued. "Well, what is less well known is that I was there when he was killed."

"Oh god, Mia."

Mia held her palms up. "But like I said, I don't remember a thing about him. Not anything from that night either. Everything I know is what I've been told or read, but there isn't anything I know just from my own experience. Apparently, I walked in right after the intruder shot my father."

Dominique opened her mouth, decided against whatever she was going to say, then changed her mind again and asked.

"I'm sorry, and I know this isn't any of my business, and you can tell me to go to hell if you want, but—"

"He pushed me," Mia said. From our third-floor landing, over the banister, and headfirst onto the marble floor below."

"Jesus Christ."

"I should have died, and I was very near death for months after. There were years of surgeries, painful rehabilitations... therapy." Mia sighed. "And on many fronts, I've made tremendous progress."

"I think that's an understatement."

"Thank you. But when it comes to my memory...there just isn't anything before my early conscious days in the hospital after the accident. If it weren't for my sister, photographs, articles about my father and our lives, well, the public part of our lives anyway...I wouldn't have any sense of who I once was or where I came from."

Dominique looked shocked. She shook her head twice, then looked back at the portrait. "I'm so sorry, Mia. What a horrifying thing for your family to endure...and it was never solved? Is it still a cold case?"

"Yes. My mother and sister were able to give a description of the man. But he was never found."

"He's still out there," Dominique blurted. It was the same thought that ran through Mia's head every day.

"Yes."

"Doesn't that scare you?" Dominique asked, but then seemed to realize how invasive she was being. "I'm sorry. I guess I don't know what to say," she confessed.

"If it's any consolation, I'm not sure anyone else ever does either."

"You don't know me, I get that, but please know I would never repeat—"

"No," Mia shook her head. "I know you wouldn't," she lied. She expected Dominique would share the details with her friends as soon as she left. But Mia couldn't worry about that now; she needed to get through the rest of this visit. If Dominique felt overwhelmingly sorry for Mia, that may be for the best. "Of course, you wouldn't. Can I get you something to drink? More wine?"

Dominique checked her phone. "It's nearly five," she said. "And I do need to get home and get dinner started...but I could probably stay for one more glass."

"Perfect." Mia forced a smile. "I'll go grab another bottle from the cellar."

A quarter after six, Mia finally said goodbye to Dominique and Caleb and closed the front door. The relief of having them out of her house was immediate. It wasn't that she didn't like them, not at all. She felt the same way about having anyone over to the house—Mia found socializing exhausting. It didn't matter if it was one of Alexander's, far too many, New York dinner parties or this fellow mother from Sasha and Everly's class.

If she should ever be allowed to do what she pleased when she pleased, Mia might not ever speak to anyone beyond her own immediate family ever again.

She realized this put her twin girls at an incredible social disadvantage.

Both were curled next to each other on the family room couch, ten minutes into their hundredth viewing of *Beauty and the Beast*, with a bowl of popcorn between them. Despite the girls' ability to quote the movie from beginning to end,

Mia knew neither one would move more than an inch for the next hour and a half.

Mia slid her last and final pill from her pocket and into her mouth as she turned to collect her and Dominique's dirty wine glasses from the portrait room. But when she stood over the coffee table, she realized that, even though the 2012 Silver Oak cabernet bottle was empty, Dominique's glass was still full.

Mia lifted the glass to eye level and could plainly see there was not a single mark on the glass. Not a smudged fingerprint, not even a hint of Dominique's plum lip balm. Dominique had sat here, talking to Mia for over an hour, without taking a single sip of wine.

Mia placed the glass back on the table and lowered herself onto the pale blue couch. She had drunk the entire bottle herself? How had she not noticed that Dominique was completely ignoring her own glass?

Her mind spun, trying to recapture the events, the conversation, from the last hour. But it was a blurry film, overlaid and distorted by the drinking and her meds. What had they talked about?

Her eyes drifted to the portrait of her father hanging above her, and that's when she knew—they had talked about him. She didn't remember exactly, but Mia had a broad stroke of Dominique's questioning and then her own acquiescence.

Mia leaned forward, plucked Dominique's glass from the table, and raised it to her lips. What had she said? What had she revealed about herself and her family? She took a large swallow, stood up, and walked several unsteady steps toward the fireplace beneath the portrait.

With her free hand, Mia steadied herself by grasping the ornately carved white oak mantle. Then, she reached for one of the silver-framed pictures among the many on display.

Most of the photos were of the girls, she and Alexander, and their family vacations. There was also Mia, and Alexander posed on their wedding day in the Hamptons. But this photo, this photo was grainy and old. Mia tried to make her eyes focus on the subjects, the four people standing in their early 90s summer clothes at the center of the lush, green lawns of their gold coast home, Beaumar Manor.

The combination of wine and medication made it impossible to focus, and time had drained all the life and color from this photo but this was her family. Not the one she'd created with Alexander, the one she'd been born into. Her father, Raphael, her mother, Pixlie, and her older sister Holly. Years before a man broke into their home and changed their lives forever. A man who was never found and never held accountable. A man who could be anywhere.

Be anyone.

What if he was watching her?

Mia managed to avoid answering Dominque's question. *Did it scare her?*

The answer was yes. It scared her. Every minute of every day.

Mia closed her eyes to stop the room from spinning.

She needed to call her sister.

CHAPTER 3

*A*lexander untethered his MacBook from the projection cables and slid it into the padded sleeve of his computer bag. His class of Columbia University neuropsychology graduate students, were collecting their own things, talking, and filing past him on their way out the door. He kept his gaze focused on his hands, his bag, the work of leaving this room as quickly as possible before he was cornered by one of them and forced, out of politeness and professorial duty, to indulge their questions, comments, or otherwise banal blathering meant to accomplish nothing more than single themselves out from the herd of other students. They were special. They were *engaged* with their education. They were making sure to follow the brochure's advice to *get to know your professors*. They believed the university marketing material that had ensured them that *Columbia professors care about you, not only as a student but as a person.*

They always thought this especially true of Alexander because he was a doctor of neuropsychology and assumed this made him more approachable than their other professors—therapeutic even. But for Alexander Strauss, nothing could be further from the truth. Sit down. Listen to what I'm teaching you. Do the work. Now leave my class as quickly as you can. He was a doctor of neuropsychology, a practitioner, a scientist, *not* a therapist.

And this day, in particular, the additional post-class conversation was neither desired nor encouraged. He was looking forward to having an hour to spend sipping one, probably two, Macallan on the rocks at Marley's polished mahogany bar before he boarded the train that would carry him home and out of the city. He had rambunctious five-year-old twin girls and a wife who seemed to be spiraling into personal chaos. He was going to need some liquid fortitude before walking in his door.

"Doctor Strauss?" a woman's high and tenuous voice interrupted his packing. Even before he turned to face her, he knew she was nervous about approaching him from the insecure pitch of her question.

He cleared his throat to hide his annoyance, but his response was clipped, "Yes." He closed his bag and slipped the wide crossbody strap over his head. When he turned, he saw that she was young, early twenties, with long brown hair tied in a low ponytail. Her brown eyes held a question for him, but he could also see that he'd been right—she was nervous, maybe even a little afraid.

Her expression made him feel like an ass, so he dropped his shoulders a few inches and remedied his tone. "How can I help you?"

For a moment, she only stood there, staring at him with those huge, beautiful eyes. Alexander forced a smile, hoping it would help reset the interaction. Yes, he felt the stress with his teaching workload, research, and everything that seemed to be happening with Mia. But the last thing he needed was for one of his students to feel like he was not supportive. Or, much worse, discriminatory.

She opened her mouth and was about to speak, but then a look of concern stalled her attempt.

Alexander looked over her head, there were still a few other students left in the room, but they were heading for the door. He didn't want to be alone in the room with one of his young female students.

Jesus, even the suspicion of impropriety was the last thing he needed right now.

"Is there anything..." he tilted his head, trying to be *approachable. Caring. Concerned* for her wellbeing while not counting the minutes he was losing with his planned scotch.

"Doctor Strauss," she announced. Suddenly finding her voice, she appeared determined to state her purpose. "I'm Tasha Adams." She thrust out her small hand.

Alexander noticed how delicate her fingers were as he took her hand in his own for two shakes before dropping it promptly. Tasha Adams was young and beautiful. And he wished she would hurry and get to her point because the last of the other students were now walking out the door.

"What can I do for you, Tasha?" he said in his best dad's voice while inclining his head toward the door. "How about we walk and talk?" Yes, let's walk right out of this deserted classroom into the open spaces for everyone to witness their conversation.

Alexander felt he couldn't ever be too careful when it

came to appearances. As he headed toward the door, Tasha fell into step beside him.

"I'm in your class," she stated.

"Yes," he forced a smile. "I gathered."

A look of relief softened her expression. "Well, I was wondering—" She stopped short as she turned and reached into her own bag. "If you would consider signing this for me?"

When she handed him a book, he stopped walking. It was a copy of his book, *Somebody She Used to Know: Amnesia and the Journey Forward.* He couldn't help the genuine and delighted smile that spread across his face. "Well, this is a surprise."

"Really?" she asked, turning again to her bag. She pulled out a pen and handed it to him. "It was so good. I figured you must get asked all the time."

With the hardcover cradled against his forearm, he flipped open to the title page and clicked the pen. "Yes...five years ago during the book tour? Thousands of requests to sign it." He scribbled his name across the page and closed the book. "But these days? *And* by a student who's already loaded up with all my other assigned readings? No." He handed the book back to her and gave her a genuine smile. The unexpected encounter with a young fan had buoyed his spirits.

"Thank you," she said and held the book in her hands for several seconds before returning it to her bag.

"You are more than welcome," he said as he pushed open and held the door that led outside.

Tasha nodded her head in thanks for the courtesy and slipped past him. This close to her, it was impossible to ignore the intoxicating waft of her scent. And whether it was simply her or an elixir of the shampoo, soap, and perfume she used, the result was a lush, fresh aroma. A walk in the woods while holding hands.

Alexander swallowed the feeling down and followed her out the door. "Well, Ms. Tasha Adams," he said, sounding excruciating and lame even to himself. "It was a pleasure to meet you. I'll see you in class."

She nodded and dropped her eyes to the ground.

He waited for several seconds. Was she going to say good-bye? Should he walk away now? It seemed weird to leave without her saying anything but equally odd, *more so*, to stand here staring at her, saying nothing.

"Okay then," he said as he adjusted his shoulder strap. "Bye." He raised his hand and started to leave.

"Doctor Strauss?" She raised her eyes to meet his.

"Yes?"

She bit her bottom lip, hesitating, then mustered her courage. "I was wondering. Well, your book. It would be an understatement to say it's been influential for me. I might go so far as to say it's actually changed my life."

With a wide-eyed surprise, Alexander rocked back on his heels. "That's quite a compliment." Her admission took him by surprise. It had happened a few times while touring with this book. Readers would lean in awkwardly while he signed their book and gush about how his work had impacted them profoundly. He never knew quite how to respond. *Thank you? I'm so happy you enjoyed it?* Reserved platitudes that never matched the reader's fervent declarations—and then they would take their book and be gone. His words had *changed their life*, and yet he would never see or hear from them again.

But Tasha Adams was in his class. She was beautiful and smelled like youth.

"Thank you," he said.

Tasha took a breath. "I was wondering." She shrugged one shoulder. "I know you are very busy, but...would it be possible for me to buy you a cup of coffee sometime? I...well, I have so many questions about your book and your work. Getting to study with you is one of the biggest reasons I came to Columbia."

Alexander took a beat to digest her question, and this other adulation directed his way. "I'm flattered," he blurted. "And yes." It was his turn to lower his eyes to the ground. "Coffee would be great...good." He shook his head, looked into her eyes again, and tried to smile casually. "But I insist, my treat."

Her expression lit up. "Wonderful. Is tomorrow too soon?"

CHAPTER 4

*a*s his train neared his home station, Alexander closed the book he was reading on his phone and opened his contacts to Tasha's phone number and personal email address. They had exchanged information before finally parting ways and agreed to meet during his office hours in the morning. She would text him tomorrow with a few coffee shop options.

Alexander closed the app, slid his phone into his bag, and rested his head back against the seat as the train slowed its approach. From the moment he'd walked away from her, he'd been aware of the knot of nervous energy that had taken up space in his gut. He closed his eyes to the rush of scenery flying past his window that was doing nothing to help quiet his feelings of dread.

But why did he feel this way? And what was this feeling exactly? She was a student who had enjoyed his book and was interested in his specialized field of research. So what? Many others over the years had expressed similar enthusiasm and the wish to position themselves for research assistant positions. Not once had the prospect of coffee with a student filled him with anticipatory angst.

She was *very* beautiful.

But he'd had other beautiful women in his class and always done his best to pretend, believably or not, that he never noticed.

She said his book *changed her life*.

He opened his eyes and watched the platform move beyond his window as the train crawled to a stop. Was that it, then? The intoxication of female beauty coupled with her admiration? An irresistible potion for any man, sure. Especially one rapidly approaching middle age.

Jesus. Alexander scoffed at himself and shook his head at his own stupidity. Apparently, even a doctorate in psychology couldn't wholly save a man from some of the most stereotypical leanings of his gender. It was embarrassing, now, to think he had even vaguely imagined Tasha may have had, perhaps subconscious, personal interests in him that were not purely professional.

As the train came to a stop, he shouldered his bag off the seat next to him and stood up. Thankful to have come to his senses long before his coffee appointment with her tomorrow.

She was a student.

His student.

Full stop.

By the time he pulled his Mercedes into his garage, he had nearly succeeded in pushing Tasha Adams, however lovely she had smelled, from his thoughts.

A forty-one-year-old man's fantasy watered with the not

one, not two, but the three Macallans he'd indulged himself while sitting at Murphy's.

He looked through his windshield to the door leading from the garage into the house. He was late; the clock on his dash read quarter after eight. Long past when Mia and the girls would have sat down to dinner. Sasha and Everly were probably already bathed and in pajamas, begging Mia to read them just one more story before bed.

The thought made him feel equal parts guilty and relieved. He loved his girls and Mia, but the day-to-day requirements of family life were exhausting. And tedious.

The sheer repetition of children's books, children's games, children's movies and television, and children's toys every-where. The constant thundering feet, fights, tears, and refusals to eat. It had never occurred to him, and it seemed no one ever spoke about how mind-numbing parenthood could be. How embarrassingly pedestrian.

Before having children, he had always envisioned them as older, more self-reliant. Able to hold inquisitive, intelligent conversations and, if games must be played, it was chess—not Candyland.

In truth, he adored both his girls, but he was looking forward to one day sitting down to dinner with them in full control of their emotions and faculties. Considering they were only beginning kindergarten this year; Alexander realized those days were far into the future for him.

He sat for one more moment, surrounded by the very adult luxury and peace of his car, then grabbed his bag and steadied himself for however angry Mia might be that he'd left her to handle the girls alone for the night.

When he opened the door to the mudroom, he expected

the first floor to be dark and deserted. Mia would be upstairs with the girls in their bedroom, running through all their usual avoidance tactics for going to sleep.

Instead, the lights in the family room were on, and he could hear sounds coming from the kitchen down the hall. The girls' voices, dishes, and pans clanging against the marble countertops, the sound of silverware hitting the hardwood floor.

Confused, Alexander let his bag slide down his arm and to the floor in the living room as he made his way to investigate the commotion. "Mia?" he called out, listening for her voice. When he didn't hear a response, he tried, "Hello? I'm home!" The rest of the house was dark, and only the kitchen ahead of him was illuminated. "Girls?"

"Daddy?" Sasha called back, her tiny voice echoing through the main floor. Something seemed wrong; he picked up his pace toward the kitchen. "Yes," he answered back. "What is going on? Why are you girls still up? He could hear both Sasha and Everly talking rapidly to each other, but their voices were low and hard to make out.

"Mia!" he tried again, but there was still no response.

He jogged the last twenty feet into the kitchen and stopped short in surprise. The scene he saw before him made him shout, "What are you doing?"

Startled, both girls snatched their hands back to their sides. They were standing on dining chairs dragged from the table and positioned in front of the stove. With one quick scan, Alexander took in the chaos of their kitchen: a large pot of water was boiling over, a package of elbow noodles was spilled across the floor, plates, bowls, silverware, a carton of milk, a block of cheese. His two girls, in very big aprons, standing on two chairs, had orchestrated the unsupervised mess.

Without waiting for a response, he swooped in, picked up both girls around their waists, lifted them away from the hot surface, and placed them on the floor near the fridge. He then moved the pot from the burner and turned it off.

Alexander squatted in front of the girls, so he was at eye level and took their clasped hands into his own. "What on earth are you doing?" he asked, his voice more concerned now that he'd had a moment to wrap his head around his shock. "Where is mom?"

The girls started talking at the same time.

"She's sleeping," Everly said.

"And we were hungry," Sasha added.

"What? Sleeping?" Alexander asked and shook his head. "Didn't you have dinner?"

Both girls shook their heads.

"Where is mommy? In bed?"

They shook their heads again. "She's on the floor," Sasha said.

"In the portrait room," Everly added.

Alexander looked Sasha in the eye as he processed their words. "What? She..." He stood up. A slick swell of fear washed through him and made him run from the kitchen. "Mia!" his voice, loud and panicked, thundered through the too-quiet house. "Mia!" His leather-soled shoes skid from beneath him as he took the corner from the hall and into the portrait room. "Mia!" his eyes scanned the dark room until he saw her face down on the carpet next to the coffee table.

"Oh, my god." He rushed to her, turned her body over, and lifted her head and torso into his arms. "Mia." He grabbed her cheeks between his thumb and fingers and shook her head from side to side. "Mia!" he shouted into her face.

Jesus Christ, was she breathing? What happened? What should he do? "Mia!" he tried again, his voice breaking. *Call 911*. Where was his phone?

He was moving her too much; he couldn't tell if she was breathing. He needed to calm down. In high school, a million years ago, he'd been trained in CPR that summer he'd worked as a lifeguard at the neighborhood pool. He gently lowered her back to the carpet, leaned his ear close to her mouth, and watched her chest closely for any movement.

It was hard to see, all the lights were off, but he thought maybe, he felt her breath on his cheek. A warmth? Maybe? "Mia, please," he whispered. "Please, please. I don't remember how to give CPR."

He heard a small sob and looked up to find Sasha and Everly standing shoulder to shoulder next to the couch. Everly had tears running down her cheeks while Sasha stood stoically with her arm around her sister.

"Girls, we need to call an ambulance. Can you go see if I left my phone in the kitchen?"

Sasha reached out her hand to him. She was already holding his cell.

CHAPTER 5

*H*olly had just gotten into bed and was only a few paragraphs into her book when her phone buzzed on her night table.

"That must be your boyfriend texting to say goodnight," Harris, her husband, joked as he turned the page of his own book.

"Funny," Holly said, as she laid her book on the bed and grabbed her phone.

It was a text from Alexander.

At the hospital with Mia. She's going to be okay, but can you meet us here?

Holly took a sharp inhale and replied. *What happened?*

Bad medication/alcohol combo. I could really use your help with the girls.

Which hospital?

Saint Anthony

On my way.

"What's going on?" Harris asked.

Holly pressed her phone against her thigh and looked into his worried eyes. "It's Mia. She's in the hospital. Something about mixing her medication with drinking. Alexander is asking if I can come help him with the girls."

Holly watched as his worried expression shifted to annoyance, the crease between his bushy eyebrows deepening. He shook his head and returned his eyes to his book.

"She's my *sister*," Holly said.

"Who needs professional help," Harris said, placing his book down. "She's getting worse. Every time I see her, it's something else. And now look." He reached across the handmade quilt covering them both and took her hand. "She OD'd."

Holly shook her head. "She didn't... that's not what he said. It was just the combination of her meds with drinking."

Harris sighed loudly, squeezed her hand, then pulled her close to him until Holly was nestled against him, and she could feel his mid-length beard resting on top of her dyed white, pixie-cut hair. Harris was a large, burly guy. With his bushy brown hair, beard, and elaborate tattooed artwork covering both his arms, he looked intimidating, like a Viking, and probably an odd match next to Holly's spindly frame. She met him ten years ago when she wandered into his tattoo shop to get her first ink. By the time he gave her her third six months later, Harris had worked up enough courage to ask her on a date. They had been inseparable ever since.

But under his gruff exterior, he was a soft, sensitive soul. She knew it wasn't that he didn't care about Mia. He was just more worried about his wife. "So, you're going then?"

Holly tilted her head upward and looked into his pale blue eyes. "Of course, I'm going," she said. "She's my sister."

"So? Does that mean you're obligated to go running every time she falls off the rails?"

"You wouldn't understand. You barely ever speak to your brothers."

"That's because they are both Wallstreet pricks with their greedy heads shoved up their twenty-four-carat assholes. Just because you are delivered into this world saddled with the misfortune of being related to dicks doesn't mean you're required to like them...or even pretend to. As far as I'm concerned, you're all the family I need."

Holly patted his protruding belly, kissed his cheek, and sat upright. "Well, maybe you and I feel differently about what the concept of family means. It's not been easy for Mia. After her accident, she needed me. And now there's Everly and Sasha... it's a rough patch right now."

At the mention of Everly and Sasha, Harris sighed, and his expression softened into resignation. "Fine, you win. Do you want me to come?"

She smiled at him and shook her head. "No. If it takes all night, I'd rather you be here to feed all the animals in the morning."

As if on cue, Ralph, one of their rescued great Danes, popped his head over the side of the bed and looked at them with baleful eyes. Ralph was one of twelve dogs Holly and Harris were fostering on their twenty-acre property.

"Don't look at me," Harris said to Ralph. "I don't want her to go either."

Holly reached over and ran her small hand down Ralph's soft long face. "Don't worry," she said. "He won't forget to feed you."

"I wouldn't dare," Harris said, picking his book back up.

"Or you'd come home to discover they'd all conspired and were feasting on me."

Holly scooted to the edge of the bed and swung her legs over the side. "And don't forget Sophie's antibiotics."

"I won't."

"And Chester needs—"

"The heating pad on his back left haunch," he finished her sentence without taking his eyes off his book.

"Set to low," she added, changing from her pajamas into her most comfortable jeans and a tee shirt.

"Set to low."

Ralph pushed his big nose under her hand, insisting on some love. She crouched down in front of him and nuzzled the side of his face. "I'll be back soon," she promised and stood up to leave.

"Call me when you get there," Harris said. "I'll come if you need me."

Holly smiled. "I will, and I'm sure everything will be fine," she said out loud. But privately, she worried all her carefully crafted lies could collapse beneath her at any moment.

CHAPTER 6

hen Holly entered Mia's hospital room, the sight of her sister's ashen complexion and thin, gaunt features made her stop short. Alexander was sitting in a yellow, taut pleather armchair in the corner, with both girls looking uncomfortable and crowded as they tried to sleep on his lap. When he turned his head to see her, she could see the exhaustion and worry weighing on him.

Unsure if she should speak and risk waking Mia and the girls, Holly raised a silent hand in greeting.

Alexander stood with the girls and turned, trying to reposition Sasha and Everly back into the uncomfortable chair. He joined her at the door and motioned for her to follow him into the hall. He closed the door most of the way, leaving a crack so he could keep an eye on them.

"Thank you for coming," he said.

Holly nodded. "Is she going to be okay?"

Alexander closed his eyes and nodded. "Yes. But they want to keep her overnight for observation. Can you take the girls home and put them to bed? I'll stay here a few more hours just in case she wakes up."

Holly nodded again. "Of course."

"Thank you, I'll help carry them out to your car," he said and headed back into the room.

Holly followed, and after Alexander picked up Everly, she bent low and gathered Sasha's sleep-heavy body into her own arms. She had so many questions. It had only been two weeks since she'd last seen her sister, but she looked like she'd dropped twenty pounds. What happened? Why did Mia look so terrible? What drugs was she taking, and how long had she been taking them? Two weeks ago, they had been drinking coffee at Mia's kitchen island and discussing the girls' upcoming sixth birthday party. What had changed since then?

Or what had Holly not seen then?

All these thoughts raced through her mind as she followed Alexander through Saint Anthony's brightly lit hallways to the elevators, but Holly didn't think Alexander was up to being interrogated.

She unlocked the doors when they reached her pickup truck in the parking lot, and they loaded the girls into the backseat. They both immediately lay down and curled up, the tops of their heads meeting in the middle of the bench seat.

"Should we get their booster seats?" Holly wondered aloud.

Alexander sighed and seemed to weigh the effort of pulling them from his own car against the potential danger of letting child car safety slip a little—just this once. "It's only a few miles," he said. Let's just buckle them in."

Holly nodded and began threading the belt the best she could around Sasha's horizontal body, remembering that she and Mia had spent most of their childhood tumbling seatbelt free in the back of their mother's white Bentley. Once they closed the back doors, Alexander walked around the truck to where Holly stood next to the driver's side door.

"Thank you again," he said, checking his watch. "I'll be a few more hours...midnight at the latest. He closed his eyes and shook his head. "I'm supposed to teach a class in the morning," he added absently. It was both a realization and a reminder to himself.

Holly watched her brother-in-law heave a big sigh and wondered if she should give him a hug. Or at least some words of reassurance and support. Alexander stood, looking uncomfortable, with his hands shoved into the front pockets of his pants—she had never before hugged her sister's husband. Not the day he and Mia announced their engagement, not the day they got married, and not the day the girls were born. Alexander was a stiff, formal, and unfamiliar sort of man that kept an emotional distance. His body language had never invited her close enough to get within hugging distance.

And that was *before* he wrote his book, for his own selfish reasons, that exposed Mia and their whole family. It had been several years since Holly's heated accusations about his book, but the scars remained.

Tonight was no different.

"Okay then," she said and opened her door. "Don't worry about the girls. I'll make sure they get back to their own beds." It was the most supportive statement she felt her stilted relationship with Alexander would allow.

"Thank you," he said again. "I appreciate this, Holly."

When she glanced at him, she saw from his pained expression that he meant it. She wondered if maybe Alexander would have liked her to hug him anyway, give him some comfort he didn't know how to ask for.

"Of course," she said. "*This* is what family is for."

When he nodded, she closed the door, started her truck, and drove her nieces away from whatever trauma she felt certain was brewing inside Mia.

CHAPTER 7

*W*hen she made the left turn out of the parking lot and onto the road, she adjusted her rearview mirror to see the twins. They were still fast asleep, heads touching, but their hands were now also clasped. Ever since they were born, Holly could see the twin connection between Sasha and Everly. As infants, they always seemed to be touching. When they were toddlers, they explored together. Now, they frequently finished each other's sentences and often appeared to have some psychic communication only they were privy to. Even unconscious, the girls found each other in the dark. Holly returned her eyes to the road and readjusted her mirror for driving,

She thought of her own sister. Once upon a time, Mia had been a dauntless and cataclysmic force; a hurricane set loose on the world. Thinking of Mia now, shrunken and hidden, looking half-dead in that hospital bed, it was like all Mia's intensity was directed inward and set on self-destruction.

"Don't do this, Mia," Holly whispered into her truck. "Please, not again."

When Holly pulled her truck onto the driveway of her sister's house, her phone buzzed inside her bag. She shifted into park and let the engine keep idling as she reached for the long fabric strap and pulled her small, tattered purse across the bench seat. The phone's illuminated screen made it easy to find in the dark, and when she swiped for her notifications, she saw a text from Harris.

Everything okay?

She responded. *Define okay. Alexander's staying at the hospital with Mia for a few hours. I have the girls, putting them to bed.*

Want me to come over?

No, try to get some sleep. I'll probably be home before 1:00 anyway.

Let me know if you change your mind. Love you.

Love you.

She shut off the engine and shoved the keys and phone into her bag. She was just considering the logistics of how to get two sleeping five-year-olds out of her truck and into the house when she heard Sasha's small voice.

"Mommy?"

When Holly turned in her seat, she saw that Sasha's eyes were open, and she was pushing herself upright. "No honey, it's Aunt Holly," she whispered. She could see the explanation was doing little to resolve the sleepy confusion on Sasha's face. "Let's get you and Everly inside and into bed, okay?"

Sasha let her eyes droop closed again and nodded.

"Your sister's still asleep. If I carry her, do you think you'll be able to walk into the house?"

Sasha opened her eyes again, looked down at her twin, fast asleep beside her, and nodded.

"Okay then," Holly said as she slid her purse strap over her head. When she opened the door to the backseat, the old truck's rusty door hinges squealed into the quiet night. She unbuckled Sasha and lifted her out to stand on the driveway before leaning in and doing the same for Everly. With the sleep-heavy girl balanced on her left hip, Holly closed the door and did her best to guide Sasha toward the house with her right hand.

Thankfully, Alexander hadn't thought to lock the front door in his rush and confusion to follow the ambulance to the hospital. When she grasped the wrought iron door handle and pressed the lever with her thumb, the heavy door swung inward, easy and silent, saving Holly from rummaging for her copy of their house key in her bag.

With Everly's face now buried against her neck, she guided Sasha over the threshold into the dark house and closed the door behind them with her foot. At the base of the staircase, she felt Sasha slide away from her and onto the floor. When she looked down to see what was wrong, Sasha looked up the stairs and shook her head. "I'm too tired," her voice broke, and Holly knew her niece was near tears.

"Just wait here a second. I'll get Everly upstairs, and then I'll come to carry you."

Satisfied with this plan, Sasha curled up on the circular rug beneath her and closed her eyes.

Holly sighed and started up the stairs, wondering how Mia managed this life daily. By the time she had ferried both girls up the stairs, wrangled their limp limbs out of their clothes and into their nightgowns, and nestled them into their side-by-side matching twin beds, Holly's heart was pounding against her breastbone like she'd been running a race. She stood in their bedroom doorway and watched their sleepy, slack expressions for several seconds before switching on their nightlight and closing the door.

The sheer physical effort required to mother these two girls boggled the mind, and Mia had been doing it for years. And yes, she had Alexander to help—in theory. But Holly knew her sister had always done all the heavy lifting when it came to parenting Sasha and Everly. Alexander loved his girls, but Holly always imagined he considered the manual labor of child-rearing somewhat beneath him. She was sure he would never utter the words *women's work*—that was archaic. Never mind that his actions or inactions implied the same sentiment and led to the same result. Archaic or not, Mia raised the girls.

Alexander was too busy being a *New York Times* best-selling author and professor of neuropsychology at Columbia. At least, that was the general impression Holly always had. Maybe it was an unfair assessment? It's not like Mia ever complained about the arrangement, at least not to Holly.

She placed her hand on the top banister. She was about to head back downstairs when it occurred to her that she was seldom on the second floor of her sister's house and never unattended like this. The light switch for the second-floor landing was on the wall to her left; Holly flipped it on. Besides the girls' shared bedroom down the hall, there were two guest rooms, Alexander's office and Mia's and Alexander's bedroom.

The last time she'd been in her sister's bedroom was after

Mia had given birth to the girls. Mia had been propped up on a pile of pillows, looking exhausted but undeniably happy as she worked to nurse the two newborns and recover from the twenty-seven hours of labor she'd endured at the hospital. Holly had stood near her sister's king-sized bed, watching in awe as Mia learned to navigate this new phase of life—one that Holly herself was sure she wanted no part of.

Motherhood was not something she ever wanted to experience. And she had always assumed that Mia felt the same. She remembered her shock when Mia had told her she and Alexander were pregnant.

But so much had changed for and about Mia after the accident. It was sometimes hard for Holly to believe that, without any memories from her life before, Mia had essentially become a brand-new person after the near-death fall had cracked her life into two distinct and separate existences. It was as if a human's personality, thoughts, desires, and actions were predicated solely upon their individual experiences and not on inescapable inborn traits encoded within their DNA.

Nothing had convinced Holly of this more than the fact she knew, better than anyone, who her sister was before she lost everything.

There was Mia's life and who she was before the accident.

And Mia's life and who she had become after the accident.

With very little resemblance between them.

Deciding she wanted to have children was hardly the most significant difference between the two Mias. Still, it was the one change that left Holly feeling the most shocked and, if she was being honest, also bitter. All the history and reasons

Holly had for not wanting to bear the responsibility for bringing an innocent child into this world were shrouded behind a black curtain of amnesia for Mia.

The memory of Mia, content with her babies burrowing up against her milk-heavy breasts, was a stark contrast to the now gaunt and hollowed-out Mia recovering at Saint Anthony's tonight. What had happened?

Holly checked the time on her phone. It was only after ten, and Alexander had said he would be home by midnight. She glanced at their closed bedroom doors...she had time. Mia looked down the hall toward the girls' room, turned the handles of Mia and Alexander's bedroom doors, and stood back as they swung in and away from her.

Aside from the faint blue moonlight streaming through the large picture windows, the room was dark. She considered flipping on the overhead lights, but she already felt like an intruder. For some reason, snooping under the glare of bright recessed lighting seemed worse than a casual look around in the dark.

Besides, her eyes were adjusting, and the moonlight from the window was much brighter than she had first thought. The large bed was taut and tidy with square, European-sized throw pillows leaning against the grey velvet headboard and a variety of smaller rectangle and rolled decorative pillows cascading across half the bed. In concert with the custom ceiling-to-floor drapes and curated area rugs, the bedroom looked ready for the cover of one of those expensive, elegant home magazines—and just as unlived in.

There was a single dresser, filled only with a few neatly folded black shirts. The bedside tables were round slabs of marble balanced on lattice iron legs. There was nowhere she might look to find something hidden away. If Holly had been hoping to discover some clue about Mia's sudden deterioration, this room wasn't equipped to hold any secrets.

Beyond the bed on the far side of the room was the door that led to the master bath. Holly opened several cabinets and needed to flip on the lights to inspect the rows of cleansers, creams, and medicine. There were several labeled brown prescription bottles. When Holly picked each one up, she could see they were empty. All of them were prescribed to Mia: Lithium, Risperidone, Xanax, and the last, Klonopin. She had heard of Xanax and Lithium before, but the other two were a mystery to her. She pulled her phone from her pocket and snapped pictures of the labels up close so she could look them up later.

On the opposite side of the counter, she opened the other cabinet, assuming this to be Alexander's side. She only saw a few bottles of cologne, shaving cream, his toothbrush and paste, and an electric razor. She closed the cabinet and wondered what Alexander's *professional* thoughts were about all the medication his wife was taking. Did he think it was excessive? Necessary?

And how long had Mia been taking all of them? Holly had no idea.

She was about to flip the lights off and leave when something strange occurred to her—there were no mirrors in this bathroom. She stared at the expanse of wall above each sink. It was an intricately constructed tile mural in soft gray, sea green, and pale blue. It depicted a woman floating on her back down a river. It was beautiful, and Holly felt sure that Mia had hired an artist to create the work.

But artistic beauty aside, she couldn't help but wonder

about the functional loss of a mirror to stare into as you wash your face, apply makeup, or inspect your teeth. What sort of bathroom didn't have a mirror? Even though it had been six years ago, Holly knew the bathroom had mirrors the last time she'd been up here. Two large black framed ones above each sink.

She realized there hadn't been any in the bedroom either. Curious, Holly walked past the box-shaped glass shower, around the deep freestanding soak tub, and entered the adjacent walk-in closet. Her hand ran along the wall until she felt the switch. When the recessed lights on the underside of the whitewashed shelving illuminated the space, Holly could see that there wasn't a mirror in here either.

Nothing. It seemed weird to not have mirror for getting ready in the bathroom or dressing.

She stepped further into the closet. There was something else. She could see which side of the massive closet held Alexander's things. His sports coats, knitted sweaters, oxford shirts, and carefully hung dress pants and jeans. It was the other side, Mia's side, that Holly couldn't stop staring into.

All Mia's clothes. Every shirt, dress, pant, and skirt. Every scarf and shoe. Every hat tucked neatly away into its own individual cubby. Every last item was black. Holly reached out and held the sleeve of a black silk shirt between her fingers while her mind cartwheeled through what all this strangeness could mean. Was it the medication? The drinking? Maybe the stress of raising two busy young twins?

Holly didn't know, but standing there before her sister's black wardrobe, a creeping fear wound its way up her spine. What if...?

Holly shut off the lights in the closet and left.

Downstairs, Holly entered the portrait room and flicked on the lights. Alexander had told her that this was where he'd found Mia. Passed out and face down on the floor. Between finding his incapacitated wife and shepherding her to the hospital, there hadn't been any time to clear away the aftermath.

Mia's empty bottle and a spilled glass of red wine were still a testament to what had happened here hours before. The dark red stain burned irresolvable into the white wool fibers of the rug. On instinct and fueled by familial obligations, Holly rushed into the room and grabbed the bottle and the overturned glass. As her mind combed through known solutions for red wine stains, her eyes were pulled up to meet those of her father.

The portrait over the mantle.

She hated it. The feel of it. The intention behind it. Mia insisted on hanging it, pride of place, even if she couldn't recall the details of its creation.

Holly did remember.

Everything.

And she hated this portrait because those dark memories were burned forever into her mind's eye. But from the day Mia had retrieved this framed monstrosity from their parent's dilapidated estate, Holly had been powerless to explain why Mia should have left it where it had lain hidden for so many years.

To explain this portrait, the meaning behind the ferocity of their father's eye, the aggressive tilt of his head, and the unflattering swell of those jowls would mean unraveling everything Holly had tried to hide for almost two decades.

So, as she had on so many occasions before, Holly

lowered her eyes and did her best to not think about their father watching over the elaborate lie all their lives had become.

CHAPTER 8

*M*ia opened her eyes. She didn't recognize this room. Not the astringent smell, stiff bed, or limp blanket draped over her.

It was dark, but there was also something wrong with her sight. It was hard to focus her eyes.

She heard soft beeps and saw light shining through a small rectangular window in what she thought was a door a few yards from the end of the bed.

She was in a hospital, she realized. There was an IV taped to the inside of her left arm. In the chair beside her, someone was reclined with a thin blanket spread across their chest and lap.

She blinked hard several times, her sight and mind beginning to clear. It was Alexander, asleep and looking uncomfortable.

She tried to say his name, but her voice failed, and the syllables were broken and faint. She cleared her throat, which was raw, and tried again. "Alexander, "she whispered.

His chest rose and fell in the steady rhythm of deep sleep. He couldn't hear her.

A plastic cup and straw were on the tray attached to her bed. She struggled to scoot and push herself into a more upright position, then pulled the articulating tray closer. She misjudged the distance when she reached for the cup and knocked it sideways instead.

"Dammit, "she croaked.

"Mia?" Alexander asked and sat up in his chair. When he saw the overturned cup, he threw off his blanket and moved quickly to clean it up. The lid contained most of the water, but a small puddle dripped from the tray and onto Mia's hospital blanket.

Alexander headed into the bathroom and turned on the light.

"You should've woken me up, " he said as he grabbed several paper towels from the dispenser over the sink. When he returned to her bedside, he mopped up the mess. "How long have you been awake?"

Mia swallowed around the pain in her throat and noticed the angry set of wrinkles between her husband's eyes. She didn't think it was because he was annoyed about some spilled water.

"Only just," she whispered.

Alexander dumped the sopping paper towels into the trashcan and handed her the water cup.

"Your throat hurts?" He asked, matter of fact.

She nodded and took a slow pull from the white plastic straw.

Alexander nodded like this all made perfect sense to him. "They had to intubate you. They pumped your stomach."

Mia pulled the straw from her lips as her eyes slid to meet his. She didn't remember what had happened, and now hearing his words, she was afraid to ask.

Their eyes held each other's for several moments. The reality of their present circumstances was a tragedy they couldn't ignore but didn't want to discuss.

When Mia could no longer bear Alexander's visible disappointment in her, her eyes drifted back down to the plastic cup between her hands.

"I'm not sure...." Alexander started but faltered.

Mia could hear the strain his emotions were causing him. She wondered, not for the first time, if this was the end for him. If this was his final breaking point with her.

"I'll get help," she blurted.

"You've said that before," he countered.

Mia pushed herself up more. She needed to be upright, not lying flat on her back. She needed to make Alexander understand this time was different. This time she knew things had gone too far.

"I'm hiring someone to take care of the girls full-time when I'm not home," he said.

"What?" Mia croaked. "Why?"

"Why?" Alexander parroted her. His expression was incredulous. "How can you even ask that with a straight face?" he hissed. "I came home tonight and found our five-year-olds standing over a boiling pot of water, trying to feed themselves while you were passed out. Cold, on the fucking floor, Mia. Jesus Christ, I thought you were dead."

Even though the room was dark, she could see the rigid set of his expression. He meant it; there would be no more chances. She needed to convince him. Make him see reason.

"I can get this under control. It was a slip, yes. A very big one. I fucked up, Alexander. Obviously, I know it. Please don't think for one second that I don't realize how dangerous my behavior was today. But people make mistakes. I made a mistake. It's not going to happen again."

They stared at each other from across the sterile hospital room. A slick worm of fear wound its way through Mia's gut while Alexander's expression never cracked. There would be no softening, no acceptance. She could feel the determination radiating off him, the physicality of the decision that came with his made-up mind.

"This is not a discussion any longer. Our children were in danger, and it's a miracle nothing happened to them. If you think for one second, I will allow them to be placed in a position like that again...then you truly are insane."

A verbal slap. His words, their implication, what he was accusing her of, and the look of hatred in his eyes ignited her own anger, and it rose like wildfire through her core. "I don't need a fucking babysitter, Alexander," she spat.

Her own venom surprised him enough to rock back on his heels. The muscles in his neck flexed, and his jaw clenched.

Mia sat up even straighter and wished like hell she wasn't wired into place. She said she was sorry and knew she had made a mistake. Still, if Alexander thought he was going to stand there and use her guilt to steamroll her into allowing a stranger into their house to watch and monitor her every move...he was the one who was insane.

"It's not just today, and you know it, Mia. You've been coming apart for months. You refuse to see anyone with the skills to help your condition and instead hide behind your cloud of medication and wine. You're unfit," he spat.

"Fuck you," she breathed. "You narcissistic, self-involved asshole."

"You can call me every nasty name you can think of, Mia, but I'm not going to back down this time. I'm not going to let you make false promises, then run back and hide inside that back hole of a mind." He turned and picked up his coat from the chair he'd been sleeping in. When he faced her again, his shoulders were relaxed but square.

"Here are the facts," he said, his voice now calm. "Either you agree to start seeing someone who has the real capacity to help you, or you can agree to sign divorce papers that I will have drafted by the end of the week. If you choose the divorce, you should know that I will be fighting to take full custody of the girls. I'm confident I will get it given your current mental, emotional, and behavioral states."

Stunned by this ultimatum, this threat, she watched in silence as he slipped his arms into his jacket and pulled his keys from the pocket.

"I'm going to go home now. I'm going to look in on our girls, get what sleep I can, and take them to school in the morning. Then I'm going to teach my classes tomorrow. I will ask your sister if she can pick the girls up after school tomorrow and stay with them until I get home." He walked to the door, placed his hand on the knob, and stopped. With his back to her, he continued, "You have until tomorrow evening to make up your mind, but I will be hiring someone to help me with the girls either way. I can't afford to put your *special circumstances* above the basic daily needs of our family anymore. And I won't, Mia."

Mia watched as he opened the door to the fluorescent-lit hallway, then walked out on her without so much as a backward glance.

CHAPTER 9

She was released at ten-thirty the following day. Mia walked out of the hospital room, alone and in the rumpled clothes she'd arrived in, with two new prescriptions in hand. Without her purse or cell phone, she felt set adrift as she walked the long corridor to the elevators at the far end.

The discharge nurse called Alexander to let him know Mia was ready to be picked up. Alexander gave the woman Holly's cell phone number. He was in the city, he explained, teaching a class, and was unable to collect his wife.

"He said your sister would come, and I should call her instead?" Both her tone and expression were full of pity.

Mia forced a tight smile and nodded. "Yes, please call her. She'll come." The grip of Alexander's threat to divorce her and take the girls was like his hand at her throat. He'd had enough. He wouldn't even bother to pick her up from the hospital. She descended the elevator alone.

On the first floor, she saw Holly waiting for her in one of the sea-green upholstered chairs in the hospital's lobby area.

Her bare, tattooed arms and shock of clipped platinum hair were a radical anomaly within the room's neutral, soothing color scheme.

Seeing her sister there, with her gaze trained out the plate-glass window before her, Mia found no comfort. The image only hammered home the fact that her husband was in the process of abandoning her. Emotionally untangling himself from Mia's messy clutch. Pulling up his anchor, the anchor Mia had come to rely on keeping her tethered in a world that too often felt like an unpredictable swell dragging her out to sea.

The thought of losing Alexander, his steadfast reliability, terrified her.

As if sensing her, Holly turned her head and saw Mia frozen outside the closed elevator. Her worried expression telegraphed that she instinctively knew Mia was in trouble. As she rose from her chair and hurried toward her, Mia felt the clutch in her throat as hot tears blurred her vision and slid down her cheeks.

When she reached her, Holly gathered her into her arms and whispered in her ear. "You're okay, Mia. Do you hear me? You're going to be just fine. We'll get this straightened out," she promised.

Mia shook her head. She didn't believe her sister or see any easy way out of the private hell she'd created. Instead, she focused on the security of Holly's arm wrapped around her shoulders and allowed herself to be led out the sliding exit door and into the warm, mid-September morning.

When she climbed into her sister's rusted-out pickup, she'd noticed that her girls' car seats had been placed on the backseat. "Alexander asked if I could pick up the girls after school today," Holly explained as she slid behind the wheel and yanked her squealing door shut behind her. "I said I could help out for a few days. While you recover and he... well, looks for some regular help."

Mia had no response to any of this. They drove to Mia's house in silence, Holly's eyes glued to the road ahead while Mia closed hers and rested her head against the passenger window. When they pulled onto the driveway, Mia sat staring at her wood-paneled garage doors for several seconds. Once she went inside the house, decisions would need to be made, realities faced, and her personal demons addressed. Alexander had drawn his line in the sand; no more allowances would be made for Mia's *unique circumstances*.

Mia looked at Holly standing on the driveway, watching her through the windshield, waiting for her to follow the lead and open her door. "It's okay," she mouthed.

Mia had no idea if her sister really believed that or if she was just trying to get her out of the truck. Still, she nodded once, lifted the handle, and followed Holly into the house. She stood in the foyer and looked around as if only now seeing her home for the first time. It didn't feel like *her* home. It was a house. The one she'd lived in for seven years. It was filled with everything she owned, but nothing about it felt like *her* home.

Mia realized she didn't even know what her home should feel like. Did Alexander feel like this was his home? Did the girls? She had no idea.

Mia turned her head to meet her sister's worried gaze. "Did Beaumar feel like home for us?" she asked.

Holly's eyes widened in confusion. "What?" she asked and shook her head.

"When we lived there, as kids, did we feel like mom and dad's house was *home*? Like, the place we belonged and came from. A place we would want to get back to after a long trip. That sense of this is *my place* in the world. Do you know what I mean?"

"I think so," Holly answered, but there was a cautious edge in her response.

"Was Beaumar that place for us?"

Instead of answering, Holly scanned Mia's face. "Why are you asking me this?"

Mia sighed and dropped her shoulders. "Because it occurs to me that this is not my home, not in any real sense. I don't know if I've ever felt that way but maybe I did when we were growing up at Beaumar."

Holly took a breath. "Okay. Yes, Beaumar was your home, and it felt like home to us...at least it did then. I don't feel that way now. Home for me is my place with Harris."

"And all your dogs," Mia said with a smile.

"And *all* my dogs."

Mia placed her hand on the banister and started up the stairs. "I think I'm a little jealous of you."

"Mia," Holly sighed and followed her up the stairs. "You've been through so much."

"Yes, poor Mia and her broken brain," Mia said as she headed for Alexander's study. "Trouble is, I think Alexander has had enough of her." She turned the handle and opened his door.

CHAPTER 10

"What does that mean?" Holly asked as she followed Mia into the room. Mia noticed that she stopped short in the doorway like she was uncertain if they should be here while Alexander was gone.

"It means," Mia said as her eyes scanned the floor-to-ceiling bookcases. "That Alexander has given me an ultimatum. Either I get help. Real, memory jogging help or he is going to divorce me." She found the book she was looking for and turned to face her sister's shocked expression. "And he'll take the girls away from me. At least he'll do everything in his power to try and make that happen."

"He wouldn't," Holly blurted. "He's just scared."

Mia sat in Alexander's office chair and placed the book on the desk in front of her. "I don't think if you'd seen and heard him last night, *scared* is the adjective you'd choose to describe his current state of mind. Pissed off, enraged, done...any of those better encapsulate his feelings about me at the moment." She flipped the book over and scanned the author's photo and blurb.

"I don't understand," Holly said. "What does he expect you to do?"

Mia glanced up from the book in front of her and met her sister's eyes. "He expects me to get help, real help this time. He thinks my current issues are because of the memory loss. That if I work on trying to recover my memory, all of my many and assorted current mental health problems will *resolve themselves*."

"That's ridiculous," Holly said, throwing her arms in the air. "You had a traumatic brain injury. You barely survived. How can he possibly expect you to *resolve* that?"

Mia opened the book in front of her. "Alexander has come to suspect that my continued memory loss is not the result of physical trauma but more likely due to post-traumatic stress disorder. He has come to believe that I'm physically capable of getting better, but because I don't get proper therapy, I'm avoiding recovery."

Holly stood watching her for several seconds, then scanned the office and bookshelves. "That's such bullshit," she said. "Mia, please tell me you're not letting him convince you that your memory loss is what...your own fault? Is that what he's suggesting?" Holly reached out and pulled a book off the shelf herself. It was one of several duplicate copies sitting side by side, front and center on Alexander's shelf, along with its framed *New York Times* review. "And how much of this theory has to do with Alexander and his own career prospects? It's been a few years since he's basked in the accolades of the press. Any chance he's pushing this bullshit on you in an attempt to drum up new content for his next..." She read one of the blurb lines from the back of the book. "Stunning and insightful look into the mystery of the human mind and the role memory plays in shaping us as humans?"

Mia didn't want to take her sister's bait. Instead, she shook her head and flipped through several pages of the book she had in front of her.

"Mia, look at me," Holly demanded.

But Mia kept her head down and continued scanning the pages in front of her.

"He is, isn't he?"

Mia sighed. Holly wasn't going to let it go. "Is what?" she asked.

"He's writing a new book. Another one about you and the accident and...everything."

Mia hesitated. She knew what Holly was getting at. It was an old argument she would now resurrect. Her sister thought Alexander's use of her past for his book was, at best, exploitative. When Holly had learned all those years ago about Alexander's book and its topic—Mia—she had spent countless hours on the phone and in person explaining to Mia exactly why she thought it was so wrong of him.

It was wrong of him.

It was manipulative of him.

It was opportunistic of him.

At the time, Holly never seemed to understand that Mia was fine with Alexander's book. After all, she was also reaping the benefits from its astronomical sales trajectory without having to endure the media attention and spotlight herself. At the time of the book's initial release, Mia's only genuine concern was the daily care, feeding, sleep schedule, and safety of her twin toddlers. She never had the energy, or desire, to root out any malfeasance, or the breadth and depth of her husband's own ego, with regard to his use of her personal tragedy.

As far as she was concerned, it was her past. A past she couldn't even remember.

Holly had eventually tapered off on the critique but had *never* let her grievance go.

Mia placed her hand flat on the open pages in front of her and looked up at her sister's angry and worried face. "Is he writing another book? Maybe."

"I fucking knew it!" Holly said, shaking Alexander's first book over her head.

"I said *maybe*. I don't know for sure. He has been spending more time in here, early in the morning and when he's late coming to bed. Which is what it was like—" she gestured to the book in Holly's hand. "Before."

Holly tossed the copy of *Somebody She Used to Know* onto the desk where it landed with a loud slap. "You can't allow it, Mia. Not again." Her tone was calmer now, resolute.

Mia sighed and closed her eyes. She understood Holly's concern, truly. And she knew why Holly was adamant as well. Ever since the accident, Holly had been the one right by Mia's side, physically, mentally, and emotionally. Holly had encouraged, coaxed, and held her hand through those early months and years when Mia had been the most lost. Holly had been her singular and most salient connection to the past that was now lost to her, to some sense of understanding about who Mia even was as a person.

Mia couldn't remember if Holly had always been so protective of her, but since the accident, Holly had become Mia's fiercest advocate and protector. When Mia met and married Alexander, Holly's extensive and highly involved role in Mia's life became more complicated. Mia loved her sister, but she loved her husband too. And while she both understood and appreciated everything Holly had done for her, she didn't believe Holly's accusations about Alexander's intentions were correct—or even fair. Especially since, given their last argument in the hospital, Mia wasn't sure what Alexander's intentions were. Would he divorce her? Take the girls from her? She hoped that today, in the light of day and with the chance to calm down, Alexander regretted his cruel threats. But she couldn't afford to assume anything.

"Holly, right now I have one focus, and that's finding a doctor to see that will convince Alexander that I'm taking his threat of divorce seriously enough to finally get *real help*."

"But what he's asking of you isn't even fair. You *can't* remember."

Mia shook her head again. "Yes, but Alexander doesn't *believe* that."

"Who gives a shit about what he *believes?*"

"For starters? A judge might right now. Don't forget, Alexander's the one with a reputable career as a *neuropsychologist*. One who lectures at *Columbia*. I'm an unemployed wife with a significant history of traumatic brain injury and a medicine cabinet filled with enough prescriptions to rival a psychiatric in-patient. Oh, and I'm also the woman who mixed alcohol with those meds while alone with her five-year-old's. That alone gives Alexander grounds to make good on his threat. And honestly, after what happened…Holly, you must see that he's not entirely wrong. The girls—" her voice broke. "If one or both of them had gotten hurt…because of me?" A few tears slipped down her face.

At this, Holly's shoulders dropped, and the anger drained from her expression. "Oh, Mia," she said, and Mia knew that there would be no more argument from her. Because as much as Holly loved and wanted to protect her, she also loved her nieces, ferociously. And facts were facts. Mia's behavior had put them in danger. Not even Holly could deny that. "So what will you do? You've seen doctors, excellent ones, for years. If Alexander doesn't believe you or them, who will he trust?"

Mia took a deep breath, wiped her cheek, and held up the copy of the book she'd pulled from the shelf. "Erica," she said.

Holly's forehead wrinkled in confusion as she stepped closer to take the book from Mia's hand. She inspected the title, *Trauma and the Brain: Alternative Approaches to Healing and Hope.* "Erica Monae, MD, Ph.D.," Holly read aloud, then opened the book to the back cover and the author's photo. Doctor Erica Monae had a close-cropped head of silver hair. She wore a bright red cardigan over a white collared shirt, rimless glasses, and a thin gold chain with a pendant too small to make out in the photo. "Who is she?" Holly asked as she looked up to meet Mia's gaze.

"She was Alexander's doctoral advisor," Mia explained. "And the only person, I think, he's ever been truly intimidated by."

Holly raised her eyebrows and didn't bother to suppress a grin at the thought of her brother-in-law being brought down a notch or two. Mia watched her sister read over Erica's author bio; her medical degree and Ph.D. in neuropsychology were from Harvard, and she was a senior faculty member at Columbia University. "You know her?" Holly asked.

Mia nodded.

"And she'll help you?" Mia asked.

"I hope so," Mia said. "And if what Alexander has told me about Erica's latest research is true, I think there's a pretty good chance Erica will *want* to work with me, too."

Holly closed the book and placed it back on the desk. "Why?" she asked. "What is she researching?"

CHAPTER 11

*W*hen Mia first explained to Alexander her plan to work with Erica, he scoffed and shook his head. "Erica hasn't worked with private clients in years. She's too busy with research and her class load. Plus," he added as he grabbed the bottle of Macallan from the top of their liquor cabinet and pulled the cork. "It would be a conflict of interest." He poured the amber liquid into a crystal tumbler. Mia watched as he raised the glass to his lips. "We work in the same department, and I think that could be an example of a dual relationship," he added matter of fact and took a long swallow. His expression as he stared at her over the rim of his glass barely concealed his contempt. *Was she stupid to even consider such an idea?*

Mia cleared her throat. "She won't be seeing me as a private client. I'm joining a clinical trial. Which will not be run by her directly but by one of her supervisees. I spoke with her this morning. She explained there are enough layers of separation between Doctor Ty Yun and myself. She has no reasonable expectation that my being your wife could lead to impairment, exploitation, or harm. So it's already been decided," Mia said, then walked from the dining room without further explanation.

Seconds passed as Alexander processed this new information. "What?" he blurted and followed her into the kitchen.

The girls were sitting at the expansive marble island eating their dinner of macaroni and cheese and sautéed broccoli florets. Mia noticed that Sasha's cup of water was empty. "Do you want more?" she asked, reaching for the cup.

Sasha nodded as she pushed another floret into her mouth.

"Mia?" Alexander asked. His tone was direct, but she could also hear the undercurrent of fear. "What do you mean? You can't join Erica's clinical trial."

"Excuse me," Mia said and gave Alexander a quick smile as she scooted past him on her way to the fridge. "I can," she explained as she filled Sasha's cup with filtered water from the fridge's door. "And I have." With the cup now full, she passed Alexander again. "Excuse me," she repeated and placed the cup back in front of Sasha. She turned to face Alexander and took a deep breath. "You made it very clear that I would need to find someone with the capacity to *really* help me. So, assuming any more can be done for me in that particular arena, there isn't anyone better working in the field today than Erica. I found someone, the best someone, to try and help me. What's more, she's actively doing research in a therapy I have not tried." Mia turned to the sink, pulled her long black sleeves off her hands, up onto her wrists, and turned on the water. "Honestly, Alexander... I've only done exactly what you asked me to."

As she washed her hands, she kept her eyes trained on her girls finishing up the last few bites from their food-segregating plastic plates and waited to see if Alexander could construct some additional argument against her plan. She felt his eyes boring into the non-scarred side of her face, but he didn't seem able to come up with anything more to say.

She turned off the water, dried her hands, pulled each of her sleeves back down to the base of her fingers, and began clearing the girls' now empty plates. "All done?" she asked them with a smile and a bright tone.

Without question, Mia needed help. From a strictly logical viewpoint, she could see that her recent behavior, and particular avoidances, were not grounded in reason. She was spiraling and knew Alexander was correct when he said she was getting worse. But it seemed to her, for the first time ever, that Alexander was not standing beside her and looking to solve this new problem with her.

No. Ever since he delivered his ultimatum, it had become increasingly clear that Alexander was standing before her, resolute in his judgment, and waiting to see if she could get her shit together, finally, on her own. And if not, well, there would be consequences this time. It was both baffling and terrifying to imagine that this might be the beginning of the end for their marriage. More so because she would have no one to blame but herself. If it had only been the two of them, if it were only the dissolution of their vows at stake, Mia could maybe face that. Alexander had his flaws, but she loved him, she always had, and if he left her alone, now, after everything they had been through and built together, the physical and emotional pain of that would be indescribable. She would hurt for a long time.

But not forever. She loved him with everything she had, but she would survive a divorce.

However, Alexander had threatened far more than just divorce. And if he thought she was going to allow herself to be steamrolled with his threat of taking her girls away—well, there was no way she would lie down and wait to see if he meant it.

Reaching out to Erica Monae was Mia returning Alexander's threat to his own court. Because if he did mean it, if he was ready to leave Mia and take everything she held most dear, Erica was the person she needed to align herself with to keep Alexander in check. Mia felt confident in her decision, tactical in her approach to both accept Alexander's ultimatum and ensure that he didn't overreach or make any drastic moves.

It wasn't until two days later that she had any doubts.

CHAPTER 12

*H*aving taken the Hudson Line to Marble Hill station in the city, then the number one subway line from South Ferry to 168th Street station, Mia ascended the concrete steps into the thrum of a city she hadn't navigated alone since her own abandoned graduate school life at Columbia over a decade ago.

It was the third week in September, and the temperature in the city was broiling just below one hundred degrees. The heat and humidity commingled with the aroma of dried urine emanating from the underground station; reflexively, Mia lifted her hand to her nose and mouth in a futile attempt to filter the nauseating stench. Once upon a time, Mia raced along the city's interconnected networks as fluently as any other native New Yorker. Back then, she wouldn't have even noticed the smell.

She exited the stairwell and did her best to look natural as she picked up her pace and entered the current of other humans spilling onto the sidewalk. With her elbow clamped down against her black Fendi purse, Mia headed for the meeting she had scheduled with Erica and Doctor Ty Yun.

Erica's office wasn't located on the main campus. Like many other practicing university neuropsychologists, she conducted her research and met with patients at The Neurological Institute. Which was part of the Columbia University Irving Medical Center, two and a half miles and five subway stops northeast of where Alexander was lecturing right now. Alexander also had an office within the medical center, so Mia made sure to schedule her appointment with Erica and Ty when she wouldn't run into him.

Mia stood on the sidewalk next to the stucco planters that flanked the wide and shallow curved concrete stairs that led up to the main entrance and lobby area of The Neurological Institute. On the street, cars pushed along Haven Avenue and darted around an illegally parked gray suburban. The driver of a battered blue Camry right behind the suburban seemed intent on getting the large vehicle to move by engaging in an indecipherable series of morse code honks: short, short, short, long, long, short, long bleats emanated from the exhausted looking vehicle while the woman leaned out her driver's side window and screamed at the suburban to, "Move the fuck out of the way!" as she slapped her hand hard against the outside of her own door.

Mia considered, for a short moment, letting the woman know that the suburban was empty. Then she remembered that, in general, it was best to allow the city to carry on in its own chaotic and intense way without unnecessary interference. She turned away, pulled her black sleeves to the very tips of her fingers, and started up the stairs.

After confirming her appointment with the man behind

the front desk and being cleared to enter the building, Mia headed down the hall and up the elevator to Erica's office on the eighth floor.

Years ago, when she and Alexander had first met, but before he had his own office here, Mia had spent a considerable amount of time in this building, but she hadn't stepped foot inside in over five years. As she passed Alexander's closed and locked office door, she did not turn to acknowledge it or his brass nameplate, Alexander Strauss Ph.D., mounted to the wall.

In all the years that had elapsed since her voluntary withdrawal from her own Ph.D. program in which she had specialized in Jungian psychology, Mia only experienced some vague regret on a handful of occasions. Usually, those occasions coincided with the tangible evidence of Alexander's own ascension within this professional world she had chosen to step away from. Ever since the birth of the girls, it had been easy to never find the time to get into the city to meet him for lunch or happy hour. She no longer had to pretend that she never, *ever* wondered *what if* she hadn't given up and walked away. Had she made a different choice that day all those years ago, would Mia's name and credentials be the one mounted to some wall in another department building? Sharing an office floor and engaging in relationships with her own colleagues instead of, again, submitting herself to being a subject for research and study?

Mia inhaled through her nose and pulled the turtleneck at her throat up until it brushed the bottom of her chin. She didn't regret her choices, she reminded herself. Besides, that life was a long time ago.

Along with Erica's name and credentials, her office door had a sign.

If you have an appointment
Please come in and take a seat

Which Mia believed was the same sign that had been hanging on Erica's door for over a decade. She let herself in, closed the door behind her, and took a seat on the forest green chenille fabric couch that Mia knew for sure had been sitting against the same beige wall and under the same framed reproduction of Claude Monet's Water Lilies and Japanese Bridge since Erica had moved into this office. It was clear that interior design and office decor were very low on Dr. Monae's priority list. But Mia found that the place's banal familiarity helped ease her anxiety.

She hoped that Erica, like her office, would prove to be the woman Mia remembered her to be.

Mia had hardly settled her handbag onto her lap to wait when the door that led from Erica's outer office to her treatment room opened, and Erica herself appeared in the doorway.

"Mia!" she exclaimed, then moved past her unoccupied desk and toward Mia with outstretched arms.

Mia stood to greet her, opening her arms to accept Erica's full-throttled hug. "Erica," she said as her chin slipped over the woman's shoulder. "Thank you," Mia added as she backed out of the embrace. "For seeing me...taking me on."

Erica stood back and held Mia's upper arms in her hands as if to get a good look at the woman she had become. Mia noticed that, as part of the visual assessment, Erica gave Mia's arms the barest of squeezes as a brief hint of worry flitted across her expression.

Erica would think that Mia had grown far too thin—and she was without a doubt correct. But Mia gave her a big smile and pushed ahead. "You're sure it isn't too much trouble to add—"

"Trouble? Are you kidding?" Erica scoffed and motioned for Mia to follow her into her interior room. "Do you know how difficult it is to find viable and willing candidates for this type of research? Your call was like a miracle from heaven. I might have begged you to join it myself if you hadn't reached out. Although truth be told, I think of you every time I start one of my more out-of-the-box projects." Erica shook her head and motioned for Mia to sit in one of the club chairs positioned on the opposite side of the coffee table from a young and very handsome man.

"Mia, this is my extremely talented research partner, Doctor Ty Yun. Ty, this is Mia Strauss."

Ty stood and reached his hand across the table. "Mrs. Strauss," he said. "It's a pleasure, and an honor, to meet you."

Mia raised her eyebrows and her hand to greet him. "An honor? Well, I must say I don't often hear that," she quipped with a smile but wondered why this very accomplished young, and handsome man would show her any deference. Unless, of course—.

"I've read several of your husband's research articles," he said. Then added, "Doctor Strauss." As if Mia might have forgotten who Alexander was.

"Yes... I've met him," she attempted a joke.

Ty wrinkled his brow, her statement obviously confusing him.

"I'm kidding, of course," she smiled.

Ty smiled too, but she got the impression that he still

didn't see how silly it was for him to clarify that her own husband and Doctor Strauss were one and the same. Mia sighed and reminded herself about the sometimes stunted social skills that seemed to plague these type-A, top-of-the-food chain Ivy League brainiacs.

It was a component of Alexander's personality that Mia had never been able to effectively translate for Holly so that she could understand; Alexander wasn't really an asshole, but Mia could see why her sister thought he was.

Mia imagined Ty and Alexander spoke the same social language. Complete with longwinded monologues, poor listening skills, and an inability to read the room.

"Please," Erica came to the rescue. "Let's have a seat, take a few minutes to chat, and review a few things before you and Ty head downstairs to get started."

This surprised Mia. "Started?" she said as she lowered herself into the chair behind her. "Today? I figured we'd just be meeting and signing consent paperwork."

Ty, who now looked nervous and off his game, glanced at Erica and then back to Mia. "Well, yes. We will do all that. But I would prefer.... Of course, if you have the time and are available.... There are quite a lot of intake questions we could get started on. Since you're here? It would take about two hours."

Erica, who seemed nonplussed by all this, picked up the folder on the coffee table in front of them. "Yes, sorry if that wasn't clear when we spoke. Can you stay for a bit longer today? Since you're joining the study a few weeks behind the others, it would mean that Ty could get up and running with your treatment sooner."

"By Monday," Ty clarified.

Monday? That was only three days from now. Mia nodded. She was the one in greater need here. "Of course. Not a problem. I'll ask my sister to pick my girls up from school today."

Their expressions relaxed, and they settled into their respective chairs across from her. Erica opened her folder across her lap.

"Okay," Erica started. "So I've given Ty the most basic details, but I couldn't delve into the specifics about your history without your signed consent." She pulled several sheets from the folder and slid them across the coffee table to Mia, along with a ballpoint pen. We'll need a few signatures on the standard paperwork, which is this, and then we should review some of the more unique aspects, consents, and legal rights regarding the nature of this *particular* study."

Mia nodded again as she picked up the pages and pen and pretended to read all the many paragraphs of legalese she would agree to. After she had spoken to Erica on the phone, she knew they would be moving along the process quickly. However, she had assumed there would be a bit more time to adjust and mentally prepare herself to start such an intensive therapy.

Something that she had never even considered trying before.

Mia laid the pages flat on the table and began initialing and signing all the highlighted areas.

"This one," Erica stopped her on the third page. "Is about any current medications you are taking."

Mia met her eyes. "I have already stopped taking them like you said."

"That's wonderful," Erica said. "But we'll still need you to list the specifics here. Name, dosage and frequency, and the last day you took each one. We'll want to be very careful about potential interactions, as some may still be clearing your system. As you come off them, we will need to monitor you and your symptoms."

"I don't want you to worry, Mrs. Strauss," Ty interjected. "While I would love for us to get going on Monday, we'll only get into administering the drug component if you are stable and we get the all-clear from Doctor Monae once she has reviewed your lab work."

Erica smiled. "Yes. There isn't any way we'll be starting the psilocybin on Monday if we don't think you're ready physically, mentally, and emotionally.

"Well." Mia wrote down the name of one of her meds, uncertain if she was spelling it correctly. She wished she had the bottle with her to check. "That is reassuring," she said, but privately worried that maybe she was making a huge mistake. When she thought about taking the psilocybin and subjecting herself to intensive psychoanalytic treatment while under the influence of a powerful psychedelic with a young man she didn't even know—well, it wasn't hard to understand why Alexander had his reservations.

They went through several more pages of specific consents and acknowledgment of rights, each requiring Mia's signature in multiple places.

When Erica turned over the last page, collected all the sheets together, and returned them to the folder, Ty stood up as if on cue. "Well then," he clapped his hands together and gave Mia an excited smile. "Shall we head downstairs and get started with the intake?"

"So enthusiastic," Erica laughed.

Mia nodded, slipped the handles of her handbag over her shoulder, and stood. As a fresh wave of adrenaline washed through her nervous system, she couldn't help pulling her sleeves to the tips of her fingers and her turtleneck up to her chin.

Ty noticed her behavior, gave her a sympathetic smile, then turned toward the door.

CHAPTER 13

*T*asha Adams was seated at a corner table near the front of the busy coffee shop, waiting for Alexander. When she saw him enter through the glass door her arm shot into the air, and she waved to get his attention.

She need not have bothered. He had spotted her through the plate glass from across the street.

Now inside, their eyes met, and her entire face lit up with youth and expectation. This unsettled Alexander at his very core. He gave her a restrained smile as he wove his way through the shop's disorderly arrangement of wobbly tables and mismatched chairs, but on the inside, he was bursting with a joyous thrill he hadn't experienced in years. As he pulled out the chair across from her, he forced his eyes to veer hard and fast away from the expanse of skin revealed by her blue V-neck tee that accentuated the delicate slope of her neck and the small swell of her breasts. He cleared his throat and hoped like hell there wasn't any way she could detect his heart hammering against his chest.

This was a huge mistake.

He took a breath. "Hello, Tasha," he said with exaggerated enthusiasm, like a distant uncle she might only see at Christmas dinner.

"Professor Strauss." She beamed at him. "Thank you so much for agreeing to meet with me." She pushed a bowl-shaped cup on a saucer across the table toward him. "The line here can be terrible, and they're so slow, so I ordered you a coffee." She then slid a small metal creamer across to him and gestured to the box of assorted sugars and artificial sweeteners like it was Alexander's first time at a coffee shop. He noticed a tremor in her hand—she was nervous.

Why was *she* nervous? Was it just because she was meeting her professor outside of class? Could it be something else? Alexander didn't allow himself further speculation about what that something could be. To do so would be to admit, if even only to himself, how much he would like it if this young, attractive, vibrant woman was interested in something other than how Alexander could help her academic career and trajectory at Columbia. What it might mean if she was, in some way, interested in him as a man.

"Thank you," Alexander said as he picked up the creamer and poured a small dollop into his coffee. "But I think I should be buying you coffee, of course." He smiled.

"Oh well, you can get it next time," Tasha said and waved her hand in dismissal.

Next time? It meant nothing, Alexander assumed. Unless it didn't. Unless she really did think there would be more of these times in their future, across from each other at shared tables in busy coffee houses. The idea of this, meeting her again, was both thrilling and terrifying. But why? Because he could honestly say that the idea of meeting any of his current or former students, even exceptionally attractive females, had never impacted him this way.

In the past, Alexander had always felt these personal, time away from campus interactions were nothing more than additional obligations on his thinly stretched time. He lifted his cup to his lips and took his first sip, and as he did, he lifted his gaze to meet Tasha's large brown eyes across from him. What was so different, so intriguing about this young woman?

"So," he began, doing his best to mimic the tone, intonation, and body language he would have used at every other student meeting he'd ever had. "How can I be of service to you, Ms. Adams?" He gave her what he hoped was a fatherly smile, despite the fact he was feeling anything but.

Careful. Careful. Careful, he thought. Because this was precisely how long, successful careers smashed themselves against the sheer cliffs of blind, misguided lust.

Tasha nodded once, then turned toward the back of her chair where her tote bag was hanging. A moment later, she turned back with a notebook and the copy of Alexander's book she'd asked him to sign when she'd first approached him after class. She lay both items on the table in front of her and placed her palms reverently on each, like they were sacred and on an altar before her. "Well." She gave him a brief smile. "Actually, I was hoping we could talk about your book."

Surprised, Alexander sat back in his chair. "Really?"

Tasha nodded again. "Yes. I mean, if that's okay with you. Obviously." She opened the notebook and paged through the first half of the pages that Alexander could see were filled with neat, careful notes. When she reached the first blank page, she picked up her pen and wrote: *Meeting with Alexander Strauss* at the top.

Alexander took several more sips of his coffee, which was delicious, and explained how and why the long line and terrible slow service were tolerated by so many. He tried to wrap his head around Tasha Adams's angle. Most students asked to meet for coffee, and the bolder ones invited him for a drink, so they could get a foot in the door for research opportunities. This could lead to a co-publication credit and help their careers.

If this was what Tasha was also hoping for, her focus on his decidedly non-academic publication was certainly a different approach. Was she hoping to win him over with flattery? Or, perhaps, stand out by doing something completely different?

"Like I said before, this book." She pointed to the cover with emphasis. "Has completely changed my life."

Alexander smiled at the compliment, but his mind was working to dissect her motivation. Ferret out any signs of disingenuity. Because while he appreciated the sentiment, he found it hard to believe she meant it. "Well, again, that's quite a compliment."

And yet, as he watched her staring back at him, her face so open and sincere, he knew she was telling him the truth.

"Do you mind if I ask you some questions? Things that came up for me while reading that weren't addressed in the text itself?"

Alexander shook his head. "Please." He gestured with his open palm. "Ask away. I'll do my best to remember the correct answers. It has been a while since I wrote that one."

"Is there another one?" She asked.

"No…well, not exactly. But I am working on something new. Sort of."

"Really? Same topic? About Mia?"

Hearing his wife's name slip from Tasha's mouth with such casual familiarity was startling. "Um…yes, sort of." Although why should it be surprising? He referred to Mia by her first name throughout the book. Of course, Tasha would as well, just like any other character in a book she'd read.

Mia's name didn't conjure a real woman, a real weight, for Tasha like it did for Alexander.

"It's just bare bones, the beginning of a concept. I've scratched out a few chapters. If you could even call them that. I'm still waiting for the book to find its legs, so to speak."

Her face fell a fraction of an inch, and Alexander had the distinct impression that she had maybe been on the verge of asking him to read this practically nonexistent new work. "But what did you want to ask me about this book?" He redirected.

Tasha nodded once, picked up her pen, and turned back a page in her notebook. Alexander could see that she had several bulleted questions, but the notebook was upside down and far enough away that he could not read them without putting on his glasses. He watched as Tasha scanned the page, looking for a place to begin. She seemed to be weighing something in her mind, although Alexander couldn't begin to imagine what.

She had a list of questions. Why not just start at the top?

Her eyes stopped scanning, and he assumed she'd decided on her interview entry point. She was very nervous, it was obvious. What was less obvious was the why.

She turned the page back to where she would take notes

and positioned her pen to write. "In the book, you shared that Mia lost her memory at eighteen after experiencing a tragic attack that caused her to suffer a traumatic brain injury. At the time of writing the book, it's clear that Mia had yet to regain any of her memories prior to the assault, but you remained hopeful that, with continued therapy, she might one day be able to recall partial memories. Maybe even a complete recovery. It's been a few years since the book was published; has she experienced any breakthrough memories of her life before the loss? And if so, is that what your new book will focus on?"

Alexander sat a little straighter in his chair while he worked to process Tasha's complex question and the odd discomfort it had ignited in him. "Well," he stalled. "To answer the first part, no. She has not yet, made any further progress."

What was it about her question that was rattling him?

"Which, I guess, then also answers the second part. No, the new book isn't about any additional recovery." He shrugged. "Since there hasn't been any."

Tasha nodded and scribbled a few quick notes. She turned to her questions, scanned them, then flipped back to her notes page.

"You briefly mention that Mia grew up on the north shore of Long Island at Beaumar Manor. Even though there isn't much mention of them in the book, obviously, this would have been with her parents, Raphael and Pixlie Renaud?"

"Yes," Alexander interjected. "And her younger sister." He took a sip from his coffee.

Across from him, Tasha's pen remained frozen above her page even as her eyes remained glued to it. She was surprised but trying to hide it for some reason. He watched as she wrote a single word he could clearly make out, even without his glasses.

Sister.

She underlined it.

When Tasha did look up to meet his gaze, her expression was easy and relaxed again, but there was an intensity in her eyes that was impossible to miss.

What, exactly, was all this about? he wondered. Because it was feeling less and less like Tasha was working up the courage to ask him for a research assistant position.

She smiled and picked up her own coffee, and took a sip. "That's interesting," she said as she returned her cup to the table. "I guess I didn't realize Mia had any siblings. There's no mention of her sister in the book at all."

And there was a reason for that. Several, actually. Alexander was initially reluctant to include any information about Mia's family in the book. After all, when he'd written it, he'd focused solely on the facts and details regarding Mia's extraordinary condition. He had worked hard to marry his clinical expertise and understanding with the personal side of her story. To him, the fact that she was also the daughter of one of the most famous film directors and his actress wife, admittedly a washed-up alcohol-addled actress, was incidental. His original book did not mention Mia's parents at all. In fact, he had not even used Mia's real name.

It was on the advice, and to be frank, insistence of his literary agent that these familiar factoids be dropped into the book. It would mean the difference between a six-figure advance from a major New York publisher and languishing in obscurity with a university press. "And that's assuming I'll be able to sell it at all," his agent had warned him.

So, with Mia's permission, he indulged in a few tastefully added name drops, including Mia's.

But Holly? Holly had refused. Holly had *adamantly* refused and had even campaigned hard for Mia to not allow any details about herself or their family to be included. In fact, Holly had been so upset by it all that she had accused Alexander, in his own kitchen, of being *opportunistic*. Of *trading on our family's tragedy and fame*. Nothing short of *using Mia for your own self-interest and ego*. She had actually called him a *fame whore*.

An accusation that had, although he would never admit it out loud, cut him to the quick.

And it did not matter that he denied it all. That he had tried to explain it was *what the publisher wants, not me*, Holly would not be persuaded. In her mind, Alexander was using Mia and their family history—she would not allow herself *to be manipulated by him*.

Needless to say, Alexander and Holly's relationship was a tense, unfriendly one.

"And," Tasha continued. "Is there even anything online about Mia's sister? I feel like I would have come across that in my research?"

"Yes," Alexander stalled. Given his already prickly relationship with Holly, he wasn't sure he should get into any details along this vein with Tasha. Something about all this was still unsettling him. "Well, the family, Holly in particular... they're very private people. And people in charge of Raphael Renaud's legacy, and the family estate, work to keep anything more than the most basic of facts off the internet. I mean, as much as they can, given Raphael's notoriety."

He watched Tasha write down another word.

Holly.

This made his unsettled feeling bloom into dread. He shouldn't have mentioned her name.

"And actually," he added as he pointed to the notebook. "If you could not. I shouldn't...could we maybe move on from this? Mia's sister would really not appreciate me talking about her at all in connection with my book."

Tasha gave him a big, broad-mouthed smile that showed her straight crystal-white teeth. "Oh, absolutely," she said as she shook her head. "Absolutely, and please forgive me. I'm sorry if I've been intrusive. Honestly, I don't want that *at all.*"

And then, as if to prove a point, she took her pen and drew a single sharp line through Holly's name in her notebook as if it erased the entire subject.

For some reason, even crossed out, the sight of Holly's still legible name in this woman's tidy script left him feeling like he had made a grave miscalculation. Even if he had no idea why.

Tasha picked up her notebook and folded it back on itself so that only one side, the fresh blank side, was now visible. Her previous writings were out of sight but not really out of mind.

"Of course, the entire world knows about Raphael's tragic murder," she continued. "But there isn't much more information about what became of Pixlie."

Alexander picked up his coffee and drained the last few swallows. Maybe he hadn't been clear? It wasn't just Holly he felt he shouldn't speak about. "She's doing very well. Living a quiet life." His tone was curt. "Out of the spotlight. Pretty normal, boring...retired. She likes to watch old films...that sort of thing. Did you have any questions that weren't about my wife's family that I could answer for you? Anything on your list about memory research? Directions within the field? Are you interested in applying for one of my assistant research positions? I don't mind telling you, it can be competitive, and spots fill up quickly, but I'm certain you'd be an excellent candidate if you were looking to throw your name into the ring."

Tasha nodded her head once like they had made some unspoken agreement. "I'm so happy you brought that up, professor." She closed her notebook and replaced the cap on her pen. "Yes. That is exactly what I would like to do. I hope I wasn't too obvious. I wouldn't want you to think I was being pushy or opportunistic by inviting you to coffee. But yes, a chance to join one of your studies is what I would love to happen." She flashed him another one of her big smiles right before she finished her own cup of coffee.

Alexander's shoulders relaxed a fraction of an inch. Maybe he was only being paranoid?

"So, what would you suggest my next steps be?" She said as she gathered her copy of *Somebody She Used to Know*, her notebook, and pen, then turned in her seat to repack them into her bag hanging from the back of her chair.

Alexander ran his hand reflexively over his mouth and short beard while he considered her new question and what best advice he could give her.

While she waited, Tasha checked the time on her phone, and her eyes drifted to the window behind Alexander's shoulder before she folded her hands on the table in front of her and resettled her attentive gaze on him.

"Well, to start...."

Alexander spent several minutes laying out how Tasha should best proceed in order to be considered for one of the positions he would be filling. He also encouraged her to look into what several of the other professors were currently working on as she might find that their research was a closer match to her current interests.

And for the entire ten minutes he spoke, Tasha kept eye contact, nodded her head, she even smiled at his attempts at humor. The meeting ended as expected for this sort of discussion, even if her initial questions seemed out of left field and not pertinent to their purpose.

By the time they stood up, shook hands, and said, "See you in class." Alexander felt relieved of his earlier, probably unfounded, suspicion.

That, for some reason, this woman was lying to him.

CHAPTER 14

*M*ia called after lunch. Holly was in her *backyard* wearing her blue, mud-caked Hunter boots, a threadbare green flannel over a limp t-shirt, and her favorite work jeans. She was bent over Roger, *attempting* to clip his nails, when her cell rang in her back pocket.

She and Harris called it their *backyard*, but it was twenty acres. They had installed extensive fencing when they decided to foster dogs so they could let them run when the weather was nice. She was *attempting* to clip Roger's nails because he was a two-year-old German Shepard mix that kept yanking his paw away every time she got the safety clippers within two inches of his overgrown nails.

"No," she said, keeping the dog between her legs. "You're not going anywhere," she added as she pulled her phone from her pocket. It was Mia calling. Holly tapped answer and pinned the phone between her shoulder and ear while she kept wrestling Roger.

"Hello?" she said.

"Holly, it's me. God, I'm so sorry this is last minute, but is there any way you could get the girls from school today?"

"My goodness, you are being a total pain today," Holly said in frustration.

"What?" Mia asked. "Well…. Look, I'm sorry. I know you've already done so much, and I probably shouldn't have—"

"What?" Holly took hold of her phone and turned her full attention to what Mia was saying. "No. Not you, Mia. I was talking to Roger." She gave the victorious Shepard a disapproving shake of her head and signaled for him to go ahead and run off to play with the other dogs.

"Roger? Oh, is that one of the dogs? I've caught you at a bad time."

Holly sighed. "No, it's fine. I needed the break anyway," she said as she watched Roger gleefully play with Barret, the one-year-old black lab mix with more energy than his previous owner had bargained for. "What's up now? You want me to get the girls?"

"Yes. If you can. I'm at the institute, and they would like me to get started on a few things today. I was not expecting it at all, so I had no plans for the girls after school. If you're busy…I mean, I could call Dominique. She wouldn't mind, but we're not that close, and I would hate—"

"Mia," Holly interrupted her sister's frantic rambling. "It's not a problem, really. I'll get them. Three-thirty, right?"

She heard Mia let out a sigh of relief. "Yes. And thank you…again."

Holly dropped the nail clippers into her grooming bucket along with the variety of brushes, combs, and various other tools she used to keep the dogs in good shape and headed toward her back porch stairs. "By the way," she asked. "How's the hunt for a nanny going? Or has Alexander let that go since you've agreed to start up with the new therapy?"

"Terrible, and no, he's not letting that one go. It just feels impossible to find someone. Well, someone good anyway, on such short notice, especially now that the school year has already started. There don't seem to be many *qualified* people interested in so few hours. The girls are in school all day, and it's only from three-thirty until Alexander gets home from work, which is usually around seven...or thereabout. Alexander thinks I'm being difficult because I don't *want* to find anyone. Which is true. It's insulting, not to mention embarrassing. Because let's face it, they'll also be a babysitter for me."

Holly pulled off her dirty boots, dropped them in the tub next to the back door to be cleaned, and opened the screen door leading to the kitchen. She wasn't sure what she was about to suggest was a good idea. Plus, she had only vaguely dropped hints to Harris about offering, to which he had scoffed, shook his head, and said, "You know, it's not your life-long duty to take care of every stray animal and person on this planet that crosses your path. You can't be responsible for *everyone*."

And Holly sighed and walked away, saying, "She's my sister, Harris. Not some stray person." No definitive conclusion had been reached, but Holly knew her husband better than he probably knew himself. He would understand.

"What if I do it?" she blurted into her phone before she could think better of it.

"What?" Mia asked. "Be the girls' part-time after-school nanny and my adult babysitter?"

"Well, I was thinking more along the lines of being the girls' *aunt* and your *sister* and helping you all out for a little while. It would save you the headache of hiring someone you don't know and get Alexander off your back...maybe."

The line was silent for a moment; Holly assumed her sister was thinking over this possibility. "It would be nice," she finally said. "You know, to not have a complete stranger in my house, in my space...someone I'd have to explain everything to. Just thinking about that makes me exhausted. Actually, yes. I would love it if you could do that, but are you sure? What about Harris?"

Holly grabbed the electric kettle from its base on her counter and headed for the sink. "Don't worry about Harris. I talked about it with him, and he thinks it's a good idea too. After all, what is family for if not to help each other out when we need it."

"Yes," Mia said. "But you know as well as I do that the need in our relationship has been pretty one-directional."

Holly turned on the faucet. "It's settled. I'll get the girls today and for as long as you need me to."

"Thank you, Holly," Mia whispered into the phone. "You are the best sister on the entire planet. I don't know how I could be as lucky as I am to have you. I probably don't deserve you at all, but I am grateful for you every day of my life."

Holly's mouth went dry. "Stop it," she tried to joke in order to brush off Mia's serious and sincere sentiments. "Don't you have some therapy to get started? Don't worry about the girls. I'll be there."

"Thank you," Mia said.

"You're welcome. Now bye."

"Bye."

Holly hung up her phone and slid it into her back pocket, Mia's praises still echoing through her mind. Holly wished Mia hadn't said all she did and wished even more that her sister didn't really feel it. The truth was Holly had her own reasons for wanting to keep close to Mia right now. And while she highly doubted that this new experimental therapy would crack the vault that kept Mia's memory from her, Holly wanted, no needed, to make sure her sister was kept safe.

Alexander was either pushing Mia for his own egotistical needs or because he thought he was helping her—it didn't matter either way.

Holly had spent the better part of the last two decades trying to keep her sister safe; she wasn't about to stop now.

Through the window above the sink, she had a direct view of the largest red maple tree on the property. Its leaves turned to their full crimson glory. Sweet Ralph, with his long great dane legs sprawled out in front of him, was fast asleep on his side in the still green grass. His big chest expanded and contracted with his every breath, and his paws twitched in pace with whatever he was chasing in his dream.

She would end up keeping him for herself, she knew. It was next to impossible to not fall in love with all the dogs that came under her care. It was her natural inclination to feed them, heal them, love them, and then want to keep them, unfortunately. And while she always loved it when one of the dogs found a loving home, and she was extremely picky about who they went to live with, she always spent that evening in tears. Worrying about whether their new family would be patient, kind, and love them just as much as she had. Because no matter how much she interviewed, investigated, and worked to make sure these often already once abused or abandoned animals found extra-loving forever homes, there was always a part of Holly that feared she'd made a mistake. Missed something. Been fooled by an externally kind facade that hid a person's true tendency toward cruelty.

The thought of these animals, any animals, being harmed by someone sometimes kept her awake at night. The flip side of her natural inclination to save was that she could never, really, trust anyone.

Because if her life had taught her one lesson, it was that almost anyone was capable of almost anything.

CHAPTER 15

*W*hen Holly picked Sasha and Everly up from school, they seemed genuinely happy to see her. Excited, even. Which surprised Holly.

She had expected them to be shocked to see her instead of their mother, maybe even unsure and unwilling to leave the school with her. So when they ran into the school's front office and flung themselves at her body while they jumped up and down, Holly took a step back and signaled for them to *stay down,* just like she would with overly excited dogs.

Thankfully, none of the other adults in the office noticed or realized the meaning of her instinctual hand command, and Holly managed to collect herself before barking out the command, "Sit!"

She didn't have much experience with children.

Sasha yelled, "Aunt Holly!"

While quiet little Everly just gave her a beaming smile while bouncing on her toes.

"Are we going to your house? To see the dogs?" Sasha begged. "Please, please, please!"

Ah, so that explained it. Holly opened her mouth to respond but was interrupted.

"Oh, hello there!" a woman's voice said.

Holly felt a hand on her upper arm and turned toward it. It was a tall woman with perfectly styled hair. Her white silk business blouse let Holly know this woman lived in a world far removed from a pack of wrestling rescue dogs and muddy boots. "Hello," Holly replied and did her best to return the woman's big, if maybe not entirely genuine, smile.

She told her sister she would pick up the girls and take care of them. She had not anticipated interacting with the monied, elite adults that could afford to send their children to a private academy like Beacon Hill.

"I'm Dominique Richards," the woman said as she pressed her expertly manicured hand to the center of her chest. "A friend of Mia's. And this," she added while she pushed out into the open the small boy clinging to the back of her legs. "Is my son, Caleb. He's in Sasha and Everly's class. They are all very good friends." She smiled again and nodded. "Did I hear correctly, you're the girls' aunt? Mia's sister?"

"Um, yes." Holly found her manners and stuck out her hand. "Holly."

"It's so nice to meet you," Dominique gushed. "I know this will sound weird," she lowered her voice. "But I've actually seen your picture. On Mia's mantle? When you were children…the one taken at your parents' estate? I mean, you were so young and hard to make out in the distance and under the shade of that big ol' tree." Dominique laughed. "So it's not like I *recognize* you, obviously. But Mia did tell me about you, so when I heard the girls just now...well, I just *had* to say hello."

What, exactly, was happening here? Holly's brain was cartwheeling through everything this woman had just said and trying to land on an appropriate and polite response that would also get her out of this situation as soon as possible. Her heart was racing like a greyhound on the track.

How the hell did Mia do this shit? Seriously, all this inane talking. With *people.*

Holly's eyes shot wide open, and she did her best to smile. "Well, then... it's nice to meet you as well...Dominique." She leaned slightly right. "And Caleb," she added to the boy who had successfully slipped back behind his mother's legs and buried his face into the expensive, camel-colored fabric of her tailored pants.

"Is this a one-time pick-up, or do you think you'll be around the school more often? Oh, do you have children of your own? You know, I'm the PTA president. If you're looking to get them in, I could help convince the board to allow Sasha and Everly to count as." She lifted both her hands and made air quotes. "Siblings. You know, for the preference list," she whispered as she leaned in.

Holly swallowed. "Oh, no. No kids. Just dogs. But... thank you for the offer."

"Oh well... someday, right? Anyway, if you do pick up the girls more often, Caleb and I love to get together for play dates after school. Isn't that right, Caleb?" She asked as she dragged her shy son back out from his hiding place. "It really is so important for kids to socialize outside of school and build those relationships. I know Mia agrees with me on this and that it was one of her top priorities this fall. And, of course, the girls' birthday is fast approaching now. I know Mia is hoping for a big turnout."

At that moment, Dominique's phone rang in her hand, and she glanced at the screen. "Oh, you know I have to take this. *Work*. Anyway, think about what I said, and let's get something on the books. Okay?" She finished her sentence as she swiped her phone and segued into her phone call. "Hello, this is Dominique."

Holly managed to nod a few times as Dominique waved goodbye to her, all while continuing her phone conversation and leading Caleb out of the double-doored main entrance.

Somewhat stunned, Holly watched as the woman stood on the sidewalk in her five-inch, nude stilettos while she and Caleb waited for the crossing guard to stop the traffic and signal for them to enter the road. Did her sister really live this sort of life? Like, every day?

Holly had watched Mia's life since the accident develop along a path that would have been unfathomable to her younger self. From her major in college and her choice of a husband to getting pregnant and the home she lived in—if pre-accident Mia could see how her life would eventually turn out, she would never have believed it. Holly, who had stood here in the middle of it and watched the progression of it unfold from its tenuous beginnings in that hospital bed all those years ago, could hardly believe it.

Mia was *friends* with this Dominique Richards—with her designer clothes and enormous diamond ring. She *chose* for her children to attend this school, with its impossible-to-crack waiting list, elitist parents, and over-funded resources. And she *married* Alexander Strauss. A man who…well, the fact that she had decided to *marry* anyone, really.

Mostly Holly just tried to roll with all the many and assorted ways her sister had become a woman practically unrecognizable to her. But some days, today, the glaring complexity of the differences was simply too astounding to ignore.

Holly loved her sister and was every day thankful she had survived her injuries. But sometimes...there were parts of Mia, long lost Mia, that Holly grieved.

"Can we go see your dogs now?" Everly asked. As always, her voice, when it could be heard at all, was quiet and small.

Holly looked down into her nieces' eyes, physically identical yet very different in many ways. "Yes," she said. "Let's go play with some dogs." Holly took hold of both their hands and guided them toward the crosswalk that led to the school's parking lot, where her beater truck stood out like a sore thumb among all the washed and waxed Land Rovers and Mercedes.

When she opened the back door, it squealed loudly on its rusty hinge, causing the dad in the next parking space to glance up from buckling his own kid into a booster seat. *Shit.* She didn't have boosters for the girls.

"Okay," she said as she lifted Sasha first and then Everly into the cab. "Here's the deal. Your mom asked me to get you, but I don't have your seats. So it's just the seatbelt today." She reached across Everly and plugged in her belt. In the next seat over, Sasha grabbed her seatbelt and clipped it in without needing help. "But I'll be sure to get that worked out for next time."

"We don't have to have them," Sasha said, matter of fact.

"Hmm. I'm not sure your parents would agree." Holly gave Everly's leg a light squeeze and shut the door.

CHAPTER 16

*a*t the house, Holly guided her three most mellow dogs into the fenced-off play arena. Ralph, her gentle giant. Gibby, an eleven-year-old Maltese that had been surrendered by his family when they moved into an apartment that wouldn't take pets. And Joey, an estimated five-year-old terrier mix with an unknown history. He'd been found wandering alone in an ally on 34th street in Manhattan. With no tag and no chip, there was little hope of finding his owner, but Holly had scoured the Lost and Found section of the paper every day for weeks. Sadly, Joey had likely been abandoned and left to either fend for himself or die in the street.

Some days, Holly hated people with a deep and ugly passion.

"Can't we play with *all* the dogs?" Sasha asked as she entered through the fence Holly held open for her.

"Probably not the best idea. Some of them get pretty

excited and are still learning how to behave. Especially with little kids."

Sasha furrowed her brow and looked sideways at her aunt. "We're not little. I feel bad for the other dogs." Sasha said. Both girls looked beyond the play arena to where most of the other dogs had free run within the largest corralled arena.

"I think they want to play, too," Everly whispered.

Holly smiled at Sasha's sassy expression and Everly's concerned one. "Okay. Well, I'm sure you're right. But we're just going to play with Ralph, Gibby, and Joey today. Maybe next time will give some of the other dogs a chance too. And hey, maybe you can even help Aunt Holly teach them how to behave and be calm with little...um, I mean, with kids. That will help them find good homes, you know."

Inside the fence, the three dogs ran up to the girls, but not one of them jumped up or plowed them over. Their butts wiggled, and their tails wagged with wild abandon, but all three of these dogs restrained themselves and waited patiently for the chance to be petted and played with by the girls.

Everly went straight for Joey, cupping his face between her small hands while Sasha gave Gibby scratches behind the ears. So he didn't feel neglected, Holly bent over and gave her big Ralph a few good rubs along his haunches. Once introductions were established, the girls ran toward the dogs' play park equipment, and all three dogs gave a gentle chase after them.

Holly watched them all run around the equipment, up the ramps, through the tubes, around the tires, and over the jumps. Harris had bought most of the stuff secondhand from an ex-dog trainer that had retired and moved to England two years ago with his husband. He had picked up a few of the items, like the dogs' paddling pool, from a big box store. The pool was empty now, thank goodness since the kids and dogs kept running through it. She could only imagine explaining to Alexander and Mia what would have surely been a muddy mess caked into the girls' burgundy and white school uniforms.

In the distance, a lone, long howl pierced the air, followed by a series of siren-grade barks. When Holly looked over, she could see that Barret, the one-year-old black lab mix, was losing his mind on the other side of the large arena fence. All the other dogs, realizing they were not going to get to come see the girls, had given up and were either lying in shady spots or playing amongst themselves. Only Barret was throwing a tantrum. Demanding to be included.

He didn't realize that his very behavior, the way he leaped six feet into the air while yowling to wake the dead, was exactly why he was not yet ready to be set loose with two very little five-year-old girls.

Still, Holly felt terrible for him. Also guilty, even though there was nothing at all wrong with Barret. To hear him, you'd think someone was removing an organ from his body without anesthesia.

The girls were throwing tennis balls for the dogs, who would retrieve them and then drop them again and again and again at the girls' feet. This could go on for over an hour, Holly knew.

She lifted the latch on the gate and slipped out quietly so as not to draw Ralph's attention—he insisted on following her everywhere.

Over in the large arena, Barret saw her approach and stopped throwing his body against the chain link. "What are you doing?" she asked. "You're being absolutely ridiculous."

He sat his butt down on the grass, his entire body vibrating with the potential energy of a lit firework. Holly sighed at the sight of him—he really did need a lot of training before he'd be ready for adoption. She smiled at him and reached her hand through the diamond-shaped links to stroke his head. "I promise I will take you on a very special walk tonight after the girls go home. I'm sorry you can't see them today, buddy. One day, I promise." She knelt down and put her nose to the fence, and Barret put his snout through and gave her a big lick. Holly stood up and wiped her dog-slobbered face with the sleeve of her flannel. "Go on, now. Go play with Roger," she said and turned back to the play arena.

She was halfway across the field between the two arenas when she realized—Everly was not with Sasha. Picking up her pace, Holly's eyes scanned the play equipment, the far corners of the arena, and the shady spot under the red maple. When she still didn't see her, Holly started to run.

"Sasha!" Holly called. "Where's Everly?"

The gate to the play arena was open.

Sasha looked up from where she stood, extracting a soaking wet tennis ball from Ralph's soft mouth. She raised her free arm and extended her finger to point. "In the barn," she yelled back.

Holly stopped dead and spun around to face the faded red barn behind her; one of the large doors was cracked open just enough for a five-year-old to slip through.

That's when she heard the barking start.

Then the screaming.

CHAPTER 17

"*E*verly!" she shouted as she ran toward the barn as fast as she could. "Come out right now! Everly!"

Jesus Christ, what was she thinking, leaving them alone for even a minute. When Holly reached the barn door, she yanked it hard and wide, then bolted inside. It took her eyes several seconds to adjust to the light, but she made her way toward Everly's screams.

At first, she couldn't tell where she was but then saw her niece crouched low and backed into the corner to the right of the doorway. Her hands pressed to her ears, and her eyes squeezed tight.

There was blood.

It was running down the girl's arm. Holly swept Everly into her arms and carried the clinging, still screaming child past the large cage in the center of the barn. As they passed, Holly glanced into the black eyes of the white American Pitbull that was kept there. His snout was retracted, exposing all his teeth as he continued to bark and snarl while leaping against the side of his cage. Everly screamed even louder, and Holly clutched the back of her head and pressed her closer to her chest.

Outside the barn, Holly closed the door behind them and saw that Sasha was heading toward them with Ralph, Gibby, and Joey following her. When she heard her sister's screams, she stopped in her tracks.

When Holly reached Sasha, she placed Everly on the ground beside her. She took her small arm in her hands and first inspected where the blood was coming from, a deep graze on the back of her hand, and then carefully looked at Everly's face and the rest of her arms and legs. There was nothing else, thank God.

Jesus, Joseph, and Mary, Harris's Catholic mother, would have said. Thank God.

Holly sat on the grass and pulled Everly into her lap. She had stopped screaming and was now sobbing with the occasional hiccup. "Are you okay?" Holly asked as she cradled Everly's head against her chest and rocked the girl back and forth.

Sasha crouched down in front of them. Her expression was pensive as she stared at her sister and tried to decipher what was wrong. Sasha took Everly's hand in her own, then whispered something into her ear.

Everly stopped crying immediately, and a second later, she whispered something back into Sasha's ear. Sasha's eyes went wide, and she nodded.

"She said there's a bad dog in the barn, and it bit her."

Holly nodded at her niece. "Yes, he did bite her. And I'm so sorry, Everly. I never thought either one of you would go in there. I should have warned you. I should have...I just didn't think—" Holly couldn't help the tears that rose up like a flood. Her throat constricted, and her skin felt cold. Now that the crisis was ending, her body shook from the stress.

She took a deep breath and squeezed Everly again. What the hell was she going to do now? Of all the things to go wrong today, this was the worst thing that could happen.

Not exactly the worst. Her mind spun. Because the bite could have been much worse than a tooth graze, even if it was deep enough to draw blood. That dog, Holly knew, could have gotten hold of Everly's small hand and ripped the whole thing off.

God, Jesus, Joseph, Mary, every saint she didn't know because she wasn't religious and never had been—thank you, thank you, thank you, for it not being any worse than it was.

Holly took Everly into her arms, Sasha by the hand, and headed for the house. "Let's go get you cleaned up," she said.

Everly gave a slight nod as she expelled one last shaky sob. She was calming down and would be okay.

But Holly knew Mia and Alexander would likely lose their shit over this.

"Why do you have a bad dog?" Sasha asked. She rested her hand on Ralph's head, a perfectly good dog by any standard.

Holly's eyes looked up to the bright blue sky above her as if the answer to this seemingly simple question, which was actually fairly complex, could be found up there somewhere. Why, indeed, did she have that dog? How could she explain it so that Sasha and, poor, injured, and rightfully terrified, Everly could understand?

"The thing is..." she started as they headed up the porch steps. What? What was the thing? "I know this will be hard to understand, but, well, he's not a *bad* dog." She shifted Ever-ly's weight in her arms to free up a hand to open the screen door. "He did a *bad* thing. Trying to bite Everly."

"He *did* bite her!" Sasha retorted.

Holly exhaled. Yes, he did, technically, bite her. That's what animal control would report if Alexander or Mia called them. And let's not forget Harris. No. Harris never wanted that dog here and had zero faith that any attempt at training would end in anything but a complete disaster.

"And what if he gets away from you and attacks one of the other dogs? Hell. What if he attacks you, Holly? That dog could kill you!"

Harris would also be livid about what happened today.

Holly led both girls to the bathroom, placed Everly on the counter next to the sink, and pulled her first aid kit from the cupboard. "He's had a very hard life, that dog in the barn. I don't think a single human has ever once shown him even a little kindness." How much do you tell five-year-old's about things like this? Holly had no idea and was completely out of her depth here. "The people that used to own him were very, very mean to him. They forced him to fight with other dogs all the time."

Yes. And they starved him and beat him and kept him in a locked kennel for nearly twenty-four hours a day, seven days a week, for his entire life. Unless he was being "trained" through abuse to learn to fight, or actually fighting, he was kept locked away in a dark basement with forty other dogs that were similarly tortured daily. But this, Holly did realize, was a level of detail unsuitable for five-year-old's.

"So," she continued. "I believe, I hope anyway, that I can help him learn how to behave like a good dog so that one day he will know that people aren't only going to hurt him and that other dogs won't all try to fight him and maybe he can have the happy life filled with love that he always deserved but never got." She was crying now, tears running hard and fast down her face. Both girls were staring at her, and then Sasha started crying too. Which then triggered Everly's tears to start back up again.

Christ. Holly closed her eyes and shook her head. What a mess. She'd only been in charge of the girls for less than two hours; look what a disaster it had already become.

"It's not his fault he's a bad dog?" Everly whispered through her tears.

Holly sighed and wiped first her face and then both the girls' cheeks. "No."

"You're going to help him?" Sasha asked as she looked into Holly's eyes, her expression doubtful. Sasha and Harris always did get along famously—he, too, doubted anything could be done for that dog.

"I'm going to try, yes." She said as she opened the first aid kit and removed the peroxide, some Neosporin, and a band-aid. Thank God she had called the vet as soon as she'd brought the dog home and ensured he was up to date on all his shots. She soaked a cotton pad in peroxide. "This might sting a little. I'm sorry."

Everly nodded once, like she both knew this fact already and had been through this particular war trench of childhood before. When Holly placed the wet pad on the wound, Everly flinched but didn't cry again. Satisfied to see the solution bubbling white on the skin, Holly blew it dry, squeezed on some Neosporin, and secured the band-aid. "How's that?" she asked.

Everly cradled her injured hand to her stomach and gave another nod, content with her treatment, so Holly lifted her from the counter and placed her two feet back on the floor.

"What's his name?" Sasha asked.

Holly turned her attention to her other inquisitive and outspoken niece. "He doesn't have one. Not yet."

"Why not?"

Because what if she was going to have to take him in to be euthanized because Harris was right? What if the damage was too great? What if he couldn't be saved? "Well, the man who had him before—"

"The bad man," Sasha clarified as her eyes narrowed into two slits.

"Yes. The dogs weren't pets to him. They had numbers on their cages, and that's how he kept track of which one was which. But they didn't have names."

"What are *you* going to name him?"

Holly hadn't dared to even consider one yet. The dog had only been here a week and had needed to be tranquilized for the vet to even evaluate him and administer the necessary vaccines and blood tests. He was scheduled to be neutered next week. "I don't know," she said.

"How about Stevie?" Sasha suggested brightly. And at the mention of this name, Everly's head swiveled fast to look at her sister in surprise.

Holly looked between the two girls. This name clearly had some meaning for them. "Why Stevie?" Holly asked.

Everly rolled her lips between her teeth, but Sasha spoke right up. "He was a boy that got kicked out of our school."

Holly didn't hide her surprised expression. "Really? Was he in your class? In kindergarten?"

Both girls nodded. "He sometimes would hit other kids," Sasha explained.

"And throw chairs," Everly whispered, her shoulders rising closer to her ears.

"He was on red every day," Sasha said.

Holly had no idea what being 'on red' meant, but it wasn't hard to figure out that for a kid that hit and threw chairs and eventually got kicked out of kindergarten, it probably wasn't a good thing.

"But usually, he was nice," Everly said. "He always shared his markers with me."

"So, you should name that dog Stevie. Because the real Stevie didn't mean to be bad either, I think." Sasha concluded, and Everly gave a decisive nod of agreement.

"He would also push me on the swing before I learned to pump my legs," Everly added.

Holly let out a breath she didn't realize she was holding and stood up straight. These two girls had whole lives she knew nothing about. Did Mia know about this Stevie kid? She wondered.

"Okay, well, I'll think about it. But in the meantime, how about we go get some ice cream? I think we could all use a treat."

And both girls seemed to forget about fighting pitbulls, dog bites, and little boys named Stevie who got kicked out of school as they bounced excitedly up and down. "Yes! Yes! Yes!"

Great. Problems temporarily forgotten. But Holly knew it would take more than a trip to the ice cream parlor to win over Mia and Alexander.

Not to mention Harris.

CHAPTER 18

"Okay then, how about we start with your earliest memory," Ty prompted.

For the last half hour, they'd reviewed the basics of her life: husband, kids, sister, mother, and the factual information about her father's death.

"I was eighteen when it happened," she shared.

"And you have no memory at all of your father?"

Mia shook her head in response.

"The first thing I remember happened two months after I woke up in the hospital. It was my sister, although I didn't know her as my sister at the time. I didn't know her as anyone at all. I remember it as a woman with spiked, white hair walking into my hospital room. She wore jeans, a faded red t-shirt, and a silver necklace with a small pendant. She could have been anyone or no one at all. I didn't know her at that moment, even though she'd been to my hospital room every day since the accident—I don't remember any of the prior visits from her. But that day, for whatever reason, my brain decided to start logging my days and working again. Sort of."

In the chair across from her, Ty scribbled notes in his notebook even though all their sessions were also being recorded by video.

Mia glanced up at the camera mounted in the corner of the room and wondered how many people would be viewing the footage and dissecting her every word, her every movement, in the foreseeable and unseeable future.

Their sessions would be happening in both this room and the one adjacent, on the basement floor of The Neurological Institute. And apart from their initial meeting earlier, she would have no further contact with Erica Monae or with any of the other assistant researchers. When they began the drug sessions, there would be a nurse present.

"A *female* nurse," Ty had specified. Who would help monitor Mia's vitals and be ready to assist should any, "... medical complications arise. Which, of course, is highly unlikely. But it's not impossible, so we want to ensure you're safe."

Mia assumed it was important to make clear it would be a female nurse since, given the nature of the drug sessions, Mia would be in a highly vulnerable state. Certainly, the nurse served as two-way protection from Mia being assaulted by Ty and from Mia making false accusations about any imagined assaults from Ty. Just like the videotaped sessions would be used for the research itself and as an exacting record of what took place.

Mia had a hard time imagining Ty, with his model good looks, muscled chest, and arms, needing to get his kicks from inebriated late-thirties women in his research study. In fact, she felt reasonably confident that Ty had no problem at all with all sorts of young, attractive, consenting women wanting his hands to run all over them.

Of course, Mia knew you could never be sure, and someone's physical characteristics had nothing to do with who the person really was beneath the facade. Especially a carefully crafted one. For some people, the biggest turn-on was power and control, which had nothing to do with consciousness or consent. And clearly, the Neurological Institute's legal team would agree, given all the precautions to "ensure you're safe."

And keep themselves out of court, of course.

"And after that day, your memory from that point forward, you would say your recall of events was fine from that point?"

Mia shrugged. "Mostly? They had me journaling my days, then reviewing my notes repetitively. I kept pictures of my sister, Holly, and my mother and documented what they told me about themselves...and myself. So it's hard to say if my memory just started working again, at least as far as new memories, or if it was trained back through all the practice. Basically, my life was rebuilt starting in 2004. Everything before that, things I know about who I was, my family, my father—only stories I've heard from my sister.... Oh, and what I've read online about my father and his career. His movies. Articles people have written. Interviews with actors that have worked with him. But I imagine it's like anyone else reading about someone famous—it's distant and holds no meaning for me. I can't say that I even have any emotions for or about him. As if he really were a stranger and not my own father."

Mia looked up from her lap, where she'd been staring at

her clasped hands. "I've never told anyone that before. Not even Alexander." She shook her head. "Practically, the entire world knew who he was, the movies he created, and loved him for his work. For me to admit that I feel nothing for him...I guess I was always afraid that people wouldn't understand that. Especially since they did love him. Or were in awe of him, at least."

Ty considered her for a moment before speaking. "I don't think it's strange at all. As far as your emotional guidance system is concerned, Raphael Renaud was a nobody on the street. Just because you know *factually* that the man was your father doesn't mean you're automatically encumbered with an equal weight of relational context. As far as your mind is concerned, you don't know him. Not at all."

Mia gave Ty a small smile. "Thank you."

Ty smiled back and wrote down more notes. "You don't have to thank me, Mia. This is therapy, after all."

She closed her eyes and let out the smallest of laughs, which felt so good. She couldn't remember the last time she'd laughed about anything.

"And," he added. "If it makes you feel any better, I don't think you are correct in your assumption that the *whole world* loved Raphael Renaud. Personally, I don't particularly care for his films."

Mia scoffed, then smiled so big she covered her mouth on instinct.

"Whew," Ty joked. "I must say, it's a huge relief to get that off my chest. I'm the world's only Raphael Renaud non-fan. I trust you won't tell anyone? Because I don't think my Google reviews could take that degree of one-star blowback if we're being honest."

Mia crossed her heart. "I'll take it to the grave."

"All right, then. What if we shift focus, move past that first year in the hospital. Talk to me about what happened when you left. You're, what?" He checked his notes. "Nineteen? You're out in the world again...." Ty shook his head like it was impossible to imagine a person completely rebuilding their entire life and identity at age nineteen without any foundational history or experience to rely on. "What did you do next?"

Mia cleared her throat. "My life was pretty non-eventful. If you can believe that. I kept close to my sister, who I leaned on for everything. And I mean absolutely everything. She didn't want to return to our family home and insisted that I not either. She rented a two-bedroom apartment in the city and moved me into it with her. She took a few jobs here and there, volunteer stuff at animal hospitals or shelters." Mia tilted her head and raised her eyebrows like she needed to be apologetic for what she would say next. "I mean, she didn't *have* to work at all. We've been well provided for financially. So Holly made me her full-time career for those first few years. I was out of the hospital, and I mean as an in-patient. But there was no end to the minor follow-up surgeries, therapy, and progress monitoring. For years after I *left* the hospital, Holly and I still spent a tremendous amount of time *in* the hospital."

Ty nodded and kept writing.

"For a few years, my only focus was the physical healing. That and trying to learn as much as possible from Holly about our past. Who I was. Even just how to live."

Ty held up his finger. "Now," he interjected and looked up. "You say that Holly was your primary caregiver during this time. What about your mother, Pixlie? What was her role in your recovery?"

Mia took a breath and let it rush out quickly. "I mean… my mother isn't the sort of person…well, to make a long and complex answer short…she didn't have one? After the accident, and when I could hang on to daily events in my mind, my mother didn't visit me often. I could count on one hand the number of times I saw her at my bedside that first year, and that was likely only because Holly had forced her from Beaumar and driven her into the city."

Mia watched as Ty continued to scribble away in his notebook, writing down the facts and sad tragedies of her life. What was he thinking, she wondered. He was a professional, yes, but a human as well, with thoughts and opinions that likely still formed judgments regardless of his training. Mia wished she could ask him and get a straight answer, but she knew that Ty would never tell her what he really thought about a mother like Pixlie. A mother that left her teenage daughter to heal from such a devastating, life-altering trauma without helping her.

CHAPTER 19

*T*y finished his note, and when he looked up, his eyes connected with hers across the room. "What that must have been like, I wonder."

Mia shrugged. "I think, like my father, I have no memories of my mother before the accident. She was a stranger to me, and she has remained a stranger. I know what I *should* feel for her, logically, because she is my *mother,* but I don't have those feelings. I suppose it's because there wasn't any relationship built between us after the accident. Whatever I once felt for Pixlie, I don't remember it."

"But with Holly..." Ty led. "It's different."

"Because I came to love her as my sister after the accident. There was a logical understanding of what I should be feeling coupled with the redevelopment of our relationship. Plus, Holly was the one that tried the best she could to rebuild the narrative of my life with pictures, stories...physical evidence of who I was before. It had always been obvious to me that my sister loved both the Mia I was before the accident and the Mia I have become since the accident."

Ty nodded once, wrote what appeared to be a single, brief sentence, then said, "Okay, I'm sure we'll explore each of your most important relationships more thoroughly as we progress through the treatment, but this gives me a good baseline for understanding the timeline of events and the connections you both had and have. Let's move forward a bit more. Tell me about your years at the university and the beginning of your relationship with Professor Strauss...sorry, I mean, with your husband, Alexander."

Mia smiled briefly, then took a breath. "Actually, I met Alexander under circumstances nearly identical to what we're doing right now."

Ty's forehead wrinkled momentarily, surprised and maybe a little shocked. "Really?" he blurted.

"Well," Mia explained, realizing how her admission was perceived. "I don't mean to say that Alexander was my doctor, no. But we did meet during a research trial he was assisting on like you are here." She inclined her head toward him. "Of course, there was nothing personal between us then, at the time of the research, I mean. He asked me out months after the trial had ended."

It had actually been the very next day after they had concluded the research, but Mia wasn't going to share that fact with Ty. At the time, Mia had been flattered and excited by the idea that someone as handsome and successful as Alexander had, perhaps, secretly been attracted to her the entire time they had been working together but was unable, for ethical reasons, to act on his attraction. It made her feel desirable and sexually attractive for the first time since the accident that had left the right side of her face so disfigured. Her scar had never seemed to bother Alexander. It was almost as if he didn't even see it when he looked at her.

She had been twenty-five years old. What had Alexander's attention and interest in her meant to her at that time? Everything, if she was being completely honest. She had tragically lost her father, and her mother was a shell of a woman. Holly was the only person in the whole world Mia had back then, and when she gazed at her fractured face in the mirror, it was easy to spiral into the fear and belief that she would always be alone.

Ty nodded and scribbled some notes on his pad. Mia had the impression that her admission had in some way impacted his reverence for the esteemed Doctor Strauss. *It wasn't like what you're thinking,* she wanted to say. But would that make whatever he was thinking better or worse? "I owe Alexander a lot," she whispered. "He saved my life."

At this, Ty looked up and met her gaze with an expression of genuine empathy. When he opened his mouth, Mia assumed he was about to say something in agreement. Then he took a moment, seemed to think better of it, and only nodded once, smiled, then glanced at the clock on the wall behind her head. "That's probably enough for today."

Oh. Now, Mia definitely had the impression that the young and handsome Ty saw Alexander in a skewed light.

"So long as all your labs come back looking good, we will begin with the medicated sessions on Monday."

Mia rolled both her lips between her teeth and nodded.

"But a big component of what we'll be doing together is still grounded in cognitive and behavioral therapy techniques.

Given that, I have some homework for you to start over the weekend."

Mia took a silent deep breath and let it rush from her nose. She was no stranger to cognitive behavioral therapy homework. He was likely about to suggest—

"I'd like you to find a journal—"

She *knew* it.

"And start writing down free associations about your childhood, family, and anything that would have occurred before the accident. And I realize you don't have any memory of that time, and that's okay. Just write down your thoughts about that time. The hope is that this will eventually be a space to record actual memories that do occur should that happen."

Mia had zero faith in journaling. She had filled shelves of journals after her accident, and not one contained a genuine memory of her own from before the accident. "I'll get started on it tonight," she promised as she slung the strap of her purse over her shoulder and stood up.

"There's one more thing," Ty added. "Your mother, Pixlie."

At this, Mia froze and raised her eyes to meet Ty's.

"You mentioned that she still lives at Beaumar but that you've spent very little time there, or with her, since the accident."

Practically none. Pixlie hadn't even seen Everly and Sasha since their fifth birthday, nearly a year ago.

"I'd like you to also find some time to return to the house. Speak with your mother and also journal about whatever comes up for you, if anything, while you're there."

Mia stared at Ty and realized her heart was beating hard

inside her chest. Absently, she reached for her hair and drew it over her scar.

Ty watched this, then repositioned his eyes onto her unhidden one. "Is that something you'll be able to do?" he asked.

Mia hesitated and wondered privately about the slick of fear coursing through her. She forced a smile. "Of course. I'll see if she's available." She shrugged, like what he was asking her to do was nothing. "This Sunday."

Ty gave her a closed-mouth smile and rolled his pen between his fingers before positioning it back onto his notepad. "Great. I'll see you Monday then."

"Till Monday," Mia said. Then she turned and left the room while Ty bent his head over his notes and wrote down whatever private thought had just occurred to him.

CHAPTER 20

The shadows cast by the shifting sun had stretched when Mia exited the Neurological Institute's double glass doors. It was only just after four o'clock, but the mid-September days were already beginning to give way to earlier evenings and cooler temperatures. A breeze blew over her, a chilled draft through the still-warm air.

Summer was ending.

She was half a block from the subway entrance that would begin her journey home when she slowed her steps and came to a halt. It had been a long time since she had been to the city.

Ty's questioning today, remembering those years when she and Holly lived in their two-bedroom apartment two blocks from Central Park, had ignited her nostalgia for a city that she now avoided. Those days she had spent fully focused on recovery while walking the park's expansive tree-lined paths, an oasis from the strum, churn, and noise. There was also her favorite deli across the street from their building, the bagel shop on Lexington, and when she was well enough, glasses of wine with Holly as they sat in their rooftop garden and watched the sky grow dark and the lights of the city come alive all around them.

She now thought of the city as an overwrought combustion of constant activity, a nauseous elixir of adrenaline and cortisol that bred stress—she had forgotten the beauty. The early mornings before the sun rose and set the clock ticking on the collective rush to hurry up and get ahead. The shared experience of living in a capital of the world, both loving and loathing its multifaceted presence.

Mia turned away from the subway entrance that would begin her journey home. She felt like taking a walk, alone, down these streets she had once known like the back of her own hand. Holly had the girls, she reasoned. Besides, she wouldn't stay long. If her job was now to remember, to dredge and troll for those images buried beneath her brain's black mud, the city that birthed her resurrection felt like the most logical place to start.

Mia entered the flow of people on the streets. Not quite as fast and not at all purposeful, but she kept a steady pace and didn't imagine she stood out. In New York, being fully cloaked in black attire, even when it was still near ninety degrees outside, didn't warrant even casual interest. It wasn't even unique.

And despite being surrounded by swarms of other people, Mia's shoulders dropped a fraction of an inch, and a sigh of relief exited on the breath she'd been holding for what felt like years.

In New York, she realized, she could be truly invisible.

She thought that once she'd had enough exploring, she'd

just dip down into the nearest station and make her way back to the route that would take her home. In the meantime, she allowed her pace to quicken and discovered that she would suddenly need to take a right turn, then a left. She was moving, legs pushing, heart pumping. When was the last time her muscles had experienced any real physical exertion?

With her blood now coursing through her veins, she felt more alive. How could she have possibly forgotten how good this felt?

She had no idea how far she'd gone or even where she was, but it seemed people were leaving work now. The sidewalks swelled, people hailed cabs, and crowds descended the subway stairs for the connected cars that would take them home.

It was getting late. Past five now, for sure, but Mia didn't want to look at her phone to check. Her phone would verify precisely how long she'd been gone. It might contain messages from Holly or Alexander, checking on her. Wondering where she was and what time she would be home. Maybe even a worried text, *Everything okay?*

And with confirmation of their expectations of her, the magic of this moment, this endorphin-laced high Mia was relishing, would be broken, and she would slip down into the nearest subway entrance and do what was expected of her. Go home.

So, she left her phone in her purse.

She would go home soon, but she couldn't stop now. She *needed* to walk one more block.

And when she had, Mia found herself standing on the sidewalk facing the glassed entrance of an art gallery.

Its bright white space illuminated by the halogen lights on

the ceiling. Each one directed so that it focused on the many framed artworks hanging on the walls.

Time and space zeroed in on her as she stared through the gallery's glass walls. The city around her was darkening—a stark contrast to the gallery's bright interior. She was vaguely aware of people rushing past her on the sidewalk. Inside, a handful of individuals gazed at the art on display.

She knew this place.

And she didn't.

It was a feeling. Gazing into the display before her, she felt excitement, expectation, and also fear. But why? She had no idea. She felt certain she knew this place while also having no memory of it.

"Excuse me," a man said politely, breaking her spell as he reached for the door.

"Oh, I'm sorry," Mia said and fell back a step. "I'm blocking the whole door."

"No worries," the man smiled at her. He wore a white oxford button-down shirt with an open collar tucked into black jeans. He was carrying a large package wrapped in brown paper and shifted it to his other arm as he held the door open with one of his black laced boots. He inclined his head toward the gallery's interior. "Are you coming in for the show?"

Mia blinked once, and her eyes flicked to the large poster in the gallery's window. It was an advertisement for an art show opening tonight. "Um...yes," she decided on a whim. "Thank you," she added as she slipped past him and caught a whiff of his warm and woodsy cologne.

"My pleasure," he said as he followed behind her, then

passed by as he carried his package to the back of the gallery and disappeared behind a rear door.

Maybe the gallery owner? Or manager? Mia wondered as she picked up one of the full-color information brochures from the pedestal near the entrance. It detailed the artist's biography and provided information about several of the works. Mia flipped the cardstock front to back, scanning more than reading, then looked up and considered the space she was in.

Why was she here?

It was all so random, and yet, that feeling of familiarity persisted. Mia was nearly sure she had never been here, not since the accident anyway. Attending art galleries was not something Holly would have ever had any interest in, so it was certain that she wouldn't have accompanied Mia to one during those early years when they lived here.

And Alexander? The mere mention of anything art related made his eyes glaze over.

Mia wondered if—

"Hello," a young woman said as she leaned into Mia's distracted field of vision. "Can I help you?"

The thread of her thought vanished as Mia focused her eyes on the woman before her. She, too, wore a white blouse, but it was tucked into a black pencil skirt. Her long red hair was tied back in a low ponytail at the base of her neck. Her bright blue eyes evaluated Mia. Probably trying to determine if Mia was a "just-looking" type of visitor or could afford to plunk down the degree of cash required to remove one of these framed pieces and relocate it to a private collection.

"Well..." Mia returned the woman's smile. Suddenly Dominique's advice came back to her. "Maybe?"

The woman settled her stance, clasped her hands in front of herself, and waited for Mia to continue.

"I have this portrait—"

"I'm afraid we don't deal in consignment." The woman stopped Mia's explanation cold. "But if you like, I can give you the list we keep of all the local dealers. If you'll follow me." She turned and waited for Mia to make a move.

Mia raised her hands wide in front of her and shook her head. "No, *I'm* afraid you've misunderstood. I'm not looking to sell the piece, it's a portrait of my father, and far too dear to me to ever part with. What I'm looking for is some help identifying the artist."

The woman raised her eyebrows and gave her a lopsided smirk. "Do you have the provenance?"

Mia opened her eyes wider. "I'm not sure what that is?"

The woman set her lips in a straight line. Mia had the distinct impression that her ignorance was seriously trying this young woman's patience, despite the fact, there were only four other people in the gallery, and all of them appeared to be entertaining themselves just fine. "You know what, forget I said anything. Thank you for your help."

"Of course," the woman said, her tone a confectionary of falseness. "If there's nothing else?"

Mia shook her head and turned to go. This was a mistake, just some weird happenstance. Why had she even come inside?

"Leaving so soon?" a man's voice called out.

CHAPTER 21

When Mia turned back, she could see the man who had held the door striding toward her with the young redhead, who now looked decidedly less smug. Mia could only assume this was her boss.

When he reached them, he gave Mia a big warm smile. "But you haven't even seen the collection yet."

"She's not here for the show," the woman responded as if trying to preemptively explain why she had failed to make Mia feel welcome.

"Thank you, Courtney," the man said. "I'll take it from here."

The girl shrugged and headed over to an older couple discussing a large, blue and black canvas on the back wall.

"Now," he said as he resettled his piercing gaze on Mia. "If not for the show, what does bring you in this evening?"

Mia glanced at her shoes, wondering how to answer such a simple question when it didn't have a simple answer. What *had* brought her into his art gallery? Random rambling?

The lights from their window reflecting onto the darkening sidewalk outside? Or the notion that she *knew* this place but held no discernible memory as to why or how.

Mia decided to stick with the reasoning she'd given Courtney. "I own this piece, but I'm unable to identify the artist. I shouldn't bother you with it...."

The man waved this away. "Don't worry about that," he said as he glanced back at Courtney, seeming to recognize that the young woman was the reason Mia was unsure. "My daughter is young and still learning the fine art of excellent customer service. I tell her all the time, art sales are a marathon, not a sprint. Maybe I help you today, and you buy a piece two years from now." He shrugged as he smiled. "I'm Gary Surrey, owner of this gallery. How can I help? Do you have a picture of the piece in question?"

"No, I," Mia began to explain but then remembered. "Wait! Actually, yes," she said as she shifted her purse to the front of her body and pulled out her phone. "I nearly forgot, which is ridiculous because the whole reason it came up, not knowing the artist, was because we were reworking our insurance and well...you don't need to know all that, I'm sorry."

She opened her photo app and first clicked on the grouping from June, and proceeded to scroll through all the photos she had taken for the insurance documentation. "Basically, no estimated value could be determined for the piece because I didn't have any documentation regarding who the artist was." She found the photo, clicked on it to enlarge it, then handed her phone to Gary."

Gary plucked a pair of black-rimmed glasses from his breast pocket, settled them on his face, then peered at Mia's screen. A second later, he glanced up over the rims. He pointed at the phone with his free hand. "Is this who I think it is?"

Mia nodded. "Yes, Raphael Renaud." She lowered her voice to a whisper. "He was my father."

Gary's eyebrows rose a fraction of an inch as he gazed at the phone. He enlarged the photo and zoomed in on the signature. Mia watched his forehead furrow as he stared at the signature, then he leveled his gaze at her from above the rims of his glasses. "You should come with me to the back office," he said, handing her phone back.

"You know this artist?" Mia asked as she dropped the phone back into her purse and followed Garry's lead through the gallery.

"I wouldn't say that. But I have something that may interest you and might be able to help." Garry raised a hand and nodded as they passed the older couple in hushed conversation in front of the blue and black canvas. The man gave Gary a warm smile, but the woman's expression looked pinched. Mia had the distinct impression the couple did not agree on this piece and were quietly arguing over the purchase.

Gary held the door at the back of the gallery open for Mia. On the threshold, she hesitated. Her hands curled into loose fists and gathered the cuffs of her long sleeves into her palms. Through the doorway, she could see the cluttered back office. It had several large tables with stacks of framed art in various stages of either being wrapped or unwrapped.

She had the sensation of standing on a precipice. If she had headed for her subway station after leaving the institute, she would be home by now. Making dinner for the girls and waiting for Alexander to get home. Holly was probably getting worried— she would surely call her cell any moment now. And if she didn't answer, would she then call Alexander? Alert him to the fact that Mia was still not home? How would she explain her strange wanderings? What was she doing here?

"Everything okay?" Gary asked.

Mia shifted her gaze to his face, and she could see the concern in his eyes. She considered waving her hand, dismissing the attempt at identifying the artist of her father's portrait with a swift, *oh, never mind*, and leaving this gallery and its helpful owner without so much as a backward glance.

Gary's expression opened up into an easy and reassuring smile. "I know it looks like a disaster back there." He nodded toward the office. "But hand to heart, I swear that's not where I keep my bodies. You'll be perfectly safe." He leaned toward her. "Unless it's where my daughter keeps her bodies," he whispered. "I can't make any promises about her," he said as his eyes darted to where Courtney was again standing with the older couple. The rigid set of her spine gave away her annoyance with their indecision over the piece.

Mia laughed, and her unfounded anxiety evaporated under Gary's charm. She was being ridiculous. This constant dread, worry, and suspicion ignited her central nervous system; these emotions were what she was supposed to be working to recognize and dispel before they sent her spiraling. She shook her head once and entered the office space, promising herself she would record this very episode in the journal Ty had asked her to start keeping so they could review it at her next session.

Gary followed behind her and flicked the light switch on the wall to his right, flooding the messy spaces before them in bright white light.

He carved a path ahead of her, working his way around tables and stacks of art on rolling carts. "It's just here," he said as he rounded an enormous scarred and beaten mahogany desk shoved into the far corner, its top littered with papers, pens, takeout containers, and catalogs. The detritus measured over two feet high in some places, and Mia wondered if Gary usually allowed customers behind the curtain of the show-room facade out front.

"Sorry, this is such a mess," he said when he noticed Mia staring. He ran a hand through his hair and took in the sight as if only now considering the precise perspective of his working condition exposed under this particular lighting. "I keep meaning to clean it up," he added as he worked his way past his ripped office chair and reached for one of the small canvases that hung on the wall to the right of the desk.

Mia watched as Gary repositioned his thick-rimmed glasses and peered into the lower right-hand corner of the piece. He nodded several times to himself before raising his eyes to hers. "Can I see that photo again, please?"

Without a word, Mia handed him her phone with the portrait still visible on the screen.

"Thank you," he said as he took the device in one hand and held his canvas in the other. He studied the two for several seconds, his eyes darting rapid-fire back and forth. He enlarged the photo several times and examined the signa-ture on his piece under a magnifying glass that he pulled from one of the desk's creaking drawers. After what felt like an eternity, Mia watched as a small smile lit the corners of his mouth, and he finally raised his excited gaze to meet hers.

He nodded his head several times. "I'm almost certain...

of course, we'll need you to bring the original in, but I feel pretty confident they're the same."

Mia shook her head at him. "What are the same?"

"The signatures. The artists." He handed Mia her phone and the small painted canvas.

She studied them side by side for a few seconds. She was no expert, but they looked the same to her. "That's great," she said. "Who is it?"

Gary's face broke into a broad grin as his head slowly shook back and forth. "I don't have the faintest idea."

Confused, it was now Mia's turn to shake her head. "I don't understand."

"That piece." He pointed to the canvas in Mia's hand. "It was a gift for my mother. She owned and operated this gallery for fifty years. She knew everyone, and I mean everyone, who was anyone in the art world. She'd pick up the phone, and they'd be having lunch the next day. She passed away five years ago."

"I'm sorry," Mia said reflexively.

Garry nodded. "Thank you. I'd been living in Dallas. Making my own art." He shrugged off this confession as irrelevant. "But she left this place to me. Hoped I'd be able to keep it going the way she had. And that's neither here nor there other than to explain that that piece has been hanging in that spot next to this desk since before I took over the place. I have no idea if there's any documentation for it. All I know is that the artist inscribed the back of the canvas to my mother."

Mia flipped the canvas over and saw words painted in blue.

For Millie, thank you for everything 2003

I've always assumed it was a personal gift to her from one of the artists that showed here. I have no idea who painted it, but it was special enough for her to hang it right next to her desk. I never took it down. And until today, I've never seen another piece with the same signature."

"But if you don't know who it was...."

"But I do know it was someone associated with my mother. She was always taking an interest in new talent, trying to give them a chance by showing their work. I'd bet money the artist showed here at some point. And if that's true, it's only a matter of digging through my mother's old documents and matching the signature on a contract to the one on these paintings."

Mia couldn't believe she was this close to finding the person responsible for creating her father's portrait. "Is that something you're willing to do? After all...the time it could take." Mia handed the painting back to Gary.

"I mean," he said as he hung it on the wall beside his mother's desk. "I can't promise I'll figure it out tomorrow, or even this month, if I'm being honest. But my mother kept *everything*."

Mia nodded as she glanced around. She assumed Gary was more like his mother than he might want to admit.

"And we at least have a date to start with, 2003. I'd bet money that some document in her files links our artist to a decipherable name carefully typed into a contract with this signature underneath. Leave me your number," he said, handing her a stack of pale pink sticky notes and a pen. "I'll call you the moment I discover anything."

Mia wrote her name and number down, shaking her head at her great good luck to have stumbled into this exact art gallery with this exact portrait. She handed the stack of notes back to Gary and watched as he peeled the top one off and placed it in the breast pocket of his shirt. "I don't know how to thank you," she said. "I only wish dear Millie Miller were still alive so I could hug her and thank her myself for keeping that picture."

Gary smiled but then looked puzzled. "How did you know her last name was Miller?"

CHAPTER 22

*A*lexander pulled his Mercedes into the garage and let his head fall against the headrest. As the double garage door rolled shut behind him, he closed his eyes and mentally prepared himself to enter his home.

He felt loose and uncertain. Between his strange encounter with Tasha this morning and the knowledge that Mia had her first session as part of Erica's new study—everything felt off. Unpredictable.

Like he wasn't driving the bus, and he could see it heading for a cliff.

Everything felt at stake. His marriage, his professional career...his integrity. For the tenth time, he wondered if he should just move forward with separating himself from Mia regardless of her many promises to pull her shit together. What if he went into the house, straight up the stairs, packed a bag, and just left?

Walked out. Right now.

What would that feel like?

What would it look like?

He had no idea. Normally so centered and sure, he suddenly felt like his internal guidance system was malfunctioning. Failing him on every front.

And now that Mia had involved Erica. Alexander shook his head. How could he even think of walking out on Mia when she was now seeing Erica and doing the one thing he had asked of her as the condition for him *not* leaving.

Alexander banged his head against the leather headrest several times, grabbed his bag off the passenger seat, and got out of his car.

He couldn't leave. It was ridiculous to even entertain the thought of returning to the city tonight, unfettered and free. He had responsibilities, the girls to consider.

Besides, he suspected that when he wasn't consumed with frustration over her present state, part of him still loved Mia.

When he opened the door to the house, he could hear the girls and Mia in the kitchen having dinner. He closed the door to the garage quietly behind him and let his bag slide silent and slow off his shoulder and onto the mudroom bench. Alexander stood in the dark room, eyes closed, and wrangled his thoughts and emotions into a state that would allow him to face his family with an outward demeanor that wouldn't tip them off to the fact that he was spiraling on the inside.

After several deep breaths, he opened his eyes, constructed his face into a practiced smile, and strode toward the kitchen, where he would face his wife and accept the girls' loud and always overzealous greeting.

As he rounded the corner into the kitchen, both girls looked up from their dinner plates at the counter. Their expressions were surprised—and maybe scared? They didn't say a word to him and immediately returned to eating their food. Not a single screamed, "Hello, daddy!" from either of them.

Even more surprising—it wasn't Mia with her long sheath of jet-black hair standing on the other side of the kitchen island orchestrating the meal. It was Holly, her short shock of bright white hair the complete opposite of what he was expecting.

"Holly," he blurted as his eyes darted around the kitchen, and his mind attempted to put all the mismatched pieces of this puzzle together into a scene his brain could understand. "Why are you here? Where's Mia?"

Holly seemed to hesitate before turning to face him, almost as if she hadn't heard him. She took a moment to dry her hands on the dish towel before turning around. "Hello," she said, her tone distant and practiced, like a stranger or a telemarketer who knows you don't want to be hearing from them.

Both the girls had their eyes glued to Holly's face like they knew something was up and were waiting to see what might happen next.

"Mia's not back yet from her appointment in the city," she explained. "She called around two and asked if I could pick the girls up from school. Apparently, the doctor asked her to stay longer."

At the mention of Mia's doctor—Erica—Alexander's back stiffened. He wouldn't say outright that he was intimidated by Erica, and certainly not that he was afraid of her, but the woman was a pillar in his field. Her influence knew no bounds. The thought of his wife sitting across from her, or even one of her research assistants, sharing vulnerable details about herself and their life made him sweat.

Unable to express himself, the anxiety crawling through his gut, Alexander only nodded at the information. "Thank you," he said. "For getting the girls, feeding them." He motioned with his hand to the plates of spaghetti the girls hadn't touched since his arrival. It was then he noticed a large gash on the back of Everly's hand.

His brow furrowed as he rounded the counter and took her small arm in his hands. "What on earth happened?" he asked and tried to look into Everly's face for an answer, but her head was turned toward her sister.

Sasha sighed. "She fell."

"Fell? How? Where?" Alexander now directed his questions to Sasha as he inspected the gash on Everly's hand. He was unable to imagine how she could get such an injury, on the back of her hand, from a fall.

"On the playground," Sasha said. "At school during recess. "She fell off the climbing frame and scratched herself."

"At school?" Alexander clarified and glanced at Holly for confirmation. "And they didn't call. Did they call Mia?" He met Holly's gaze across the counter and watched as she shrugged in response.

"I'm not sure. She didn't mention it when she called, but she didn't have much time to talk either." Holly's gaze shifted to Sasha, who was nodding.

"They called mommy," Sasha confirmed.

And Everly nodded, glanced up at Alexander for a moment, then dropped her eyes like she was in trouble for something.

He let go of her arm, wondering if maybe he had scared

her with his surprise and concern. He sometimes miscalculated and came in too hot with Everly. Sasha was so brash and outspoken; it was easy to sometimes forget how extremely sensitive Everly was. How rapidly she shrunk before sudden movement or loud sounds.

"Okay, well. As long as they called mommy, I guess. I'll give them a call tomorrow. Make sure they know they can call me too. I do have a phone."

"Oh, they know," Sasha added. "I told them they didn't have to bother you. She was going to be okay." Sasha leaned over and put her arm around Everly's shoulders. "We decided."

Alexander stared at Sasha. "*You* decided?"

"Me *and* Everly."

Alexander nodded at her—something felt weird here.

He looked at Holly, but she turned on the kitchen faucet and was busy clearing the girls' dinner plates. "I think I'll head out now," she said. "Harris is probably wondering if I'll ever come home."

"Oh, right. Of course. Sorry, you had to stay so late."

Holly turned off the water and began drying her hands again. "No worries. I loved spending time with my nieces today." She smiled at them both. "But I should get going now." She rounded the counter and kissed both Everly and Sasha on their heads. "See you guys Monday?"

Both girls smiled and nodded.

"Bye, Alexander."

"Bye," he said and watched as she gathered her bag from the end of the island and rounded the corner. He followed her to the front door and watched from their front porch as she crossed the street to her truck parked on the opposite side. He was so consumed with his thoughts he'd missed seeing her truck when he pulled into the garage. As she hoisted herself onto the bench seat, she waved her hand. Alexander waved back and closed the door, unable to shake the feeling that something was off.

"Daddy!" Sasha yelled from the kitchen.

"Yes?" he asked, letting his suspicions slide away.

"Can we watch a movie?"

Alexander groaned to himself. A movie meant something brightly colored and animated, for sure. "Yes!" he called back as he headed into the dining room to get his bottle of Macallan. "Go ahead!"

In his front pocket, his phone buzzed with a text message. He pulled it out and took his reading glasses from his shirt pocket so he could make out the tiny words.

It was from Tasha Adams. It was impossible to deny the surge of electric excitement that shot through him.

Instead of reading her message right away, he plucked one of the crystal tumblers from the bar cabinet and poured himself a generous glass of scotch. "Daddy will be in his office!"

"Okay!" Sasha yelled back. "We'll be in the family room!"

Alexander shook his head at Sasha's precocious personality. "Good to know!" he yelled and headed for the stairs and the privacy of his office with his drink in hand and Tasha's message in his pocket.

CHAPTER 23

$\mathcal{H}$olly waved to Alexander, standing on the porch watching her leave under a cloud of suspicion. She could feel it. When he waved back, turned, and closed the door to the house, she shut her driver's side door and let her head fall back against the seat.

Sasha had lied to her father. Bold and outright. Sasha knew it, Everly knew it, and worst of all, Holly both knew it and allowed it to happen.

Sasha had done it to protect the dog, now named Stevie. Even at five, she understood that her father would not have allowed Everly to be harmed without retribution against the dog. Holly pulled her keys from her jeans pocket and closed her eyes as she started the geriatric engine. She had to pump the gas and crank the key twice before it finally turned over and came to life, disrupting her sister's silent, eco-car neighborhood with the roar of nineteen-sixties diesel technology.

She popped the emergency brake, pushed the clutch, shifted the stick into first gear, and allowed the truck to slow roll away from the curb and down the street, never above the posted fifteen miles per hour.

It was wrong. She knew it. She felt it. She should have spoken up and told Alexander the truth about what happened to Everly's hand today.

But the thought of what would most likely happen after a confession of that magnitude was too much to bear. She didn't know if she could for sure save Stevie, but she didn't know for sure that she couldn't either. But if Alexander knew the truth about what had happened today—if Harris found out—Stevie would be out of the barn and waiting for euthanasia first thing in the morning.

And maybe he should be. It terrified her to think about what might have happened today. What if Everly had been a little closer, pushed her arm through the cage a little farther? Holly couldn't bear that thought either.

As she reached the stop sign that would lead her from her sister's neighborhood and onto the main road, Holly considered turning the truck around and stopping the lie right now. No matter what the consequences for Stevie. Alexander and Mia had a right to know what happened to Everly.

And what sort of example was she setting for her nieces? She didn't ask Sasha to lie, but she certainly didn't step up to stop her. Where was the lesson in that? Holly put her blinker on, ready to make the U-turn and confess everything to Alexander as soon as the car approaching from the opposite direction was clear.

Holly watched as the headlights crossed through the intersection in front of her. As it rolled past her, she recognized the white Volvo XC 90 that stopped beside her—Holly made eye contact with Mia, and they rolled down their windows.

"I'm so sorry you're here so late," Mia said right away. "I swear next time will be earlier."

Holly shook her head. "It's fine. It was nice to spend the day with the girls. Alexander's home now." Holly hitched her thumb in the direction of the house.

Mia scrunched her nose up. "What's his mood like?"

Holly considered the question and how to answer it, then shrugged. "Fine...I think. There was one thing...."

Mia watched and waited to hear what was waiting for her down the block.

"Today...Everly got hurt."

Mia's eyes looked alarmed, but she didn't interrupt.

"The back of her hand, there's a pretty bad gash. She's okay. It's been cleaned up and has a bandage."

"What happened?" Mia asked.

Holly licked her lips and swallowed. "Something...something at school. On the playground, I think. Apparently, they tried to call you?" she lied.

"Really?" Mia picked up her phone from the seat next to her and glanced briefly at the screen before shaking her head. "I must have...it was such a bizarre day." She shook her head. "I'll call them tomorrow."

"It's fine," Holly blurted. "She's fine, and Alexander already knows. I don't think you have to worry about it."

Mia's shoulders dropped, and she looked at Holly with such unbridled gratitude Holly had to look away. "Thank you again. For today, for everything." Mia shook her head.

"Don't thank me. I loved it, really. Now get home. You can tell me all about your psychedelic therapy later."

Mia smiled, blew Holly a kiss, and drove away.

Holly shifted into first gear again and continued through

the intersection that would take her home. "Not everyone needs to know everything," she whispered and shuddered.

It was something she and Mia had often heard throughout their childhood. One of Pixlie's favorite lines and excuses. It made Holly sad to think that it would mean nothing if she'd said it out loud to Mia. Holly alone carried the weight of it.

CHAPTER 24

ia slowed down, flipped on her blinker, and turned the Volvo left onto the hidden gravel drive. Large, evenly spaced red oaks lined the entire mile that stretched from the turn-off to the fifteen-foot wrought iron gates that guarded the entrance to her childhood home, Beaumar Manor.

"This is where Grandma lives?" Sasha blurted from the backseat.

"Yes," Mia said as she turned to see her daughters leaning from their booster seats to get a better view through the windshield. "And it's also where Aunt Holly and I grew up," she whispered.

She leaned out her window and entered the nine-digit gate code into the silver keypad. A second later, the two large gates swung inward, the old, rusty hinges squealing into the silent autumn air.

Mia wondered if her mother could hear the sound inside the house and worried it might frighten her.

Pixlie didn't know Mia was coming today. Mia *and* the two girls.

She had tried calling her mother several times yesterday and this morning, but Pixlie never answered the phone.

"Do you think everything is okay?" Mia had asked Holly when she called to tell her that their mother wasn't picking up.

"I'm sure everything is fine. She's probably just on one of her old movie jags in the theater room. You know how she is."

Only Mia didn't know how her mother was. Not even a little bit. But she didn't remind Holly of this. "Okay. Well, I just thought I'd run it by you."

"Why are you calling her anyway?" Holly asked, the pitch of her voice climbing ever so slightly.

"I just thought I'd check on her...I don't know. I thought maybe I'd invite her to the girls' birthday." It was a lie. She was calling Pixlie to let her know she would like to visit on Sunday. As Ty instructed, Mia intended to spend some time both at Beaumar Manor and with her mother in hopes that maybe some shred of her past might reveal itself to her.

But she didn't want Holly to know she was going. Mia knew Holly would insist on coming with her, and Mia needed to do this without her. She wanted the opportunity to view Pixlie and their childhood home from her own perspective without Holly's constant commentary on everything.

"Well, I don't think I'd invite her. To be honest, it would probably be a disaster. And embarrassing, if you know what I mean."

"Yes, well... you're probably right. I'll think about it."

Mia rolled her window back up and drove through the

wide gates. From her rearview mirror, she watched as Everly and Sasha craned their necks to see the gates close behind them until they reconnected with a clang.

"Grandma lives in a castle," Sasha stated.

Mia smiled at them through the mirror. "Kind of. It *is* a very large house." It occurred to her that neither of them had any memory of this place, and Mia tried to remember when the last time was the girls, or any of them for that matter, had been out to visit the property.

It had been years, not since they were toddlers. The house was such a claptrap of wonderment and danger for curious girls; keeping their tiny hands from placing every god-knows-what into their mouths had been challenging. Which was nothing and might have even been handled by both her and Alexander watching the girls like hawks. But when little Sasha picked up a gun—a *real* gun, a *loaded* gun—from a side table in the library, they had left immediately.

"Oh, that," Pixlie took the gun from Alexander's shaking hands. "It's nothing. Mia and Holly grew up with guns all over the house." She had waved her hand around absently. "Children will learn to not mess with things if given a chance."

Alexander's restraint was a testament to his reason. Pixlie wasn't a well woman.

Mia and Alexander both decided Beaumar Manor and Pixlie herself were so far beyond what might be considered toddler proof it was best to avoid taking the girls there again until they were older. Much, much older.

As a result, the girls rarely saw their grandmother since the women could only be pried from the house under extreme circumstances. Alexander and Mia's wedding. The birth of the girls.

Thinking about it now, as she pulled the Volvo to a stop on the disheveled circular driveway, Mia felt a twang of guilt for not making an effort to visit her mother, out here all alone, more often.

She would make a point of getting out here at least once a week from now on.

She turned in her seat and looked into the girls' faces. "Ready?"

Wide-eyed and excited to enter the *castle* where their mother grew up, they both nodded.

"And what do we do if we see a gun?" Mia asked.

"Don't touch it," both girls said.

"Good girls. Now let's go."

Sasha unbuckled herself and then helped Everly with her seatbelt; the stiff orange button was still a struggle for her to press. Everyone closed their doors, and the sound echoed off the estate's large, gray, roughhewn bricks.

Mia took a deep breath as she glanced up, taking in all four stories and the multitude of windows above her. The girls flanked her sides, each grasping one of her hands.

As they approached the front door, it occurred to Mia that maybe the reason Pixlie hadn't answered the phone was because she could not answer it. What if she was walking into a scene her five-year-old's shouldn't be seeing.

Mia was deciding if she should have the girls wait in the car until she had gone inside herself and confirmed that Pixlie was alive and well when the front door opened before them.

"Can I help you?" the woman standing in the doorway

asked, her accent heavy and Russian. She looked about sixty and wore a floral, dark green blouse over tight brown trousers.

"Um... we're here to see Pixlie. My mother?" Mia answered, uncertain who this strange woman was and what she was doing here.

"Ah, okay. Come in," the woman said and stood to the side. "She didn't say you were coming." The woman shook her head, tapped her temple, and gave Mia a knowing look. "Must have forgot."

Mia smiled, nodded, and allowed this woman to believe that was what had happened, not that Pixlie never had any idea they were coming in the first place.

"She's in treatment for another twenty minutes. But I'll let her know you're here." The woman turned and walked away across the black and white checkered floor, leaving Mia and the girls standing in the foyer. Obviously, she assumed that, as Pixlie's daughter, Mia would know how to make herself at home.

Mia stood stock still with both girls glued to her sides, uncertain of what to do next. She grew up in this house but felt like a stranger within its walls.

"Mom," Everly whispered.

"Yes?"

"I'm thirsty."

Mia nodded. "Okay, let's get something to drink from the kitchen while we wait for Grandma." It was a task to focus on. Mia tried to ignore the fact she felt like a trespasser in a stranger's home. Surely Pixlie didn't think of her as a stranger. Did she?

Mia shook her head. "This way," she said and guided the

girls through the foyer, past several cluttered, jewelry-toned rooms trimmed in thick mahogany, and eventually into the kitchen at the back of the house.

Like everything else in Beaumar, the kitchen was enormous, but time here had stopped somewhere in the late eighties. In the center, a massive island anchored the room with a butcher block top, while above it, copper pots and pans hung from racks attached to the large wood beams that crisscrossed the ceiling. When Mia flicked on the lights, she could see that all the hanging cookware was covered in a dusty film and was connected by an elaborate network of thick cobwebs.

Apparently, Pixlie wasn't big on cooking. *Or cleaning*, Mia thought, as the rest of the kitchen's filth came into focus around her. The tiles used for the walls of the island matched the tiles above the countertops and behind the stove; six-inch, sapphire blue hexagons that, like the archaic appliances, were once the height of modernity but now made the space appear dark and cramped.

But maybe that was mostly due to the clutter and grime that filled every usable space. Unwashed dishes piled in the sink with what looked like weeks-old food cemented in place. Half-drunk glasses of water, juice with a layer of mold, lipstick-stained coffee cups, and crystal tumblers everywhere.

Mia wasn't sure she should allow the girls to even be in this biohazard, let alone get them something to drink from it.

"It stinks in here," Sasha said loudly.

"Shhh, that's not polite," Mia said, waving her hand at her daughter's rudeness. She had no idea where Pixlie was or when she might appear.

"But mom, it *does* stink," Sasha repeated, this time in a whisper.

"I know," Mia said. "But you shouldn't say so."

Everly stood wide-eyed, taking in the scene. She didn't blurt out her thoughts like her sister always did, but her gaze seemed to catalog the environment and draw conclusions she kept to herself.

Mia opened several cupboards looking for a clean glass but found that they were mostly empty. One was filled only with an assortment of protein bars. She opened the industrial-sized fridge next, slightly terrified of what she might find, and discovered that this space, to her surprise, was immaculate. It was empty except for three bottles of Beefeater gin, single-serve cans of tonic, and a package of water bottles.

Relieved, Mia reached in and grabbed two of the water bottles, and shut the door. She unscrewed the caps and handed the bottles to Sasha and Everly. The girls still inspected carefully what they were drinking before bringing the bottles to their lips, despite the fact the containers had been sealed.

Mia didn't blame them.

She gazed around the kitchen one last time before ushering the girls into another, hopefully tidier, part of the house. She wondered if she should spend her time today rolling up her sleeves and managing this. As one of Pixlie's daughters—should she do something about this? How long had this been going on? Did Holly know?

Mia felt sure that if her brain wasn't so damaged, she would have many emotions about seeing her mother live this way. If she had her memories and history with Pixlie, she would feel emotionally compelled to take care of all this.

As it was, Mia felt like she'd stumbled into a stranger's

chaos and was primarily embarrassed for them to be so exposed.

"Come on," Mia said to her daughters. "Let's go find somewhere else to wait for Grandma Pixlie."

She would talk with Holly later tonight about what should be done about all this.

CHAPTER 25

*A*s she guided the girls through the house in search of somewhere to sit, the enormity of the situation began to come into focus.

The kitchen was by far the worst, but every room they passed was also cluttered with collections of things, from books to shawls to candle sticks. Statues, photo frames, lamps, and discarded jewelry. Loose papers, cards, mosaic bowls, bells, a violin, and a set of wooden crutches. It went on and on. Mia felt like she was browsing the world's most over-crowded and disorganized secondhand shop.

She steered Sasha and Everly into the library and motioned for them to take seats on a blue velvet couch in front of the ash-filled fireplace.

The room was a library. With a high ceiling that boasted two enormous crystal chandeliers, all four walls had floor-to-ceiling mahogany bookshelves loaded with leather and cloth-bound hardbacks. Considering the amount of dust and visible cobwebs that coated them, Mia assumed they had not been touched in years—maybe decades.

On the east-facing wall in front of the blue velvet couch, an enormous stone fireplace was the only feature to interrupt the grand shelves with its smooth stacked gray and white stones and once glossy mahogany mantel. Above the mantel hung an oil portrait of Pixlie, a very young Pixlie, that Mia guessed was created sometime in the late 70s or early 80s. Her willowy frame was adorned in a gauzy cream fabric. The talented artist had captured the illusion of the dress being barely there, nearly transparent. Pixlie's image glowed, and she looked every bit the starlet she had been. It was the only item in the whole room that was free of the dust and dirt that had settled into every crevice of this room. Of the entire house, Mia assumed.

Both girls sat straight backed on the couch, their hands clasping their plastic water bottles between their knees. They seemed afraid to move or speak, as if they were uncertain of their safety in this strange place. Mia was about to reassure them when a noise behind her, a gentle cough from the doorway, made them all turn to see who was there.

It was Pixlie.

She was posed in the wide doorway, one hand resting high against the wooden frame, the other positioned lightly against the jutting bone of her hip. Behind her, Mia could see the Russian woman who had been giving Pixlie her *treatment*, shouldering a large bag and lugging a folding massage table toward the front door.

"Same next week, Mrs. Renaud?" The woman called out from down the hall.

Pixlie raised the hand from her hip. "Yes, Vera. Until next

week," she called back as a goodbye to the woman without ever turning her head or taking her eyes from Mia's. Only when the front door had closed behind Vera did she speak again. "This is such a lovely surprise," she said, her hand floating back to her hip.

Mia heard the words and understood the sentiment they were meant to convey but felt that Pixlie was perhaps parroting an appropriately polite greeting that would be expected of any host. Mia wished she could gauge Pixlie's facial expression, but she was just far enough away, and the lighting throughout the house was dim because Pixlie kept all the large windows closed off behind heavy, dusty drapes. "I did try to call," Mia explained. "Several times. Is the house phone not working?" Mia came around from her side of the blue velvet couch and approached her mother, extending her arms as she drew closer to hug the woman.

When she was still a few feet away, Mia could see Pixlie's face more clearly. Mia wasn't sure what treatments Vera performed, but it had to involve injecting a significant amount of facial filler and Botox into Pixlie's face. Additionally, it was apparent Pixlie recently had plastic surgery to lift and round out her features. Or rather, she had *more* plastic surgery to *further* lift and round out her features. Mia knew Pixlie had been under the knife several times before.

This would be yet another topic to discuss with Holly when she next spoke to her. Was she aware that their mother was continuing to have these procedures performed?

"Hello, mother," Mia said as she embraced Pixlie and felt the contours of her bones beneath her airy and elegant kaftan. "It's good to see you."

"Hello dear," Pixlie replied and returned Mia's hug. Her

spindly arms provided barely-there pressure before she quickly released Mia and took a step back. Her eyes shifted over Mia's shoulder. "I see you've brought the children?"

Mia turned and saw both Sasha and Everly peering over the back of the blue velvet couch at their mother and grandmother.

"Yes. I hope that's okay. They wanted to see you and the house."

Pixlie floated her hand into the air again. "Of course. You are all always welcome. But I'm afraid you've caught me without my face on." Pixlie shifted her chin, pursed her lips, and lifted her hand to frame her face. "So if you give me a few minutes to compose myself, I'll be better prepared to play the proper host to you all."

Mia took a moment to digest Pixlie's words, then nodded. "Of course." She shrugged. "Should we wait in here?"

"Darling, this is your home." Pixlie smiled and rested her hand on Mia's forearm for the briefest of moments, like a butterfly landing, then lifting off again. "Go wherever you like." Her arm arced wide as she swung it over her head. "The girls would prefer exploring to sitting in the library, don't you think?"

Mia nodded. Yes, it was true, the girls would prefer that, but Mia felt a sickness at the pit of her stomach rise up at the thought of them rambling through this claptrap.

"It's settled then. You show them around, and I'll be back before you know I'm gone." She leaned in and pressed her balloon-like lips to the side of Mia's face. When she turned to leave, her kaftan billowed out around her as her kitten-heeled alligator slides echoed against the hardwood floor.

Mia turned back to look at her girls and saw Sasha dragging Everly by the hand, her excitement barely contained. Everly pulled back, her brow furrowed in worry, and maybe fear, as she resisted her overzealous sister.

Undoubtedly, both girls had heard every word their strange and eccentric grandmother had said, and they had wildly different reactions to that information.

"I want to play hide-and-seek," Sasha said. She pulled Everly the last few inches and held her hand firmly so she couldn't escape. "You'll never find me," she whispered loudly in Everly's ear. "Never, ever."

Everly grasped Sasha's arm and pulled herself free from her ironclad grip. "I don't want to play hide-and-seek. This place is scary."

"It's not scary," Sasha declared. "And there are so many places to hide!"

"I thought you said it stinks," Everly shot back.

This reminder made Sasha pause and wrinkle her nose in remembrance, but it didn't deter her. "The kitchen will be off limits."

Mia sighed and knelt down in front of them both. "I don't think Grandma Pixlie would like you squirreling around and hiding in her house," she said. But the truth was, *Mia* wouldn't like it. The idea of her girls hiding somewhere in this enormous and cluttered house was a little terrifying. "How about if we explore it together? Especially since this is our first time here, and we don't know where anything is. It will be an adventure we can have together."

Both her girls stared back at her with confused expressions. Everly stated, "But mom, it's not *your* first time here. You lived here."

Mia held her breath. It was a slip. They were getting old

enough to notice these continuity errors between what they thought they knew about her and her life and statements like this that contradicted that presumed knowledge. "Of course, yes...I meant it's *your* first time. That you remember, anyway." The girls didn't know about her accident or memory loss, and Mia didn't know how to tell them or when.

But she knew, eventually, the truth would come out.

Sasha reached out her hand and placed it on Mia's face, right over her scar. "Okay, mom. We can play your game instead."

CHAPTER 26

*M*ia stared into Sasha's eyes. With the warmth of her daughter's hand against her scar, Mia wondered what her girls were beginning to think about her disfigurement now they were getting older.

"Can we see your room?" Everly asked.

Sasha dropped her hand, and Mia turned her gaze to Everly. "Um…sure," she said, trying to keep her tone light and easy. Of course, her daughters would want to see the bedroom where their mother grew up.

The problem was Mia didn't know where to find her childhood bedroom.

She had been to the house since her accident, but only a handful of times. And always with Holly. Holly would orchestrate the exceedingly brief visits with their mother, usually less than an hour while keeping them mostly confined to the library.

Mia held the girls' hands and stood up. She wondered if it was strange that she hardly came here, and when she did, it was always and only with her sister. Holly insisted that their mother wouldn't want to visit long because she tired easily and was so unaccustomed to visitors, even her own daughters apparently, that she would only tolerate brief check-ins.

"Should we head upstairs?" she whispered conspiratorially to the girls, who nodded enthusiastically. "Okay, let's go explore. This should be fun," she smiled wide at them—an attempt to hide her growing apprehension. In truth, she felt the urge to leave Beaumar. To make some excuse to her girls and walk them right out the front door without waiting for Pixlie to *put on her face.*

Maybe there was a reason Holly always insisted they keep it short…and confined.

She led the girls out of the library and back to the black and white marble-checkered foyer. When they were only a few feet away from the grand mahogany staircase that led to the upper floors, Mia stopped as a cold realization swept through her like a ghost.

She looked up, past the enormous crystal chandelier covered in dust and cobwebs, beyond the second-floor and up to the banister railing that guarded the third-floor landing.

The height of it was astounding. Her own body had traveled that distance in free fall, landing on the stone-cold marble slabs beneath their feet. Mia now looked down. Her body had once laid here, bled here, and almost died here.

She wondered if the tile had needed to be repaired or replaced. Or were they strong enough to survive the blow of her body crashing into them? Her own flesh and bones, not these stones, absorbed the force and split wide after she was pushed over that railing so high above.

"Mom?" Sasha asked.

Sasha's voice pulled Mia back and ground her in this present. "Yes?"

Sasha wrinkled her brow; whatever she saw on her mother's face worried her. "Are we going upstairs?"

Mia nodded and redirected her attention toward the staircase and the task of finding her old bedroom without tipping the girls off to the fact she didn't know where it was.

Both girls ran ahead of her, their short legs working hard to navigate the tall and wide steps while their hands kept their balance with the curved handrail. Mia let them fly ahead while she took her time, considering each step that carried her into the upper reaches of her childhood home.

As she climbed, she paused at the works of art that punctuated the expanse of off-white plaster wall above the mahogany wainscoting. Maybe she would find something familiar, something to jog her memory. She passed by these same gold-framed oil landscapes several times a day throughout her childhood—did they seem even a little familiar?

No. Mia sighed and continued up the stairs, her hand trailing the worn wooden handrail.

When she reached the landing on the second floor, she could see both her girls darting in and out of rooms that lined the hallway before her. Whatever they found in each room didn't capture their interest for more than a few seconds. When Mia poked her head into the first room on the right, she saw an elaborately decorated bedroom with a plump red bedspread that matched the large pillows against the heavy wooden headboard and the drapes that hung in a measured swag in front of the large windows.

It was a beautiful room, or it would have once been

considered one. It now had the neglected feel of a dated spare room. Neither Mia nor Holly had lived in this room, she was sure. And she was equally certain about the next four bedrooms and three bathrooms she glanced into on this floor. These were guest spaces, Mia knew. Given the layer of dust that coated everything, it must have been at least a decade since anyone had stayed here.

Two other hallways branched off the main one, and the girls were about to head down the one leading left when Mia called after them. "It's not there. Our rooms were upstairs." She pointed to the ceiling above her head. And somehow, she knew it was the truth, felt that it was right—even if she had no idea *how* she knew it. An electric thrill ran through her. Was this a memory? Or the beginning of one, at least? The girls gave up exploring and ran back down the hall toward her. They each grabbed one of her hands and dragged her back toward the staircase.

"Let's go, mom," Everly, her voice usually so quiet and small, insisted. She had caught Sasha's urgency to see as much of the old house as possible.

Once they reached the staircase, both girls abandoned Mia so they could run up ahead of her, racing to be the first to open each door and see what lay behind it. Mia glanced back down to the first floor. How long did it take Pixlie to make herself presentable? Would she be wondering where they were? But there was no sign of her in the foyer, and Mia didn't hear any sounds rising up from below. They probably had at least another fifteen to twenty minutes before Pixlie would come looking for them. Mia didn't get the impression that Pixlie's makeup and hair routine had a quick version. Nor did she imagine Pixlie was the type of person that felt she should rush just because she had unexpected company.

Pixlie would take exactly as long as she would take and not a minute less. The world would wait for her—it always had and always would.

This thought about her mother stopped Mia midway up the stairs. It was another truth; she felt it and knew it but couldn't explain how.

Along with the knowledge that she and Holly's bedrooms were upstairs, this knowing felt like the echo of a memory. The vapor of a vision just beyond her mind's current reach. Would a real and distinct memory come to her if she just sat still with this feeling, on the brink of this knowing?

Mia continued up the stairs, determined to keep her mind and emotions open to whatever else might strike her. The sense she had about her mother's peculiar personality wasn't a sentiment Holly had ever expressed. Holly rarely spoke of their parents, and Mia had always assumed that the topic was likely too painful for her. After all, Holly hadn't lost *her* memory. She was also there the day their father was killed and mourned the loss of him. And while Mia grieved the concept of her father, the closeness of the man who had raised, guided, and protected her, Holly missed the real Raphael. The man Holly could actually remember as their talented, larger-than-life father who was murdered in this very house.

Mia sometimes felt jealous of Holly's known history, but she now wondered if maybe Holly envied Mia's lack of genuine grief. It occurred to her that, amazingly, she had never sat down with her sister and discussed how she felt about everything that had happened since that terrible day.

Holly had always cared for Mia—but there wasn't any way Holly wasn't equally in need.

As she reached the highest stair, a profound sense of shame swept through Mia. She was so accustomed to Holly being the strong one, Holly taking care of everything, Holly knowing what needed to be done next. How had it never occurred to Mia that Holly might need her just as much?

The realization brought on a tidal wave of anxiety. She was selfish. Blind to her sister's needs. Incapable of taking care of herself, her children, her family. Broken and unfixable... this new therapy wouldn't work any better than any of the others. Alexander was tired of her and her problems. He would leave her and take her girls away from her.

And she deserved it.

On instinct, Mia closed her eyes and grasped her neck between her palms. As she squeezed, she could feel her pulse pound beneath the heel of her hands as her heart pumped hard and fast within her chest.

It's just the anxiety, she reasoned. She'd been off her meds for several days now and was vulnerable to these episodes. A rush of dizziness made her sway, and Mia wondered if she was about to pass out. She opened her eyes, grasped the banister next to her for support, and forced herself to take big breaths.

This was it, she realized. This was the place. Right here. Eighteen years ago, Mia had been pushed from this very spot. Over this railing. Shoved by the hands of the man who had shot her father only minutes before, leaving him to die.

Mia grasped the railing with both hands, her fingers curling around the polished dark wood, and forced herself to look. As she stared at the black and white tiles below, an oily, slick fear rolled up through her so quickly she thought she might be sick. Her skin crawled with the sense that someone was behind her, watching her, preparing to send her again over the edge and to her death below.

Some part of her, the thin thread of rational thought still trying to make her see and feel reason, knew she was safe. These feelings—it was trauma. The ancient history that lurked beneath her every waking moment, infiltrated her subconscious, and infected her with a sub-current of fear that felt impossible to root out.

"You're fine," she whispered, but no part of her believed it.

"Mom!"

Mia jolted and spun around, her every nerve now wild and set to explode. It was Sasha, standing outside a room down the hall. She looked astonished, like she had discovered something.

"What is it?" Mia managed, her voice ragged and on edge.

But Sasha was too excited to notice her mother's distress. "Come look! We found it!"

"Found what?"

"Your room!" Sasha pointed toward the open door next to her. "Before you even showed us. I found it!" Sasha yelled with excitement.

"I found it," Everly countered from somewhere inside the room.

Sasha turned her head toward the open door, "Did not!" she screamed at Everly.

"I did so," Everly replied calmly.

They were going to get into a fight any moment now. Mia could sense it. It didn't happen often, and it was almost always instigated by Sasha, but it was about to happen right now, and Mia was not in any condition to deal with that.

"I'm coming," she said, hoping that would take Sasha's mind off the argument with her sister.

Sasha rushed down the hallway, grabbed Mia's hand, and pulled her toward the room. "It's amazing," she said. "You were so lucky!"

CHAPTER 27

$\mathcal{A}$lexander sat at his desk, staring at the student paper on his monitor he was supposed to be grading. He had reread the wordy and convoluted first paragraph three times; it was impossible to keep his mind from floating away after only a few sentences.

Frustrated and unable to focus, he closed the document and grabbed his cell phone instead.

Mia had taken the girls to visit her mother for the day. A development that had stunned Alexander, but he silenced his questions when he learned this day trip was an assignment from Ty Yun. Alexander was having trouble conjuring the man's face and didn't think he had ever met him. He had intended to dig around online to learn whatever he could about the man but had been distracted by the singular topic that had taken up residence at the forefront of his mind.

Tasha Adams.

Alexander leaned back in his office chair and again pulled up the last text she'd sent him.

Thank you again for meeting with me and answering my MANY questions. I'm looking forward to having more of these opportunities in the future.

It meant nothing. He knew that. And yet he had kept returning to this text, again and again, since first reading it on Friday night. Each time he would spend an unreasonable amount of time deciphering any possible hidden meaning, the words like tea leaves at the bottom of a cup. Was Tasha *really* looking forward to seeing him again? And when she thought about these *opportunities* to see him again, were they frequent? Maybe regular? Did she imagine, eventually, reaching across the small coffee table that divided them and casually holding his hand? Would they, sometime in the future, sit side by side, their arms brushing against each other's while, beneath the table, their knees touched?

Alexander placed his phone face down and closed his eyes against these thoughts. His typically logical and pragmatic mind vacillated between a desire to be wanted in this way by a young, beautiful, intelligent woman and the fear that he was being ridiculous.

He leaned forward in his chair, clicked open his university mail account, and created a new message. He quickly typed a general but friendly greeting.

Dear Tasha,

Per our conversation last week, here are the links to apply for the available research assistant positions on my current projects.

He then proceeded to add some additional information about other faculty projects that were currently recruiting assistants. So as to seem impartial and as if he didn't care one way or the other if she applied to his. Although he did very much hope she didn't end up being more interested in the other projects and wondered for a moment if he should delete them from the email, just in case.

But it was better to at least appear impartial, he decided, so he left them in and just hoped she wouldn't end up applying for them.

Sincerely,

Alexander Strauss

He reread the message, considered his choice of *Dear Tasha,* and replaced it with a *Hello Tasha.* Satisfied with the switch, he then typed her first and last name into the address line, clicked on her university email address that auto-filled, and hit send.

A thrill of excitement ran through him. Was it the idea of seeing her? Not really. He would obviously see her in class. Maybe the intimacy of working together on a project he cared about? That was it. The idea of teaching her, mentoring her—coupled with her being attracted to him, his thinking, his work. He imagined her admiring him and that admiration getting tangled up with sexual desire.

It was a fantasy. He knew that. But thinking about it filled him with an energy, a lust for life, for her, that he hadn't felt in years. Was that so wrong? To feel alive like this, even if it was all, most likely, in his head?

He could get them a hotel room when they wanted one, somewhere nice—somewhere expensive, so the encounters never felt tawdry. And if it continued? Became something more between them? He could afford to rent an apartment in the city. Of course, he'd have to be careful. Take steps to ensure none of Mia's money was ever used.

If it ever went that far, he'd set up a separate, private bank account.

As his mind conjured ways in which he could secretly siphon money into a private account to pay for his imaginary affair with Tasha, Alexander leaned back and rested his hands on the round protrusion of his belly—that he fully intended to do something about starting this afternoon. Forty-one wasn't old, not anymore. Forty-one today wasn't like his father's forty-one. His father, whose hair had thinned into pale gossamer threads that the man cautiously combed over his fallow field of a bald head that expanded every year. His father, who wore cheap suits his mother bought him from J.C. Penny. A man whose greatest pleasure was an early dinner at Applebee's and a frosted pilsner glass filled with Budweiser. His father who worked his entire life selling Chevys at the same dealership in Columbus, Ohio, that had hired him the summer after his senior year in high school.

His father who had died at the age of forty-two from a heart attack that struck him on a Sunday while he watched the third quarter of the Denver Broncos and the Green Bay Packers in his favorite leather recliner. A half-finished Budweiser and a plate of homemade nachos going cold on the TV tray beside him.

Alexander had been seventeen and in his senior year of high school. At the funeral, his mother had stood on one side of him, crying uncontrollably into a wad of damp tissues, while his younger brother stood, shocked and silent, on his other.

At his graduation in the spring, Carl Tomlin, the owner of Tomlin Chevrolet, where his father had worked his entire life, shook Alexander's hand, told him how proud his father would have been, and offered Alexander a job.

"We can start you out cleaning the cars, just like your dad

did. But I'm sure you'll be on the selling floor by December." Carl shook his head and smiled. "Your dad was the best goddamn car salesman I've ever seen." He clapped Alexander hard on the back. "Come on down and see me next week."

Sometimes Alexander would lie awake at night, staring at the ceiling above his and Mia's bed, the proximity of Carl Tomlin's offer haunting him. His mind unfurled the life choices that would have fallen like dominos. His chest would grow tight at the thought that in some alternate universe, some other Alexander was still selling Chevy's in Columbus, Ohio, married to Debbie, his high school girlfriend, raising four kids, and falling asleep in front of the television every night.

That Alexander did not graduate from Columbia with his doctorate in neuropsychology. He didn't become a professor at Columbia, write a *New York Times* bestseller, drive a Mercedes, travel all over the world, or live in a house that cost more money than his father had ever made in his entire life.

Staring at his ceiling, he sometimes wondered if that other Alexander would also be dead at forty-two.

Then he would turn his head and gaze at Mia sleeping beside him because, of course, that other Alexander would never have even been in the same room with Mia Renaud— never mind married to her.

Even as the Alexander he had become, well educated, better dressed, and more self-confident, he had been utterly awed by Mia Renaud when they first met. Back then, he was the research assistant to Erica Monae, and Mia was working on her Ph.D. in clinical psychology with an emphasis on Jungian theory. Mia, who had a long history with both Erica and the Neurological Institute by then, was one of the participants in Erica's latest study. It had been Alexander's job to do the intake.

Meeting her that first time all those years ago, she was a perfect storm of mystery, intellect, infamy, and beauty. Of course, he already knew all about her father. The whole world knew about Mia's father. And there he was, the son of a Midwestern car salesman sitting across from the daughter of Raphael Renaud, taking her history—what little of it remained inside her fractured brain. He had to remind himself every few minutes to stop staring at her and be professional.

Alexander was pragmatic, even in his twenties, and if you had asked him if he believed in an occurrence as absurd and romantic as love-at-first-sight, he would have laughed, shaken his head, and asked the questioner, "Are you *serious?*" But how else could he describe the swift and drastic change his entire life outlook took once he met Mia? It was an emotion, a pull and attraction, that transcended all rational thought. Back then, all he ever wanted was to talk with her, be near her —he fantasized about waking up in his bed with her beside him. Getting through the six weeks of that study, being so close to her while maintaining a strictly professional demeanor toward her, was an agony unlike any he had known.

On that last day of the study, he had practically chased her out of the building. Both his heart and head desperate for her to agree to dinner with him that night. And when she had smiled, big and genuine, before she had developed that habit of tilting her head to hide her scar, and said, "Yes. I'd love that." Alexander had levitated onto another plane of reality.

He had never before wanted anyone, or anything, as much as he wanted Mia Renaud.

In all the years since, Alexander never parceled out his attraction to Mia. He never considered to what degree he pursued her because of her intelligence, beauty, and charm versus the fact she was the daughter of Raphael Renaud. If he had ever been asked, and he hadn't, Alexander would say that Mia's connection to A-list fame and money had nothing, not one thing whatsoever, to do with his love for her. He loved Mia for who she was, not who she was connected to.

He believed this. His whole sense of identity clung to this assertion about who he was, as a man, because the alternative version, a version of himself where Mia's proximity to extreme fame and fortune measured into his love, aligned directly with Holly's accusation of him being a "fame whore."

The memory of which still made him squirm.

He was not superficial; this was another of his most steadfast self-beliefs. The evidence for this, he secretly considered but would never say aloud, was as plain as the colossal scar disfiguring the entire right side of his wife's face. Would a superficial, fame-whore of a man be capable of seeing beyond something so *impossible* to not see?

No, Alexander felt certainly not. Alexander believed he didn't care about Mia's scar at all, that he didn't even really see it—anymore.

He did, however, wish she would stop trying to hide it. It wasn't something to be ashamed of. Quite the opposite, Mia's scar reminded the people that knew her history of what she had endured. What she had survived.

It reminded people, particularly at the Manhattan dinner

parties he was frequently invited to—and that she would now rarely attend—exactly who Mia was.

When Mia slept, her black sheath of hair fell away from her face and exposed the white scar that, when she was awake, she was so very careful to keep hidden. Even from him. Over the years, he had come to believe that she was unaware of the hiding behaviors. The way she kept her long hair always in front of her right shoulder. The tilt of her head to the right and slightly lowered so that her unscarred side was always most prominent. But most disturbing and inconvenient had been the way she had begun to even avoid her own reflection over the years and the slow eradication of every mirror within their home.

It was when she had the master bathroom remodeled last spring, and she'd commissioned a tile artist to create a piece where their vanity mirrors once were, that Alexander realized things had gotten really bad.

"How are we supposed to get ready?" he had asked.

Mia had shrugged. "The same as we always do. You shave in the shower. What do we even need enormous mirrors in here for?"

"Oh, I don't know," he said sarcastically. "To make sure we don't look like train wrecks before we leave the house."

Mia had given him a gentle smile. It was the same way she looked at the girls when they were upset over something ridiculous and Mia was being patient with them. "You never look like a train wreck," she said and kissed his cheek.

"What about you? How will you do your hair and put on your makeup."

Mia shook her head. "I haven't worn makeup in years, and I hardly need a mirror just to brush straight hair.

Honestly, Alexander, I don't know why you're making such a big deal about this. I think the artistry here is amazing. Wouldn't you much rather see this every morning than our own aging faces," she joked.

She had tried to laugh it off, make it seem like this was no big deal, and Alexander was being absurd. And maybe if Mia had been any other woman, a woman without her particular history and trauma, Alexander would have been convinced.

But standing there that Thursday evening last May, stock still and processing the fact that Mia had installed tile artwork that bore a striking resemblance to John Everett Millais's depiction of Ophelia floating on her back in a river just before she drowns—Alexander didn't need to be a clinical psychologist to see the association.

Mia was getting worse. Every year, every month, she was disappearing before his eyes. Falling in on herself, being eaten away by whatever it was she was trying to hide from—her physical scars were the least of it, he felt sure. At that moment, all the pieces clicked together like tumblers in a lock. Alexander suspected for the first time that his wife's psychological struggles had little to do with her physical injury anymore.

Alexander clicked on the file in the bottom right corner of his desktop and opened a long list of files organized by date. He clicked on the most recent one from last April and watched as the black, grey, and white image filled his screen.

It was the MRI imagining from Mia's last brain scan. She had one every year as part of her continued monitoring and assessment. For years and years, the imaging had looked exactly the same.

Perfect.

Physically, Mia's brain looked healthy. No dark shadows, no white tumors, no missing elements. Which, of course, in itself didn't necessarily explain anything. Often, traumatic brain injury doesn't show up on imaging. So neurologists also conduct a multitude of assessments: cognitive, executive functioning, memory, attention, behavioral, and emotional, to explain dysfunction that doesn't always show up on a screen.

Alexander clicked open the file labeled with the same date as the MRI and the extension: ASSESSMENTS. And there it was, Mia's most recent neurological report detailing those tests she had taken every year since her accident eighteen years ago. He had read them all, even the ones from before he met Mia. And while the ones from the years immediately after her injury showed delays in memory, executive function, and some cognitive decline regarding her processing speed, they had predominantly been within the normal range for the last ten years.

Except, this wasn't entirely true because, in fact, Mia's full-scale IQ score had consistently been at or around the mid 140s. Extremely High. Higher than his own score of 133 even —a fact he kept to himself. Her performance on measures of memory and executive functioning were all above average.

But if you asked her today who the president of the United States was in nineteen ninety-five, she would pause and work hard to remember. Not as a memory she could connect to her own experiences from nineteen ninety-five, but as a fact she had worked hard to learn, a historical detail like World War II or the Magna Carta. Often, she would need to look it up on her phone.

"Bill Clinton!" she would read, with as much attributed

context as Abraham Lincoln or Dwight Eisenhower. "He was the one with the sex scandal...right?"

Mia persisted in not remembering a single detail prior to that night in 2004. Despite the physical and psychological data, that suggested there wasn't anything wrong with her brain anymore.

Because of all this, Alexander now firmly believed that his wife could remember her past. He scrolled and scrolled through fifty pages of facts that all pointed to Mia being capable of remembering.

Data did not lie.

Still, he knew the brain was a mysterious organ. Modern technology and tests can look, measure, and calculate so many of its functions. But how do we measure the mind? The universal expanse of unknowable terrain that was Mia's consciousness. Because Alexander now believed that this was the foggy atmosphere they now needed to explore for answers. Mia's mind held the keys, he knew.

And he knew this because his wife talked in her sleep. And when she spoke from her unconscious, she spoke of her past. Conversations with either her sister or a friend as they watched one of Raphael and Pixlie's lavish parties take place on the lawns outside Beaumar Manor. She spoke about specific guests, what they wore, and the cars they drove. On many occasions, Alexander had grabbed a notebook and pencil from his side table and scribbled notes as fast as he could in the dark. The next day he had been able to look up several archived society articles that confirmed many of the details—these were Mia's memories; not stories she'd been told. Mia narrated her past in her sleep. Not fiction, remembered instances from her childhood.

So, if Mia's dream state mind could remember her past, he held that her waking brain should also be capable. The problem was, he didn't think she wanted to.

Alexander shook his mouse awake and pulled up the internet browser. From his saved links, he clicked on the address for the Manhattan Psychiatric Center. Their main page displayed a photo of the facility, an enormous block of a building designed sometime in the nineteen fifties that was supposed to evoke an art deco feel. He already knew what Mia would say.

"It looks like a prison."

Obviously, he would dissuade her from thinking in these terms, but privately he would agree. The building did, in fact, look like a slightly nicer prison.

Or an insane asylum from a movie set.

Regardless, when Erica's treatment failed to bring about any real change in Mia, and she reverted to coping by popping pills, drinking, and negligent behavior, the Manhattan Psychiatric Center was what Alexander had in mind to help his wife make a *real* recovery.

Erica could pump microdoses of synthetic psilocybin into Mia all day every day, and Mia may experience exactly the breakthrough in resurfaced memory that Erica was hoping to achieve with her study, so long as Mia was under the influence of the drug.

But Alexander thought Mia's chances of carrying those memories into her normal conscious waking state were close to zero.

Not because she couldn't but because she refused to.

Or because she was lying.

An email notification slid onto his screen; for a moment,

he had a small hope that it would be Tasha already responding to his email. It wasn't, but it was even better. It was his literary agent.

Alexander clicked open the message.

Amazing news! I just got off the phone with your editor and she said the whole house is buzzing about a follow-up to Somebody She Used to Know. *If you're able to pull it off with all the intimate details you outlined in the proposal, the stuff about Raphael and Pixlie, they'd kill for it! I don't have any exact numbers yet, but Alexander, we could be looking at a seven-figure advance for this one.*

Did you hear that? 7!

CHAPTER 28

$\mathcal{M}$ ia stood outside the room and tried to make sense of what she saw. The room was awash in a sea of pink and white fabrics. Directly across from the doorway, the space was anchored by an enormous white wood, four-poster canopy bed draped in heavy rose-pink brocade fabric.

Mia watched as Sasha made her way up a wooden step stool positioned next to the side of the tall mattress, then flung herself backward into the center of the plush bed. She moved her arms and legs like she was making a snow angel in luxury while in the far corner of the room, Everly knelt before an enormous dollhouse. Its multi-chimney roof stood as tall as her, and when she pulled open the two doors that cracked open the exterior siding, she let out a small gasp. She placed her fingers over her mouth when she saw the many splendid rooms, furniture, and complete family hidden inside.

When she turned her head toward Mia, her eyes were wide. "Can I touch it?"

Mia took a breath as Everly's question sank in. *Could she touch it?* Mia wasn't sure.

Sasha stopped making fabric angels and pushed herself up and onto her knees. "Of course, you can," she said, matter of fact. "It's *mom's* dollhouse."

Everly glanced at her sister, then back to Mia with her still questioning expression. Everly knew, better than anyone, that her sister was not always right in all things. Mia gave Everly a reassuring smile and nodded her head. "Yes, it's fine," she whispered. "Of course."

And with this, Everly reached into the house and began exploring the people and furniture. Sasha bounced twice on the bed and then leaped onto the floor with a loud thud before rushing to investigate the house herself.

Mia watched them both for a moment, giving herself a chance to feel out this space. Was it familiar? Had she spent her childhood here? She walked slowly into the room, her eyes lingering on the details. The carved wood of the bed frame, the drape of the window treatment, the white wallpaper with the palest pink damask design repeating over and over and over—would she have chosen this?

Was this her taste as a child? Or would her parents have left it entirely to the discretion of an interior designer? Because none of this felt remotely like herself, who she was or might have been. It wasn't only that she didn't recognize this room or have that same *knowing* sense, like how she *knew* their bedrooms were on this floor. It was that she actively disliked everything about this space.

Sasha and Everly may have thought that this bedroom was every girl's dream come true, but to Mia, it was a cloying, overdone exaggeration of stereotypical girlhood. She not only found it difficult to imagine being the girl who had this room and liked it, but practically impossible.

Mia walked to one of the large, framed windows and gazed out at the scene below. They were high up on the third floor, but Mia could still tell that the large expanse of lawn was no longer properly cared for. The menagerie of topiary animals were overgrown, their individual species now indistinguishable from each other.

In the distance, she could see the large willow tree where she had once, as a child, posed for a picture with her whole family. That picture was now situated on her mantle in the portrait room at her home.

Mia turned around and faced the bedroom again. Where were all the pictures? Her mind rolled back to her time spent on the first floor. There were framed photographs everywhere. Some were professionally taken; others were candids snapped with a personal camera. There were shots of Pixlie posing on a red carpet. Raphael accepting an Academy Award. There were countless photos of her parents with other celebrities: having cocktails, dancing, shaking hands, signing autographs, on the top of a mountain in ski gear. The house was littered with photographic evidence of Raphael's and Pixlie's famous lives.

What Mia couldn't recall seeing was a single shred of evidence about their lives as parents. Maybe she was mistaken —she must be—but Mia couldn't think of another single picture of her family besides the one on her mantle at home.

There weren't *any* photos of Holly and Mia?

Mia's fingertips touched her scar. How was that possible? It wasn't. Mia considered the dearth of photos she and Alexander already had of Sasha and Everly, mountains of them, and the girls were only five.

Of course, Pixlie and Raphael didn't have smartphones, and Pixlie wasn't the motherly type, but there simply wasn't any way they didn't have any family photos.

The girls were still occupied with the dollhouse; the story-line they had going for the miniature family inside involved a mother and father allowing the children to adopt a dog named Stevie. Mia began inspecting the room more closely. She scanned the bookshelves, opened drawers, and shuffled through old clothes. She even got down on her hands and knees and lifted the white lace bed skirt hanging from the box spring to the floor.

Under the bed, there were a few, once clear, plastic storage boxes that had yellowed with age. She was about to grab one and pull it out when she noticed something else. Pushed farther back, flat and rectangular, it was hard to make out in the dark. She scooted close to the mattress, reached her arm as far as she could, until she felt the edge of the item with the tips of her fingers. She pressed harder against the bed, stretching her arm another inch until she took hold of and slid the object toward her. Before she even had it out in the open, Mia knew it was a book.

She slid it under the bed skirt and sat with her back against the bed, and the book against her knees.

It was a large, black hardback. Mia ran her fingers over the gold embossed letters on the cover.

Riverside Academy

2004-2005

It was her high school yearbook. Mia's senior year, if she hadn't spent it in a hospital. She pressed her hand to the closed cover. She didn't even realize this was something she had owned. Holly, or her parents, must have received the book for her, and somehow, over the years, it ended up lost and discarded under her bed.

Nobody thinks much about a yearbook when their daughter or sister is fighting for her life in the intensive care unit. Not to mention dealing with the chaos and grief surrounding her father's murder.

But sitting here, eighteen years later, Mia was curious about what this book might show her, if anything, about who she once was. There was no point getting her hopes up; given the timing of her attack, August of 2004, there wasn't likely to be much about her in this book. She opened the cover to the title page.

A Year to Remember!

It struck her as catastrophically ironic.

She grabbed the stack of thick glossy pages. She thumbed the page edges, like shuffling a deck of cards, until she found the senior portraits.

Most were shot outside, with the students standing on a bridge, under a tree, or in front of a lake. Some kids leaned against their expensive car or truck; others chose portraits that looked like something from a company website.

When Mia reached the R's, she scanned the page but didn't expect to find her own photo. She had no idea if or when her senior photo had been taken. And even if it was before the assault, would the school include her here when she couldn't attend?

She didn't find a picture of herself, but she did register a familiar name.

Holly Renaud.

"What?" Mia whispered as she inspected Holly's photo.

She was confused. Had she read the years wrong? Wasn't

2004-2005 Mia's senior year? Holly would have graduated the previous year. Had the school made a mistake?

Mia brought the book closer. It was Holly's face. Younger, yes. Her features were rounder, her eyes brighter, but the hair had thrown Mia. It was short, chestnut brown, and hung straight to her shoulders.

Mia rested the tips of her fingers against the photo as she tried to work out what she was missing. It was inconsistencies like these that, even all these years later, made her starkly aware of how broken her brain was. It was impossible, she rationalized, that the school had made a mistake.

She closed her eyes. Which meant Mia was making a mistake. Either she'd muddled the dates or forgotten a fact.

Mia opened her eyes. She wasn't wrong. She was almost eighteen in August of 2004. She was born October first of, 1986. Holly was born on September thirtieth, 1985. These were some of the many life facts she had rehearsed while working to rebuild her life during those months and years of recovery.

She wasn't wrong.

So how could she explain this yearbook? 2004-2005 would have been Holly's first year in college.

Mia flipped past the photo of Holly to the back of the book. On the last pages, she ran her finger down the index of last names until she found what she was looking for.

Renaud, Holly: pg. 87, 124, 132, 140

And then,

Renaud, Mia: pg. 89

Mia sat up straighter and quickly turned to page 89. It was the last page of the senior photos.

Not Pictured

And there, along with six other names.
Mia Renaud

CHAPTER 29

*S*he stared at her name on the page for several seconds, willing the logical answer to make itself known to her. Like several other facts about her past, she felt the truth was beyond her reach. It was somewhere between the words on this page and the dusty gray mass of her memories that, now she was spending time in her old physical spaces, felt disturbed.

She couldn't see the answers, but she felt their presence. Here in this space, within this book, between the walls of this house, the echo of her past was here. And today, without Holly's ever-present guiding, explaining—remembering for her—Mia could feel the edges of her past for herself.

Why wouldn't Holly have *ever* mentioned that they were in the same grade?

As soon as she asked the question, she knew it was wrong. Because it wasn't that Holly never mentioned this apparent fact, it was that she had actively lied to Mia.

Mia ran a finger over her own name in the book. Why would her sister lie about this?

Mia closed the yearbook and stood up. Sasha and Everly were still playing with the dollhouse. "Girls," she said.

They both turned their heads toward her.

"Let's go, okay?" Mia said as she tucked the yearbook under her arm.

Both girls moved the dolls and furniture back into the house, and Everly closed the two doors until the exterior siding reconnected.

"Where can we go now?" Sasha asked as she ran up to Mia's side and grabbed her hand.

Mia gave her a weak smile. "I think it's time we head back downstairs and find Grandma Pixlie. I'm sure she's wondering where we are now."

Sasha wrinkled her nose, and her shoulders slumped as she pouted. "Nooo," she argued. "Please, just a few more rooms. We haven't seen anything."

Mia took a deep breath. "One more room," she said.

"Five," Sasha countered.

"That's too many and will take too long. We can always come back another day. Two rooms."

Sasha thought about this for a second, and Mia thought she was about to agree when she said, "Three...and we won't take long. This one just had the dollhouse."

Mia took another big breath. It was astonishing, Sasha's dogged determination when it came to getting what she wanted. It was a trait so counter to her own personality Mia often felt out of her depth trying to parent Sasha. She loved her girls equally, but secretly she found Everly's quiet, shy temperament easier to identify with. Mia understood the way Everly almost always took the backseat and let Sasha run the show because Mia was exactly the same. Confrontations with Sasha felt like negotiations with an opposing attorney—or a used-car salesperson.

"I have a better idea," Mia said as she pulled her phone from her pocket. "How about I set my timer, and you'll have five minutes to look into as many rooms on this floor as you like. We do need to get back to Grandma Pixlie, but you can at least look into several of them this way."

Sasha glanced back at Everly, who nodded. "Okay," she agreed as she grabbed Everly's hand, and they both started running for the door before Mia even had her timer set.

Mia could hear the girls opening the door across the hall as she tapped in the time and pushed start. Only a few seconds passed before Sasha could be heard to exclaim, "This is boring. Next!" When Mia entered the hallway, careful to close the door to her childhood room behind her, she barely caught a glimpse of the girls, still hand-in-hand, disappearing into the next room down the hall.

Mia froze.

The image of them running away together in this hallway. It felt familiar, like something she'd experienced before. Not a memory because the girls hadn't been to Beaumar since they were toddlers. It was more like deja vu.

Mia tucked her phone into the back pocket of her black pants and trailed after her two girls. Before she reached the room they had disappeared into, they came running out again. With bright eyes and smiles, their laughter echoed off the plaster walls. They took no notice of their mother staring after them as they ran and disappeared again into a room farther away.

Mia's chest felt tight. The book slid from beneath her arm, and its spine landed with a thud against the hardwood floor. Splayed open, a two-page spread of perfectly aligned student photos was exposed. She glanced down at the book, surprised she had dropped it but making no move to retrieve it. She curled her hands, damp with sweat, into two tight balls at her side as her throat constricted.

Mia could hear her girls' voices, but they sounded distant and muffled. As if she was hearing them through a fog. She closed her eyes against the panic rising within her.

She forced herself to breathe deep, but her heart thundered like a racehorse inside her chest. Adrenaline poured into her nervous system, igniting her every nerve—the urge to scream rose like a wave.

The girls were running straight down the hall now. Farther and farther away from her. Heading for the door at the end of the hall.

Mia moved quick. The thin leather soles of her black flats slid beneath her as she increased her pace from a quick walk to a run.

"Stop," she commanded. Her voice, louder than she intended, reverberated down the hall.

Both girls turned to face her, their expressions shocked and scared. They froze, eyes wide as frightened rabbits as Mia barreled toward them. When she reached them, Mia positioned herself between them and the closed door they had been about to open. She leaned against it, blocking the way. "Time's up," she stated. "We have to go right now. Back downstairs."

Sasha reached for and found Everly's hand, then both girls stepped back. Mia's eyes met Sasha's, and she waited for the argument to begin. The timer in Mia's pocket had not yet gone off. She knew it. Sasha knew it.

Mia's hand gripped the door handle behind her back. Her heart still flew like a frightened bird inside her chest. She needed to get out of here, get her girls out of here. On the brink of panic, Mia felt like the walls and ceiling would collapse around them at any moment.

"Okay," Sasha whispered as she nodded.

Sasha was afraid. It was why she wasn't arguing. Her eyes were fixed on Mia's face, watching, waiting to see what would happen next.

Mia took a ragged breath of her own, not in control of her emotions right now. Mia stepped toward the girls and reached for their shoulders to guide them away and back toward the stairs.

But Sasha pulled away before Mia could touch her and began walking back down the hall, dragging Everly along.

Mia stood and watched. Only seconds before, they had both been excited. Thrilled and happy to be exploring. Mia's behavior had extinguished their enthusiasm in an instant. It was obvious—both girls were now scared.

What was less obvious was if Sasha and Everly were afraid *for* their mother or *of* her right now. Mia watched as they neared the far end of the hallway. Before they rounded the corner that led to the stairwell, Everly stopped. She pulled Sasha's arm and forced her sister to stop. "Mom?" she asked, looking back at Mia.

Mia could hear the worry in her voice. "I'm coming," she whispered.

Everly nodded, then allowed Sasha to keep pulling her around the corner and out of sight.

Now alone, the house's heavy silence rushed in and filled the space left in the girls' wake. Beaumar was created from a forest's worth of solid timber, an ocean of plaster, and miles of fabric—the collective weight of it capable of robbing her breath, crushing her bones to dust.

She could hear the girls on the stairs. She should catch up with them, apologize for being so intense. Mia pushed herself away from the door behind her and took a step.

Fear cascaded down her back. She closed her eyes. It felt like a presence behind her. As if a hand might, at any moment, materialize from the wood and touch her shoulder, grab her neck.

She turned to face the door and kept it in plain sight as she walked backwards down the hall. Her eyes trained on the black metal knob, her body primed and ready to run if she saw it turn.

This was what had scared her as the girls ran from room to room, laughing and happy. Watching them reach for the door at the end of the hall was like watching them dance blind at the edge of a cliff.

She stepped on something and stopped. Mia glanced, saw the dropped yearbook, and crouched to pick it up, her eyes still trained on the door.

When she reached the end of the hall, she froze. The idea of turning her back, taking her eyes off the door, made her nauseous with fear.

"It's not rational," she whispered. "There's nothing to be afraid of."

But reason had always been a poor match against her panic.

Mia placed one trembling hand on the wall beside her, felt a single tear run down her cheek, and forced herself to turn away.

She wanted to run as fast as possible. Down the stairs, out the front door, and straight to her car. Instead, she took one measured step after another until she reached the third-floor landing. Her hand gripping the very rail her body had tumbled over eighteen years ago as she made her way to the stairs.

With every foot of distance she created between herself and the door at the end of the hall, Mia felt her heart decelerate. When she reached the second floor, she could still feel beads of sweat rolling down her back, but her breathing had returned to normal.

"There she is," Pixlie's voice called up. Mia looked down and saw her mother standing in the black and white checkered foyer with Sasha and Everly beside her. Pixlie rested a hand on each of the girls' shoulders, her bony fingers, tipped in bright red polish, curled around their shoulders and pulled them close to her side.

The sight of them together brought on a fresh fear Mia couldn't explain. She continued down the stairs and kept her eyes riveted on her girls. When she reached the last step, Mia fought the urge to tear both girls from Pixlie's possessive grasp and charge for the front door.

"The girls would like to see one of my films!" Pixlie announced. "Isn't that right?" She glanced first at Sasha, then at Everly before gently shaking their shoulders. "Mia, you take the girls to the theater room, and I'll get the projector spooled up. I thought *The Midnight Hour* would be a good choice. I have that fantastic monologue and the close-ups! No one else ever captured me so well as Ambrose."

Mia stared at Pixlie's excited expression and found she was unable to ignore the way her fake eyelashes fluttered, crooked and misshapen, on her heavily shadowed eyes. There was a small drop of dried blood above her lip—the result of the treatment she had received from Vera. It occurred to Mia that Pixlie's efforts in front of her mirror were doing her no favors. Pixlie's interventions, with both needles and makeup, produced the opposite of her intended effect. The thick foundation, too-bright rouge, and lined red lips aged the woman beyond her years and highlighted the cartoonish nature after plastic surgery.

"Mia?" Pixley asked, her bright red smile turning down only slightly at the corners. "Did you hear me? Would you prefer they watch *The Train to Belarus* instead?"

Pixlie's question jarred Mia from her trance. She wanted to leave. Her every cell felt like this visit was a colossal mistake.

But wasn't that why Ty had assigned her this task? To be in these spaces, near her mother, closer to the environments and people from her past, hoping it would help resurrect some memories? "Yes." Mia shook her head and planted a fake smile to reassure the woman. "I'm sorry. I was just... thinking. *The Midnight Hour*, that's fine. I've never seen it."

Pixlie widened her eyes, and Mia suspected her forehead would have wrinkled in surprise if it had been utterly immobilized by Botox. "Of course, you've seen it! Probably more times than you can count." Pixlie released her grip on both girls and waved her hand as if the very idea were utterly ridiculous. "Now, get them settled in the good seats while I spool it up."

And before Mia could say another word, Pixlie turned with a flourish. Her colorful kaftan billowed around her as the sound of her low-heeled slides clicked across the marble floor. When the woman was out of earshot, Sasha turned her face to Mia. "Do we *have* to?" Her earlier excitement and sense of adventure quelled by both Mia's panicked behavior and the prospect of spending more time with this wax figure of a grandmother.

Mia pursed her lips and fought off the urge to leave the house now, with no explanation to Pixlie. "We can't be rude," Mia whispered. "Besides, don't you want to watch a movie your very own grandmother starred in?"

"Is it a *boring* grownup movie?" Sasha asked.

Sasha and Everly would, undoubtedly, think it was a boring grownup movie. "We don't have to stay for the whole thing," she whispered and began corralling the girls down the hall in the direction Pixlie had headed. "We'll just watch for a bit...to be polite." And give Mia more evidence, more time to wrap her head around her own unexplainable emotions. "Now, let's figure out where this theater room is," Mia added as they passed through the messy kitchen.

Both girls looked up from either side of her. "Don't you know?" Sasha asked.

No, Mia thought. *I don't have the faintest idea.* "Of course. It's just...been a long time, and this is a very large, confusing house."

The excuse made even Everly skeptical, but neither said anything about it. Her girls were intelligent and inquisitive. Mia knew her half-baked explanations about inconsistencies wouldn't fly for much longer. She would have to tell them the truth about her past, probably much sooner than she had imagined.

She only hoped she could figure out what that truth was first.

CHAPTER 30

*H*olly sat cross-legged inside Stevie's cage with his head resting on her lap. She stroked his large, square-shaped face and watched his barrel chest rise and fall with every one of his sleep-heavy breaths.

The vet had assured her he would likely be out for at least another half hour.

At the door to the barn, Harris and Dr. Allen spoke in voices low enough that Holly had a hard time hearing but not so low that they could be accused of conspiring against her. She knew what they both thought.

Attempting to rehabilitate Stevie was a lost cause, and he should be euthanized.

Dr. Allen had agreed to come out and neuter Stevie on their property, but she had spent most of her time lecturing Holly about the dangers and difficulty of taking Stevie on.

Unfortunately, Harris had been there for every word of it. He now had even more reason and ammunition in his lobbying effort to end this. He didn't believe she could do it.

She didn't care. Holly knew she had to try. She watched Harris and Dr. Allen shake hands. The doctor gave Holly and Stevie one more glance as if she were leaving against her better judgment, then turned and left. Harris watched the doctor walk away until she reached the house, then came back and stood outside Stevie's cage.

Holly kept her eyes on Stevie, her fingers running over the scars on his body that told of the horrors he had endured before being rescued. She heard Harris let out a long and worried sigh.

"Holly."

She looked up into his concerned face. "I already know what you're going to say."

Harris shook his head. "Believe me when I tell you that your huge heart and desire to save everyone and everything in need on this planet is one of the things I love about you most. Right up and until I see you putting yourself in real physical danger. I know this dog is breaking your heart, but don't you think it's possible you're not being realistic in this particular situation?"

Holly looked away from him. "Is that what you and Dr. Allen were whispering about by the door?"

"We were not whispering."

"Well, you certainly *were* having a conversation about me that did not include me."

Harris sighed again. "I was asking for her honest opinion on the feasibility of all this. Holly, I don't think you even begin to understand how terrifying this is for me. Every day, I worry I will come home and find you mauled to death."

It was her turn to sigh. "That's a bit dramatic, don't you—"

"It's not dramatic!" He raised his voice. "People get attacked by dogs every day. Dogs that don't have half the behavioral problems that one has!"

"It's not his fault."

"Of course, it's not. I understand that. And I wish to God no dog or animal or person for that matter ever had to endure cruelty at the hands of these fuck-wits that make me so mad I could kill them. But that doesn't mean I want the one person I love more than anyone else on this whole fucked up planet to be risking her own life and safety just to save one dog that is probably too far gone to be saved in the first place."

Holly set her jaw and felt the tears welling up. She ran both her hands over Stevie's face and ears. "I'm sorry, Harris," she whispered. "I don't want you to worry or be scared. But I'm simply not going to give up on him yet. I have to at least try."

"And if you can't? If he just won't or can't change?"

Holly swallowed. "He will. I know he will."

Harris didn't say anything more. She didn't look at him, but she could feel his eyes on her. "If he doesn't," he continued, his voice softer. "If he doesn't make a noticeable change, and soon…if he ever tries to attack you or one of the dogs, if he ever bites, even once…Holly, I'm so sorry, but I will have that dog put down myself. I need you to hear that because I will do it. For your own safety."

Holly stopped stroking Stevie's head as Harris's threat came fully into focus. She thought of the tenuous lie she and her two nieces were keeping about Everly's injured arm.

He would do it. She believed him. And Dr. Allen would support the decision. Dr. Allen would have done it today if

Holy had allowed it. "I hear you," was all she could manage to say.

In her back pocket, she felt her phone vibrate. She leaned forward and pulled it out. It was Mia.

"My sister is calling me," she said, preparing to swipe and answer the call.

Harris took a deep breath. "I have an appointment and have to get to the shop. Promise me you'll be out of there long before there is any possibility of it waking up."

Holly nodded once, then answered the call. "Hi, Mia." From the background noise coming through the phone, she guessed her sister was in the city.

"Hi," Mia said, her voice clipped. And with that one word, Holly could tell something was wrong. She had spent her entire life attenuated to her sister's every emotional fluctuation—she knew how to read her winds.

Holly's spine straightened. She hoped Mia was just stressed about starting the new therapy. "You have your first appointment for the new treatment today. I didn't forget," she said. "I'll be sure to be at the girls' school by three thirty."

"Thank you," Mia said, still with an edge. "But there's something else I want to speak with you about."

Holly closed her eyes as dread washed over her—Mia had found out about the bite. Either the girls had let it slip or she had spoken with someone at the school. Whatever the case, Holly felt sure she would have to find a way to defend the undefendable Stevie. "Okay. What's up?" Holly said, her voice sounding fake even to her own ears.

There was a pause on the line; Mia was hesitating. Holly could hear only the rush of the city for so long, she wondered if there might be something wrong with the connection.

"I took the girls out to Beaumar yesterday," Mia said.

Holly opened her eyes. The dread she'd felt about getting caught in the lie about Everly was swept aside by a new terror. Since the accident, Mia had never been to the house without Holly there—why would she suddenly do this? Her mind raced through the possibilities and questions she had. *Why? What were you doing out there? Did Pixlie say anything?* And the most disturbing—*Did you find anything?* She couldn't ask any of this without complicating this conversation more. There was a chance, however small, that Mia wasn't about to pull back the curtain on everything Holly had worked so hard to keep hidden.

"How's Pixlie?" she asked, hoping the fear rooted in her stomach wasn't evident in her tone.

"She's fine...well, no. Actually, she's anything but fine, and that's another thing we need to discuss. But that's not the main reason I'm calling."

Holly absorbed her sister's clipped tone and braced herself for whatever could be coming next.

"Yesterday, at the house...the girls wanted to explore...."

It seemed to Holly that Mia was hesitating. Either she was unsure of what to say or how to say it.

In Holly's lap, Stevie made a noise. She could see his eyes darting back and forth beneath his lids. He was dreaming. When she stroked his face, his lip curled and exposed his teeth.

"We ended up in my old bedroom," Mia said, her tone accusatory.

If they had made it up to her old bedroom, Mia would have questions. Holly knew she should have locked that room away. Why, why, why hadn't she bolted that door shut? Holly let out a sigh and felt like she might cry. She didn't think she could have this conversation over the phone; it was too much. She would need to be *with* Mia for this. Look her in the eye as she tried to explain the unexplainable.

"I found a yearbook. *My* senior yearbook," Mia's voice cracked, and Holly knew her sister was crying. "And apparently, it's also *your* senior yearbook. Can you explain that to me, Holly? Can you explain to me how we were both in the same grade, and yet you've never, not once in the last eighteen years, told me that."

Holly sat so still she could feel Stevie's steady breath as he inhaled and exhaled, his chest rising and falling beneath her hand. She swallowed and thought carefully about her next words. Because if a found yearbook was the extent of Mia's revelations—Holly could fix that with very little collateral damage.

"I was held back in school." Holly's mind cartwheeled. She didn't like lying on the fly. A good, solid lie needed to be carefully thought through. It needed to stand the test of inquisitive investigation and fall in place with other known factors. A shitty lie stuck out on the landscape of a life. It drew attention to the fact that it didn't make sense in context with other verifiable knowledge. But Holly didn't have time right now to consider the multitude of variables that could spin from this lie. And she needed this one to stick and mollify her sister.

She couldn't afford to lose Mia's trust. Everything depended on it.

"In kindergarten," she added and was immediately glad she thought of it. It would help explain any other potential discoveries—not that Holly would encourage or allow that to happen—as to why they were always in the same classes. "They thought I wasn't ready to move on. So when Pixlie enrolled you the next year, the headmaster suggested I repeat kindergarten with you. I'm sorry I never thought to tell you, Mia. It's just one of those things. I guess, given everything, I just never thought it was important. I'm sorry finding the yearbook upset you. You said you found it in your old room?"

Mia let out a shaky breath. "Yes. The girls were playing with my old doll house, and I found it under my bed."

Holly closed her eyes and allowed herself a small smile of relief. "Of course. That makes sense." If the girls had been playing with a dollhouse, they hadn't been in Mia's old bedroom. They'd been in Holly's. "It must have been upsetting. I really am sorry, Mia."

The line was quiet; Holly couldn't even hear the sounds of the city anymore. "No, I'm the one who's sorry now. I shouldn't have jumped to conclusions. For some reason...I don't know. I guess I was terrified that you'd lied to me. And I couldn't figure out why. And it just, I don't know. The venerability of being so utterly dependent on someone for relaying even the most basic facts of your entire existence." Mia sobbed now. "I'm sorry."

"Don't be sorry. It makes perfect sense. Look, why don't we talk more about it this afternoon when you get home. Are you at your appointment now?"

Mia let out another loud sigh. "Yes. And that's the other thing. Starting this first trial today...I thought I'd be fine. I mean, it's not like I haven't been through a hundred different treatments, right? But for some reason, I'm shaking. My whole body, I can't stop it."

"It's going to be okay, Mia. And you know, it's not too

late for you to back out of this. You don't have to do this. I'll support you. Harris too. There isn't any way in hell we'd let Alexander take those girls from you. It still infuriates me that he would even—"

"I have to go now, Holly. You've got the girls after school?"

"Yes."

"Thank you," Mia finished and hung up.

Holly lowered the phone from her ear and stared at the time on the screen for a moment, processing the near, catastrophic miss. It had been easier to curate Mia's life story when it had only been the two of them. But now there was Alexander and the girls with their sharp curiosity and endless questions. Holly needed to be more vigilant about keeping up with all their life changes. All those outside variables that were now also influencing Mia.

It was only nine o'clock. It gave her plenty of time to get over to Beaumar and take care of some things before she needed to be at the girls' school for pick-up.

Holly shifted her weight so she could slip her phone into the back pocket of her jeans. As she did, Stevie's head rolled a few inches in her lap.

His eye opened.

Holly froze, wondering if she'd waited too long to leave the cage, distracted by Mia's call. She stared back into his black eye, afraid of making any sudden movement.

He stared up at her as her heart kept time with the seconds that ticked by. She should have left the cage with Harris. But Stevie's breath was still heavy and evenly paced, and a moment later, his eye slid shut again.

Holly slipped her hands under his big head, scooted out

from under him, and rested his head on the edge of his dog bed. She picked up the soft cone and fastened the Velcro around his neck to keep him from licking the stitched incision where his testicles had been, then left the cage and locked it behind her.

On the other side of the barn, Holly opened the top drawer of the battered chest she used to store various odds and ends that didn't have immediate use but were still useful and might one day come in handy. She shuffled through the detritus of loose screws, rusty hammers, rubber stoppers, and dusty tapes until she found something that would help her carry out her plans at Beaumar this morning.

A steel lock and key.

CHAPTER 31

On the basement level of the Neurological Institute, Mia followed Renee, the nurse who had greeted her at the front desk on the first floor and taken her vitals. They were headed down a narrow hallway with a low ceiling. Mia felt confident that if she reached up her hand, the tips of her fingers would brush against the rough textured finish that was likely blown into place sometime in the nineteen sixties.

They passed doors every twelve feet on either side of the hall, painted the same pale hospital blue you encountered everywhere in the medical industry. Mia knew the shade and hue were supposed to have a calming effect on patients. It instilled feelings of trust, or so she'd been told at one time or another.

Mia couldn't help but wonder if other patients like her, patients who had long and traumatic medical experiences and were always swathed in this particular shade, learned to feel anything but calm and trusting over time. Seeing the color now generally had the opposite effect because she knew the next several hours, weeks, and sometimes months would involve needles, injections, hospital beds, monitoring machines, feeding schedules, and an endless parade of medical professionals who would always and forever be in her life.

Mia would probably never entirely escape hospital blue.

The whole body shaking she'd described to her sister over the phone had subsided into an internal tremor. Her bones quaked, but she doubted there were any obvious external signs. If nothing else, Mia was usually pretty great at hiding. When Renee had greeted her upstairs, there wasn't even a shadow of concern that flitted across her expression at the sight of Mia.

And now, down in the belly of the institute, Renee finally stopped their trek down this tight artery of a hallway and opened one of the doors.

"Here we are," she said brightly. "Room zero two two."

Mia followed her through the door. She saw the room had a single-sized bed in the center with two low-slung, midcentury brown leather chairs on either side. There was another door on the wall next to the bed.

Renee motioned for Mia to take a seat in one of the chairs.

"I'll let Dr. Yun know you're ready," she explained, then headed through the other door.

Mia held her purse in her lap and tried to relax. She leaned back into the awkward angle of the chair, which she imagined was designed with the idea of comfort, but in fact, made her feel vulnerable. Like she was exposing her underbelly when predators were near. She much preferred chairs that encouraged you to sit fully erect. Spine tense, eyes open, ready.

She felt her hands shaking again, the palms sweating into the leather of her purse. Mia forced herself to take a deep breath right as the door Renee had exited from reopened, and Ty Yun stepped into the room.

"Hello, Mrs. Strauss. It's good to see you again."

She managed to make eye contact and gave him a brief smile before she dropped her eyes back to her lap and pulled her sleeves to the tips of her fingers.

She could feel the weight of his eyes on her and knew he would be inspecting her, calculating her behaviors, facial expressions; everything she said or did, or didn't say or didn't do, potentially meant *something*. She was being observed, and those observations would be recorded, analyzed, and conjured into seemingly relevant data.

Now, her hands longed to also unfold the neck of her black shirt, pull it all the way to her chin, stretch that fabric clear over her face.

But that behavior, certainly, would be noted and discussed at length with Erica later.

"It's normal to feel apprehensive, Mia. Do you mind if I call you Mia? Once we begin the session, using your first name may help you feel more supported and connected."

She shook her head. "I don't mind," the words came out in a whisper.

"Great. And if you're comfortable with it, please also call me Ty."

Mia nodded.

He took the seat across from her and explained that all her tests and labs from last week had come back normal. He was happy to report they would be able to begin treatment today. He explained that Renee would return in a moment with a pill, either a microdose of the psilocybin or a placebo, depending on whether Mia had been randomly placed within the experimental or control group. Then they would wait fifteen minutes for the drug to begin taking effect. Renee would help get Mia situated in the bed and connected to a few monitoring devices to track her vitals throughout the session. Renee would remain with them throughout the session, and everything would be recorded. He pointed to the small camera mounted in the corner of the room.

"Do you have any questions?"

Mia shook her head. Renee reentered the room with a small paper cup and a bottle of water. She gave Mia a warm smile and handed her the medication.

Mia took the cup between her fingertips and looked down at the blue pill. More trusting, calming, comfortable blue. She tipped the cup to her mouth and felt the pill land on her tongue.

Renee unscrewed the top of the water bottle and gave it to her.

Mia held the bottle for a moment, feeling the shape of the pill resting on her tongue—it wasn't too late. She could still pluck the pill from her mouth and place it back into the paper cup. Stand up from this chair, walk out that door, down the hallway, and ride up that elevator that brought her here.

She could still change her mind.

She looked into Renee's face and saw that her warm expression now had the barest hint of curiosity. Mia was taking too long, and Renee was wondering what she would do next. Mia felt that Renee probably didn't care one way or the other if Mia swallowed this pill or bolted for the door. It wasn't her experimental trial, after all. Babysitting Mia for the day was just a job; Renee's skills would be used elsewhere should Mia decide to remove herself.

"Is everything okay, Mia?" Ty asked.

Mia raised the bottle to her lips and felt the water wash the pill off her tongue and down her throat. "Yes," she answered and handed the bottle back to Renee. "I'm fine."

Because what were her other options at this point? What would Alexander say, what would he do, if she backed out now? She either needed to make real progress toward remembering her past or gain Erica's support in concluding that memory retrieval was physically impossible for her now.

And the only way to arrive at either of those two conclusions was this.

CHAPTER 32

*Ol*lexander stared out the window of his second-floor faculty office and watched students walk, ride bikes, or skateboard through the courtyard below. He was procrastinating. He returned his attention to his laptop and shook his mouse until the screen lit up.

He stared at the blank white page of the document he had created. The document that was going to be the start of his new book. The book that, according to his agent, could mean a seven-figure advance from his publisher.

His intention for this book, like his first, was to explore memory and trauma and the potential for recovery based on current evidence-based practice and research.

His *publisher's* intention, he well knew, was to use that framework as a legitimate way to unearth more never revealed information about Raphael Renaud, his family, and the tragically unsolved murder that still fascinated an ever-growing segment of the population that salivated over true crime stories—especially the unsolved variety.

"Seven figures," he whispered. He sat back in this chair, wondering about that sum of money and how many intimate details of his wife's family he would need to divulge to get it.

Intimate details that he neither knew nor had much hope of learning because his wife couldn't, or wouldn't, remember them. And his only other source, Holly, would never sit down with him and share her childhood memories. If she found out he was even thinking about writing another book about her family—

He placed his hands on his keyboard and quickly typed *fame whore* onto the blank white page. He didn't want to think about how her accusation would be impossible to discount should he agree to write this book. He would be accepting an enormous amount of money in exchange for private and traumatic details about their lives—it didn't matter how academic he made the subtitle.

If he did this, he was committed to writing a tell-all whose marketing campaign would heavily involve tabloids that line the grocery store checkout lanes. He would make a lot of money from it and again be a *New York Times* best-selling author. He would also become someone who traded on their hard-earned academic legitimacy for fame and a fast buck. And he didn't imagine there was any way for his professional reputation to recover from that.

He would be stepping into a different circle of existence. Losing the respect of the Erica Monaes of the world in exchange for public admiration. There would undoubtedly still be Manhattan dinner parties, but the guest list would be significantly different.

Alexander glanced at the clock on his desk. It was just after two. He had taught one class this morning and suffered through an hour-long faculty meeting, all while his wife was only blocks away, presumably having a psychedelic experience in a basement with a man who was familiar with Alexander professionally and was likely about to learn more than Alexander wanted him to know about his personal life too.

He hadn't spoken to Erica since before Mia's announcement that she would be joining the trial, but they were both in attendance at the faculty meeting this morning. Maybe it was only his imagination or paranoia, but it had seemed to him that Erica had avoided making eye contact with him. And when he moved to approach her as soon as the meeting ended, she had slipped out the door and was halfway down the hall before he could make his own way out.

It was then, as he watched her determined stride, so quick that her cardigan billowed in her wake, a worm of real fear began to slither in his gut. Was Erica Monae, one of the most distinguished and influential people in their field, actively avoiding him?

What, exactly, had Mia already shared about her life? About *their* life? He felt sure that whatever it was, it had impacted Erica's opinion of him. If that was the case, there would be far-reaching implications for both him and his career trajectory. It hardly mattered that the research was bound by confidentiality—he well knew that academics still whispered and gossiped at their cocktail parties and behind closed office doors.

What would they say about him? What did they imagine they knew about his life with Mia? He stared at the two words on his screen—did they think he was a fame whore? A sellout? A gold-digging climber?

Was he, right now, at the beginning of the end of his

academic career? Of course, it was unlikely that anything would ever be said to him outright. It's not like he would or could be fired because Erica had decided she didn't *like* him. But he had watched other tenured academics get the collective shut out and shut down. They kept you fed, but you were still, for all intents and purposes, kicked out of the herd. Opportunities within the university were rooted in networking. Anyone who was cut out was essentially fucked.

Alexander sat back in his chair, closed his eyes, and tried to imagine his life without the university and its prestige. Without the oppressive course load, the students and their never-ending needs, the papers to grade, the TAs to supervise, the politically-fueled faculty meetings, the grant writing, the intense pressure to get research published...the fucking commute on the spastic MTA every day.

He had worked so long and hard to get himself out of Ohio, and he'd always imagined being a doctor, with a position at Columbia, as the peak of his career Everest. But the truth was, now he'd scaled this mountain and sat atop it for several years, he wasn't sure this was the view he wanted for the rest of his life.

Alexander sat forward in his chair, opened his personal email, and pulled up the one his agent had sent over the weekend. Seven figures. To write another book. A book that would again place his name on every meaningful bestseller list and launch him onto another multi-city book tour where people would line up to both buy his book and shake his hand.

This other world would welcome him with champagne and open arms. All he had to do was say yes.

He thought about Tasha. The way she had practically

gushed about his first book changing her life. And at the coffee shop last week, those notes and questions—Tasha had been so interested in this side of his career. He imagined how excited she would be if he told her that, yes, he was now for sure writing a follow-up book. It was all confirmed and contracted, and oh, did he happen to mention the size of this advance?

Yes, it was huge and ridiculous...would she like to go to dinner with him to celebrate?

She would have so many questions for him. He wondered if Tasha might enjoy coming with him for a few stops of the book tour. She probably looked amazing first thing in the morning.

Maybe it was time for a change. No, a complete overhaul. If he was honest with himself, he'd felt adrift and unhappy for a long time. It wasn't only Mia and all her spiraling issues, although yes, that was a main factor. But there was simply no ignoring the fact that he didn't exactly love his career anymore. Maybe he never had. Now that he had achieved what he'd set out to do all those years ago, he realized there were many aspects of his current position he loathed.

How many people got an opportunity like he had to pivot midlife into millions of dollars?

Alexander clicked the reply button on the email.

This sounds amazing. Tell them I can have a proposal and rough outline for them by Thursday.

He hesitated for only the briefest of moments—this would mean committing himself to an entirely new way of life.

Send.

CHAPTER 33

*M*ia waited in the lobby of the Neurological Institute with Renee. She had a clear view of the entrance from her chair. She watched through the tinted glass doors as Alexander made his way up the concrete steps outside and reached for the door.

When they had first met, it was his good looks that first caught her attention. His square jaw, blue eyes, and thick brown hair that was wavy when he let it grow too long. Back then, she loved how his jeans rested on his hips, and the tight V of his abdominal muscles as they disappeared into the denim. She had felt giddy, alive, and sexy when he pulled her into his arms.

Her fingers used to clutch fistfuls of that thick, wavy hair when they had sex.

Alexander saw her sitting in the lobby chair and gave her a brief nod before turning his attention to the woman at the front desk.

It had been over two years since they'd had sex.

Mia watched him from behind as he leaned against the tall reception desk and negotiated her leaving under his care. He was softer, rounder around his middle, and his hair had sprouted gray strands at his temples—but he was still a handsome man. Despite the current chasm between them, Mia still wanted her husband. She would like him to pull her again into his arms. She would like to look into his face and see that hunger he once had for her. Lust and love, raw and naked, for all the world to see. Back then, Mia never questioned it. He had so obviously wanted her.

Mia pulled the neck of her shirt to her chin. What did he see when he looked at her now? What was he thinking? She didn't have any idea.

"Looks like your ride is here?" Renee asked, clearly eager to be able to leave herself.

"Yes," Mia confirmed. "I'm all good. Will I see you on Wednesday?"

"Yes." Renee stood up and gave her a warm smile. "I'll be here."

Mia nodded and dropped her eyes to her lap. "Have a good night."

"You too. And by the way," she added in a whisper.

Mia looked up and met Renee's gaze.

"You did amazing today."

Mia nodded and returned her eyes to her lap. "Thank you."

Renee walked away. She slipped her badge against the reader on the wall and disappeared behind the interior double doors that led to the main clinic.

Alexander turned from the desk and approached her. "Ready?" he asked.

She nodded, stood up, and walked silently by his side to the exit.

They pushed through the doors, and the late afternoon heat and humidity enveloped them like a wet blanket as they joined the pace of harried pedestrians streaming through the city. Mia quickened her pace to keep up with Alexander as they headed toward the subway entrance.

"I need to make a quick stop," she said.

"What?" Alexander asked over his shoulder without slowing.

"On the next block. There's a stationary store. I'm supposed to journal this process, and Ty suggested I buy a new one that feels special to me."

Alexander, unable to contain his contempt for the stereotypical therapy assignment, rolled his eyes. "Of course."

They stepped into the street. Once upon a time, Alexander would have reached for her hand, a protective reflex that had apparently atrophied over the years.

"Where is this place?" he asked.

"Just ahead. Halfway down the block."

Alexander stopped in his tracks, annoying several people behind them who were forced to go around. "While you shop, I'm just going to pop into Murphy's across the street and say hello to Tony." He tilted his head in the direction he would be heading. "That way, you won't be rushed."

And you can scotch your way through the rest of this afternoon. "Okay. I'll call you when I'm ready?"

"Perfect. See you in a bit." He headed back toward the intersection they had just crossed. "Take your time," he called back, then joined the crowd crossing to the opposite side of the street.

She watched him for several seconds as he stepped onto the sidewalk opposite her and headed up the street. Mia started walking again, keeping a pace parallel to her husband while the New York traffic crawled between them until he slipped down a flight of steps and into Murphy's basement-level bar. She had never been there but had seen the charges on their bank statements enough to know this was a regular stop for Alexander on his way home from work.

She paused at the entrance to the stationary store and stared at Murphy's scripted flashbulb sign. An electric arrow pointed the way to the stairs. Did Alexander know people there? The regular people that congregated nightly. Was Alexander considered a *regular*? It suddenly occurred to her that her husband had a whole life she knew nothing about.

Was he, right now, greeting a friend she had never met?

Maybe another woman, even?

She had avoided the city and its chaos more and more ever since the girls had been born, but Alexander's life here had continued on without her. So busy with the girls, their home, and her own medical and mental health needs, Mia realized she had never thought much about the details of his existence once he left their home.

Was his sudden and drastic breaking point with her possibly about something more than her collapsing on their living room floor?

Her phone buzzed. She pulled it from her purse; it was a phone call from the art gallery.

"Hello?"

"Mia? It's Garry Surrey."

"Yes, hello."

"I wanted to let you know I looked through all of mom's

contracts from 2003. I think I've found one for the artist who painted your father's portrait and her gift."

"Really? That's wonderful news." Mia wondered if it was someone famous, maybe even a name she would recognize.

"Well, not exactly," Garry said. "My mother always filled out the contracts with artists herself. In meticulous detail. Except for this one. This artist had three pieces that were included in a 2004 spring show, that much I can tell. She *always* typed in all the demographic information, but on this one, instead of typing it in, she allowed the artist to sign their name. Which is the same as on both paintings, an indecipherable scrawl. Everything else, address, phone number. It's blank. She just drew a line through it."

"What? Why?"

"For whatever reason, my mother seems to have wanted to keep the identity of this artist a secret," Garry explained. "I'm sorry. I have a few people I can call that worked at the gallery then. They may know something or remember something. But if my mother was helping this person stay anonymous...."

"She probably did a good job."

Garry sighed on the other end. "Yes. There was a reason she was one of the best in her field."

Mia thanked him for his time and for trying. "If I'm ever in the market for a new piece, I'll come to you first," she promised.

"You know where to find me," Garry said.

Mia dropped her phone back into her purse and pulled open the door to the shop. She relished the blast of air conditioning that rushed over her as it drove a chill across her sweat-damp skin.

"Hello. Can I help you find anything?"

Mia saw the young woman. She stood behind the cash register and placed her phone, which she'd been scrolling through, face down on the counter in front of her.

"Do you sell journals?"

The woman nodded and pointed into the store. "Along the back wall. Next to the restrooms, in the corner."

Mia smiled and nodded once as the woman picked up her phone and began scrolling again.

Mia entered an aisle displaying the most extensive, colorful assortment of pens and pencils she had ever seen. Single, packaged, ballpoint, gel, rollerball, marker, black, blue —every color known to exist on earth. Mia glanced at the small pieces of paper mounted mid-shelf where people had tested various pens. Amongst the squiggles and signatures, someone had written, *You are fucking lost* in a practiced looping cursive.

She imagined some teen trying to be funny, but the message struck her as personal. Like the universe had left it there for her alone to stumble across. Mia adjusted the strap of her purse on her shoulder and refocused her gaze on the back of the store.

Like the pens, the store carried a wide variety of journals. There was even a guide posted on the wall that explained bindings, paper weight, texture, and color. The first journal Mia selected off the shelf because it had a smooth, black leather cover surprised her when she opened it to discover it also had black pages inside. She flipped through the paper, letting the gilded silver edges rush past her thumb. She wondered which pens behind her she would need to hunt and select for this particular journal to be functional.

White ink? Maybe silver?

Mia sighed and replaced the book.

Alexander hadn't even asked her how her session went. *How did she feel? Any strange reactions to the treatment? Was she okay to be left alone on the street and navigate this store alone, given she'd just spent hours in what was potentially an altered cognitive state working to conjure memories that had been buried in her brain for over eighteen years?*

Not one question from him. Only a statement: He'd be having a drink at his favorite bar while he waited for her to take care of this homework assignment from her doctor.

Given Alexander's insistence that she get some real help, it seemed to her that the first thing he might have asked was, "*Did you remember anything?*"

To which Mia could have answered, "Yes. In fact, I did remember something, Alexander."

It was only a brief image that had floated to her halfway through the session—a red sequin dress. Mia didn't know if the dress belonged to her or someone else, but she knew she had a long-buried memory of it, and that dress had been resurrected from her mind today. She intended to record this memory in whatever journal she selected as soon as she got home today.

She reached out and took hold of a white, cloth-covered journal with a small silver crescent moon on the cover. It was one of the larger sizes. She slipped off the protective sleeve and opened the cover, testing the feel of the paper between her fingers. The thickness and texture satisfied her, although she couldn't articulate why it should matter. But this journal felt like it might withstand the heft of her thoughts as she navigated this strange process.

Mia tucked the journal under her arm; this was the one.

She was heading back toward the register when a display in the opposite corner of the shop caught her attention. A cardboard rainbow arched above a closed display case filled with white tubes.

Unleash Your Inner Artist was printed under the rainbow's arch in black block letters.

A moment later, Mia stood in front of the display, opening the case and inspecting the tubes one by one. They were oil-based paints, at least fifty different shades.

And she wanted them.

Mia retrieved a basket from the front of the store and, when she returned to the display, began dropping tubes into it. At first, she only selected primary colors, figuring that would be enough to experiment with. But when her fingers touched the ochre, the magenta, the French ultramarine, she realized she, in fact, needed them all and so decided to buy one of every color.

Next to the paint were a multitude of brushes in various sizes and shapes sorted into bins like floral arrangements. She plucked ten of them without knowing what each could or would be used for, but she felt confident in her selections.

On her way to the register, she grabbed four canvasses from a nearby rack without giving much thought to their sizes. She figured it didn't matter since they were all likely to end up looking like something Sasha and Everly would bring home from kindergarten.

When she left the shop with her large bag and enormous receipt, she did not text Alexander that she was done. Instead, she headed straight for the crosswalk and Murphy's front door. Having had a glimpse of the outside, Mia was now curious to see for herself what her husband's New York life was like.

Not to mention, if he did have friends there, female or otherwise, Mia would like to walk in unannounced and see for herself. She followed the blinking flashbulb arrow that led the way down the concrete steps to a heavy wood door painted red. The two windows on either side were so darkly tinted Mia was unable to see inside.

For all she knew, Alexander was on the other side and could see her approaching anyway.

CHAPTER 34

*S*he grasped the long-wrought iron handle with her free hand and pulled the heavy door, flooding the entrance with bright outside light. It took a second for her eyes to adjust, but when they did, she immediately saw Alexander.

He sat in profile near the far end of the bar. Slouching over what was sure to be a half-finished double of Macallan on ice.

Far from the suspicious image in her mind of imaginary friends and bar regulars reminiscent of a *Cheers* episode, Alexander sat alone with only his phone for company.

Not even the bartender, who was busy scrubbing glassware in the sink, was speaking to him.

"Hello." The bartender glanced up to greet her. He was young, muscled, and looked like he probably spent his free time at auditions and was waiting for his big break. "What can I get you?"

Only then did Alexander's attention break from his phone. He looked right and saw her standing at the door.

"Mia!" he exclaimed as he stood up from his bar stool.

Mia waved off the bartender's offer and headed toward her husband.

"I thought you were going to text me?" His tone held an edge of accusation as he glanced between her and his half-finished drink on the bar like he was trying to decide his next move.

Mia shrugged and pulled out the bar seat beside him. "I thought I'd have a drink with you." She paused before taking the seat. "I mean...*If* that's okay with you?"

Alexander looked incredulous. "Well...of course...but." He sat back down and seemed to think about what to say next. "Well, quite frankly," he whispered as Mia sat beside him. "*Should* you be having a drink? What are the instructions from the doctor? *Mixing*, I mean. The drugs...and alcohol?" He asked the last question while glancing up at the bartender to make sure he wasn't being overheard.

As if the bartender gave two shits about what they were talking about.

"I don't think it's an issue," Mia whispered as she signaled for the bartender. "But how about I play it safe, just in case." She added and turned from Alexander to meet the bartender's bright, deep-set blue eyes. "I'll have an iced tea. Unsweet, please."

"Iced tea, coming right up." He gave her a gorgeous, perfectly corrected, whitened smile, then spun to his left and began filling a tumbler with ice.

"Actually!" Alexander called out, stopping the bartender mid-scoop. "Never mind that." He cut his hand through the air, waving off Mia's drink order before picking up his own glass from the bar. "Just the check will do, Garret," he said, then threw back the rest of his scotch in one long swallow.

Stunned and a little embarrassed, Mia looked sideways at her husband. "There isn't any rush—"

"We should get home to the girls anyway," he interrupted her. "I don't think hanging around in a bar in the city is exactly what we should be doing." He flattened his lips and shook his head as if disapproving of the very idea.

But this was your idea, Mia nearly pointed out.

She watched as Alexander signed the credit card slip and slid his card back into his wallet. He was angry. She could feel it radiating off him. But she didn't have any idea why.

Or how to ask him why.

"Thanks, Garret," Alexander said, then rapped his knuckles twice on the bar top, and stood up.

Garret raised his hand absently and continued rinsing out the knobby bar mats that captured all the overspill from the taps.

"I thought you said his name was Tony?" Mia asked.

"What?" Alexander said.

"Earlier, you said you wanted to come in here and say hello to someone named Tony."

"Oh...he wasn't working. What is all that?" Alexander asked, now noticing her enormous bag from the stationary store. "I thought you were buying a journal?" His tone was curt, condescending—bordering on shitty, actually.

Mia paused before answering him because her knee-jerk desire was to be shitty right back—which would lead them into a fight she didn't feel like having right now.

"It's some art supplies."

"What are those for?"

Mia thought about his question because, really, what were they for? "I'm going to unleash my inner artist," she said with a flourish of her hand.

Alexander wrinkled his brow and stared at her. "Are you okay? Are you still high or something?" The way he was looking at her, it felt like contempt.

"No, not high." She raised her eyebrows and widened her eyes. "Just trying to embrace this process the best I can. I guess I figured maybe I'd try some at-home art therapy in addition to the psychedelic mind fuckery. It can't hurt, right?" she smiled, trying to lighten the mood. They still had a long train ride ahead of them.

But Alexander did not smile. He looked at her stone-faced for several seconds like he was trying to figure something out, then shook his head and sighed. "I'm tired, Mia. I just want to go home, okay?" Then he headed for the door and pushed his way out, not bothering to wait or even check to see if Mia was following. She stood and watched it close behind him as he ascended the concrete stairs without her.

"Goodnight, ma'am," a voice called out to her.

Mia turned her head and gazed into Garret's sympathetic eyes. This kid didn't miss a beat; she could tell.

"Goodnight," she whispered. "And thank you."

He nodded once, and Mia left.

CHAPTER 35

"*H*olly? Is that you?"

She had only been picking up the girls from school for two weeks, but Holly already recognized the high-pitched, lilting quality of Dominique Richard's voice when she was asking an obvious question to which she already knew the obvious answer.

Holly turned slowly and met the woman's ever-intense gaze. In her defense, Holly *did* try to smile at the woman. But she knew the expression sat upon her face like a Halloween mask. No one with any sense would imagine Holly felt even remotely welcoming toward this woman.

No one, that is, except Dominique Richards herself. The woman was either completely oblivious to social cues, which was unlikely given her current social status among these elite. Or, she was an expert at not giving a shit about how you felt if those feelings impeded her current agenda.

Holly was almost certain it was the latter.

"That *is* you! I just knew it," she said as she sidled up with her skinny, shy son in tow.

Holly had successfully avoided almost all forced social exchanges with the other parents since she had figured out she could simply drive through the pick-up lane to collect the girls. But today was different because both girls had large poster board projects and needed help getting them from their class to her truck.

"I've been on the lookout for you." Dominique waggled her finger and gave Holly a wicked smile. "I think you've been hiding from us," she flat out accused, as if daring Holly to deny it.

Where Dominique miscalculated was in assuming that Holly gave a shit, in the least, about what she or any of the other parents thought about her. She had almost no skin in this game.

"Well, yes," Holly admitted. "That's about right. I guess private elementary schools are not exactly my scene."

If she had imagined that bold-faced truth would cow or somehow put the likes of Dominique Richards in her place, Holly had herself sorely miscalculated because Dominique Richard's expression lit up like someone had just challenged her to the duel she'd been waiting for.

"I knew it," she breathed. As if they were now coconspirators. "How refreshing to find another parent—well, not a parent, but maybe that's the point—that feels so...I don't know." She waved her hand in the air like it might be able to capture the thoughts and words that were eluding her just on the edge of her consciousness. "Different?" Dominique leaned in and whispered, "It's so exhausting to watch all these people *trying* so hard, don't you agree?"

Holly met Dominique's gaze and wondered if this woman, who was wearing a suit that cost more than most people's monthly mortgage, was joking, blind, or simply taking a chapter from *How to Win Friends and Influence People* —whatever the case, Holly had no idea how to respond. Dominique was the queen of this kingdom. That she tried to convince Holly otherwise with her Birkin Bag slung over her shoulder was ridiculous.

"I'm sorry. I really do need to get to the girls' classroom. How can I help you, Dominique?"

Dominique raised her perfectly manicured hand and waved away the very idea. "I only wanted to let you know how absolutely ecstatic everyone, and I mean *everyone*, is that Mia will be holding the girls' birthday party at Beaumar." She leaned in again and whispered. "I have parents with kids in other grades calling me *day and night* asking if there is any way, any way at all, they could possibly get on the invite list." Dominique pulled away and gave Holly a mock sad expression as she shook her head. "As if. Can you imagine? But they really are desperate to not miss out on the chance to see the infamous home of Raphael and Pixlie Renaud."

Holly stared at Dominique as her brain worked to process the meaning of her words. What on earth was this woman talking about? Because there was no way Mia would invite hundreds of strangers to Beaumar Manor for...well, for anything. Would she?

As the seconds of silence passed between them, Dominique's expression shifted from coconspirator to confused. She placed her fingertips on her chest. "Wait, you didn't know? I...well, I just assumed."

Now it was Dominique's turn to be confused.

"I have to go," Holly said, walking away from Dominique without another word.

"I hope I haven't—" Dominique called after her, but whatever social faux pas she feared she'd committed died on her lips.

What was Mia thinking? And why wouldn't she have run this by her? Holly strode down the kindergarten hallway, dodging the tiny humans streaming toward the exits, bags bouncing against their backs as they headed for the main entrance.

Holly had been collecting the girls on Monday, Wednesday, and Friday afternoons for the last two weeks—which was more than enough time for Mia to share her plans for a birthday party at Beaumar.

But she hadn't breathed a single word, not even hinting at its possibility. Because if she had, Holly would have shut the idea down immediately. Holly stood to the side and let the ten children rushing from Everly and Sasha's classroom exit through the door before she entered.

She watched them pass, then peered into the classroom. Sasha and Everly were standing with their teacher, packed and ready to leave, identical girls clutching their large trifold displays and waiting for their aunt to arrive and help.

Not since before the accident had Mia kept anything from Holly. And as she watched the girls chatting with their elderly teacher, Holly realized there was only one reason Mia would have kept the party plans a secret.

Mia must have known Holly would object.

Which was absolutely true. And in fact, Holly would do more than simply object. Had Mia shared her plans, Holly would have forbidden it.

Holly would *still* forbid it. She didn't care how many nosy Beacon Hill Academy parents would be disappointed. There wasn't any way Beaumar would ever be opened up, so strangers to gawk, gossip, and guess about exactly where and how Raphael Renaud had met his infamous end there.

Mia must have known this was the only reason these people were coming to her daughters' party. How could her sister do this? To Pixlie? To their family?

To herself?

Everly and Sasha looked up at the same time as if on cue. Holly knew it was those strangely synced twin minds sensing her presence together. Their faces lit up, smiles beaming, and they bounced on their toes the way they always did when they first saw her.

Her heart, it was impossible to ignore the way it now swelled when they looked at her this way. Holly smiled back and raised her hand. She had never wanted to have children of her own, she was sure. But spending this time with her nieces sometimes made her wonder, *what if?*

As Holly helped them carry their poster boards out of the school and to her truck, Sasha and Everly only had one subject on their minds. "Today? Is he better yet? Can we see him today?"

Holly forced a smile as both girls climbed from the rusted running board and into their respective booster seats. "We'll see. Maybe."

"Does he play with the other dogs?" Sasha asked.

"Not yet."

"Will he let you pet him?" Everly asked.

"Almost. I think. I bought a special glove so that I can

keep trying, and if he bites, it won't hurt. Well, not too much anyway."

"Does he still have to stay in his pen?"

"Yes. But…you know, when I walked in the barn today, he didn't bark at me. And I think he might like some of the toys I've given him. So, we can go in and visit him and take him a treat. That's good for him, and it helps him to learn that not all people are bad and want to hurt him. But you can't get too close yet. And don't be surprised if he lunges at the cage and snarls."

Both girls nodded; their expressions were serious, but their eyes were hopeful. They had become very invested in Stevie's recovery these past few weeks. They probably wished for Stevie to turn the corner even more than she did.

Or maybe, being children, they more firmly believed in the possibility of it. Her eyes flicked to the still pink scar on Everly's hand where Stevie's teeth had grazed her. Holly was beginning to have her doubts.

CHAPTER 36

*W*hen they arrived back at her house, Holly had barely set the truck's parking brake when both girls unlatched their booster seats and exploded out the rear doors.

"Wait!" she called as she fumbled to pull her key from the ignition and grab her purse from the seat beside her. She slammed her own door shut. "Don't you go into that barn without me!" she yelled as they both disappeared around the side of the house and through the gate. Neither indicated they had heard her warning or intended to follow it. "Damnit," she breathed and ran to catch up with them. By the time she made it around the house, the girls were already halfway across the expansive yard, headed straight for the barn. "Girls!" she shouted.

Their little legs kept running.

Ralph, sleeping beneath his tree, rose and loped towards them. While all the other dogs in the far pen either lifted their sleeping heads or ran to the fence to see what all the commotion was about. Holly was catching up, but they would still make it to the cracked barn door before she did. "Sasha! Everly! Wait!"

It was times like this, when her nieces didn't listen, that Holly's doubts about not having kids evaporated. She loved them and was thankful for this time with them—but children were mentally and physically exhausting.

She was ten feet away when the girls reached the barn door, along with Ralph, and all three of them stopped in their tracks and turned to look at her.

When she reached them, out of breath and heart pounding so hard she felt like she might pass out, Holly placed her hands on her knees and doubled over to catch her breath. After several seconds of heavy breathing, she looked up and gave them all a stern look. "I thought I told you to wait?"

"We did!" Sasha said.

Holly closed her eyes and sighed before standing up and opening the barn door. "Go slow," she whispered. "It's best not to startle him." She turned to Ralph and pointed to the ground. "You stay here."

Ralph sat his butt down, his long tail thumping the dirt so hard a cloud of dust rose up. Holly ran her hand over his head and down his long face. He really was the sweetest dog ever. "Good boy."

Holly led the girls into the barn, holding each of their hands to ensure neither made any sudden movements or got too close to the cage.

Stevie sat on his large dog bed, spine erect, ears alert, his black eyes watching their every move from the moment they entered his space. "Who's a good boy?" she said, even though none of her endearments ever elicited the slightest observable reactions in him. Still, she liked to imagine her care and kindness were slowly chipping away at his learned defenses.

"Okay, stand right here. Don't move," Holly said and dropped the girls' hands. She removed the plastic lid from the old Folgers can she kept on the tool bench next to the door and took out two bone-shaped biscuits.

Stevie's ears twitched, and he stood up off his bed.

Holly handed each girl a biscuit and scooted them a foot closer to the cage. "Now, one at a time, tell him he's a good boy and toss the cookie into his cage."

"Me first," Sasha declared. "Good boy, Stevie," she called and threw the biscuit underhand. It flew through the wire and landed less than a foot from Stevie, who bent his head and gobbled the biscuit at once. He had hardly swallowed before he was looking at them again, his black eyes intent on Everly and that last biscuit.

"Your turn," Holly nudged her niece.

"Good boy...Stevie," Everly's voice wavered, and when she threw her own treat, the overhanded attempt caused the biscuit to fall a few inches short of the cage wall and land in the dirt. "I missed," Everly said and moved to get the treat.

Holly gripped Everly's shoulder. "No. Let me do it." She walked slowly, speaking softly to Stevie as she neared the cage, crouched low, and picked up the cookie. When she lifted her head, she met Stevie's eyes, only inches from hers. He had approached the cage wall and stood stock-still, staring her down.

Holly felt a shiver of fear wash through her. It was impossible to read this dog. She had no idea if he had come closer in an attempt to greet her or eat her. Holly lifted the biscuit to an opening in the cage and held her breath as Stevie leaned his head forward and took it from her. He chewed once, twice, then turned away from her and returned to his bed, where he sat and continued to stare at them.

When Holly turned back to her nieces, they were wide-eyed and smiling. "He was so nice," Everly whispered.

Holly nodded, stood back up, and led the girls outside to play with the other dogs before taking them home.

And ask her sister what the hell she was thinking by planning a party at Beaumar.

CHAPTER 37

"*M*ia?" a voice called from the floor above her.

Mia's hand froze mid-stroke. She stared at her painting as the physical space jarred her into present reality.

"Mia? Are you home?" Holly called.

"Mommy?" Sasha yelled.

Mia could tell they were at the top of the basement stairs.

"She's probably painting," Sasha said.

She heard their feet on the unfinished wooden stairs descending into her space. Mia's eyes flicked to the small clock on the bench against the wall. It was nearly six o'clock —she'd really let the time get away from her this time.

And now, because of that slip-up, she would have to explain all this to her sister.

"We're home!" Sasha yelled, her shrill voice ricocheting like a knife across Mia's nerves. She took a breath and placed her brush, still loaded with crimson paint, into the tray before her. She wiped her hands on the crusted rag she kept in her apron pocket and turned to face them.

"Mia?" Holly asked. "What are you doing?"

"This is her studio," Sasha said with pride. "Isn't it wonderful?" she added as she rushed into the room and twirled. Her hand brushed against a picture Mia had just propped against the table to dry, and her fingers smeared a line of blue and green paint across the canvas.

"Sasha!" Mia barked. "Look what you've done. I've told you, you're not allowed down here."

Sasha halted her twirl on the spot and snatched the offending, paint-stained hand to her chest. Which compounded Mia's annoyance when she saw the oil paint was now all over the front of Sasha's shirt.

"I'm sorry," Sasha said as Everly came to stand at her side, positioning herself to help absorb some of the blame.

Mia looked at them both and gave an annoyed sigh. "It's fine. Just go upstairs and wash up for dinner." She dismissed them. "I'll be there in a minute."

They both turned as if one and ran for the stairs, their feet making just as much noise going up as they had coming down. Mia winced at the racket and then noticed Holly staring at her with a strange expression.

Mia closed her eyes and let out another loud sigh. The annoyance at being interrupted, yanked from that deeply creative mind space so suddenly, made her nerves crawl. Still, as the seconds passed, she knew she was being unkind to the girls and her sister. She was the one who had lost all track of the time. When she opened her eyes, she met Holly's now stunned expression.

"What are you doing?" Holly whispered.

"Painting...obviously," her tone still clipped and laced with sarcasm. Where was all this attitude coming from? She never spoke to Holly, or her girls, like this. She picked up her paint-heavy brush and kept her hands busy wiping it on her rag.

"I can see that," Holly answered, her voice now also sharp as a blade. "What I mean is...I guess I didn't realize—"

"Yes, well." Mia placed her brush handle down into one of the mason jars on the bench beside her. "The doctor asked me weeks ago to start journaling as part of the therapy. I guess I decided to do this instead." Mia turned her back on Holly and faced the many canvases she had filled over the past two weeks. Looking at them all now, seeing them as Holly must be seeing them for the first time, Mia realized how shocking it must be. But she didn't feel the need to explain herself, not to Alexander, not to Holly, not to anyone. This place and space, and what she was doing down here, was the only thing she'd found, besides the litany of drugs she'd been prescribed over the years, that quieted the riot of anxiety and flood of emotions that were forever threatening to wash her over the edge of sanity. It was the only thing that felt completely right to her. Gave her some goddamn peace.

"It helps me," she offered by way of some small explanation, hoping that would be enough for her sister while knowing it would never satisfy her.

Holly's involvement in Mia's life had been all encompassing for the last eighteen years. Maybe longer. Maybe Holly had always been this deeply rooted and entwined in Mia's existence—but Mia couldn't fucking remember.

The thought brought on a fresh wave of anger. She untied her smock, yanked it over her head, and dropped it in a heap in front of the easel. "Well?" Mia asked as she turned back to face Holly. "What do you think? It's kind of shocking." She shook her head once. "Don't you think? I mean, you must think that based on the look on your face."

Holly stared at her, her eyes wide and her face pale. "They're good," was all she said.

Mia nodded and looked at her feet before returning her gaze to her sister. "I know that. When I'm standing here, brush in hand, I know exactly what I'm doing. But I don't know how I know. Do *you* know how?"

Holly broke eye contact with her and scanned the twenty or so paintings Mia had completed. After several seconds, she shook her head. "No. But obviously, you have a talent," she breathed.

"Yes," Mia said. "Obviously, there's that. But did I before? Before the attack. Before this?" Mia slapped the scar on her face, bringing Holly's attention back to her in a flash.

"Don't do that," Holly commanded.

"What? Don't do what?"

"This." She threw both her hands up at Mia. "Whatever this is. The anger, the barely veiled accusations—and about what, I have no idea. What are you asking me, Mia? What do you want to know?"

"Did I always paint? Before? Did I always have this talent?"

Holly bit her lip and shook her head. "No, Mia. You have not always had this talent. Anything else?"

Mia narrowed her eyes and shifted her weight. "Why did you lie to me?"

Mia watched Holly's expression harden, her jaw muscles flex. "About what?"

"About Everly. About how she got hurt at your house. She was bit! By one of those goddamn feral dogs. And you tried to tell me that she got hurt at school? And even had *them* lie to *me*." Mia threw her hand toward the ceiling and shook her head. "What the fuck were you thinking? Allowing them to be in that kind of danger, and then coaching them to—"

"Mia, that's not how—"

"I heard them. They were talking in their room last night when they were supposed to be going to sleep. Sasha telling Everly that the bite was all better and that *Stevie*—a fighting dog—didn't *mean* to hurt her! For fuck's sake, Holly. How stupid are you? Did you think I wouldn't find out? They're five!"

Holly stood before her, frozen and looking shell-shocked. She opened her mouth, about to say something, but then snapped it shut again. She shook her head, and Mia watched as the tears rose in her sister's eyes.

Mia clenched and unclenched her fists at her sides, trying to calm down, trying to take hold of a thought that could carry her through this raging storm of emotions that compelled her, begged her, to start swinging her arms, kicking her feet—she wanted, so desperately, to destroy something right now. To fracture a thing beneath her hands felt like the only way to make this rage leave her body.

"What is happening?" Holly asked. "I'm sorry about Everly, Mia truly. And you're right. I never should have lied or allowed the girls to lie. Please know I never asked them to. I would never...not that. But I didn't stop them, and I should have, and I went along with it for reasons that seemed, well, never mind that. The point is you're right, and I'm so sorry. But right now. All this." She shook her head as two tears streaked down each of her cheeks. "It's like you're a completely different person right now, Mia. And it's scaring me."

Mia dug her nails into the palms of her hand. The pain offered some release from her fury. She swallowed hard as Holly's words sunk in. "Honestly, Holly? I *feel* like a different person."

Holly nodded, but she still looked frightened. "Is it the therapy? The drugs?"

Mia shook her head, her shoulders lowering a fraction of an inch as she flexed her fingers. "I don't know. Maybe. Or maybe it's being off my regular drugs. Who can say at this point?"

"If it's making you feel this way…have you considered quitting? You know you can leave the treatment, at any time. Alexander can't force you—"

"Alexander doesn't even want me in this study. Working so closely with Erica makes him vulnerable and less able to maintain his threats." Mia bent over, picked up her smock, and hung it on the hook beside her workbench.

"So then, there's no reason for you to continue this. If it's making you feel worse?"

Mia gathered her long, unruly hair and piled it onto her head. She didn't care about her scar, feeling exposed, or even if Holly now heard the truth. "It's working," she said, driving one of her sharp-tipped pencils through the thick bun she'd created on the crown of her head, anchoring her voluminous black hair into place.

Holly's brow furrowed. "What do you mean? Your memory?"

Mia took a deep breath and nodded. "Yes. It's not

specific. Feelings, images, like half remembered dreams I once had years ago. It's frustrating, but also the closest I've ever come to regaining anything. And the painting is helping. Or feels like it's helping. But I don't know where the images come from or what they mean. When you look at these." Mia motioned to all her recent works scattered around the room. "Do you see something? Recognize anything, anyone from our past?"

Mia watched Holly scan the paintings briefly, her eyes lingering for the briefest moment on the one Mia had just been working on, still positioned on the easel. It was the back view of a young woman in a red dress with waist-length blond hair facing an ocean.

"I'm sorry, Mia," Holly quickly declared. "No. Nothing at all."

Mia watched her sister for a moment more before asking her next question. "And you're sure you never saw or knew of me painting before?"

Holly's eyes flicked once more to the portrait of the young woman, then she shook her head. "Maybe there's some neurological explanation? Something to do with the injury or the drugs activating areas of your brain. What does your doctor say about it?"

"I haven't told him," Mia said.

"What about Alexander?"

"I haven't told him either?"

"Not even about the paintings?" Holly asked.

Mia shook her head, and Holly's eyes grew wide. "How have you managed to keep all this a secret?" She held both her palms up. "I mean, even the girls know."

"I've asked them not to tell him."

Holly looked startled. "So, you've asked them to lie to their father."

"Which is nothing at all like you asking them to lie to *me* about an *injury*."

Holly stood, silent, staring at her like she hardly recognized her. "I never asked them to lie to you," she said. "Or anyone else, for that matter. I just didn't stop them from doing it...and I should have. But since we are on the subject of lies, and I can see how passionate you feel about them... when exactly were you going to tell me that you're planning to hold the girls' birthday party at Beaumar?"

Mia felt the muscles in her face twitch; she hadn't prepared herself to broach this subject with her sister yet. "I don't need your permission, Holly. I may not remember it, but I grew up there, same as you, and have just as much right to it as you do."

"No one is questioning your rights, Mia. But you saw the state of that house yourself. It's a disaster. And what about Pixlie? What are you planning to do with her while all your private school mummies and daddies are poking around, speculating...gossiping about our *family?* About *you?* You may not remember, but I do! The nightmare all our lives were after dad's death. The endless photographers, journalists, the fucking fanatic tourists who wanted the chance to observe our private hell on earth like it was some goddamn sideshow created for their amusement. While you were recovering, barely hanging onto life yourself, *I'm* the one who had to live through all that. *I'm* the one who had to find ways to protect myself, Pixlie—to protect *you*, Mia. And now you think you're just going to invite that chaos back into our lives so you can be the most popular mommy at school? I don't fucking think so."

Mia turned away from Holly and busied her hands, cleaning her brushes. "Now, who's unrecognizable, Holly? I may not remember what life was like before my assault, but I do know that my life since has been continually and persistently conducted under your ever-watchful eye. Maybe you believe it's your job to protect me, or maybe you've just always been this controlling over me. But believe me when I tell you, it ends now."

"You don't have any idea what you're talking about. You think this new therapy is helping you? You think a few half-remembered images," Holly threw her hand and gestured to the painting still drying on the easel. "Holds all the answers to your lost life? I'm the answer, Mia. Me. So, believe me when I tell you, if you keep pushing this, if you insist on opening that house back up, you will regret it. I can promise you that."

Mia turned back to her sister and squared her shoulders. "I appreciate—"

"No, you don't," Holly shook her head. "Because you are incapable of it."

"Mia!" Alexander shouted down the stairs. "Are you down there?"

Mia's eyes shot to the stairs. "Shit," she breathed. The last thing she needed right now was for Alexander to come downstairs and see all this.

"Yes!" she called back. "I'll be right up!"

"Why are you hiding this from him?" Holly asked.

"I don't know," Mia said as she yanked her apron over her head, pulled the pencil from her sloppy bun, and repositioned her hair to cover the right side of her face. "I'm just not ready for him to see this. Okay? So, I know you're angry with me right now, but please, Holly, don't mention this to him when we go upstairs."

Holly looked at her, her expression incredulous, and shook her head.

"What?" Mia snapped. "You can't do me this one small favor?"

At this, Holly scoffed. "After all this time, you still don't get it. I won't tell Alexander anything. I am your biggest protector, Mia. But you are right about one thing," she said as she turned toward the stairs. "You're not ready. Not for any of this."

CHAPTER 38

$\mathcal{M}$ia watched her sister ascend the stairs without another word. When she reached the top, Mia could hear Alexander and Holly talking, but their voices were too low to make out the specifics. Holly was mad, but Mia didn't believe her sister would betray her—especially not to Alexander, whom she barely tolerated.

She quickly inspected her clothes for any evidence of paint and was relieved to find none, but her hands were covered in it. Surely, he would notice and ask about what she'd been up to. Her mind cartwheeled for an excuse—the only logical answer was to tell him the truth.

Sort of.

Alexander already knew she had purchased all the supplies for painting. He was with her the day she'd bought them. He just didn't have any idea about what had come of it. As far as he knew, Mia likely spent all that money at the art store simply to let all her purchases gather dust in a closet. If he were to happen to come downstairs, he would be shocked to see how much time she was spending on this new hobby.

And if he had any sense about art, which he didn't, he would be floored to learn how good she was at it.

Mia took a deep breath and headed up the stairs to greet him. If he asked, she would explain that, yes, she had been painting, and she wouldn't elaborate further. He had been so wrapped up in his own work and world just lately there was a chance he wouldn't even think to press her any further about it.

She was halfway up the stairs when she stopped, turned around, and gazed at the painting still resting on her easel. When Mia first asked her sister, Holly claimed she didn't recognize anything in the paintings. But in anger, she called Mia's new work *half-remembered images*, and this painting, of the young woman on the beach, seemed to unnerve Holly the most.

Many things about her past were confusing and frightening, but what scared her the most right now was this persistent and ever-growing sense that she couldn't trust the one person she had relied on the most for the past eighteen years. Her whole life was built on a foundation of beliefs that her sister had helped her to construct, and for the first time, Mia could feel the cracks. If she couldn't trust Holly now, what did that mean about these past eighteen years? If you had asked her a month ago if her sister would ever lie to her about anything, Mia would have declared *absolutely not*. But Holly *was* lying to her. There was no denying it. About little things…and maybe big things too.

When she reached the top step, it was just in time to hear their front door closing behind Holly as she left. Mia rounded the corner, expecting Alexander to be coming back to greet her, but instead, she found him heading up the stairs to the second floor.

"Hello," she said.

Alexander stopped in his tracks. "Oh, hi," he said, not turning around. "Holly just left, and the girls are in the front room watching a movie with a snack."

"You're home early," she said.

Alexander nodded and gazed up toward the second-floor landing. "Yes. I have a lot of work to catch up on. I figured I might be better able to concentrate away from the constant disruptions of my campus office."

It wasn't her imagination; he was avoiding eye contact with her.

"So." He glanced at his feet and gestured to the stairs. "I'll be in my office," he said, then continued up without ever looking at her. When he reached the top, he stopped. "Oh, I'm sure they probably won't, but if the girls come upstairs—"

"I'll keep them away from your door," she finished his sentence.

He nodded. "Thanks."

Mia stood at the bottom of their staircase and listened until she heard him close his office door. She imagined him switching on his lamp and settling into the large leather chair behind his desk.

She needn't have worried about Alexander noticing and questioning her about what she was doing in the basement. He hadn't looked at her. Not even once.

Mia gazed down at her paint-stained hands. It didn't feel like she was the only one keeping secrets in this house.

CHAPTER 39

$\mathcal{A}$ lexander opened his eyes to the sound of his wife's voice. Their bedroom was flooded with a soft blue light. The moon was full and bright tonight, and they had both neglected to close the drapes.

When he turned his head, he could see Mia's profile. She was lying flat on her back, her black hair spilling above her head across the stark white sheets, her scar plainly visible to him. Her eyes were closed, but her lips were moving.

"No, Natalie," she whispered. "Don't go."

Alexander sat up, careful not to wake her, and slid his legs over his side of the bed. He picked up the notebook on his side of the bed, turned to the next empty page, and began to write down everything she said.

Mia had always talked in her sleep. Mostly she rambled about people and events he was familiar with. For years, he assumed she was processing her daily life while she slept. Occasionally she had what could only be described as a reoc-curring nightmare. She would shake, cry, and go on and on about eyes. The best he could figure out was that the dream was about watching someone—or maybe being watched. Early in their relationship, he felt sorry for her and would wake her up and ask if she was okay. But Mia never remembered the nightmare and didn't know what it could be about. They were infrequent enough, once every few months. They increased while she was pregnant with the twins. One of her many doctors suggested that Mia was perhaps processing the trauma of witnessing her father's murder. Mia's eyes had watched it happen, they reasoned.

Alexander had thought that particular doctor, one of the few he felt was actually trying to get to the root of Mia's troubles instead of only prescribing ever-increasing doses of drugs, was onto something. He encouraged Mia to explore the possibility that this doctor was right, but she found a reason to stop seeing them soon after the hypothesis was posed. She never seemed to really want to address the burden of her father's death.

The nightmare continued to ebb and flow from her unconscious, and the sleep-talking continued. Alexander hadn't bothered to wake Mia for years. Now, when she woke him up, he would take his pillow and move into the spare room so he could at least get some uninterrupted sleep before work.

Things had changed since Mia had joined Erica's trial. The night after her first session, Mia spoke in her sleep, and it was the first time Alexander didn't know what, or who, she was talking about. "Natalie, don't go. Stay here."

That night had been the first time Alexander had heard mention of Natalie. It was also the first time Mia spoke about *watching* without it being in conjunction with her reoccurring nightmare. Maybe this new psychedelic therapy really was going to be the ticket to helping Mia recover some of her lost memories. He had considered waking her up. Maybe she could now remember or make sense of her dreams.

But that first night, when he reached out to shake her shoulder, he thought about the new book. If he woke her, there was a good chance Mia wouldn't remember anything anyway. If he let her keep dreaming and talking, she might reveal some insights into her past. Insights that could help him piece together some truths about her family for himself.

"Natalie," Mia whispered again. "Please, don't go down there."

Alexander scribbled down her words and waited for more. When several minutes went by, and all Mia did was sigh and roll away from him onto her side, he knew the dream had passed. She was unlikely to say anything else.

He glanced at the time on his phone; it was three fifty-seven. It was both too early to get up and too late to get back to sleep. He rubbed his face with both his hands and stood up. He could use this time to get some work done on the new book before heading into the city for the day.

Downstairs in the kitchen, he pulled a coffee pod from the drawer and made himself a cup in the dark. As the cup filled and the roasted, rich scent filled the room, Alexander wondered how he could figure out who this Natalie was. He felt positive it was someone, a real person, from Mia's past. It was the way she spoke in her sleep, as if she were her younger self. Natalie was someone from Mia's childhood. And he felt sure she was someone significant. Otherwise, why would Mia's recent dreams be filled with her?

After the machine hissed and spat out the last few drops,

Alexander took his scalding hot cup and his thoughts back upstairs to his office.

Once behind his desk, he placed his coffee onto the coaster beside his keyboard and flipped on the desk lamp. He pulled up the file he was keeping for the new book but decided to check his email before diving in.

There was an email from Tasha.

Just thought I'd reach out and see if you had any further thoughts about moving forward with your new book? If so, I would love to be involved...if that's possible. I could be a huge help to you with any research, notes, etc. Please think it over. I would love the opportunity. I know you're very busy, but any chance we could meet for coffee again to discuss it?

Reading her words—the excitement he felt was impossible to deny. He reached out to his keyboard to reply immediately, his eagerness to see this woman again momentarily overriding all sense and reason. He had typed out his first enthusiastic sentence before his fingers recoiled from his keyboard into two tight fists.

He glanced at the antique brass desk clock next to his lamp. It wasn't even four o'clock in the morning. He imagined what she would think, young, beautiful, cool Tasha receiving a desperate to see her email before the sun had even risen on the day. Alexander used his pointer finger to delete every letter he had typed and closed his email.

Eight o'clock. That was an acceptable time to be up. A normal time to respond to emails. Still early enough to ensure they could find a time to meet today. He was about to pull up the outline he had started for the new book when a thought occurred. He opened his email back up and reread Tasha's exact words. He had assumed she was responding to his earlier email letting her know about the massive deal he would be signing with his publisher, but her email made it clear that she either hadn't read or received his earlier email. She didn't know that the new book was happening.

He pulled up his sent messages and scrolled until he found the message he had sent to her university account. It didn't appear to have bounced back, but there was no way of telling if she had opened it. When he went back to look at her response, he could see that it wasn't a reply, and when he clicked on the address, it hadn't been sent from her university account. This was her private email.

Maybe she didn't check her university account very often? Although that seemed unlikely given the sheer amount of information he knew all of the professors cranked out to students every day. Was there more to this? Was there any chance Tasha, if her interest in him was more than professional, was taking precautions to keep their communication off the university's channels? And if that was the case, should he follow her lead and also use a private account to communicate with her?

The very thought, the need for secrecy and clandestine communication—the burn of excitement he had felt erupted into an inferno of lust. Also fear. He was sailing, rudderless, into unchartered waters without a map.

It made him feel alive in a way he hadn't in over a decade. He wondered if this thing with Tasha became serious, he should see about getting a burner phone. Then wondered, where one would go to get a burner phone discretely? And if that became necessary, should he also consider setting up a separate bank account or a credit card? One Mia didn't know about?

He shook his head; he was getting way out in front of the situation. He was a thinker, an over-thinker, actually. He would worry about all that later. He would text Tasha from the train to set up a time to meet later. Right now, all he needed to do was focus on completing the new book's outline.

It would be good to share it with Tasha over coffee. Or maybe even lunch.

CHAPTER 40

*L*ater that evening, sitting next to Tasha at the mahogany bar in Murphy's, Alexander again felt the intoxicating rush of desire steeped in unease. Tasha was thrilled to hear the new book had a green light from his publisher. She was also clearly impressed when he casually let drop the ballpark number of the expected advance.

"You see!" she gushed. "I'm not the only one who can't wait to get their hands on the next one." As she reached for her glass of Chardonnay with one hand, she rested her other on the back of his hand on the bar. When she pulled it away and used it to brush her long hair behind her shoulder, Alexander smiled and wondered if she would do it again and if he could also find some innocuous way to touch her.

Talking, laughing with her—being near her made him feel alive and young, as if her energy had awakened his own long-dormant sense of vitality. His virility. There was no denying what he was feeling. He wanted to hold this woman, kiss her, see her naked body, and make love to her.

Which all felt miles away from a casual, friendly touch on the back of his hand. It had been an eon since he had volleyed on the court of sexual innuendo. He had no idea how to gracefully get from sitting politely side by side at a bar to sweaty, breathless, and tangled naked in white sheets.

"So, what do you think?" she asked, cocking her head to one side and giving him a smile.

Alexander brought his full attention to the moment. "I'm sorry," he said and picked up his scotch. "My mind." He shook his head. "I missed what you said." He took a sip to try and disguise his nervousness.

"I knew you weren't listening." She pushed his shoulder gently.

Jesus Christ, he wanted to smash his face against hers, pick her tight ass up off that stool, and carry her out of this bar and down the street to the Marriott on the corner. Right here, right now.

"I said, what do you think about me coming on to help you with the book? I'd be great at helping with the research. I'm meticulous about note-taking. And you can trust me to be discreet," she finished with a whisper and a knowing look that left Alexander wondering if she was still only talking about working on the book or implying what he desperately hoped she was implying.

Alexander glanced down at his glass and was surprised to see it empty. They had only been here about thirty minutes, and this was his second glass. He swirled the giant ice cube around the tumbler and signaled the bartender to bring him another. He wanted to choose his next words carefully. No matter how much he hoped Tasha wanted what he did, he didn't want to risk exposing himself and jeopardizing everything if he was wrong.

As the bartender exchanged his empty glass for a full one, Alexander nodded like he was mulling over her proposal. "I think you'd be great," he said and ventured to look her in the eye. "And I really could use the help, especially from someone already committed to the concept, subject matter, etcetera, etcetera. But I would be remiss in my duties if I took you up on this offer without first discussing how this could, and would, impact your ability to devote your time to assisting on a research project. A project that would, in all likelihood, benefit your academic career far more than helping me to write this book."

Tasha, who had been leaning into him waiting for his answer, sat back several inches and finished off the last of her glass of wine.

"Would you like another?" he asked. And when she nodded, he signaled to the bartender again. It wasn't Tony behind the bar tonight, but Alexander recognized this guy. He was working the day Alexander had picked Mia up after her first session with Ty. As he poured Tasha more wine, he glanced up and met Alexander's gaze with a furrowed brow. Maybe he was being paranoid, but the look on the guy's face seemed to convey condemnation—or, at the very least, judgment.

Did this guy remember Mia coming here? And did he now think Alexander was hitting on this younger woman?

"Can I be perfectly honest with you?" Tasha said as she picked up her glass and took a sip.

Alexander returned his attention to her and tried to push aside his worry about what some thirty-year-old bartender was thinking. "Please do." He smiled.

Tasha took a deep breath and began to shake her head. "I don't want to continue my studies at Columbia."

Alexander widened his eyes and reached for his drink.

"You're shocked," she said.

"Well...yes. I mean..." Over the past several weeks, he'd checked Tasha's academic progress. In his class, obviously, but then also into her other current courses. Her past courses. Then the entirety of her academic record, at least the parts available for him to view. It was impressive. Astounding, in fact. She currently had the highest grade in his class. He would bet she was also at the top of all her other classes. But he didn't want her to know he knew all this. "You're so successful," he said. "At least in my class. I imagine you do well in everything?"

Tasha averted her eyes for a moment, then shrugged. "Yes, I guess so. But just because you're good at something doesn't mean you want to spend the entirety of your life pursuing it." She laid her hand on her notebook, resting on the bar. "What I want to do is this."

Alexander let out a small laugh. "Take notes on my books?"

Tasha didn't laugh back. "Investigative journalism."

Alexander took a moment to digest this declaration. His immediate reaction was to think, *what a waste*. Tasha was brilliant and would have an extraordinary career ahead of her as a neuropsychologist. Why would she throw all that away to languish in obscurity within a dying field? But he couldn't say any of that. "Well, that certainly is a one-eighty. Have you discussed this with your advisor?" he said, hoping he didn't sound too much like a *dad* but feeling reasonably sure that was precisely what she was thinking.

Tasha shook her head and took a drink. "No. I don't need to discuss it with anyone. I *know* this is what I'm meant for, and it's the only thing that really lights me up. You know?"

Alexander nodded at her enthusiasm and palpable excitement, but actually, he did not *know*. He was driven, focused, and desired to be very successful. He was even becoming more comfortable with the idea that, maybe, he did want to be famous. But he couldn't say that he had ever experienced anything career related that lit him up the way Tasha claimed to be. He could never bring himself to feel such exuberance about a job that likely held little to zero significant-sized carrots at the end of such lengthy and oppressive sticks.

As an investigative journalist, what were the odds Tasha would achieve much in the way of compensation, renown, recognition, or even thanks? Additionally, was she aware that she would be trading the respect and authority that life as a doctor would give her?

"So, you won't see me on campus after this semester. I've already decided to drop out. This is why I would prefer to work with you on your book instead of one of your research projects. There's just no future in that field for me."

"Of course," Alexander said, then took a drink to buy himself some time before responding. A part of him suddenly felt undeniably offended by the fact that Tasha didn't seem to regard the field, and presumably himself, with quite the reverence he felt all his hard work, struggle, and, quite frankly, sacrifice over the years should be afforded.

Then again, if Tasha was no longer a student at Columbia, one of the most frightening complications preventing him from having a non-professional relationship with her would not be a problem once this semester ended. So, instead of defending his own career and life decisions, Alexander swallowed his ego and said, "It sounds like you've thought it through and know what you want." He took another drink and was alarmed to see he'd now nearly finished his third scotch. "I admire that," he added for good measure and was rewarded for the lie when Tasha's face lit up a few watts.

"So, does that mean you say yes?"

"Yes?"

Tasha's shoulders slumped in exasperation. "*Yes*, to me, working on the new book with you?"

"Oh, yes. Of course. But we should work out some sort of stipend or fair hourly rate for your time."

Tasha waved her hand and then picked up her wine. "Of course. Whatever you think is fair. But more importantly, when and where do I start?"

Alexander considered his empty glass. He definitely should not have any more to drink, but he signaled the bartender anyway and had a new scotch on the rocks in front of him in the blink of an eye. "Well," Alexander started—was it his imagination, or did that come out slurred? He swallowed and started again, focusing more on the shape of his mouth and the pronunciation of his words. "To be honest, my publisher is pushing for more details about Mia... that's my wife, but you already know that, I forgot, but anyway, they really want this book to focus, even more, on the family history. Particularly on the unsolved murder of Mia's father."

Tasha sat staring at him. She didn't move at all.

"And well, that's actually presenting me with a bit of a problem because, as you know from reading my first book, Mia doesn't remember her past."

"What about her sister?" Tasha asked.

"Yes, well, let's just say there isn't an ice cube's chance in hell that Holly will help with this. Not at all. In fact, and maybe I shouldn't say this...but you and I, we are what? We're like partners now...right?"

Tasha nodded. "Exactly. Complete partners."

"Complete," Alexander echoed, and had a vague thought that maybe he wasn't making as much sense as he would prefer, but the thought blew away from him before it had a chance to land anywhere and really stick enough to stop him from picking up his scotch and taking another big swig. "So, yeah." Alexander shook his head. "No help from her."

"And Pixlie?" Tasha said.

Without a second thought, Alexander tapped his temple with his index finger and shook his head slowly. "Nutter."

"Surely she can't be that bad," Tasha mused. "It sounds like she would be the only option at this point. It couldn't hurt to try, and maybe it would lead to something? Like she might mention another person, a connection to the family you either don't know about or never considered? Someone that's more lucid."

Alexander shrugged. "I mean, I don't know." But maybe Tasha had a point. Pixlie, while utterly unreliable herself, could very well still have connections to individuals that had first-hand knowledge of the family. "You could be right, though. It's worth giving it a shot."

"Is there a way to get out to Beaumar and meet with her?"

Alexander nodded slowly. "Actually, there is the perfect opportunity happening next week." He finished off the last of his scotch and signaled for the check. He was going to have a hard time not stumbling to the subway. "Mia is having the girls' sixth birthday party at the estate. It will be *crawling* with people. It's the perfect chance to have a conversation with Pixlie without drawing too much attention."

"That's perfect!" Tasha gushed. "Can I come?"

Alexander was about to blurt, *of course*, but realized just in time how awkward it would seem to invite this beautiful, young, very sexy woman to his daughters' birthday party. "I think it's probably best if I handle this alone. It's a family thing, after all."

"But you said it would be crawling with people. Nobody would even know who I was or what I was doing there. I could—"

"Not this time," Alexander interrupted her as he signed the credit receipt for their drinks. "But we will definitely work together to utilize whatever information or connections I can figure out." He placed the pen back inside the black plastic folder, closed it, and touched Tasha's shoulder. "Sound good?" He badly wanted to pull her toward him, wrap her in his arms. If she moved a little closer, gave him any sense that she was making the first move here—that was all he needed.

Tasha dropped her eyes to her lap. "Yeah. Sure, I get it."

He let his hand linger for a few seconds too long in case she was about to reach out or lean into his arms. Alexander pulled his hand away when she reached for her purse hanging on the back of the stool.

"Good then. Great." He stood up to leave. "I'll be in touch tomorrow with some ideas about paying you and what

I have so far for the outline. You can let me know what you think. Oh, by the way. I meant to ask sooner—are you getting the emails I'm sending to your university account? I got the impression that maybe you weren't reading them?"

"Oh." She waved her hand to dismiss this. "Yeah, I have tons of problems with that. They say it has something to do with the servers or something. I mostly use my private account. So, send it to me there, okay?"

"Sure." He stuffed his wallet into his back pocket. "Should I send your class stuff there as well? I don't want you to miss any of that material."

"Um." Tasha turned toward the door. "I mean, yes. That's probably a good idea. Is it possible to send it to both? Until I get it fixed by IT."

"Absolutely. Not a problem." They walked to the exit together. He felt the sleeve of her shirt brush against his bare arm. He stopped so she could walk up the stairs ahead of him and forced himself to look away instead of staring at her perfect ass. One day soon, he imagined he might cup those two perfect cheeks in his own hands.

Outside, the sun had already set, and the lights from the city illuminated the streets all around them. "You're all right to get home safe?" he asked.

"Yes." She smiled. "My station is just the next block."

"Okay then." He looked down into her eyes and wished she would raise her hand, touch his chest, and give him the barest of excuses to believe she wanted him to make a move.

"I look forward to getting your email tomorrow," she said as she turned away.

"Until then," he said, and watched her walk several steps,

raise her hand in goodbye, and pull her phone from her back pocket.

He ran his hand through his hair and closed his eyes as he turned himself and headed for the train that would carry him out of the city and back to the house, and life, he suddenly had no desire to go back to.

CHAPTER 41

*M*ia stood at the front door of the estate and watched as the last of the cleaning crew closed their van door and started the engine. She glanced at her watch; it was only two-thirty. She had plenty of time to finish up here, say goodbye to Pixlie, and get to the school to pick up the girls. As the van pulled around the circular drive and headed down the private lane, she shut the door and turned around to fully take in the changes she, and the crews she had hired, had made to Beaumar over the last week.

Given the state of the house before, with its four decades of film star memorabilia, heirlooms, tapestry, art, kitsch, photos, and general mess from Pixlie's day-to-day living all covered in dust and cobwebs—the end result of all their cleaning and organizational efforts looked like a miracle. Beaumar looked the way Mia imagined it had when her father was still alive. Stately and classic with its heavy wood trims and marble floors. But with all the framed personal photos of famous people, original classic film posters, and actual memorabilia from some of the greatest films ever made, the estate still maintained a very eccentric feel.

It was exactly the type of home one would imagine Raphael and Pixlie Renaud would curate for themselves.

A movement to her right caught Mia's attention. When she turned her head, she saw Pixlie emerging from the dark hallway off the foyer that led to her personal suites on the first floor. She had one arm crossed over a turquoise and gold kaftan while her other carefully balanced a half-full martini glass. "Have they finally gone?" she asked before raising the thin glass to her bulbous pink lips.

"Yes," Mia said.

"For good now? They won't be returning, yet again, to disrupt me with all their noise and chaos?" Pixlie closed her eyes as if she had just survived a personal turmoil of epic proportions.

"Yes, for good." Mia took a deep breath and sighed it out. Dealing with Pixlie's peculiarities and specific idiosyncrasies over the past week had required all of her patience. "But remember, you did say it was okay for us to hold the girls' birthday party here next week. There will be many more people here for that," she warned.

Pixlie's dour expression brightened in an instant. "Oh, but a *party* is nothing at all like having your home, your personal belongings...your precious and invaluable collections, rifled through by a bunch of *laborers*. The party will be a glorious event," Pixlie declared as she raised her martini-free hand into the air above her head with a flourish.

This mini-performance, from this woman who was both her mother and a stranger, gave rise to a tight fist of dread in Mia's stomach. Having the party at Beaumar seemed like an excellent idea when Pixlie suggested it as Mia and the girls were leaving after their first visit. It was the perfect excuse to help Pixlie out by getting the house cleared up and cleaned out. But the more time Mia spent with her mother, the more she realized Holly was right.

Pixlie was not a well person.

It went beyond the overly dramatic speeches and flamboyant dress and behavior. What she had done to herself, physically and permanently, with excessive plastic surgery, both minor and major, that had left her features overblown and deformed in a way that practically any sane person would tell you was infinitely more terrifying than the normal wear and tear of aging. Mia felt fairly confident that Pixlie, in preparation for the party, had been doubling down on her visits from Vera and her needles filled with fillers and Botox.

Mia was more than a little afraid of what Pixlie might do at the party in front of all the Beacon Hill Academy parents. What might she say if some of the more curious ones began asking questions about her and her life with Raphael? Maybe Holly had been right, Mia wondered. Perhaps none of them, especially Pixlie, were up to handling this type of exposure.

"Are the girls excited?" Pixlie asked as she twirled across the marble floor in her kitten heels. "Oh, what a silly question. Of course, they are! Of course, we all are. It's going to be just like the old days. Remember Mia when Gracie Howard and Steve Kelly and Adrian Harlow...oh, just everyone would come for the whole weekend, and we would drink and laugh and smoke and so much more." She laughed, and her voice echoed up to the ceiling, but the sound was hollow and gave Mia the chills. Pixlie stopped her twirl abruptly and gave Mia a serious look. "Not that you and Holly were allowed. Obviously." She smiled wickedly. "Because there was almost nothing happening at a Renaud party that children should see." She winked at Mia, her lashes so heavily coated in mascara it looked like a tarantula was nesting on her eyelids. "Not that this party will be anything like that. We will all need to behave. It's a children's party, after all."

Mia wasn't sure who Pixlie was speaking to. It no longer felt directed at her; it was more like an out loud dialogue in Pixlie's own head. Mia wondered if, over the years of living alone in this enormous, dilapidated mansion, Pixlie had simply gotten used to speaking to herself. Preferring the prattling noise of her own, mostly unreasonable, words to the terrible, deafening silence.

"Pixlie," Mia interjected. "I'm going to run upstairs and check on how the other floors turned out, then go pick the girls up from school. Is there anything you need before I go?"

Pixlie gave her a smile, but behind all the pancake makeup, Mia could see the pain in her mother's eyes. If nothing else, the time she'd spent out here over the last several weeks had shown Mia just how alone and lonely, Pixlie had been all these years. She regretted not realizing it sooner and wondered how Holly could have disregarded it for so long. "Oh dear, I'm just fine." She raised her glass and gave Mia another wink. "I'm going to pour myself one more of these." She raised a single index finger for emphasis. "And put one of the movies onto the projector. Maybe I'll even start up the popcorn maker, like in the old days when you and Holly were little...that is, if I can figure out what those *laborers* have done with the machine."

"All right," Mia said. She chose to ignore Pixlie's derogatory remarks for a second time and moved toward the stairs.

Mia had been making an effort to spend more time here at the house and with Pixlie, she still needed to figure out what was an appropriate level of involvement between them. Pixlie was her mother but also enough of a stranger that Mia didn't feel comfortable chastising or correcting her. "I'll see you later this week," she said as she climbed the stairs.

"Tomorrow?" Pixlie asked. The hope in her voice was palpable.

"No." Mia stopped halfway up the stairs and turned to look at Pixlie, who was staring up at her from the center of the foyer. "I have my appointment in the city tomorrow. I'll be back on Thursday. In the morning, after I drop the girls off at school. Okay?"

She nodded, swallowed the last sip of her drink, and turned away. "Whenever you have the time," she said with a forced, noncommittal tone that belayed her disappointment far more than tears would have. "Until Thursday, then." She waved her hand over her shoulder and walked away toward the theater room where she would pull out one of her old films from thirty years ago and, once again, imagine herself living the life she'd once had.

Mia sighed and tried to push past the guilt she felt rising. This was likely one of the reasons Holly rarely came here. No matter how much time was spent with Pixlie, it never seemed to be enough. And unless you were going to bring her home with you, you eventually had to say goodbye to her and leave her alone all over again.

Mia headed back up the stairs; they should try to reconnect Pixlie to the outside world again. Surely there were still some of her old friends around that she could contact.

On the second floor, Mia poked her head into one room

after the other. The decor was all still faded and dated, but the cobwebs and dust that had coated every surface were now gone. Only a week ago, these musty, shut-off and forgotten rooms were uninhabitable. Now they were so clean, they were almost quaint. Mia imagined people would flock to Beaumar should they ever decide to turn it into a bed and breakfast.

What an idea that would be, she thought as she closed the door to the last room. It would be something to keep Pixlie both busy and entertained with guests. When she and Holly got past their current disagreements, Mia would bring the idea up. Maybe it could even be a family business they were all involved in.

Alexander would then see her in a different light, wouldn't he? Instead of this broken, struggling-to-function version of Mia he had been living with and tolerating all these years, there would be a new Mia. Productive and confident Mia.

Business owner Mia.

The very idea of it stopped her in her tracks at the top of the stairs on the third floor. To have Alexander look at her again the way he once did. With desire and an insatiable need to be near her. Even with all they had been through, as distant as they'd become over these past years, Mia still wanted her marriage to work. She still wanted Alexander.

And she wanted him to want her.

It hit her with blinding clarity that if she didn't keep trying to turn herself around, she would lose him. Soon.

Mia balled her hands into fists at her side until she could feel her nails, sharp and painful, against her palms. She strode down the third-story hall and into her old bedroom. Once inside, Mia shut the door behind her and stood in the center of the room. She had spent her entire childhood within these walls. She should be able to remember something, some fragment, some feeling of who this girl was...who she was.

The therapy was working. Every session with Ty brought more images, more knowing that felt real. Alexander had been right after all. The physical ability for her brain to conjure her past was there. It was her mind, that inexplicable space neither tangible nor scannable, that stubbornly refused to let her conscious self dig up what it had long ago buried.

The sense that the memories were there, they existed, that even now they were only just beyond her cognitive reach, brought on wave after wave of frustration every day. She now believed she could remember. She would remember. She only needed to keep beating on that locked door hard enough and long enough—eventually, she would bring it down.

Mia crossed the room to the far corner where an oval framed mirror sat propped up on a metal frame. She stood to the side for several seconds, watching the room's reflection in the glass. This mirror had witnessed all the parts of her life she could not remember.

Without allowing herself another thought, Mia stepped into full view of herself. She stared straight ahead into the eyes of the woman she had become and willed herself to see the girl she'd once been. She had seen her, probably every day, in this same mirror. She had to still be in there somewhere.

Mia would find her.

She lifted the mirror from its frame and carried it from the room.

CHAPTER 42

When Mia heard the door to the garage close, she glanced at her bedside clock. It was after ten, and Alexander was only now getting home. She had texted him. Twice. Once when she and the girls were sitting down to dinner, and again after she had put the girls to bed— he hadn't responded.

She listened and lay perfectly still as he walked up the stairs and entered their bedroom. In the dark, she watched him cross the room. He stumbled, lost his balance, and fell against the dresser. It slammed into the wall with a bang.

"Shit," he whispered.

Mia sat up. "Are you okay?"

"Yes. Yes," he said, waving her off with one hand. "I just tripped."

He'd been drinking. The tripping made it obvious, but she could also hear it in his voice. She imagined he'd stayed at Murphy's much later than usual before catching the train.

She lay back down as he navigated their master bathroom

in the dark. She listened as he used the toilet, flushed, then ran the water in his sink as he washed his hands and brushed his teeth. Maybe it was better, she reasoned. Him being drunk. It would make what she had planned feel less awkward.

She heard him slide open the top drawer of his dresser and then watched him remove his clothes and put on his pajamas. He pulled back the duvet and sheet on his side of the bed and lay down with a sigh. Flat on his back beside her, Mia could now smell the scotch he'd been drinking. He should not have driven home from the train station. She was about to say this, to chastise him for not calling her to come pick him up. But if she started down that road right now, there was no way they would ever do what she had in mind.

Under the covers, Mia reached her hand across the mattress and placed it on his forearm. She let it rest there, felt the warmth of his skin, the hairs on his arm, allowing him a moment to adjust to this uncharacteristic physical contact before her hand migrated to the soft round of his belly.

He said nothing, and Mia wondered if he had passed out. He was so late; he probably had several drinks beyond his usual two or three. She considered waiting for another night.

But to what end? When she'd thought about doing this on her drive back from Beaumar today, Mia realized it had been almost two years since she and Alexander last had sex. It astounded her. How was it even possible? When had they both given up? She never made any sexual advances or indicated she was interested.

When was the last time he had attempted to have sex with her? She couldn't remember, and it scared her.

She rolled onto her side and faced him. The way the

shadows fell across his face, it was impossible to tell if his eyes were open or closed. Her hand circled his belly twice, then shifted down until her fingers played over the elastic of his waistband and came to rest on the mound of his penis. It was soft and folded forward inside his boxer briefs.

Once upon a time, Alexander would get an erection just being near her. Of course, tonight, he'd been drinking—quite a lot. So, this might take more effort than she had at first imagined. Today at Beaumar, she realized she wanted to reconnect with her husband. To feel close to him again, be a partner with him again, like when they were younger. She sensed he was still awake and wondered if he was surprised she was making a move on him, given how desolate their marriage bed had been.

She moved closer to him, slipped her fingers inside his pajama pants, and held his still-soft penis in her hand. She stroked it several times, trying to coax it to life. "Alexander?" she whispered.

He sighed and opened his eyes. "I'm tired, Mia," he said, his tone flat and without emotion. He reached down, grasped her wrist, and pulled her hand from his pants. "I have a lot going on at work right now. I just want some sleep." He rolled away from her and faced the wall. "You understand," he added.

Mia stared at the back of his head, stunned, hurt…mortified. "Of course," she whispered and retreated to her side of the bed. "I'm sorry," she said, without knowing what she was sorry for. She lay flat on her back and stared at the ceiling above her as she tried to process the chasm of worry and shame that Alexander's rejection had just cracked open at her core.

He didn't say anything else. Not that he was sorry too, or that she shouldn't apologize, not one word to try and ease the blow. Within minutes she could hear him snoring; he'd passed out. She tried to reason with herself—this wasn't a big deal. She knew he was drunk. He likely wouldn't even remember this in the morning. But then her mind wandered into thoughts less consoling.

He was very busy at work, and she hadn't made his life any easier for years.

Because she was so broken, their relationship had deteriorated.

Of course, he wasn't attracted to her anymore. Why would he be?

She was barely hanging onto this life with him, and tonight was proof—wasn't it?

He had been trying with her for years, and because she was incapable of getting her shit together, now she'd lost him.

Because he had never, ever, not once rejected sex from her. This actually was a big deal.

She tried to stop, manage her mind, think of something else, anything else, and go to sleep. But her brain insisted on cartwheeling through a deluge of negative, self-loathing, and ultimately catastrophic thoughts. Sleep would not come. And because she no longer had a single pill in this house that might bring her some relief, Mia's heart thundered on, driving her to the brink of panic. There was no escape from the four closed walls of her own thinking.

When she realized she was dripping in sweat, she sat up, got out of bed, and headed to the only place in the house where she might find some relief.

The basement and her painting.

The temperature alone, at least fifteen degrees cooler than upstairs, was a relief. Even so, Mia pulled off her sweat-soaked pajamas. She left them in a pile on the floor beside the stairs, slipped her apron over her head, and tied it behind her naked back.

She removed the painting of the anonymous girl facing the ocean from her easel and placed a new canvas before her. Mia poured and mixed colors without thought, plucked several brushes from her jars, and began this new piece with only her emotions to guide her.

When she put her brush down, Mia could see she had created an image of a young girl standing before a broken window. In it, the girl could see her own reflection. But from the perspective of someone viewing the entire painting, it appeared to be two girls facing each other with the glass between them. The broken glass distorted the facial features of the girl on the outside.

She stared at it for a moment. She felt sure this was not a memory but a truth nevertheless.

The sleepless night hit her all at once. Exhausted, she left the still-wet brush and exposed paints on her messy bench and headed for the stairs. She would clean up later. Right now, she only wanted to catch a few minutes of sleep before getting the girls ready for school.

Upstairs, Mia could hear the shower running in their master bathroom. She glanced at the clock on her night table; it was only four-thirty.

Why was Alexander up so early and getting ready? She knew she had put him through a lot, especially lately. Still, his own changes in behavior, his basic routines even, suddenly struck her as very odd.

It made her suspicious.

Alexander usually went to Murphy's before his train ride home but never stayed out as late as last night. With the shower still audible from their bathroom, Mia picked Alexander's phone up off his charger and punched in his code.

She had never searched his phone before. It was such a violation of privacy. But she had never before wondered if he was hiding something from her. Given the current climate of their marriage, and his recent, and not idol threats of leaving her and taking the girls from her...Mia couldn't help but think there must be more going on with him.

She found his messaging app and opened it. The most recent thread was with someone named Tasha Adams.

The water in the shower stopped, and Alexander opened the shower door.

She only had a few seconds. She clicked open the thread.

The shower door closed, and he pulled a towel from the rack.

Of course, I would love to meet up for drinks and discuss your new book. I can't wait. See you at 6.

"Mia?" Alexander called from the bathroom.

She backed out of the app and scrambled to get his phone back onto his charger.

"Yes?" she called back. "I'm here," she said as she sat back on her side of the bed. She pulled the sheet over herself right as Alexander opened the bathroom door. He had one towel secured around his waist and used another to dry his hair. Was it her imagination, or had he lost some weight?

He looked at her, his brow furrowed like he was trying to work something out. "Where did you sleep last night?"

"I was hot," she lied. "I went to the guest room down-stairs. You're up early."

He raised his eyebrows and looked away from her and at his phone on the bedside table. "Yes. There's so much going on at work right now. I'm up to my eyeballs," he finished as he walked to his side of the bed and plucked his phone from the charger. "I'm going to head in early and see if I can crank out a few things before the day gets away from me."

Mia nodded and watched as he put his code into his phone and began scrolling through whatever he was looking at. She hoped she hadn't left some app open or an obvious sign that she'd been snooping. He read something, then swiped left, likely deleting whatever it was.

Mia felt confident it was the message she'd just read from Tasha Adams.

Whoever that was.

CHAPTER 43

*H*olly stood outside Stevie's cage and opened the latch. "Hey there," she said, her voice light. "Who's a good boy?" she added. She held a treat in her gloved left hand as she pulled open the door with her right. "I thought we could try something new today," she kept talking to him. "How about we see if we can trust each other without all this wire between us?"

In addition to the gloves that covered her arms to her shoulders, Holly wore a padded body suit and a helmet with face protection. He hadn't barked at her in over a week, and for the past two days, Stevie would come to the cage door when she brought his food or treats. She had even been able to pet him a few times. Although, she never put more than the tips of her always-gloved fingers through the mesh and never anywhere near his face.

This morning, she had woken up and decided that today was the day to take a real step forward with him. She felt confident that he had come to trust her and knew she wouldn't hurt him.

He sat and stared at her for several seconds, then got up and approached the open cage door. His focus was mainly on the treat in her glove, but his eyes darted to her face like he was waiting for a trap or a trick from her. "It's okay, Stevie," she whispered. "I wouldn't ever hurt you, boy."

When he reached her, his body stopped a foot away, and he extended his neck to first sniff and then take the treat from her glove. Once he had it, he took it back to his dog bed to eat it.

He didn't appear to have any desire at all to leave his now safe space.

Holly sat in the dirt outside his cage and watched him watching her as he crunched up the biscuit with a few bites and swallowed it. She sighed. "Stevie," she tried again. "Come here, boy." She patted the dirt before her and wondered if all her protective gear was freaking him out.

"It would freak me out, too," she told him. She thought about the wisdom of it for only a few seconds and then removed the helmet and placed it on the dusty wood floor next to her. "Is that better?" she asked him.

He looked at her as if interested in this new version of her but then lowered his head back onto his dog bed. He wasn't having it.

Holly unbuckled the body padding she was wearing on her chest and pulled the straps loose. She lifted it over her head and placed it next to the helmet. It made her feel vulnerable and a little afraid. She wondered if Stevie could sense this because he lifted his head up and watched her.

"Will you come to me now?" she asked.

He stared at her.

The desperation she felt about this dog—it was becoming increasingly hard to believe she was right and that Harris and everyone else was wrong. It killed her to imagine giving up on this dog. "Stevie, come here. Please." She patted the floor in front of her. "Please. I'm begging you. I want to help you. I want you to heal, to get better, and I know you have no reason at all to believe me or any human after what you've been through. But if you want to have any kind of a life, you're going to have to meet me halfway."

To her complete surprise, he stood up. Holly watched as he cocked his head to one side, like he was trying to make sense of both her and her words, then took a few steps closer. Then a few more. And finally, he was standing within arm's reach of her.

Slow and without any sudden movements, she turned her gloved hand palm up and extended it toward him. "Stevie," she breathed. "You're such a good boy. I just know it. Let's show everyone else what a good boy you can be."

Her heart pumped hard, carrying a flood of adrenaline to her limbs that now tingled with the fear she couldn't deny. Her hands were gloved, but the rest of her whole body was exposed. And should this dog suddenly decide to attack her, Holly knew she couldn't fight him off for long enough to get away without serious injury.

He could even kill her.

Stevie sniffed at her hand, probably detecting the remnant crumbs and dust from the biscuit she had given him earlier. When he realized there wasn't another, Holly expected he'd turn back again, but he let out a sigh of his own and sat down.

"Can I pet you?" she asked. Holly rotated her hand, a fraction of an inch at a time until her palm was sideways and beside his protruding jawbone. "I won't hurt you. I promise." She touched him on the side of his face. She stroked him once, twice, so gently her glove barely grazed his fur. He neither retreated nor leaned into the affection. He sat, seeming to tolerate it. Holly let her hand glide further, up and over his head, down along his neck. She scratched behind his ear.

After several minutes, he lay down in front of her.

And Holly cried.

Without warning, Stevie's ears perked up. The hackles on his neck and back rose. Behind her, she heard the barn door creak open on its rusty hinges. Within an instant, Stevie was up on all fours, teeth barred, his bark vicious as he hunched into an attack stance, ready to lunge at whoever was coming through that door.

"Holly!" She heard Harris bellow behind her, his heavy boots running toward her and the frightened dog.

Stevie snarled; frothy white saliva streamed from his mouth. He had no idea why this huge man was running at him; he only knew what his history had taught him. Men would bring violence. Men would bring pain. This man was here, and all Stevie knew was to hate men.

Stevie lowered his stance, opened his mouth wider, and sprang, ready to rip Harris apart.

Holly slammed the cage door shut and threw all her weight against it right as Stevie's body slammed against it. She slid the bolt into place and scrambled back on all fours as quick as she could.

Harris rushed to her and grabbed both her arms. His

expression was wild and terrified. "Are you okay? Holly! Answer me! Are you okay?" he yelled, trying to make himself heard over the deafening sound of Stevie raging, his every bark ricocheting off the barn's metal interior walls and ceiling.

When she didn't answer immediately, Harris dragged her to her feet and picked her up in his arms, intent on carrying her out of the barn and to safety. He got her as far as the door when she managed to come to her senses.

"Put me down," she insisted. When he kept walking with her, Holly squirmed until he lost his grip and was forced to drop her legs and allow her feet to hit the ground. "I said, put me down. I don't need to be carried. I'm perfectly fine." She twisted the rest of herself free until she stood on her own and faced him outside the barn door.

Harris's face shifted from scared to angry in an instant. "What the hell do you think you were doing in there?"

"Why the hell did you come barging in like that?" she shot back.

Harris shook his head. "That goddamn dog was this close." He held his thumb and index finger together. "To ripping your face off."

"Stevie was perfectly calm until you came storming in, guns blazing. I was petting him, Harris. Petting him. Not through the cage but with the door open. He was lying there."

"He was snarling and lunging at you. If I hadn't walked in when I did—"

"You upset him!"

"I upset him? Holly, you have completely lost all reason when it comes to this dog. For the life of me, I can't figure out what you imagine you're going to accomplish here besides a lengthy stay in the intensive care unit. And that's if you're lucky! There is no fixing this one. I'm sorry, but he is too far gone to be saved. Anyone with two eyes can see it, but for whatever reason, you insist on remaining blind to the facts here. I'm sorry, and I know you will hate me for this...." He hesitated and shook his head. "But for your own safety, I'm putting an end to this. I'm calling the vet right now and asking her to come out tomorrow. I'm not going to come home from work and find my wife—" his voice cracked, and Holly could hear the tears he was holding back. He cleared his throat. "I'm not going to find my wife dead because of some dog," he finished, turned away from her, and headed back across the yard to the house.

But not before she saw a tear slip from his eye and down his face.

Speechless, Holly placed her hands on her head and watched him walk away. Behind her, she could hear Stevie snarl, bark, and throw himself against the cage door. She turned and watched him, terrified she'd lost what progress they had made and that Harris might be right.

"Oh, Stevie," she whispered. "I wish you could lose all your terrible memories too."

CHAPTER 44

*W*hen Renee opened the door to the treatment room, Mia was surprised to see Ty was not alone. Erica was seated next to him in one of the low-slung chairs that faced the bed.

"Hello, Mia," Erica greeted her with a smile. She rose from her chair and moved across the room to embrace Mia in a hug. "I've been monitoring the sessions, of course." She gestured up to the camera positioned in the corner of the room. "But I wanted to be in the room with you all for today's session. I hope that's okay with you."

Mia laughed at this. "Erica, it's your study. Of course, it's okay with me."

Erica held both of Mia's hands and nodded. "We are moving beyond the microdosing phase, upping the micro-grams of the psilocybin today. It's very likely you could have a profound experience today. I feel it's important for me to be here to support that journey."

Mia smiled back at Erica's sincerity. Since the beginning

of the trial, Mia had felt fairly certain she had been randomly placed within the control group and had only received the placebo. Although she knew that, even as part of the control group, Erica would still need to treat both groups exactly the same.

So, if she were inserting herself into the sessions of the participants who had been receiving the psilocybin, she would need to do the same for the participants, like her, who were only getting the placebo.

"Of course. With the number of these studies I've participated in over the years, I understand how this works."

Erica squeezed Mia's hands once, then released them without another word. It was vital that the specific script she said to every participant remain the same for Mia, regardless of their longstanding relationship. "I'll just sit over here. Out of the way," she explained as she picked up her clipboard and took the seat tucked into the farthest corner of the room.

"Hi Ty." Mia now directed her attention to him as she pulled back the blankets and positioned herself onto the bed.

"Hello, Mia," he said with his usual warmth. "Before we start today, let's go through the usual questions?"

"Sounds good," Mia said as she lay back on the pillows and made herself comfortable.

"On a scale of zero to one hundred, with zero being not anxious at all and one hundred being extremely anxious, how would you rate your anxiety right now?"

Mia took a breath. She thought about Alexander coming in late and the text message she'd read that morning from the unknown Tasha Adams. "Eighty-five."

She had never before rated herself that high. Ty raised his eyebrows.

"But not because of what we are doing here today," she explained. "I recently discovered...well, let's just say I have a personal issue that is bothering me right now."

Ty lowered his clipboard with his questionnaire. "Is this something we should discuss before our session?" he asked.

Reflexively, Mia's eyes flicked to Erica, who thankfully had her attention directed to the clipboard on her lap. As frustrated as Mia was with Alexander, she didn't think bringing up this particular issue with him in front of Erica was wise. "No," she said. "It's not anything critical. Or about my past, my memories, or this treatment at all. If I'm being honest with myself, I'm probably making a mountain out of a molehill."

Ty tilted his head, made a note on his page, and nodded. "Okay then. Moving on, have you experienced any significant thoughts, emotions, or new memories since our last session?"

Mia took a breath. "Actually, yes. At least I think so."

"Really?" Ty said. "Would you like to explain them?"

"Well, I think it began as far back as our first session. But I couldn't be sure, and I'm still not, but...well, when you instructed me to get a journal and start writing down my thoughts, I ended up painting instead."

"Painting?" Ty wrote down several things. "Interesting. Please go on."

"Well, as it turns out, I'm quite good at painting. And over the past few weeks, I've completed over thirty works."

Ty put his pen down and looked at her. "I'm sorry. Did you say thirty? As in three, zero."

Mia nodded.

"That's a lot of painting," he said with a smile. "You must enjoy it?"

"Yes...well, yes and no. Honestly, it's more like I have this compulsion to paint. Like, it's not entirely a choice. And then there are the subjects in the paintings. I don't really know what I'm doing or creating. Not consciously. But I have this incredible frustration when I'm doing it. It's like I know exactly what I'm doing, but that knowing is happening behind this thick black curtain that I can't see around. Everything is happening beyond my senses, yet I'm the one doing it."

"That's interesting," Ty said.

"Yes," Mia agreed. Erica had put her own pen down and was staring at Mia.

"Do you feel like these images you are creating could be memories?"

"I think so. But I don't have any proof or way to verify that."

"Could your sister, or maybe your mother help with that?"

"Holly didn't recognize any of it." At least, that was what she claimed. "And I haven't asked my mother yet." She hadn't even considered asking Pixlie. "But we are having a birthday party for the girls at her house this weekend. So maybe that would be a good opportunity to show her some pictures of what I've done."

Ty nodded and smiled at her. "I think that's a great plan," he said, gesturing to Renee. "Okay. Do you feel like you're ready to get started here?"

Mia nodded and watched as Renee carried over the small paper cup with the blue pill and bottle of water.

Mia saw there were now four pills instead of one.

She noticed that while they were essentially the same size

and shape as the pills she had been taking, these appeared to be a slightly different shade of blue. She placed the cup to her lips and tilted it until she felt all four pills on her tongue. She washed them down with the water, and handed the cup and bottle back to Renee. Mia picked up the sleep mask and the over-ear headphones, which she put on before lying back down.

If nothing else, Mia reasoned, these sessions were undoubtedly relaxing. She would lie here, as usual, listening to the sounds of Bach played on cellos while her mind wandered, and she tried to conjure memories from her life prior to the day her father was murdered.

She wasn't sure how much time had passed, but Mia felt, then heard, a cracking sound emanate from inside her head. And even though she was still wearing the sleep mask, she could see the fracture was occurring along the fault line of her scar. It was the color of red-hot lava, and the opening began at her forehead and slowly split down her face.

It was shocking, but she found she wasn't afraid or even alarmed. She had a sudden knowing that this was where the new growth would erupt from. A moment later, she saw the first sprout of greenery, plants pushing from their seed casings, filling the slit in her head that had only a moment ago been a trickle of lava. They multiplied and spread, merging into a dense mass of shrubbery. The growth accelerated upward, then began to spread around her head, down her neck, and across her chest. She felt the cool green leaves cover her arms and legs until it had enveloped her in a protective cocoon of branches and leaves, and the world all around her was black.

She was suspended, weightless, and protected. This was

where she lived. A habitat of her making. Around her, the vines pulsed with the same blood running through her veins. The leaves were made of the same molecules that were her skin. Her thoughts manifested everything that was in creation, and she was creation itself. She inhaled space and exhaled the darkness.

One of her leaves turned a coppery orange, then rusty brown. Before her eyes, it decayed, dry and black, until it crumbled into dust. Then, like an infection, this change spread from this first leaf to all the others until her once verdant green shell had died, and when each leaf and vine exploded, dust scattered into the winds all around.

And Mia saw that she, too, had decayed and was blown into dust.

She had died and disappeared.

All that was left was the perfect, silent black that stretched out in all directions and continued on into infinity. It was a relief to see it all gone. To remember how ephemeral an existence truly was.

A pinprick of light, bright and white, illuminated out on the horizon before her. Mia watched it float. It doubled itself, then doubled again, and again, and again until the expanse before her was a blanket of white lights, like stars throughout the universe. And she was one of these singular points, tiny but bright, and she felt herself separate into two. Her light grew and took shape, and she watched the other half of her do the same. Connected, but individual. They watched each other form from the chaos of space and light until they were again whole, hearts beating, lungs breathing. And Mia remembered a truth she had long forgotten.

She was not alone in this universe.

She was forever connected.

We all are.

Her other half took her hand and guided her through the starry night. With a sweep of her arm, she cleared them all away, pulled back the black night, and revealed to Mia a door.

"Go inside, and see for yourself all you have locked away."

Mia stared at her other half and then at the door.

"I don't think I'm ready," she said.

"You've been gone long enough," her other half said. "We wouldn't be here if you were not." She took Mia's hands in her own, and she could feel the force of life, of creation itself, coursing through them and radiating out in all directions. She was ready. She understood that now.

When she pulled up the sleep mask and opened her eyes to the treatment room, she saw Ty, Erica, and Renee staring at her. She sat up, removed her headphones, and placed her hands over her face.

"How are you feeling?" Ty asked.

Mia took a moment and tried to find words to explain what she had just experienced. There were none. "I feel...like I've just had the most profound experience of my life."

Both Erica and Ty nodded and then scribbled things into their notes.

"And did you recall any specific memories from before the loss?" Erica asked.

"No," Mia admitted. "But I know where to find them."

CHAPTER 45

O n the morning of the girls' birthday party, Mia stood and stared at her reflection. When she'd returned home from her last session with Ty and Erica, she'd placed the mirror from her childhood on its metal frame in her and Alexander's bedroom.

When he noticed it the following day, Alexander stopped and stared at it for several seconds.

"That's new," he said.

"Yes," she replied.

And that was all that was said. She figured Alexander didn't feel like probing deeper into this monumental development. Which was fine because Mia didn't have any answers for the uniquely personal phenomena she had experienced during her last session.

She had a new outfit for the party. It still had long sleeves and a high neck, but it was an A-line shirt dress that belted at the waist. Not black, but a deep orchid that flattered her dark hair and pale skin. She paired it with a new pair of burgundy riding boots.

She was still covered up, but this was progress. She pulled a simple black hair tie from her wrist and gathered her long hair into a low ponytail, fully exposing her scar. She didn't know exactly who she had been, but Mia wanted to stop hiding from who she was now.

She left the bedroom and walked down the hall to Alexander's office. He had been up since before dawn, behind his closed door, working on something. Mia assumed it was the new book he had yet to tell her about.

She didn't know for sure, but given the message she had seen from Tasha Adams, whoever that was, and the secrecy, she thought it probably had something to do with her. She would find out. One way or the other. But starting a potentially volatile conversation with Alexander hours before they would both need to play gracious hosts to all their guests wasn't a good idea. If her years of marriage had taught her anything, it was knowing which battles to choose and when. She planned to wait until after the girls' party to thoroughly investigate everything going on with him. That way, if there was a blowup or blowout, they would have the space and time to deal with it without an audience.

She knocked on his door. When he didn't answer, she knocked harder and opened it. He was sitting behind his desk, hunched over, his face illuminated by his laptop screen. He lifted his eyes to her. "I've asked you to knock," he said.

Mia shifted her jaw. "I did knock. Twice. I don't believe you heard me, though." He heard her just fine, she knew. He had ignored her and expected her to go away. "I won't keep you from your work, but I wanted to remind you that I'm heading to Beaumar early to ensure everything is ready for the guests. Can you please make sure the girls are dressed and ready to go on time?"

Alexander sat up straight and glared. "Aren't we paying an army of people to *ensure* the party is set up and ready on time? At the prices they're charging, I should think we wouldn't need to do anything more than show up and try to have a good time."

Mia forced a smile. "Well, I leave that luxury to you, darling. Meanwhile, I'll go supervise. You're good with the girls?"

He nodded and returned his attention to his screen.

Mia almost prodded him, *What are you working so hard on, dear?* He would lie about it, make up something to do with Columbia or the Neurological Institute. There would be no point other than the satisfaction it might give her to see him caught off guard and squirming for a few minutes.

She sighed, quiet and unnoticeable. This urge toward pettiness didn't feel like her. Yet more and more, she found aspects of her life annoying and provoking in ways that had never bothered her before. "I'll leave the door open," she said as she headed back into the hall. "So you can hear the girls if they need you."

Alexander didn't look up. Instead, he lifted his hand to let her know he'd heard and continued typing.

Downstairs, Mia cleared the girls' breakfast, got them started on a movie in the family room, and let them know that daddy was upstairs in his office. Their birthday dresses were laid out on their beds, and she would see them at Grandma Pixlie's in a few hours."

"What about our hair?" Sasha whined as she held up some of her tangled locks.

"Daddy can brush your hair," Mia said.

Sasha shook her head. "He doesn't do it right," she declared. "We'll bring the brush to Grandma's."

"That's fine," Mia said, kissing them both on their foreheads. "I'll see you soon."

CHAPTER 46

*W*hen Mia pulled her Volvo up and around the circular gravel drive, she could see the party rental company had already arrived. Several people dressed in matching navy polos were unloading the tables, chairs, and the white tent that would be erected on the south lawn. The caterers pulled up behind them in their black van.

Good. Now all that was left to arrive were the decorators and the DJ. She glanced at her watch—she didn't expect them for at least another hour. She grabbed her handbag from the passenger seat and got out of her SUV. As she headed into the house, she checked in with both teams to let them know she was now on the property and to please direct any questions they might have to her.

"I would ask that you not involve my mother. She can get confused easily, and it's unlikely she would be much help solving any problems that may come up."

"Of course, Ms. Strauss," they all promised.

Mia nodded, thanked them, and said they could contact

her on her cell phone. She then pressed the heavy latch on the front door and entered Beaumar.

She had been working, with teams of help, as Alexander liked to remind her, to get the house cleaned and back into what could be considered a livable order for weeks. For the party, yes. But also for Pixlie. When she had come here weeks ago and seen the deplorable conditions her mother had been living in—the guilt had been nearly unbearable.

She had yet to talk with Holly about it. Mia couldn't understand how her sister, who had always been much more aware of Pixlie's current state, could have allowed the house to spiral into such a terrible condition. Maybe it wasn't fair to blame only Holly. After all, for years, Mia had been capable of showing up here and being more engaged. She never had. For whatever reason, this place had always felt like Holly's territory. And it always seemed like Holly didn't want Mia to come here alone. She never suggested or encouraged it.

In fact, Holly had been shocked to learn that Mia and the girls had been spending time here with Pixlie. As if Mia needed her permission to visit her own mother.

Mia realized how controlling Holly had become over the years. Had it always been this way?

The house looked beautiful now. It was dated, and there was still plenty of clutter from Pixlie's many mementos. But it was clean and certainly more organized. The house was eclectic—like Pixlie, but it was also fascinating. Mia knew their guests today would roam the rooms and hallways and marvel at the art, the film memorabilia, and the photographs of Pixlie and Raphael, looking so young and posing with some of the greatest actors and directors of their generation.

As she scanned the house, she imagined how others would

see it when they arrived today. Mia felt a swell of pride balloon in her chest. Her parents were amazing people who had lived extraordinary lives.

She only wished she could remember being a part of it.

Or at least, she wished there were more photos of her and Holly growing up. Mia walked to the arched entrance of the library and let her eyes scan the collection of framed prints scattered across the mantel and every table in the room. Hundreds of photos were in this room alone, a veritable archive of Raphael and Pixlie's glamorous life through the seventies, eighties, and early nineties.

And yet, not one single photo of either Holly or Mia.

"You're here!" Pixlie exclaimed behind her.

Mia turned and watched her emerge from the hallway to her master suite. She wore a soft cream-colored kaftan with a chaotic, golden swirl pattern. The airy fabric billowed out behind Pixlie's still-bare feet. Her toes were painted the exact same shade of fiery red as her long fingernails and meticulously lined lips. "I'm nearly ready," Pixlie said as she fanned her hands up and down her body. "Just a few finishing touches, and then I'm all yours to help with the preparations."

Mia smiled to see how excited Pixlie was to entertain people at Beaumar again. And while it was true there wouldn't be a single academy award winner among today's guest list, Mia could see Pixlie was still working to put on a grand showing of both herself and her home.

Mia faced Pixlie and took both her hands in her own. She couldn't remember a single instance of physical contact with her mother, at least not in her recalled history. Not a hug, pat on the back, or even a handshake. She would like to be closer to Pixlie. Hear her stories, learn about who she had been, and get to know who she was now. Holding her hands, Mia felt they were warm, the skin loose and papery, and her fingers long and delicate.

Pixlie did not pull away, but her facial expression was suddenly confused. As if something were happening that she did not understand or comprehend. She glanced down at their clasped hands, and when she looked up, Mia had the impression that Pixlie was suddenly afraid.

Mia dropped her mother's hands and smiled, hoping to reassure the confused woman without having to speak about what had just passed between them. Mia needed to remember that Pixlie had lost her husband in the most tragic of ways. And she had nearly lost one of her daughters as well. Ever since that night, she had lived alone, and the busy, sensational life she had once lived faded further and further into history with each passing year.

Rebuilding a relationship with her, a real one, would take time, Mia reasoned. Of course, it would. "There's no need to help," Mia reassured her. "You take as much time as you need to get ready. Between all the hired professionals and me, I don't think there is a single thing for you to worry about."

A smile returned to Pixlie's red lips. Whatever had frightened her flitted away from her thoughts as quickly and mysteriously as it had arrived, and, not for the first time, Mia wondered if Pixlie was experiencing some early onset dementia symptoms. It made her sad to think she was only now working to reconnect with a mother she would probably lose again within the next few years.

"Well, if you're sure," Pixlie said as she turned back toward her room.

"I'm sure. Oh, but there is one thing."

Pixlie stopped and turned back with a smile.

"I've been thinking, there are so many amazing and beautiful pictures all around the house, but I haven't seen any photos of Holly or me from when we were young. Do you keep them somewhere else?

Mia watched Pixlie's smile evaporate as her look of confusion returned. She shook her head twice. "You have them all, dear."

Mia was surprised. Pixlie must be mistaken. She should be careful not to press or upset her, especially since so many strangers would arrive in only a few hours. She only shook her head. "Well, there must just be some misunderstanding. I'm sure they're around here somewhere. After all, this house is so big, and there are a million places they could be stored.

But why would they be stored away, Mia wondered.

Pixlie gave Mia a sympathetic look as if Mia were the one in need of placating. "No, dear. They've been gone for years now. Holly took them all shortly after you were released from the hospital after the...well, after the unfortunate events of the past that we need not speak of." Pixlie waved her hand about her own head. Whether she was referencing Mia's traumatic brain injury or Raphael's fatal one, Mia couldn't tell. "She put them all over the apartment you shared in the city. To help with your recovery. She said you took them with you when you moved in with Alexander, hoping you'd see those photos and remember one day. So, you see, you do have them. You've had them for years."

Mia stared at Pixlie as she absorbed this information. Mia had exactly one photo from their childhood, the framed photo on her mantel at home that sat beneath the portrait of her father. She had seen other pictures. Early in her recovery, Holly had sometimes shown her a handful of photographs. But Mia did not have them. She never had them.

"All I have is the one photo album I kept for myself."

"An album?" Mia asked.

"Yes," Pixlie smiled. I know Holly thought it was important to have all the photos. 'It's impossible to know which one may spark something,' she always said. And honestly, I would have given her the album, too. It's just that I had completely forgotten about it. It wasn't until you had all those laborers here, picking over everything and displacing things, that I found it again. It was buried under a stack of old magazines." Pixlie shrugged.

"Where is it now?" Mia asked.

Pixlie pointed into the library behind Mia. "I put it up on a shelf next to the fireplace. I figured Holly would want that too, so I didn't want to lose it again."

"I'd like to see it," Mia said. "Right now."

"Of course, dear. I mean, Holly will give it to you anyway." She turned away again. "Now I really should finish getting ready."

Mia nodded. Everything Pixlie had shared with her was confusing. Why would she think Mia had all the old family photos unless Holly had led her to believe such a thing? It was true, over the years, Holly had shown Mia several pictures from their childhood—but no more than a handful. Pixlie made it sound like there were many, many more.

Why would Holly have kept these from her? And why would she lie about it to Pixlie?

In the library, Mia scanned the shelves on both sides of the fireplace. They were filled with old books that she doubted

Pixlie had ever even touched, never mind read. She saw it on the third shelf from the bottom, on the right side of the fireplace.

It was white or had been at one time. Its cover had yellowed over the years. Mia pulled the album from between the books on either side and carried it to the velvet couch.

She ran her hand over the cover and tried to quell the nervous fear inside her. It was impossible to know if she was afraid of what she might see in this book or terrified that her sister, the one person she had relied on the most since her attack, had been lying to her for years.

What did it mean to now know that she couldn't trust Holly?

The very idea made Mia want to cry.

Mia lifted the cover and stared at the blank first page for several seconds before she turned it and revealed the first spread of photos.

There were four mounted onto the thick page. Each corner was tucked inside triangle slots that held the faded photos in place. They were all of Pixlie, young and pregnant. She wore a red and white striped bathing suit with a loose, knotted tie across the top of her breasts. She posed in the sand with the ocean behind her. Her long, shapely legs extended, toes pointed, head tilted back as she laughed, blew a kiss, gave a sexy pout, and in the last one, contemplated the horizon.

Her belly was enormous. Under the striped suit, it looked like a huge circus ball. Even still, Pixlie had been incredibly sexy—and she obviously knew it. Mia turned the page to see more pictures of Pixlie pregnant. In their garden, Pixlie wore a gossamer sheath that showed the nude outline of her body. Standing at the kitchen counter, hair in a bun, laughing as she ate ice cream from a tub. In a black dress that hugged her curves and belly, lounging across a couch at a party, her high heels discarded on the floor beside her. And finally, Pixlie in a hospital bed, clearly about to give birth.

Mia turned the page...and stared.

She reached down, removed the first photo from its mount, and held it in her own two hands.

It didn't make any sense.

Unless...of course. Mia shook her head as the truth took shape in her mind.

Why would Holly lie to her about *this*?

CHAPTER 47

*M*ia turned the photo over in her hands. There, written in loopy blue cursive, were the words that confirmed the truth.

Holly and Mia Renaud. Born September 1st, 1986 (with their mother, Pixlie Renaud)

"Twins," Mia whispered into the silent library. She and Holly were more than sisters. They were twins. Mia lowered the photo and stared across the expanse of the library before her as a heaviness, like a large stone, pressed on her chest. Her throat tightened. Mia shook her head and found she couldn't help the grief—the sense of complete betrayal—that rose up and broke loose.

She turned the album's next page, and then the next, and the next, and the next. Photo after photo of her and Holly. As newborns, as toddlers, dressed alike, playing together, running across a lawn, under a Christmas tree that had stood in the corner of this very room. Mia flipped through the pages and realized that every photo Holly had ever shared with Mia had been carefully curated—they were never together in the pictures Mia had seen.

It was *always* Mia alone.

The last photo on the last page showed them sitting side by side at a dining room table in front of a giant cake with two sets of four burning candles.

Happy Fourth Birthday Holly and Mia

It was printed in white across a swag of pink fabric high on the wall behind them.

They were identical, just like Sasha and Everly. Staring at the photo of them poised to blow out those candles, Mia had no idea which one was her and which was Holly.

Mia closed the album. Her fingers gripped the edge of the book so hard her knuckles ached.

Could Holly tell them apart? Mia wondered. When she looked at all the old photos she had hidden away somewhere, could she point and say, "That's me, and that's my sister, Mia." Did she have the luxury of knowing who she was, her history, her identity?

Yes, of course, *she* did.

All these years, Holly had led Mia to believe she was helping her. And Mia had trusted her sister with every cell in her body. For all these years, Holly had kept the truth. Now Mia wondered if Holly may have contributed to her worsening condition. How many times had Holly hindered Mia's progress as she stood ready and on the precipice of a breakthrough? Instead of nudging Mia forward, encouraging her to keep exploring her own mind because, "Yes, that is something, Mia. You're on the right track." Holly had denied every single glimmer of a memory Mia had ever shared with her.

And Mia had let the feeling of familiarity, the shadow of a

memory, pass away from her—it was nothing because her sister had said so.

Years ago, when they were living in their apartment in Manhattan and not long after Mia left the hospital, she had said to Holly, "Bring some pictures of you next time. That might help too."

"Oh yeah! That's a great idea," Holly had agreed. The next week, Holly presented her with the photo that now sat on Mia's mantel, framed in silver. It was the whole Renaud family standing at a distance and in the shade of the weeping willow on the lawn behind Beaumar. Mia and Holly were together in that photo, but the details were distorted due to distance and light. No one would ever be able to detect anything as definitive as *looking exactly alike*. Mia now knew Holly had selected that picture specifically to hide the fact they were twins.

Mia never would have believed Holly was capable of this.

Her phone vibrated and pulled her back to the present. Outside, the professional party organizers were preparing for the fifty guests arriving in only a few hours. How was she supposed to get through this day now?

She heard her cell chime and vibrate inside her purse. She reached in and grabbed it—the text message was from Alexander.

Traffic is terrible. Won't be there for about an hour.

Mia typed, *Okay,* and dropped her phone back into her purse. She was relieved she would have a little extra time before the girls and Alexander arrived. It would give her time to pull herself together and figure out how to handle all this right now.

Maybe the best idea was to not handle it at all. At least,

not right now. She should get through this day. Smile, nod, and make small talk. Give the girls a fantastic birthday party.

This mess wasn't their fault.

But what would she do if Holly showed up? She hadn't spoken with Holly since their last argument. Holly had been adamant about the party not taking place at Beaumar, and now Mia understood why. But that didn't mean Holly wouldn't come.

She wasn't sure she could face Holly right now and not confront her. How was she supposed to look into Holly's eyes, for even a single day longer, and not say to her, "I know you've been lying to me for the past eighteen years. What I want you to tell me right now is why."

Mia stood up from the couch and clutched the album to her chest. Why would Holly work so hard to deceive Mia if she didn't have something to hide?

Mia looked out the nearest library window. It overlooked the back lawn, and she could see that the large white tent was already constructed; the tables and chairs were being arranged beneath it. The decorators had arrived. They were pulling wagons filled with pink and purple embellishments across the grass—Sasha and Everly's favorite colors.

Mia stared at the tent, the center poles lifting it like mountain peaks into the gray skies above. She should have styled this party after a circus, she thought. Instead of this stark white tent, it could have been red and white stripes. They could have hired acrobats and performers who would mingle among the guests in brightly colored costumes.

The guests themselves could have also dressed up. Someone might choose to be a lion tamer, another a high-wire walker. It would have been more fun, more colorful, more engaging. Mia could see it now. On the lawn before her, an enormous red and white striped circular tent. Its entrance flaps pulled open, the warm yellow glow from the lights inside illuminating the night sky. A man appears in the doorway. Backlit, his defining features are in shadow, but when he exits, Mia can see it is the circus ringmaster.

Dressed in his red velvet tailcoat with gold epaulets, a black tophat, and riding boots. He strides across the lawn, his black whip in hand, and when the light from one of the lawn torches illuminates his face, Mia recognizes him.

"Dad," she whispered, and when she heard herself, the scene evaporated. It was replaced by daylight and the return of reality. The simple white tent she had rented situated where her imagined circus had been only moments before.

Only it wasn't her imagination. It was a memory.

Here, at this house, on the lawn she now gazed at—there had been a party. A circus party. And her father had dressed up as the ringmaster.

She remembered it.

Or parts of it, at least. She had never seen a photo of that day, and no one had told her about it—she was sure. This was a genuine artifact from her own head about her life, and she remembered it all alone.

Mia sat back down on the couch and closed her eyes. It was so vivid. More than just visual, she remembered it had been a brisk night; the air seeping in through the open window before her caused a chill in the library. There was the scent of the kerosene burning in the lanterns outside. The sound of hundreds of people laughing and talking. Music was playing. She had no idea when it had happened or how old she had been. She only knew she had stood in this room and watched from this very same window.

And she had not been alone.

Mia opened her eyes. Someone had been here with her at that moment. Was it Holly? It seemed likely that her sister would have been here too, but Mia felt that wasn't the truth.

It was someone else. A girl with long blonde hair. A friend, not her sister.

She could almost picture her standing before the open window and watching the party. In Mia's mind, the girl turns around.

But Mia can't see her face.

CHAPTER 48

*H*olly buttoned up her best pair of jeans and pulled her favorite blue knit sweater over her head. It had been two days since Harris had threatened to bring the vet to the house and put Stevie down. The vet had not arrived, and they hadn't spoken since their argument in the barn.

Every day since, Harris had gotten up early to leave for the tattoo shop and not come home until Holly was already in bed. She had not given up. She wasn't going to let him and Dr. Allen kill Stevie. Harris couldn't see it, but Stevie had made progress. There was hope for him.

He just needed more time.

More love.

More trust.

So, every day since their fight, Holly had returned to the barn and continued working with Stevie. If Harris and Dr. Allen showed up, they'd have to fight her and the dog.

Holly ran her hands under the cold water from her bathroom faucet and scooped it up over her face and through her short white hair. She dried off with her towel and then used her comb and some gel to make her short, spiky locks less messy. The problem was that today was Saturday—Sasha and Everly's birthday party at Beaumar. She needed to be there to celebrate with the girls. Yes. But also because she was getting more and more paranoid about Mia. Holly needed to be there to better understand what was going on with her sister.

She was losing control of Mia. Holly had only been slightly concerned when she had begun her new therapy. After all, there had been so many over the years that hadn't made any difference, as far as Holly could tell. But when she had walked into that basement and seen all those paintings— Holly knew that whatever she was doing in the city was having an impact.

And a big one. One Holly may not be able to pull her sister back from.

But she couldn't be there trying to manage Mia and also here trying to protect Stevie. Holly sighed and examined her own reflection in the mirror. She knew Harris had been upset by Stevie's behavior. But would he follow through on his threat? And would he really wait until she wasn't around to carry out his plan? She didn't want to imagine he could or would and didn't want to think she was married to someone capable of it.

If he was so angry with her that he wouldn't even be coming to Beaumar with her today, then she would need to talk to him before she left. She needed to know Stevie would be safe if she left him.

"Holly?"

She turned and saw Harris standing at their bedroom door with Ralph at his side.

"You're getting ready for the party?" he asked.

She nodded.

"Can we talk?"

I was thinking the exact same thing, she thought. Instead of saying so, Holly crossed her arms over her chest. "Not if all you have to say are more threats about putting Stevie down."

He sighed, and she could see that her defensiveness was also making him defensive. She knew he had come in here trying to make things better—but there was only one way she was letting that happen: with assurances that Stevie be given more time. "No," he said. "Not more threats. Actually, there's someone downstairs I would like you to meet. Someone who I think can help us both."

Uncertain about what solution he might have devised, Holly hesitated for a moment. She hated fighting with Harris. He was more than just her husband; he was her best friend. Being on opposite sides of anything with him was painful. She unfolded her arms and followed him and Ralph out of their bedroom and down the stairs.

When she entered the kitchen, Holly saw a woman sitting at their table. She stood when she saw Harris and Holly. She was tall, at least six feet, and had long gray hair that hung loose to the middle of her back. The woman smiled at Holly, creating a network of wrinkles that radiated from her eyes and across her forehead. She looked to be somewhere in her late sixties.

"Hello, Holly. I'm Tabatha Pines." She extended her hand as she introduced herself.

Holly glanced at Harris as she shook Tabatha's hand. It

was large and warm; Holly could feel the strength this woman commanded in her grip. "Hello," Holly said.

"She's come to take a look at Stevie," Harris explained.

Holly dropped the woman's hand. "What do you mean, look? Are you a vet?" Holly asked, unable to keep the defensive edge from her voice.

Tabatha gave Holly a smile that could only be interpreted as sympathetic—it did nothing to quell Holly's suspicion. "No, not a vet. But I am an expert on canine behavior, and I have worked, for over twenty years, to end dog fighting in this country and rehabilitate dogs rescued from those circumstances."

"Doctor Allen gave me Tabatha's number. I explained our situation, and she was kind enough to come here today to see if she and her organization can help us," Harris explained.

"You think you can help, Stevie?" Holly asked. "Not just euthanize him?"

Tabatha's smile evaporated. "I don't know," she said. "I would like to take a look at him. Spend some time with him, if that is okay with you. But Harris has explained your feelings about this dog, and I think it's only fair to be honest with you. I've been doing this a long time, Holly. We work to rehabilitate the dogs that still have a chance for that. But I would be lying if I told you we've been able to save every dog over the years. Some are simply too far gone. That's just the truth." She shook her head. "I can't say what the situation may be with Stevie until I've had a chance to evaluate him."

Holly thought about the compromise Harris was offering her and what this woman's help could mean for Stevie. Holly had taken him on, but even she knew she was in over her head with him. "He's made progress," she said. "I'm sure you are amazing at what you do. It's certainly commendable devoting yourself to helping these animals. I would like your help, but you should know I won't give up on him," Holly said. "You can see him, evaluate him, but if you decide he's too far gone...." She couldn't help the hard lump of grief in her throat at the thought of losing him now.

Tabatha didn't argue with her, but Holly got the impression from her patient, sympathetic gaze that she thought she knew better. As Holly led the woman and Harris out the back door and across the yard to the barn, she worried that Tabatha might be right—given all her experience, she probably did know better.

She unlatched the barn and pulled the wide door toward them. "How long do you think your evaluation will take?" Holly asked. "It's my nieces' birthday party today, and I really need to be going soon." Harris met her eyes and furrowed his brow. With all the silence between her and Harris over the past several days, she had failed to figure out if he planned to come with her. He adored the girls and would have originally planned on being there.

Holly watched Tabatha's profile as her eyes adjusted from the bright outside light to the barn's dark interior. She was looking for some sign on the woman's face, some tell to reveal what she might be thinking when she saw Stevie for the first time.

Her expression, curious but neutral, never wavered.

"If it's all right with you, I'll stay with him all day. As you may imagine, these things can take time. Harris mentioned you both had somewhere to be, so this will give me some time alone with him to get to know him."

All day? Alone with him? Holly's first instinct was that this woman meant well, but what assurance did she have that this stranger might not just decide on her own that there was no hope for Stevie and take matters into her own hands while Holly was away?

Tabatha must have sensed Holly's worry because her very next words were spoken to alleviate fear. "It's clear to me how much you care about him." She gestured to Stevie, sitting alert in the center of his bed on the far side of his cage. "It's obvious you've already spent a lot of time and energy working on getting him healthy." She nodded once. "You have my word; he'll be right here, safe and sound when you get back."

Holly hesitated. These assurances were what she would need to hear to go along with this plan and get out of the way long enough for *this dog* to be *taken care of.* If that were the case, then it would be Harris orchestrating the deception. She turned to him and examined his face for any traces of dishonesty.

"If you're lying to me...if we come home and he's gone or hurt, you should know I don't think I will be able to forgive you."

Clearly surprised, Harris pulled his head back. "Holly. I would never...what makes you think I'm capable...never mind capable. Why on earth would I lie to you about something I know means so much to you? I would never hurt you like that."

She turned away from him—he was telling the truth. Harris was a good man. A very decent, fair, and honest person who loved her very much. It shocked him to think she could accuse him of such deceit. He couldn't even fathom such a thing.

The pain in his eyes said it all. *Why would she think such a thing?*

The answer was simple, but like so many other things in her life, she kept it to herself. It was easy for Holly to imagine other people, even the ones she loved most, capable of mind-shattering deceptions…because she lied to everyone every day. Lies were useful. Lies were easier. Lies even kept people safe.

Her whole life was built upon lies.

Sometimes, like now, it was hard to remember that not everyone operated the way she did when they needed to get their way.

"Okay," she conceded. "We'll be back by six."

Because if Holly wanted to manage damage control and get her sister back on track, she had a feeling she absolutely needed to be at Beaumar today.

CHAPTER 49

*A*lexander turned left and pulled his Mercedes onto the private drive leading to Beaumar. Several cars were ahead of him, their tires crunching the loose gravel at a snail's pace, like they were unsure if they were heading in the right direction.

Other guests were already arriving. He glanced at the clock on his dash.

"We're late, dad!" Sasha pointed out from her booster in the backseat. He glanced in his rearview mirror at her angry expression and wild, uncombed hair. "I told you!" she said.

She had told him it was true. Several times, even. Both girls had shown up at his office door, already dressed, brush in hand. "Mom is going to do our hair before the party," Sasha said with one hand on her hip. Everly had nodded in agreement.

"Okay," he had said, glancing up from his computer. "I just need a few more minutes. Go get your shoes on, and I'll meet you downstairs."

That was when the email arrived. The notification slid onto his screen with a ding. It was from Tasha's university account.

Hello Dr. Strauss,

This is Tasha Adams. I'm one of the graduate students taking your Advanced Neuropsychological Assessment class this semester. I'm reaching out because I received an email from you, and I'm having trouble making sense of it. My first worry was that I had missed something for class...but after reading it over several times, I'm now wondering if your account may have been hacked? It is referencing something about a book deal that, purportedly, you and I will be working on together? Which, if it were real, would be amazing; however, given we have never even met in person—it stretches the imagination! I have cut and pasted the body of the email below as a reference. Hopefully, university IT can help trace the fraud. I'm sorry I didn't bring it to your attention sooner—I've been out of town these past two weeks for a family emergency and not as vigilant about checking my school emails. I should be back in class on Wednesday if you need anything else from me.

Sincerely,

Tasha Adams

He sat back in his chair, staring at his screen as adrenaline dripped slow and sickening through his system. His mind cartwheeled, trying to land on some reasonable explanation for this message.

Was Tasha trying to distance herself from him? Did she realize that his interests in her were more than professional —*way beyond professional*—and was now laying the foundation for her exit from his life? And if so, was she going to report him? File a complaint with the university?

With these thoughts, the drip of adrenaline increased to a flood. Alexander ran his hands up over his face and head until he gripped handfuls of his hair.

He was panicking, indulging in one of his worst fears—public and professional humiliation.

He forced himself to take a breath and reread the email. Surely, he had just missed something. So, he read it again. And again. He read the email five times, parsing out each sentence, the individual word choice, and the use of that exclamation point.

The blatant, easily refutable lies. They had never met? She hadn't been in class for two weeks? If she was laying the groundwork here for some sort of personal and professional attack on him, he needed to consider the evidence he had to refute her claims.

First of all, he had never, ever touched her. Never even come on to her—he was one hundred percent sure.

He had not...*had he?*

He wracked his brain, trying to recall what had happened the last time he'd seen her. It was at Murphy's—three scotch on the rocks. Or had he said 'yes' to that fourth?

Fuck.

He had thought about many things that were troublesome now in light of this email. The wonderful shape of her ass, for one. Alexander read the email again and shook his head. But he hadn't said a single inappropriate word out loud to her. Not one. He had not touched her, not once. But did she know anyway? Had his body language given him away? The tone of his voice?

A lecherous look in his eyes?

"Dad!" Sasha had screamed from downstairs. "Can we *go now?*"

He looked at the time on his computer. "Fuck," he said to himself. "One more minute!" he shouted.

"Daaaadddd!" she yelled.

"Just a minute, I said!"

God, why today? Of all days. He didn't have time to either figure this out or try and fix it. He considered responding to the email and opened a reply before considering the fact that sending it through the university system could be a huge mistake. He needed to be so careful here. This could still be nothing, he reasoned. A hasty reply might make it so much worse if he didn't take the time to consider his every word.

Maybe he should text her to ask what was going on.

Although that was hardly any better. If she was out to get him, all she would need to do was screen-shot his reply.

No, he needed to wait. Not too long, of course. But long enough to calm down and allow reason to guide his next steps.

"Dad!" Sasha screamed. "We're going to miss it!" she sounded near hysterical now. Close to tears.

"All right, all right," he yelled back. "I'm done." He closed his computer down and stood up. The long drive out to Long Island would give him time to think this over and make a plan.

But by the time he found a place to park amongst the forty other cars already lined up bumper to bumper along the driveway leading to Beaumar, he still had no idea how to handle Tasha's email. Between the girls' constant requests for him to play songs off his music app he'd never heard of and

Sasha's repeated observations about them being late, he hadn't had two consecutive minutes of peace.

It was a relief when they finally got out of the car, and the girls ran down the drive ahead of him. He wished he could get back in his car and drive away. Would anyone even notice if he wasn't there? But today was about more than a birthday party, he reminded himself. This was also a fact-finding mission for his new book. Regardless of whatever was going on with Tasha, he had planned to find a way to snoop around the house and squeeze a few stories out of Pixlie without Holly or Mia taking too much notice.

He walked up the drive, passing Range Rovers, Porsche Cayennes, a G Wagon—he checked his watch. Why were so many people already here? He was late getting the girls here, but it was still ten minutes before the party started. Weren't most of these people fashionably late, as a matter of course? More cars were filing into the open spaces behind his vehicle, and several families passed him, hand in hand and in a hurry, on the way to the house.

When he reached the fountain at the center of the circular drive, Alexander saw a young man dressed in a black polo and pants welcoming guests in through the front door. A line had formed because people were stopping to ask questions and have a chat before entering the house.

Everyone was smiling and talking to each other. There was an excitement coursing through the growing crowd that far exceeded what would rationally be expected for a six-year-old's birthday party.

Alexander stopped and watched. This was why his first book sold so well and why his second would do even better. This was why he was getting a million-dollar advance. Except for himself, Mia, the girls, and the other six-year-olds, no one here today cared at all about Sasha and Everly turning six. Hundreds of people were coming here today to explore Beaumar Manor. The home of famous film director, and murder victim, Raphael Renaud. They wanted to see the aged Pixlie Renaud. Discover the exact spot where Raphael was shot.

Locate the place on the checked marble floor where Mia had landed after being pushed from the third-floor landing.

They were here to gawk. Take photos. Relish in the ugly true crime history as if it hadn't been a family's true-life tragedy. It was a reality he had always known, a faraway fact like people dying in the streets or starving in other countries —but to see the glee on strangers' faces up close.

He had never seen or participated in this side of the family tragedy. The intersection between extraordinary fame and tragedy that turned Holly and Mia's worlds into a circus sideshow attraction for public consumption. He suddenly knew why Holly hated that he'd written his first book.

The crowd at the door waiting to enter had doubled as more people arrived for the party. Had Mia invited all these people? Alexander scanned the crowd and noticed what seemed to be an unusually high number of adults that didn't appear to have children with them.

When he turned, he saw even more people pushing up the drive. Some had kids, others didn't. What was going on here?

He pulled his phone from his jacket pocket and called Mia's cell. It went straight to voicemail. He tried again. "Hello, you've reached Mia—" He hung up. Did she have her phone turned off? He shot her a text instead.

I'm here and this is crazy. Please call me!

From the back lawn on the other side of the house, music started to play. At this distance, it was indistinguishable except for the static drumbeat of bass, the promise of a hypnotic dance rhythm. For the music to project this far, Mia must have rented huge speakers, the kind that required stands and an expert in audio equipment to set them up.

What kind of kids' birthday party was this? He had not been involved at all in the planning. And, admittedly, he had barely listened when Mia offered details about what the day would look like.

He suddenly realized that he had likely made a colossal mistake—was Mia even well enough to be in charge of all this? He had assumed it would be a typical kids' party. Balloons, maybe a piñata, a few presents. People continued to stream up the driveway toward the house—this felt out of control.

Once they heard the music, Alexander saw several people at the back of the crowd give up waiting and head around the house and directly to the party on the lawn. He was about to head around to the back himself when he saw a familiar profile talking with the man at the front door.

He kept losing sight of her behind the heads and jostling bodies, but her face and hair were unmistakable.

"Tasha!" he yelled out, not thinking or caring about the propriety of it.

She didn't hear him, and a moment later, the man gave her a welcoming smile and invited her into Mia's family home. She disappeared behind the door.

He felt sick. A dread unlike any he had ever known settled

into his bowels. Tasha was here, at Beaumar, in excruciatingly close proximity to his wife, his mother-in-law…his children.

And considering the email she had just sent him, he had no idea what she may have planned. Was she going to accuse him of something? Right here, in front of his family and other parents?

"Alexander?" a voice behind him called, pulling him from his burgeoning panic.

He turned and scanned the driveway. His eyes landed on a small woman with close-cropped gray hair and her signature hip-length cardigan, striding toward him with three of her younger children in tow.

"Erica?" he said. He forced himself to smile and return a wave as he felt every ounce of his blood drain away.

What the hell was she doing here?

CHAPTER 50

The house was filled with guests, and Mia stood alone on the third-floor landing. She watched from her perch as people filed through the door—she was waiting for the moment her sister arrived. She wanted Holly to join her up here, on the third floor, where they could be alone and talk in private. She planned to confront Holly, tell her everything she already knew, and make Holly confess to whatever she might still be hiding.

There was no sign of her yet. Just parents and children from the school—although there seemed to be many people Mia did not recognize as well. All these people are smiling and excited, anticipating the fun.

The debauchery and decadence that Beaumar was notorious for.

Surely no one was expecting *that* sort of event. This was a children's party. Her girls were turning six, and it was their birthday party. She had hired a DJ to play a curated selection of Kidz Bop songs. A corral was set up, with six beautiful and well-cared-for ponies tethered and waiting to take the young guests for rides. There was a professionally crafted and frosted four-tier birthday cake with an ombre of deep purple to pale lavender frosting. The cake remained in the kitchen and would be unveiled after the parents and kids had their fill of catered delicacies served by white-shirted waiters who wove through the party with trays held aloft.

So then why, Mia wondered, was the woman entering now wearing a low-cut evening dress? Its blue sequins shimmered under the chandelier lights. It was obvious her intention was to showcase her shapely curves and expertly augmented breasts.

And that man was wearing a tuxedo. No, not only him. All the men wore tuxedos—except for the one who preened down the hall in a velvet fuchsia suit and white leather shoes. Mia scoffed, covered her mouth with her hand, and leaned toward Holly. "So tacky," she said.

Only...Holly wasn't there.

And when Mia returned her eyes to the guests below, she saw what might reasonably be expected for a children's party. Parents wearing jeans, cardigans, kakis, and polo shirts. Boat shoes and ballet flats.

What had she just seen then? Because it had been so real, the opulence of the guests below her.

It was another memory. She saw it before her, exactly as it was years ago. Raphael, Pixlie, and their parties were legendary. Exclusive, private, and attended by only the most elite of individuals. Getting invited to a Beaumar event meant you lived at the apex of life.

And *everyone* who was *anyone* wanted to be there.

Below her, a young woman stood at the center of the

black and white checkered marble foyer, her head craned back so she could gaze up at Mia standing above her. Like Mia, her hair was long, nearly to her waist. Only hers was a deep chestnut brown, while Mia kept her own dyed black as night.

The woman raised her hand as if saying hello to Mia.

Mia did not return the gesture. Something was disturbing about this woman, familiar. Ethereal, like a memory, but made of flesh and blood. *Was this real?* Mia wondered. Or another image from her past rising up to confuse her.

The woman kept her eyes trained on Mia and headed for the staircase.

CHAPTER 51

"Are you okay?" Erica asked.

Alexander smiled and shook his head. "Me? Oh, yeah."

"Because you don't look well," she added. Her eyes pinned him with the intensity of a microscope.

"I'm just, um..." he floundered. He was just worried that he was about to get fucked from every possible direction in his life. What if Erica knew Tasha from Columbia? Because this was highly likely. What if Erica saw Tasha here? What if Erica had questions about why one of Alexander's very young, very attractive, very female students was here at a private family event?

And what if Tasha was out to get him, for some reason, and decided to express whatever the hell she was feeling to Erica? He needed to get inside that house and find her, try to talk to her, convince her that his interest in her was only ever professional.

"I'm worried," he blurted. It was the truth. "This is a

birthday party for Sasha and Everly." He gestured at the mob waiting to get into the house. "I don't understand it, but something has gotten out of hand here." He bit his lower lip as he watched her expression and waited to see if she would buy that this was *all* that was bothering him.

Erica turned her attention to the crowd. She, too, looked concerned. "Yes. I should say it does appear like perhaps there are a good deal more people here than you and Mia invited. How many were on the list?"

He had no idea. He'd had zero to do with planning this. How many kids were in the girls' class? In all the kindergarten classes? How many kindergarten classes were even in the school? He didn't know anything. "I think, maybe fifty?"

Erica's head shot back in surprise. "Well, there are at least three times that number just waiting at the door." She motioned to the driveway behind them, and the stream of people, mostly now without any children, still making their way toward the house. "And we were waiting in a line of cars for fifteen minutes before we were even able to find a parking spot," her voice had an edge of concern, and she looked at him now the way she might look at one of her teenagers—like she doubted his abilities and was suspicious of his intentions. "Where is Mia?"

Alexander swallowed. "I think I saw her...um, around back? She had, um...there was an issue, or something with the, um...caterers."

Erica gazed up into his face, her eyes in full assessment mode, taking in details, recording his every breath, sound, and movement.

"And what about the girls? Because this doesn't seem

right, Alexander. There are *a lot* of people here. Are the girls with Mia?"

He swallowed and nodded, but a fresh fear now took up residence in his nervous system. Where *were* the girls?

"Listen, it's great seeing you, Erica. Really. And..." he gestured at her children; their specific names were escaping him right now. "The kids. But, um...I better go help Mia and figure out what all this is about." He waved his hand wildly at the still-increasing crowd.

Without another word of explanation or waiting for her response, Alexander turned and headed for the side of the house and the back lawn.

"Wait!" He heard Erica call.

He didn't turn around or stop. He pretended like he hadn't heard her and picked up his pace.

He needed to find Tasha and find out what she was doing here before it was too late.

But first, he needed to find his girls.

CHAPTER 52

*H*olly leaned forward when she saw the line of brake lights ahead of them. "What the hell is going on?" she said.

Harris stopped the truck behind a dark blue Honda sedan. "An accident?" he wondered aloud.

Holly stared in disbelief at all the cars lined up before them. "Maybe. But even if there were, this road never has this much traf—"

The party.

"Oh God," she breathed, her mind trying to work out the plausibility of the only logical thought occurring to her. She turned her head to stare at Harris's profile. "It's the party. All these people are going to the party."

Harris laughed in disbelief. "No way. It's a kids' party." He shook his head. With both his hands resting at the top of the steering wheel, he pointed his index fingers at the scene outside their windshield. "Even if they invited every kid at their school, there's no way it would create a mess like this. Something else is going on."

Holly grabbed her purse off the seat between them and opened her door.

"What are you doing?" he asked.

"This is going to take forever. I need to get up to the house right away."

"We are still like a mile away from the driveway," Harris pointed out.

"I'll jog."

"Holly!" he called after her.

"I'll see you up there." She slid from her seat onto the street outside. "Or turn back if you can't get through. But I need to get there. Something is wrong."

"You don't know that. This probably has nothing to do with the party," he reasoned.

She waved him off and shut the door, the rusty hinges squealing. She didn't have time to convince him or argue with him. Something was wrong. She felt it. For her whole life, she had known when her sister needed her. They were connected. Always had been, always would be.

But she couldn't try to explain that to her husband right now.

Especially since she had never told him that she and Mia were twins.

CHAPTER 53

*A*s he scanned the scene on the back lawn, Alexander felt something drop onto his head. He brushed his hand through his hair and felt wetness. When he looked up, he saw the overcast skies had grown heavier and darker since they had arrived.

Another raindrop landed on his cheek—*perfect.*

He wiped it away and continued to look for the girls. The panic coursing through him grew with every second he didn't spot them. He shook his head. There were so many people here.

Music pumped from the giant speakers on either side of a raised platform where a DJ was taking requests. Waitstaff wove throughout the crowd with trays of food. A beverage station was set up where kids and adults could order drinks from bartenders in white blazers and black bowties. There was a circular corral with six ponies giving rides to the line of kids waiting.

He didn't spot the girls anywhere.

They might be inside the house, he reasoned. Maybe already with Mia—whom he also did not see anywhere. Sasha and Everly had been dead set on only letting their mother do their hair. That was it. It had to be it. They were inside with Mia getting their hair done.

There was no need to panic—at least not about this. The girls were safe. He would head inside right now and see them, completely fine.

He started toward the house, then stopped. A large white tent was at the far end of the lawn. Inside, people were sitting at tables draped in lavender tablecloths. On one side, a wooden dance floor had been laid out, and several kids and adults were dancing to the tunes pumping from the speakers.

It was erected in front of the path that led through dense trees that bordered the property to the beach beyond.

He didn't know why, but there were a lot of people here that were not invited. People who obviously did not have children of their own and had nothing whatsoever to do with Beacon Hill Academy.

Through the tent, he could see the opening in the trees where the trail to the beach began. He knew it was about a fifty-yard walk through the trees before it opened up again on the other side to the shores of the Long Island Sound.

Not realizing this would turn into more than just his daughters' sixth birthday party, he had allowed them to run ahead of him, out of sight and unsupervised.

What if one of these people, *any of these people,* had spotted his girls?

Led them away.

What if his girls needed him, and he hadn't *been there?*

He was being dramatic. All of this was highly unlikely, he

reasoned. But the fear of it being even remotely possible drove him into a run toward the tent and that dark, deserted path to the beach. He couldn't stop his mind from spiraling through the worst-case scenario.

And it would be all his fault for letting them out of his sight.

He was halfway through the tent, making his way past the clustered tables when he heard a voice that nearly brought him to tears.

"Dad!"

He turned and saw Sasha and Everly, their hair still wild, looking angry. "Where's mom?" Sasha barked at him, brush in hand.

At the sight of them both standing there, Alexander let out a huge sigh and felt his throat tighten as all his worry released at once. His eyes welled up, and he quickly swiped them dry as he jogged to where they stood in the middle of the dance floor and knelt before them.

"I couldn't find you?" he said, trying to control the desperate edge in his voice as he placed a hand on each of their shoulders and pulled them close.

"Hello?" a voice interjected. "Hi there."

Alexander looked up and into a woman's face, smiling big and leaning down into his line of sight.

"We haven't met yet. I'm Dominique Richards." She straightened back up and extended her hand. "Our kids are in the same class and get together for playdates. Mia and I are friends."

Alexander stood up, his legs still weak from the relief of finding the girls, and tried to process what this woman was telling him as he shook her hand.

"Hello," he said.

"This is quite the party," she said with a huge smile. "Although, it's a few more people than I was expecting. I wasn't aware that people outside of the Beacon Hill community would be coming."

Alexander stared into this woman's expertly made-up face and found he was at a loss for words.

"Well, and then I saw the girls wandering the lawn among so many strangers. And they looked a little lost. So, well, I figured we should keep an eye on them until we saw either Mia or their aunt. But now here you are! This is my son, Caleb." She pulled a young, skinny boy from behind her legs.

Sasha tugged hard on Alexander's hand. "Where's mom?" she whined. "She promised she'd do our hair! Everyone is here!"

Outside the tent, more people were noticing the light sprinkling of rain falling on their heads and shoulders and were taking cover under the tent.

"I'm not sure," he admitted. He turned to Dominique, a woman who looked like she never missed a thing and knew everything. "You haven't seen Mia?"

"Not yet," Dominique said. "I'm sure she's swamped working to orchestrate all the moving parts. I know how much work pulling off a party of this scale takes."

He held out each of his hands for the girls to grasp. "She must be inside," he said to the girls. "We'll go find her, get your hair done, and fix all this."

Several people jostled him as more and more of them squeezed into the tent to find cover from the rain. He pulled the girls closer to him.

"Well," Dominique said. "If this rain is going to keep up,

this tent is not going to be able to accommodate the number of guests you have."

He couldn't tell for sure, but it seemed like Dominique was chastising him, and Mia in her absence, for poor planning.

"To be honest with you," he said. "I have no idea what is going on. There isn't any way all these people have been invited."

Dominique's eyes grew wide as the reality of the situation fully dawned on her. "Oh...yes, of course." She glanced around with fresh understanding. "Oh my God," she said. "But *so many* crashers?"

"I think so. It's the only explanation." He shook his head. Having landed on a reasonable conclusion didn't provide him with any idea for a solution.

"I mean," Dominique continued. "The Beaumar events are iconic. Word must have gotten out?"

Alexander nodded. "I'm not sure what can be done about it now."

Dominique's eyes lit up. "Look, I'm the PTA president, and I know everyone from the school that *should* be here. I'll gather my people, and we'll work on figuring this out while you find Mia. We'll regroup in fifteen minutes?"

Alexander stared into the eyes of the expeditious efficiency before him and nodded dumbly. He had no idea who this woman was, but she seemed willing and more than capable of solving at least one of his problems right now. She asked for his phone, put her cell number into it, and then texted herself a message. "There now. Text me when you find Mia, and I'll let you know as soon as we have a plan to regain some control here. Just so you know, we may have to call the authorities, Alexander."

The police? At his six-year-olds' birthday party? He nodded again but wasn't entirely sure what he was signing off on.

"Oh, there's Courtney. We're going to need her," Dominique said, took hold of her son, and disappeared into the crowd.

CHAPTER 54

"*L*et's go find Mom," Alexander said. He pulled both girls close and pushed past people as they headed for the tent opening. Outside, the rain had increased from a smattering of drops to a drizzle. And while the tent had filled up with people that didn't tolerate any degree of bad weather, there were plenty of people still on the lawn, unbothered by the damp and wet.

Among them, Alexander recognized his mother-in-law. She wore a bright red dress that shimmered and dropped very low, *too low for a children's party*, Alexander thought, between her still ample breasts. She had kicked off a pair of matching red stilettos and stood barefoot in the grass, throwing back her head every few moments to laugh up into the sky like she didn't have a care in the world. She was a Hollywood bohemian holding court, surrounded by men and women hanging on her every word and gesture.

"I'm getting wet," Everly said.

"Daaaad, it's raaaaaining," Sasha whined.

"I know. But we're almost to the house," he said. Once they were through the thickest part of the crowd, he picked up the pace, and the girls ran beside him. When they reached the wide, brick stairs that led up to the patio, he bent down and lifted both girls into his arms and mounted the rain-slick steps two at a time.

When he reached the top, he put both girls down and stood hunched over, hands on his knees. His mouth agape, his lungs pulled hard, desperate for air, while his heart threatened to explode in his chest from the unaccustomed rigor of activity.

"Shit," he whispered.

"Dad!" Sasha scolded him.

He turned to look into both Sasha and Everly's disapproving glares. "Sorry," he wheezed. "Bad word." He shook his head at himself and watched as they both turned and headed toward the back door.

"Wait," he tried to call, but his voice was lost on his failing breath. He forced himself to stand up and follow the girls, determined to keep them safe and in his line of sight.

As he'd both feared and suspected, the house was full of people. He took hold of both the girls' hands and worked his way through the kitchen, down the main hall, and past the library. All around him, people gawked, touched, and snapped pictures like they were visiting a hands-on museum. He scanned the crowd.

He looked for Mia so he could hand off the girls.

He looked for Tasha so he could find out why she was here and what she had planned.

He never expected to find them together, deep in conversation, on the third-floor landing above him.

Alexander stood, stock still, in the center of the foyer and felt the foundation of his life shift beneath his feet.

What the hell was Tasha telling Mia?

"Alexander?" a woman's voice called from behind him.

When he turned, he saw Erica. She and her children had managed to make their way through the front door.

"Were you able to find Mia and figure out what is going on here?"

He stared, dumb and silent, into Erica's quizzical expression. With a slight tilt of her head and an upward gaze, she would see for herself his wife and Tasha Adams, a student from their graduate program, having what could only be described as an intense conversation two floors above them.

He had no idea what Tasha was telling his wife, but he imagined it was going to cost him both his job and his family within the next five minutes. He was just wondering if telling Erica a lie would buy him a few more humiliation-free moments when she answered her own question.

"Oh, look!" She pointed to the landing above them. "There she is. Oh…but something must have happened," she lowered her voice.

Alexander turned, looked up, and watched as Tasha descended the stairs. By the time Tasha made it to the second floor, he could plainly see what Erica was referring to. The young woman was sobbing uncontrollably.

Looking back up at Mia, he saw his wife staring down at them. Her expression was hard and distant. A moment later, she turned away and retreated, out of view, down the hall behind her.

While Tasha made her way down the last flight of stairs, Alexander closed his eyes and waited for the crash. At any moment, Erica would recognize Tasha. Erica would ask questions, and Tasha would explain things—at least from her perspective. Words like *sexual harassment* and *abuse of power* tumbled through his head.

How, and more importantly, *why* had he been so stupid?

Paralyzed, he stood beside Erica and watched Tasha reach the main floor and cross the foyer to face them. Here it was. There was no stopping it. All he could do was brace himself for the impact. He did wish his girls weren't standing here to witness it.

Tasha stopped right in front of him, her face red and wet from crying. She took several sobbing breaths and then finally spoke.

"I'm so sorry," she said. "Please forgive me. Please ask Mia to forgive me." She shook her head. "I shouldn't have come here," she whispered.

Confused, Alexander watched as she walked away, squeezed between a couple just entering the house, then disappeared out the front door.

Beside him, Erica had stood silent, watching the whole scene. A moment after Tasha was gone, Erica leaned toward him. "Who was that?" she asked.

Stunned, Alexander looked at Erica and almost blurted out *Tasha Adams* before considering two things.

Either Erica Monae, the head of their department who knew absolutely everyone in the Columbia Neuropsychology graduate school, somehow didn't know Tasha Adams.

Or, the woman who just walked out the door wasn't Tasha Adams.

"Can you keep an eye on the girls?" Alexander asked.

Erica nodded. "Of course."

"Thank you," he said, then chased Tasha, or whoever she was, out the front door.

CHAPTER 55

*M*ia watched the young woman walk back down the steps. Her shoulders hunched and shaking as she cried.

Mia had made her cry.

When the woman reached the main floor, she spoke to Alexander and Erica, then left the house.

Just as Mia had instructed her to do.

"Get out of my house," were Mia's exact words. Harsh and cruel in light of what the woman had taken great pains to share with Mia. She had approached Mia with a cautious smile—hope in her eyes. She politely introduced herself, "Hello, I'm Abigail Byron." She then extended her hand—which Mia looked at but did not touch.

Mia's rejection of even this most basic of niceties had thrown the young woman off. She dropped her hand awkwardly, her smile replaced with a worried frown. She had obviously rehearsed and practiced her lines. She then spoke to

Mia, carefully considering how best to begin, and eventually got to her point.

"I know this might be shocking, Mrs. Strauss, but you're my biological mother."

Mia stared into Abigail's eyes. She noted their color, spacing, and how they sloped up slightly. Then, on an impulse she could not explain, Mia had turned and stared down the hallway behind her, her eyes fixed on the closed door at the very end. "Get out of my house," Mia had said.

"If I could explain. I just—"

"Get out. Now," Mia said.

That was all it took to send Abigail Byron running back down the stairs, crying, and out the door.

Once Mia saw she was gone, she again turned to the door at the end of the hall. Her mind neither rehashed nor attempted to make sense of Abigail's statement. It swept all the syllables into a jumbled pile of nonsensical sounds and dumped them into a dark cognitive abyss behind that black curtain where Mia never looked. Behind that curtain were the realities that could neither be processed nor faced, so they remained where they did not exist in Mia's world.

Forgetting was the ultimate protection.

She could leave it there in the dark and unseen. It was tempting to erase Abigail Bryon and her words. To box her up and store her in the blank spaces of her mind.

Back there with all those other truths shrouded in lies.

The lies Holly told.

The lies Pixlie told.

And worst of all, the lies Mia told herself.

Her throat tightened like a vise, and the tears rose even if her mind didn't know why.

Mia heard the crack of the gun. So loud her ears rang. Then came the blood pouring from her father's head onto the carpet. His body crumpled and dead on the rug before her.

But when she blinked back her tears, the body and blood were gone.

It was only another image.

Another memory.

Mia stared at that door down the hall, and a terror unlike any she could remember rattled her core. She couldn't do this anymore. She couldn't allow herself to be lied to anymore.

She had to stop lying to herself.

She stepped over the place on the rug where her father had fallen eighteen years ago and headed for the door. It was time. To know the truth and face it. She felt—no, she knew, without a doubt that the only way to shed light into the darkest reaches of her mind was to open that goddamn door.

No matter how scared she was to see what was on the other side.

When she was only a few feet away, she didn't allow herself to stop or even slow down. She rushed ahead, all her momentum carrying her on to the truth. Her hand gripped the brass doorknob, turned it left, and pulled hard.

But the door didn't budge.

Mia twisted the handle in the other direction and pulled again. The door rattled in its frame but would not open.

Mia inspected the handle. It wasn't locked. She scanned the frame until her eyes found what was stopping her.

At the top of the door, someone had mounted a hinged hasp and loop and secured the door shut with a padlock. Mia stared at the contraption in disbelief. The lock was new.

Rage rose up in her. She shook the door, kicked it, and screamed in frustration as she clenched her fists to her chest.

She wouldn't let them get away with this. Not again. She strode back down the hall, her purpose singular, her focus unwavering. She was getting through that door, and she was getting through now.

CHAPTER 56

"Tasha!" Alexander shouted as he chased her down the drive. "Wait!"

But Tasha, or whoever this woman really was, didn't stop. Alexander didn't catch up to her until she was halfway down the drive. "Please," he begged. He was only a few feet behind her now. "Just talk to me for a minute. If you're not Tasha Adams, tell me who you really are."

She took a few more steps but finally stopped beside a black Ford Escape with New Jersey plates. Alexander watched as she reached into her bag and pulled out a set of keys. She unlocked the car with her fob, and Alexander thought she would likely leave without further explanation when he saw her shoulders drop several inches, and she turned to face him.

She was still crying, her usually beautiful face now a mask of pain and grief as she looked into his eyes. "I'm so sorry. Truly. You were right. I never should have come here. I guess I just thought that if she saw me, maybe, she would remember."

At this, she shook her head, her pain was palpable, and Alexander couldn't help feeling sorry for her.

"Can you please tell me what is going on? I want to help you, Tasha." Alexander shook his head. "Not Tasha...what is your name? Can we start there?"

"Abigail," she whispered. "Abigail Byron."

Alexander sighed. "Okay, Abigail. Now, what is going on? Who are you? Are you really one of my students? Do you even attend Columbia?"

She shook her head and took a big breath. "I'm sorry I lied to you. I just didn't know any other way to get close to her. And when I read your book and learned you were a professor at Columbia, I came and sat in on several of your lectures. I was working up the courage to talk to you. But that first day, when I approached you after class." She shook her head. "I got scared. I had heard another student, Tasha, talking about how she would be out for part of the semester...so instead of telling you the truth that day, I panicked and pretended to be her."

Alexander stood, digesting her confession and remembering his first meeting with her after class. How nervous she had been. How unsure. "What truth?"

Fresh tears flooded her eyes, and she dropped her gaze to the ground. "Mia is my biological mother. She gave me up for adoption when she was fifteen. The record was sealed until my eighteenth birthday. I didn't even want to know. Not at first. But then, last year...my adoptive mom passed away from cancer. I guess...I don't know why. It's not like I thought I could replace her, but...well, maybe my bio mom would want me to reach out?" Abigail shook her head. "It was stupid."

Abigail looked up into his eyes as more tears ran down her cheeks.

He stared at her, shocked and speechless, and wondered if this woman might have been running some con. But then he saw it. Her eyes, the shape of her face, the slope of her nose.

"Jesus Christ," he whispered. It had never occurred to him because why would it. But now that he saw it, a shame unlike any he had ever experienced in his life descended upon his psyche. Suddenly sick, Alexander placed his hand on his mouth and doubled over.

He had been attracted to this woman because she reminded him of Mia.

And with that awareness, Alexander heaved his breakfast and coffee onto the dirt and gravel before him.

CHAPTER 57

*S*he found Pixlie on the back lawn, surrounded by people, dancing barefoot in the rain. Mia pushed her way through the crowd. When she reached her mother, she grabbed her by the arm and pulled hard, shaking Pixlie from her revelry until her confused eyes focused solely on Mia.

A woman dancing with Pixlie protested. "Hey, you can't—"

"Shut up," Mia hissed at her, then turned back to Pixlie.

"Where is the key?"

Pixlie's eyes grew wide. "What key?" There was a nervous lilt to her voice. She smiled and shook her head like she had no idea what Mia was talking about. She tried to pull her arm free—Mia gripped her harder.

"You know what key," Mia accused. "To the deadbolt locking the door on the third floor."

Pixlie's smile faded; whether it was from Mia's words or her viselike grip, Mia couldn't say. Pixlie's eyes filled with tears. "You're hurting me. And I don't know what you're talking about. I never go to the third floor."

Mia leaned in close to Pixlie's ear. "Then who locked the door, mother?"

"I don't know," Pixlie repeated. "Your sister was here last week. She goes upstairs sometimes. She would know."

Mia released Pixlie. "Holly," she whispered. Of course, it was Holly. There wasn't any way Pixlie could have installed that lock alone. The woman couldn't lift a broom, never mind a drill.

But Holly? Holly could.

Mia turned from her mother and the crowd that rushed in to ensure she was okay. Several people shot Mia nasty looks —she ignored them. Her mind grasped for solutions as she scanned the grounds around her until her eyes landed on the small structure at the far end of the lawn tucked back into the tree line.

The shed.

Another memory rose up. She was a child, standing in the open doorway of that small building. Sunlight warmed her back as she stared into the dark and saw all the many tools carefully organized and hanging on metal hooks from the pegboard mounted to the wall.

As a child, she had marveled at the sight of the enormous sledgehammer. Its huge iron head. Its long wooden handle. She had wondered then if she was strong enough to hold it above her head and swing it against her desired target. As a child, she had never tried.

But as an adult, she was about to find out.

CHAPTER 58

The sledgehammer was where she remembered it hanging as a child. The handle was worn, and the head rusty, but Mia imagined it was still capable of what she had in mind. She grabbed it from its hook on the wall. Its actual heft surprised her. She took it in both hands, left the shed, and made her way back across the lawn and toward the house.

This time, seeing her marching toward them with her sizable weapon, the crowds parted to make room for her long before she reached them. She was back inside, upstairs, and standing before the locked door in minutes.

She trained her eyes on the lock above her, lifted the sledgehammer above her head, and swung.

She miscalculated her first hit. The iron head landed on and dented the door's wood. Undeterred, Mia lifted the hammer again, took a deep breath, and kept her eye on the lock as she swung. This time she connected, but the lock and hasp still held.

She didn't care how many times she needed to lift the enormous hammer over her head and hit that damn lock—she was getting into this room. She swung and swung and swung. Her shoulders ached, her arms shook, and her back felt like it might break, but the crack of the hammer hitting the lock continued to rack the otherwise silent third floor.

Every swing grew more difficult as her muscles weakened. Mia began to doubt her plan would work. Maybe this sledgehammer and her rage simply weren't enough to break the lock. Then suddenly, with a blow that felt like it might be her last, the hinged hasp broke away from the door frame.

Mia stopped swinging and inspected the damage. The lock was still firmly attached to the ring, but she could pull the broken hasp away.

When she turned the door handle and pulled, the door swung toward her.

CHAPTER 59

$\mathcal{H}$olly didn't stop running until she reached the circular driveway. She had seen all the people and their cars lined up and making their way toward the house. She had no idea what was happening, but seeing everyone rushing toward Beaumar had made her run faster.

Standing on the driveway, the size of the crowd seemed impossible. Holly didn't ask questions; she started shoving her way through until she stood face to face with a twenty-something man wearing a black polo and a welcoming smile. As soon as she reached him, Holly wanted to shake him and start interrogating him, but a sound coming from inside the house captured her attention instead.

A loud banging. Metal on metal could be heard emanating from somewhere inside.

"What is going on in there?" Holly asked the man.

"It's a birthday party," he said. His expression morphed from welcoming to suspicious. "Have you been invited? Because this is an invitation-only—"

"I'm the girls' goddamn aunt. Of course, I've been invited! Have you asked the hundreds of other people who are clearly *not* here for a children's birthday party if they have been invited? This is my family home and this situation." Holly threw both her arms wide above her head. "Is completely out of control."

She heard a hammer-like sound ring out through the house again. "What is that noise?" she asked the man again.

His suspicious look had transformed again as he appeared to only now consider the fact that, maybe, there were by far many more people here than should be. "I...I don't know. It started a few minutes ago. I think it's coming from upstairs?"

The sound echoed again, but Holly also heard something break this time. Something metal giving way.

The lock.

Her lock.

"Get out of my way," she said, shoving past the guy. "And start getting all these people off our property!" she yelled over her shoulder as she ran for the staircase.

The house was packed with people. They wandered all over the first floor, in and out of rooms, taking pictures, touching everything. Holly considered yelling at them all, but there were far too many. What was going on? There wasn't any way Mia had invited all these people here. Mia didn't even *know* this many people.

Holly reached the stairs and took them two at a time. The sounds from the third floor had stopped. She tried to pick up her pace, but running from the truck to the house had turned her legs to jelly. She reached the second landing and rounded the staircase to head up to the third floor.

What was she going to do if Mia had broken in?

CHAPTER 60

*M*ia stared into the dark before her, and all her rage and momentum drained from her instantly. The trapped air from the room seeped out. It smelled musty and felt cold. As her eyes adjusted to the dark interior, she could see a set of ten narrow wooden stairs leading from the door to a room positioned above the third floor.

Mia took a breath. Without her anger to drive her, all her old fear about this room came rushing back.

She knew this space. It was in her bones. The despair she felt as she stared into this space made her want to slam the door and forget about resurrecting her past.

Every nerve in her body was telling her to run. She didn't need to remember this. There were other ways to solve her Alexander problem. She could beg him to please forgive her. She could hire a high-powered attorney. She could try to convince Erica to pressure Alexander into backing off.

She could swear to give up her old coping habits. She

would never take another pill or drink another drop of alcohol again.

Mia stared at the staircase before her and fell back a step. It wouldn't work—she knew that. Because this feeling, this fear, the visceral anxiety churning at her core—it was real. It was part of her. And it would never let her go until she faced it down and came to terms with whatever truths were being kept from her.

Whatever it was her mind insisted on hiding from her.

She could pretend, continue to hide, push her past down —but she had already lived that life. It wasn't what she wanted. Not for herself. Not for her girls.

Scared Mia. Anxiety riddled Mia. Broken Mia.

It wasn't who she wanted to be. Not anymore.

She took a step forward and then another. Every foot closer to the entrance intensified her terror. A bead of sweat ran down her spine. When she reached the threshold, Mia's chest tightened. She closed her eyes and kept moving.

Her legs shook as she mounted each stair.

Her hand, slick with sweat, slid across the wooden handrail.

Halfway up, the room above her came into view. She could see the soft white light from a window illuminating the dusty floor. When she reached the top step, she scanned the space. It was a large room. The single arched window faced south. It had individual panes that were dark-framed and cloudy with grime. Mia reached for the wall on her left, and her fingers flipped a switch that her body knew was there even if her mind did not.

From the center of the high vaulted ceiling above her

head, a soft yellow glow emanated from a hanging brass chandelier.

At that instant, Mia saw it all. All that her mind had been keeping. All her sister had hidden. Every forgotten image rushed her at once the moment she saw them.

There were so many. Each different. Round, narrow, wide, frightened, confused, sorry. Every one an individual. Every one a story. They all stared back at Mia. Their truth plain for her to now see.

The room was full of eyes.

And Mia remembered them all.

CHAPTER 61

*N*ovember 2003

Mia sat, slumped and bored, in one of the four wooden chairs that lined the hallway outside the guidance counselor's office. She picked at her nails, biting off an angry hangnail from her middle finger. When Kara Robinson and Tracy Perry walked by and gave her disgusted looks, Mia pulled her finger away from her teeth and used it to flip them off.

"Fuck you," she mouthed.

Both girls gave her wide, frightened looks and scurried faster down the hall. Mia scoffed and rolled her eyes. Neither one would dream of giving her any real shit—she was a Renaud. Practically royalty.

As far as the outside world knew, being a Renaud was a mighty powerful thing.

Mia continued to bite at her nails. The truth was, Mia would give anything to *not* be a Renaud.

To never have been born.

Every day, she wished she were dead.

"Mia? You can come in now."

She looked into the hazel eyes of the guidance counselor, Ms. Parker. Mia dragged herself up and out of her chair, and followed her into her office.

Ms. Parker was young, late twenties at most. She had mid-length light brown hair and a face nearly devoid of makeup. Ms. Parker looked like where she'd come from— Kansas. She wore affordable clothes and sensible shoes and carried the same worn black leather purse to school every day.

While Kara and Tracy laughed at her poverty behind her back, Mia wished she could be Ms. Parker.

A nobody. Normal. Mia imagined Ms. Parker lived in a horrifically cramped and terribly furnished studio apartment in a shitty broken building nowhere near the upper east side. And yet, Ms. Parker seemed like a genuinely happy, or at least content, person.

She had a small, framed photo of her and a guy on the credenza behind her desk. They were smiling and kneeling on either side of a German Shepard, its tongue lolling happy and loose outside its mouth.

Mia had been in this office countless times over the past few months but never asked about that photo. She didn't like to think it was possible for some people in this world to be that happy.

It wasn't fair, and the unfairness made her both sad and angry. Even suspecting Ms. Parker of genuine happiness made

Mia want to hate her. And she didn't want to hate Ms. Parker. So she never confirmed it by asking about the photo.

Mia needed to be careful with Ms. Parker, keep her guard up no matter how close the woman sometimes came to getting behind Mia's well-crafted walls. During their first meeting in August, one of many times Mia had been caught staying out all night, Ms. Parker had asked the question.

"So why did you leave Riverside last year? I see you transferred out last September and are now back for your junior year."

Mia hadn't been prepared for the question—it caught her off guard. No other administrator had asked why her parents suddenly pulled her out of school last year, and they didn't ask why she was back this year. That information fell under the category of *private family matters*. And the kind of families that could afford to send their children to Riverside knew they could count on this institution to be, above all else, discrete.

But Ms. Parker was new.

Ms. Parker was from Kansas.

Ms. Parker didn't yet understand the rules and social mores of extreme wealth. So, she did what any counselor at any other school would do.

She asked questions.

Sitting there that day, across from Ms. Parker and her inquisitive face, it surprised Mia how much she wanted to tell the woman the truth. To open her mouth and let all the vile bile that was her life flow up and out of her. She sat in silence, unsure of what she would or could do next. The very idea of telling the truth—it was both impossible and terrifying. Everything would break—including her.

"I wanted to try a public school. So, my parents let me," Mia lied.

Ms. Parker nodded her head like she understood this reasoning. "I imagine an entire life of attending one private school can feel a little claustrophobic after a while," she empathized with a smile. "I mean...not that I would have any idea what that is like." She laughed. "It was nothing but public schools for me. So, what school did you attend?" She poised her sharp pencil over her notepad. "I'll call and ask them to send over your academic records from last year."

Which, of course, was impossible. "I think my parents have already called? They had my grades sent directly to them. I'll ask them to send what they have to the school."

"Oh, okay then. That would be easier. Thank you."

Mia had nodded—lying was second nature to her.

Now, months after their initial meeting, Mia slumped into one of the leather wingbacks in front of the desk. Ms. Parker watched her and let out a small sigh as she shook her head. "I thought we talked about the black lipstick?"

Mia glared at her, but only for a second before she leaned forward, plucked a tissue from the box on the desk, and swiped it across her lips. She balled the tissue up and kept it clenched tight in her fist while she waited to hear about whatever had landed her in trouble this time.

Mia knew there were a multitude of reasons why she could be sitting here: staying out past curfew, flipping Mr. Chase off, falling asleep in chemistry, being high at morning assembly, and turning in zero assignments all semester, were just a few reasons that came immediately to mind. It wouldn't be everything. Mia never got into trouble for everything. And the consequences would be minor—the Renaud family money pumped into this elite private institution guaranteed that. Grotesque amounts of money ensured that Mia and Holly, not that Holly *ever* did anything wrong, would never receive more than a nod in the general direction of a punishment: detention, loss of off-campus privileges for a few days, etcetera, etcetera. The school only needed something on file to show they had addressed the situation with Mia.

"Give her a slap on the wrist. Just enough in case other parents complain," she had once overheard the school director explain to the last guidance counselor, Mrs. Aaron—a decidedly not happy, frumpy, middle-aged hag who Mia had detested with every fiber of her being.

And to be fair, Mia suspected Mrs. Aaron had hated her just as much. It was written all over her face every time Mia sat in this exact same spot and glared at her ruddy, loose-jowled face. She thought Mia was spoiled, privileged, and entitled, a rotten rich brat who thought she could have anything and get away with everything.

Which was partially correct.

But Mrs. Aaron didn't know shit about Mia's actual life. Like everyone else, she saw only what she wanted to see. She was blinded by the Renaud fame, opulence, and wealth—she never even bothered to think that Mia might be a real person underneath all those external factors.

It never crossed her mind that Mia might be trapped, alone, isolated, in excruciating pain, and in need of real help. It never occurred to her that all the fame, opulence, and wealth were exactly what barricaded Mia into an existence that was both a prison and a torture. It kept her silent, and it kept others from helping.

And it protected those who hurt her most.

No, Mrs. Aaron never knew that Mia often wondered if her only possible escape was terminal. Or that Mia thought about all the ways she might be able to end her own life every single day.

"Mia, I have someone I'd like you to meet," Ms. Parker said.

Surprised, Mia shifted in her seat. This was not what she had expected when she'd been called out of her third-period world history class.

Ms. Parker raised her eyebrows and seemed to be watching Mia's reactions carefully. "It's another student. She's new to Riverside this semester. She began at the beginning of the term but...well, due to circumstances that I'm unable to share with you because of confidentiality, she will be moving rooms. And since you're currently occupying a double suite all on your own, she's going to be your new roommate."

Ms. Parker took a breath and watched Mia from across her desk. Mia noticed the pensive pinch of skin between her brows. Even if she didn't admit it out loud, she was worried about what Mia's reaction would be.

"She could really use a friend like you, Mia."

Mia cleared her throat and sat up in her seat. She already knew exactly who Ms. Parker was introducing her to and exactly why this person was changing rooms. It was Natalie, Charity Case, Cross. Which was the name Kara Robinson, Tracy Perry, and the rest of their crew of bitches had been calling Natalie all semester. Natalie had arrived in August, fresh-faced and excited, all the way from the middle of nowhere Nevada. She was one of the few students admitted to Riverside on scholarship for demonstrating some unique acuity in one discipline or another despite what might as well be a crippling degree of poverty compared to most students who resided at Riverside nine months out of the year. Natalie's gift was for the dramatic arts. She had already "stolen" the lead role for the fall production of *Cat on a Hot Tin Roof* from Tracy.

She may have been poor, but Natalie was also statuesque and thin, with naturally chiseled cheekbones, a perfect jawline, and the exact nose many of the other girls at Riverside had paid top dollar for. Her lips were full, her teeth perfect, and when she walked into a room, every head turned. To add insult to injury, Natalie was also extremely talented.

In short, Natalie Cross was going to be a star. Everyone knew it.

And practically everyone hated her for it.

Her now former roommate, Kara Robinson, was unaccustomed to feeling completely overshadowed by someone who descended from nobodies. Kara's father was CEO of a global private equity firm and always on the top twenty list of wealthiest men in America. Kara had complained to her parents about being roomed with someone she had *absolutely nothing in common with*. But everyone knew the real reason was that even with all Kara's money, she couldn't buy the natural beauty and talent that Natalie possessed. And so, to make his daughter happy, Kara's father called the headmaster. And now Natalie would be moving in with Mia.

"Well, is she here?" Mia asked.

"She's waiting outside," Ms. Parker said.

Mia got up, opened the door, and saw Natalie standing outside. Mia personally had no conflict with Natalie. She didn't care how beautiful or talented she was—she had grown up with a mother who lived the existence Natalie was chasing. Mia knew the undesirable secondhand results of that life.

It was not one Mia held any envy for.

Still, she had prepared herself to be chilly toward her new roommate. She didn't want or need any friends. Certainly not from Riverside, anyway. Mia now hung with a different crowd. Underground, New York kids that had no idea who she was or where she came from.

But seeing her now, eyes downcast, shoulders hunched, her hands clasped so hard her knuckles were white—it was impossible to not feel sorry for the beautiful Natalie Cross. Mia hadn't really dialed into all the drama that was going on between Natalie and Kara, but it was clear, just by looking at this girl, that Kara and her crew had been making her life miserable. When Natalie looked up, her eyes big, blue, and still red from crying, Mia felt the will to hold this girl at a distance dissolve.

"Hi," Mia said.

"Hello. I'm Natalie," she whispered, her eyes darting away like she was embarrassed by the admission.

Mia sighed. "I know who you are. Come on. Let's go get your shit from that bitch's room."

"Mia," Ms. Parker called from her office.

When Mia turned to look at her, Ms. Parker mouthed, *thank you.*

CHAPTER 62

$\mathcal{M}$ ia was unlike Kara and Tracy—she would never go out of her way to make anyone's life more miserable. But neither did she have any emotional bandwidth available to open herself up to Natalie. Mia would help her move her crap and settle in the room, but she had zero intention of becoming Natalie's best friend.

Two weeks later, it had happened anyway.

Natalie was the oldest of six kids. Her father worked as an installer for their local cable company, and her mother cleaned houses on the weekends and office buildings at night. It was Natalie's dream to be a famous actress. She didn't care if it was on TV or in the movies, but Natalie wanted to act her way into fame, fortune, and the ability to buy her family their own home. She wanted her mother to be able to stop cleaning other people's property day and night. She wanted a better life for her three younger brothers and two younger sisters. A future that was financially secure and included always having food in the house.

When her drama teacher at school encouraged Natalie to apply for the creative arts and drama scholarship at Riverside in New York City, Natalie didn't believe in a million years she would be the one selected. "It was an absolute dream come true...until I got here."

There was no way Natalie could have prepared herself for the culture shock. Or for being on the receiving end of such casual cruelty.

"I cried every night for the first month," she confessed to Mia. "I think it only made Kara and her friends hate me even more."

Mia had not meant to *like* Natalie. She had not wanted to *care* about Natalie. But after two weeks of hearing Natalie's life story and baring daily witness to how good, kind, and gentle Natalie really was—it had been impossible to stand by and do nothing when Kara, Tracy, and their friends were sitting together, like a mini-mob, openly talking shit and laughing about Natalie who was sitting alone, on the verge of tears, only one table away.

Mia stood and watched them cackle, her fingers curling tight around her lunch tray. She was about to throw her bowl of Waldorf salad at them when she had a better idea. Mia strode over to their table, shoved her way between Kara and Tracy, and slammed her tray down.

In an instant, the entire table went silent and stared at Mia.

"What's so funny, girls?" she asked with the fakest smile she could muster.

Uncertain and obviously scared of Mia, they exchanged looks, but no one said a word.

"Oh, now come on," Mia prodded. "Just a moment ago,

you were all howling like the pack of fucking hyenas you really are. Certainly, you must have found *something* hilarious. Well… let's see if I can guess. Maybe you were all sitting here, feeling smug and self-important, as usual, when it suddenly occurred to you how tragic each of your oh-so pathetic existences would be if the safety net of your daddies' money suddenly vanished from your lives. Say, like, if the stock market crashed. Or your dear father was arrested for embezzlement, fraud, or insider trading. I mean, what would happen? All that family money gone in the blink of an eye. And you and your sad, bored mothers with no means to support yourselves since you have absolutely zero skills beyond shopping and acting like bitches?"

Mia stabbed her lettuce, shoved the bite into her mouth, and swallowed hard.

"I mean, you're right to joke. It's so fucking terrifying to imagine. All you really can do is try and laugh it off. But, on the off chance that's not what you found so very funny, I have a bit of advice for you girls." Mia stood and picked up her tray. "If I see, hear, or find out that any of you are continuing to make Natalie's life difficult, well, you can bet I'm going to be making your lives a fucking hell."

"Jesus, Mia," Tracy said. "We were only joking."

Mia nodded and gave a sardonic laugh. "Sure. I get it. But remember what I said because the next *joke* will be on you."

Mia took her tray and headed over to where Natalie was sitting. There wasn't any way she hadn't heard every word.

As Mia placed her tray on the table and sat down, she caught her sister staring at her from across the cafeteria. Holly didn't hang out with the Kara and Tracy crowd, but she didn't hang out with Mia anymore, either. Once inseparable, their relationship had been strained and distant for years. There were things about Mia's life that Holly didn't know. Things Mia didn't want her sister to ever find out. And the only way she could think of to keep her secrets from her twin was to completely shut her out.

Mia knew it hurt Holly, but she didn't see any other way.

Mia dropped her eyes and sat next to Natalie.

"I'm sorry you got dragged into that," Natalie whispered. She sat in front of her untouched sandwich, her cheeks still wet from crying.

"Don't apologize," Mia said. "And to be honest, I pretty much dragged myself into it. You shouldn't let them get to you. Tears are like blood in the water for them."

Natalie smiled but kept her head low, and her eyes still trained directly on the food before her. "I know. But they're not really why I'm so upset. I mean, hearing them talk about me always sucks, but that's not why I'm crying." She turned and looked Mia in the eyes. "I talked with my mom this morning, and she told me—" Natalie started to cry again before getting the words out.

Mia handed her a napkin and wondered if someone in her family had died.

"She told me they can't afford to fly me home for Christmas break," she whispered. "I'll have to stay here."

"Oh, Natalie," Mia said and gave her a hug. As happy as Natalie was to have the opportunity to go to a school like Riverside, Mia knew how homesick she was. She had been talking for the whole last week about how excited she was to go home and see her parents and siblings. Her family didn't have much, but Mia could tell there was at least a lot of love in their house.

"I can't bear the thought of it," Natalie said through her tears. "Being here? Alone on Christmas?"

Mia pulled away from their embrace and looked her new friend in the eye.

"Stop crying. You're coming home with me for Christmas."

CHAPTER 63

 ecember 2003

When the car pulled up the driveway and Natalie got her first look at Beaumar Manor, she reached across the seat and grabbed Mia's arm.

"You actually live here?"

Sitting in the front passenger seat, silent and occupied with a book for the entire ride from Riverside, Holly turned her head and made eye contact with Mia. It was a brief and silent communication, but Mia knew exactly what her twin was thinking.

This is a mistake. You shouldn't have brought her here.

Mia ignored her sister. Holly was right, but she didn't know half the real reasons why. Holly, always so private, hated their parents' fame and all that came with it. She would be concerned about personal exposure and the possibility of

Natalie gossiping about the Renaud lifestyle once she witnessed what went on behind their closed doors.

Which was nothing compared to the danger of Natalie, whom Mia had already grown far too close to, finding out the truth about Mia. A truth even Holly didn't know.

A truth that Mia had tried, and failed, to scrub from her own mind.

"What is that?" Natalie asked, her voice full of wonder and surprise as she pointed out her window to the portion of the back lawn visible from the drive.

Mia and Holly followed her gaze and saw the huge, red and white striped tent constructed on the winter-brown lawn.

"That will be the setup for this year's holiday party," Holly said as she returned her gaze to the windshield before her. "Looks like mom decided to have a circus this year," she added as the car stopped and she opened her door. "Not that every party here isn't a circus," she added as she stepped out, then slammed her door behind her.

Natalie watched Holly head toward the house. "Did I say something wrong?" she asked. "Is she mad at me?"

Mia sighed, uncertain of what to say, as she watched her sister disappear inside the house. "No, it's not that."

"Because I got the impression she was kinda upset that I was coming home with you guys. I'm worried that I'm intruding on your private family time. I mean, it is Christmas, after all," she finished in a whisper.

Mia stared at Natalie. How to explain to her that none of this was an issue? Her family didn't do *private family* anything, and no one cared about the sanctity of Christmas. "If my sister is upset," Mia said. "It's because of that tent out there."

"What? Why?" Natalie glanced back at the enormous, striped monstrosity, its unsecured flap doors blowing in the breeze. "I mean...it looks like it will be amazing."

Mia bit her lip and nodded. "Yeah," she said, then opened her door. She didn't know how to explain to Natalie that these extravagant parties had never been *amazing* for her or Holly.

They were events to be avoided at all costs.

The driver unloaded their bags from the trunk, and Mia led Natalie inside. Natalie was quiet, reverent even, as her eyes scanned the ornate front door and threshold. When she first stepped into the foyer, her eyes were drawn to the majesty of the staircase, up past the second floor, beyond the crystal chandelier, and to the heights of the third floor above. "Mia," she whispered, her eyes alight with wonder over the grandeur. "It's so amazing."

Mia smiled but said nothing as she led her friend up the stairs to the top floor.

When Mia opened her bedroom door at the end of the hallway, Natalie peered into the dark space, and her expression changed from awestruck to bewildered. "This is your bedroom?"

Mia nodded and started up the stairs that led to her attic bedroom. When she reached the top, Mia pulled the heavy, purple brocade drapes to each side of the window, allowing the light from the gray overcast sky to illuminate the room.

Mia stood in the center and waited for Natalie to make her cautious way up the stairs. When she saw the room and its extensive collection, her eyes grew wide with surprise. She glanced at Mia once, then proceeded to make her way around the room as she processed all there was to see.

After what felt like an eternity, she finally said. "My God, Mia. Did you do these?"

Mia closed her eyes and nodded. She had never openly shared this work with anyone—at least, not with anyone who knew her. Over the summer, she had submitted a few of her pieces to a gallery in the city that was running a show for new, up-and-coming artists.

To her amazement, three of her pieces had been selected for inclusion. She was thrilled but terrified of the exposure because it wouldn't take much for the public to connect her with Pixlie and Raphael. Her work was too personal, and she was afraid to imagine what connections an overly astute art observer might make between Mia's art and her real life.

She had resigned herself to pulling out of the show and had expressed her gratitude and deep regrets to the gallery owner, Millie Miller. Mia didn't think she had ever wanted something this much in her entire life. Here was, yet again, another way that being a Renaud was destroying her.

But when Millie agreed to keep Mia's identity anonymous, when she swore there would not, or ever be, anyway for her identity to be revealed unless Mia revealed it herself— Mia's heart had soared.

Her work would be displayed and for sale in a New York gallery.

It was enough for her to know she was good enough to accomplish it—even if no one else ever did.

"Their eyes," Natalie said as she turned away from the portrait she'd been studying. "They're haunting."

Mia nodded and looked at the paint-splattered floor beneath her feet. "That's because they *are* haunted."

Natalie turned back to the portraits. "These are real

people?" she asked. "Who are they? What happened to them?"

Mia watched Natalie as she inspected the portraits. The concern she had for Mia's subjects was genuine. Natalie could see the confusion and suffering. Mia had captured it and communicated it through her art. And because Natalie could see it…feel it, Mia almost told Natalie the truth. She had never before, not even with Ms. Parker, ever come this close to letting it all out.

Mia opened her mouth, but when Natalie turned to face her, she couldn't say it.

"They're nobody," Mia lied. "I made them up," she added and quickly looked away from all her portraits and their observing eyes bearing witness to her deceit and denial that was yet another violation enacted upon them.

"But not that one," Natalie said, pointing to a painting propped in the shadow of the far corner. Before Mia could protest, Natalie stood in front of the picture and pulled it out and into the light. "This one is your father," she said. "Although, it's not very flattering, is it?" Natalie made the observation as a joke with a smile on her face. But when she turned to meet Mia's gaze, her smile evaporated. "I'm sorry," she said, suddenly serious. "You're upset. I didn't mean that the picture isn't good. Oh God, Mia, are you angry? I really am sorry."

Mia stared at the painting. She wasn't mad at what Natalie said, but there wasn't any way to express, not in words, how that portrait of Raphael made her feel, either. The painting *was* the expression of her emotions. It told the truth she couldn't. "He's not my father," Mia blurted as her eyes met Natalie's. She shook her head. "It's a big secret. Nobody knows but me, Holly, Pixlie." Mia nodded once at the picture. "And him. He's not our dad."

Natalie moved the portrait back to the dark corner she had pulled it from, then crossed the room and shocked Mia by wrapping her arms around her and pulling her into a hug. "I'm so sorry, Mia. Truly. Have you always known? Or just found out? It must have been such a shock. I'm so sorry you have to deal with this. I don't know what I would do if I found out my dad wasn't my real dad... I'd be devastated."

Mia was surprised to find herself hugging Natalie back. Her hands rested between the girl's shoulder blades. This caring, physical, human contact, something she had not had or sought out in years, crashed hard into and threatened to knock down the protective wall she was always vigilant about keeping in place. Later, Mia would realize it was in this moment, in Natalie's arms, with the soft gray light from the window illuminating them, in the silence, and seconds that ticked slow enough, in front of all Mia's subjects who were both evidence and witness, that Mia's opportunity to confide, confess, and yes, protect, was the most right.

She had the words. She felt their shape jagged and hard at the center of her throat. She needed only to open her mouth, force them from her.

It would have changed everything.

Natalie pulled away from Mia and looked into her face before lifting her hand to wipe away the tears on Mia's face. "Don't cry. And please don't ever worry. Your family's secret is safe with me." She held her hand to her heart in oath. "Okay?"

Mia nodded.

"Should I go get my bags from downstairs and bring them here?"

Mia nodded again.

"Okay then. I'll be right back," she promised Mia with a smile, turned away, and headed back down the stairs.

And just like that—the moment evaporated into time and space.

It was the greatest regret of Mia's life.

CHAPTER 64

*N*atalie stayed with Mia at Beaumar Manor, roaming the halls, raiding the kitchen, and marveling at what it would be like to grow up as a Renaud for three days before Raphael and Pixlie even realized she was there.

Mia and Natalie were in the library, staring out the large window that overlooked the back lawn and the teams of people taking care of the finishing touches for the Renaud circus-themed holiday party. The first guests would arrive in less than four hours.

Natalie was mesmerized by all that Mia and Holly's life appeared to be. She and Mia watched crews bring in food, speakers, stemware, and crates of alcohol. At the same time, other people constructed exterior walkways over the lawn that would lead guests to different entertainment areas that were sectioned off away from the tent. There was an arena where they could watch various performances: jugglers, fire eaters, a contortionist. Another where they could recline in Adirondack chairs around four stone fire pits that had been built only yesterday. And farther away, a shooting gallery where guests could watch a sharpshooter perform feats of extraordinary precision with rifles and pistols before having the opportunity to test their own skills against red and blue circled targets set against the tree line.

"This is going to be the best party I have *ever* been to," Natalie said. "Who am I kidding?" she added as she turned to Mia. "This is the best party I *will ever* go to in my entire life."

Mia stared into Natalie's eyes. Suddenly aware and surprised by Natalie's expectations. "We don't go," Mia said.

"What?" Natalie asked. She was still smiling with excitement, but her eyes conveyed her confused disbelief. Then she let out a laugh. "Ha, ha. Very funny, Mia," she shook her head and nudged Mia's shoulder.

Mia swayed once from the contact, but her expression remained dead serious. "No, I'm sorry, Natalie. And I should have realized you would assume…but Holly and I have never been allowed to attend. Adults only."

"But…." Natalie stared back at the scene before them, no doubt imagining all the activities and delights that would happen shortly. "I mean…you never go?"

"Never."

"So, every year, your parents hold these extravagant, extraordinary, mind-blowing parties that everyone who's anyone would give their right arm to attend, and you're telling me that you and your sister don't even go."

"Not once."

"Well, perhaps," a man's voice suddenly interjected from behind them. Startled, Mia and Natalie both turned at once and saw Raphael standing under the arch of the library's entrance. "This is the year we change that." He smiled; his eyes focused on Natalie.

"After all, you're hardly a child anymore." Presumably, he was speaking to Mia, but his gaze never left Natalie. "And who is this?" He glanced only briefly at Mia. "I didn't realize you were bringing a friend home for the holidays."

Before Mia could answer, Natalie stumbled forward with her hand extended. "I'm Natalie. Natalie Cross, sir." Her voice trembled on the words, and her quick movements and overeager approach gave away how awestruck she was.

Mia watched Raphael. His eyes sized up Natalie and took measure of all her most obvious attributes within seconds. He was an exceptional reader of people and often saw a person for what and who they were faster than it took that person to open their mouth and confirm his assumptions. Mia had watched him for years. Before the person could blink, he had collected the relevant information, sorted it, categorized it, and determined both what you wanted most and how far you'd go to get it. In short, he knew who you were better than you knew yourself.

He would note that Natalie was exceptionally beautiful—this was both easy and obvious. But the shabby wornness of her cheap clothing coupled with her eager-to-please, clearly starstruck, desperate-to-impress him approach, was what let him know Natalie was a hungry sort of girl.

"Well, Natalie," he enveloped her small hand in his large one and then placed his other hand on top of them both. "Natalie Cross," he teased and smiled and then, almost imperceptibly, pulled her the smallest fraction of an inch closer. "It is my absolute pleasure to meet you." Then he let her go and turned away. "But I had better get back and help prepare for this evening's extravaganza. After all, I don't want to get into trouble with the boss lady."

He was referring to Pixlie, as he often did. Only Mia knew what a joke this was to him—the very idea that her mother was the boss of anything or anyone was absurd. It served his purpose—hiding in plain sight behind a ridiculous wife camouflaged the fact he was an apex predator.

A lethal combination of intelligence, talent, charm, good looks, and ruthless entitlement.

Her mother had never been any match for the man she married.

"But," he stopped himself as his right hand gripped the edge of the library door. "Remember what I said. Certainly, no one could mistake either of you for children anymore. So come to the party, if you like. I'm sure Pixlie has loads of options in her costume closet that could be considered circus themed."

Natalie bounced once on her toes, unable to contain her joy.

Mia stood silent, her eyes on the floor below her feet, terrified of the pure, unadulterated power that poured off Raphael. He feared nothing, bent to no one, and didn't ever appear to succumb to the morass of everyday emotions that plagued most humans: regret, remorse...guilt. She had often wondered what went on inside his head. Or if he had any conscience or heart at all.

The man moved through the world beholden to nothing and no one. It was his. He owned it and all that it contained. Like a king in his own country—Raphael would do as he pleased.

Breathless from her excitement, Natalie gushed, "Thank you. But I could never ask Pixlie—"

"Ask Pixlie what?" And as if on cue in one of her husband's films, Pixlie entered the library, her silk robe cinched like a noose around her slender waist.

"Ah, there she is," Raphael turned to his wife. "My queen."

As was the case, practically every time he spoke to or about Pixlie, his tone had the barest hint of sarcasm. It was never enough that he could be accused outright, and his literal words always provided a case for plausible deniability. But Mia always heard it. His complete and utter disdain and disrespect for her mother.

Mia was sure the fact Pixlie never seemed to understand Raphael's true feelings about her made him detest her even more. Like the house and its furniture, she was one of the mere trappings in his life. Pixlie was something he had purchased a long time ago. Being married to her was incidental to his life and existence. Too shallow and ignorant to be a real partner, Pixlie was, at best, a very expensive pet.

Which suited Raphael just fine. A wife like Pixlie would never interfere with who he really was and what he really wanted.

"This is Natalie," Raphael introduced her. "Natalie Cross. Mia has brought home a friend for the holiday, and she wants to come to our party this evening."

Pixlie's eyes ran over Natalie and narrowed. She took a long drag from her cigarette and blew the smoke into the room.

Raphael watched his wife with what appeared to be a combi-

nation of amusement and contempt. "You will find her something suitable to borrow from that enormous closet of yours. Mia,
too…if she wants. Now," he turned away, confident that what he
asked would be carried out without further discussion. "I'm off to
make sure your party is coming together just how you like."

Pixlie looked after him as he walked away and nodded.
Imagining she was in control, in charge—exactly the way
Raphael set her up to feel. "Let's go find something quickly. I
still have a lot to do before everyone starts arriving." She
shifted her eyes to Mia. "If you're coming tonight." She
pointed her two fingers holding her cigarette at Mia. "I don't
want any trouble from you. Do you understand?"

Mia stared at her mother and suddenly felt lost all over
again. She had tried to put it all behind her. She had tried to
forget. But looking into her mother's angry, unforgiving eyes,
Mia knew she was dead to her mother.

Her mother who would not help her.

Her mother who could not save her.

And now, her mother who did not love her.

Unable to answer, Mia looked at the floor again.

"Come on then. Let's find you something to wear," Pixlie
said.

And Natalie, who thought all her dreams had come true
at once, followed Pixlie out the door. Mia watched them cross
the foyer and disappear down the hall that led to Pixlie's suite,
then she headed for the stairs that led to her own room, as far
away from the rest of her family as she could possibly get
while still being in the same house.

CHAPTER 65

*M*ia, Holly, and Natalie stood outside the entertainment arena, watching the hired circus performers warm up and practice their routines. The sun had set, and the temperature was dropping quickly. Two men started fires in the circular stone pits while several others lit the kerosene lamps that lined the walkway. The most eager guests would begin arriving any moment.

Natalie placed her hands on her cheeks. "I cannot believe I'm here. I cannot believe I am about to attend a Beaumar party." Her eyes were wide with disbelief. She stood up straight and let her arms fall to her side. "Be serious with me...do you think there is any chance, however small, that I might be..." she stopped herself and shook her head. "No, it's too stupid. Things like that don't happen to people like me."

She turned away again and watched the fires, but within a minute, she turned back. "What am I saying? Because I'm here! Right? So, things like this do happen to people like me. I'm just going to say this out loud. And please don't think

I'm stupid...I think I'm here." She lifted her arms above her head and then spread them wide to indicate this immediate time and space. "For a reason. You have no idea how much I've prayed for something like this." She dropped her hands to her side. "I think I'm going to get discovered tonight." She balled both her hands into fists and held them to her chest. "It's like I can *feel* it."

Speechless, Mia watched Natalie revel in her greatest hope for several seconds before turning away. It was Holly who managed to say, "That's so great, Natalie. And who knows? It could happen. This place will be crawling with absolutely everyone. And you do look fantastic."

Natalie did look fantastic in one of Pixlie's skintight, red sequined dresses with a slit that stopped mid-thigh. The look gave a nod to the circus theme with a small, shiny black top hat pinned into Natalie's hair, a riding crop, and a thin curling mustache expertly drawn onto her upper lip with stage makeup. If it were a Halloween costume, the label would have read: Sexy Female Ringmaster.

"I'm going back inside before everyone gets here," Mia said. Then she followed the pathway through the dead winter grass to the back door. When she passed through the kitchen, she saw that the caterers were using it as a storage area for the extra food and beverages they would need as the night went on. She grabbed a bottle of vodka, a carton of orange juice, and a tumbler, then made a beeline for the staircase before anyone else noticed her.

All she wanted was to get through this evening. Getting blackout drunk sounded like the fastest and easiest way to accomplish that.

Back in her room, Mia unscrewed the top of the large

bottle of vodka and poured it into her glass until it was three-quarters full. Before adding the orange juice, she took a swallow, testing to see if she could handle the liquor straight. It burned and made her wince, so she filled the rest of the glass with orange juice and took two long drinks.

When she lowered her glass, she stared into the eyes of all the portraits she had created over the past few years. All of them, except two, were young women. Their bodies looked thin and atrophied in comparison to their overlarge heads. The focal point of every one was the subject's eyes. Large and bulbous, the eyes communicated the whole emotion of each piece. Some were angry, some were confused, and others were simply broken. Whatever the case, the observer was given the impression that their frail, emaciated bodies could not hold the weight of such heavy emotion for long. Each subject was seconds away from collapse.

In the background, large black shadows lurked, haunting each subject. These young women, trapped in their frames, within their stories, their experiences—their perspectives—this was their reality, and it could never be escaped.

Mia took another big drink and turned away from them to stare out her own framed window instead.

The light was fading fast, but the fires and kerosene lamps illuminated the scene on the back lawn below her. More people had arrived. Some were standing near fires, and others were heading into the big-top tent. Mia was able to make out the shimmer of Natalie's red sequins. She was with a group near one of the fires, a drink in hand. Natalie's head tipped back. She was laughing. Giddy with her expectations for this night and the possibility of changing her whole life.

On the far left side of the lawn, a group of ten young

women appeared. They wore evening dresses and had professionally styled hair but struggled to keep their high heels from sinking into the lawn.

The limo had arrived.

Mia took another big drink from her glass and watched as a man, one she had seen many times before, came up alongside the girls and herded them toward the temporary walkway that had been laid out. It would save their shoes from getting ruined.

Or rather, his shoes. Everything these girls wore belonged to him.

For every party her parents held, girls like these were shipped in. They were very young, very beautiful, and they were meant to keep some of Raphael's special guests *entertained* for the evening.

Some of these girls knew exactly what they were doing here.

She turned her head away from the window and felt the weight of all the eyes she'd captured.

But some of them had no clue at all.

Mia finished the drink in her hand. The vodka was dampening her senses, but it emboldened her as well. She poured herself another drink and headed downstairs.

CHAPTER 66

*E*ven amongst all the other brightly adorned guests, it was easy to spot Natalie in her sparkly red dress. She stood alone outside the open circus tent with a glass of champagne. Mia, who wore jeans, a tank top, and an unbuttoned flannel, attracted looks from several other guests. She ignored them. She didn't care about the people that came to these parties. It didn't matter to her how important they imagined themselves to be. They were part of a world she wanted nothing to do with.

When she turned eighteen, she would change her name and leave all this behind.

Natalie saw Mia and smiled. "You decided to come!"

"No," Mia said. She allowed herself a single curious glance into the tent. Inside, people mingled as they held drinks, ate hors d'oeuvres, chatted, and watched acrobats, baton twirlers, and contortionists that made their way through the tent and performed small acts for the guests. Next to the center pole, Raphael stood surrounded by ten other guests who hung on his every word. As if he could sense her, he looked up and made eye contact. She saw a smirk play across his lips before he looked away.

He had not really expected her to show up at his party.

Mia turned to Natalie. "Come upstairs with me."

"Have you been drinking?" Natalie asked with a knowing look before taking a sip of her champagne.

Mia was slurring her words a bit. She shouldn't have poured the vodka so heavy. "Yes." She shook her head. "But that's not the important thing. Come upstairs with me. There's something I want to tell you. Something I should have told you before I brought you here."

Natalie gave her a pouty expression but quickly followed it with a big smile. "Okay, but I don't want to be gone for long." She took Mia by the arm and leaned in close to her ear. "I've already seen two directors. And those are just the ones I recognize. Not including your dad, of course. I mean...." She grimaced and shook her head. "I know he's not your *dad*. Sorry, I should have said, *Raphael*."

Uncertain about how to respond, Mia stared at Natalie for several seconds, then grabbed her hand. "Never mind. Let's just get out of here."

Mia pulled Natalie down the path to the house. "Mia, slow down," Natalie said when she stumbled a few times, but Mia kept up the pace. She ignored the glances and curious expressions of other guests as she shoved past them.

She didn't let go of Natalie's hand until they made it back to Mia's bedroom. When Mia finally stopped and turned to face Natalie, she expected her to be angry—Mia had just dragged her away from the party she'd been so excited about attending.

It surprised her to see Natalie smiling.

Breathless and red-faced from their trip up the stairs, Natalie burst into laughter. "Look, I saved my champagne!" she said as she raised her glass to show Mia it was still half full before raising it to her red lips and finishing it.

Mia watched her friend, statuesque and beautiful, her lipstick had stained the rim of her crystal glass. As desperate as she'd felt to get Natalie away from the party, she couldn't help smiling as well. Natalie had an infectious life force. Her beauty, energy, and vibrancy filled Mia's small room and instantly made it glamorous just by her presence.

Mia also saw what every guest downstairs did—Natalie was a star. Undoubtedly, she would one day be the top-billed talent in many films.

Just like Pixlie once was.

Light from the party outside illuminated the window, and Natalie was drawn to it. She peered down at the activity below and asked, "Now, why are we up here again?"

She indulged Mia because she was her guest, but Natalie obviously wanted nothing more than to return to the world of fame and champagne below.

Mia had felt so certain about getting her friend up here, away and safe. But now, as she faced her, on the verge of telling Natalie everything, Mia found the words again failed to take shape.

"It's not—" she started, but looking Natalie in the eye and confessing all she'd been through was too much. It made her too vulnerable, too exposed. After all, she barely knew this girl. Natalie was kind, as far as Mia knew. But who was to know if she could be trusted with a secret as big as Mia's? For all Mia knew, Natalie would use the knowledge as collateral. An entry ticket into the exact life she was dreaming of.

Because Mia's secret would open every locked door Natalie wanted access to. And if it got out—Mia and her whole world would be ruined.

"It's just...not as much fun as you imagined," Mia copped out. "Seriously. All those old men hoping to grope drunk girls." Mia waved her hand at Natalie in her tight dress as if presenting her as evidence. "And the women, so desperate to get their foot in the door or remain relevant. It's all so fake. *They're* all so fake. Honestly, we can have more fun on our own." Mia plucked Natalie's champagne glass from her hand and poured her some of the vodka and juice she had stolen from the kitchen. When she turned and handed the glass back to Natalie, her disappointment was palpable. All the vibrant excitement and hope had drained right out of her face.

Mia pretended not to notice and poured herself another large drink as well. "I know," Mia said with forced enthusiasm. "We can watch a movie. You love movies," Mia proclaimed as she pulled two t-shirts and a pair of jeans off the TV in the corner of her room. "And I seriously have every channel you could possibly imagine." Mia took Natalie's hand and pulled her toward the unmade bed. "Take off your shoes, get comfy, and I'll go make some popcorn." She picked up the remote control from the floor and handed it to Natalie. "You pick something. Anything at all. I'll be right back with some snacks and more drinks. I'll even see if Holly wants to come up. It'll be a girls' night."

Natalie collapsed onto the edge of the bed like her knees had given out. She looked so sad; Mia pretended not to notice. Once she had some salty snacks, a little more to drink, and was invested in a movie, Natalie would forget about the party downstairs.

Down the hall, Mia stopped outside of her sister's room and knocked gently. Several seconds passed before Holly opened the door. She had headphones on and a book in her hand. When she saw it was Mia standing outside her door, she looked at first surprised and then worried. "What's wrong?" she asked.

Mia shook her head. "Nothing." Mia knew it was weird for her to even be standing there. She and Holly had hardly spoken to each other over the past year. When Mia came home last summer, she was surprised that her once identical twin had cut her long brown hair short. Even though they shared the same face, she hadn't recognized her sister when she'd first seen her.

No one ever mistook them for each other anymore.

"Then what do you want?"

Realizing this was a dumb idea, Mia took a step back. They were not the sort of sisters that ate popcorn and watched movies together. At least, not anymore. "Nothing," Mia said. "Never mind."

Without another question or word, Holly shut her door. Mia told herself it didn't matter, she didn't miss her sister, and none of this hurt her anymore. When the truth was that everything was so painful all the time, the only tolerable solution was to go numb, be numb, stay numb.

And never, ever think about it.

When she returned to her room with two hot bags of microwave popcorn and a bottle of champagne she'd pulled from an open case in the kitchen, she found Natalie sitting back on the bed, with her glass now empty, watching a black and white film. She looked at Mia with joy in her eyes again. "*All About Eve* is on AMC. It's like my favorite movie. Ever."

Mia smiled, relieved to see Natalie happy and distracted. "Look what I found," Mia said, holding up the bottle and popcorn.

"Perfect," Natalie said and scooted over to make room for Mia in bed.

As Mia climbed in, she popped the cork on the champagne and noticed Natalie was still in her dress. "Do you want to change into something else?"

Natalie held her glass up so Mia could pour into it. "I thought about it, but this is a perfect outfit to watch this movie in."

Mia smiled, shrugged, and poured some champagne into her tumbler. Never a fan of old movies, and certainly not black and white ones, Mia had never seen *All About Eve*. But if it made Natalie less sad to be up here instead of downstairs, she didn't care what they watched. She handed one of the bags of popcorn over to Natalie and settled back against the stacked pillows.

CHAPTER 67

*O*nly minutes had passed, or so it felt like, but when Mia opened her eyes, sunlight was streaming through her window. Disoriented, she squinted against the harsh light. Her head throbbed, relentless and agonizing, inside her skull. She was home, in her own bed, and the scent of stale microwave popcorn made her want to throw up.

Her television was on with the volume muted. The empty bottle of champagne was in the middle of her bed, along with the half-empty bottle of vodka. She vaguely remembered— she and Natalie had poured glass after glass for themselves as they watched an old movie last night.

Mia looked at the empty pillow beside her. Where was Natalie?

The high heels she'd kicked off beside the bed last night were gone.

CHAPTER 68

$\mathcal{M}$ia made her way through the house. She peeked into spare bedrooms and found other guests. Their limbs tangled, sprawled, naked, and still passed out, but there wasn't any sign of Natalie. As was always the case after a Beaumar party, the house was littered with empty glasses, wine bottles, and discarded plates. Professional cleaners would be scheduled to arrive later in the day, giving all the guests who had passed out in rooms and on couches the opportunity to make their exits discretely.

Mia made her way outside. It was cold, and the frost on the lawn sparkled in the morning sun. When she reached the tent, Mia pushed one of the heavy canvas flaps to the side and entered. She stood in the center, where she'd seen Raphael last night, and scanned the interior. Without all the people, lights, and activity, the circus tent seemed smaller, and it was colder. If Natalie had stayed out here all night, she would have frozen.

The worry Mia felt grew into dread. Natalie had been

right beside her last night. Where was she now? Where could she have gone? Mia thought about Natalie, dressed and ready for a party. So confident this was how her life would change for the better. So disappointed when Mia dragged her away. The look of pure longing on her face as she stood at Mia's window and stared down at all the lights and people below them.

Natalie had left; Mia knew it for sure. Last night, she had waited for Mia to pass out, and then she put her heels back on and came down to the party anyway. Mia's dread spread through her stomach and up her spine. At the center of the circus tent, she turned in a circle and tried not to imagine what would have kept Natalie from returning to the room once the party was over.

Mia left the tent and was about to head back to the house when something on the trail to the beach caught her eye. She pulled her flannel closed against the chilled air and went to see what it was. When she was twenty feet away, she recognized it.

It was one of Natalie's heels.

Mia ran, scooped up the heel, and shouted, "Natalie!" She scanned the dense trees on either side of the path, looking for her friend or some other sign she was here—or had been. Mia kept shouting Natalie's name all the way down the path until it opened up to the beach.

Mia saw her.

Her red sequin dress shimmered in the sun.

Natalie sat facing the ocean, her arms wrapped around her bare legs pulled tight against her chest. Her hair hung loose and tangled down her back. "Natalie!" Mia yelled again as she ran through the sand.

But Natalie didn't move or acknowledge she had heard Mia in any way. When she reached Natalie, Mia saw that her black eyeliner and mascara had run down her stark white face. "Natalie," Mia said again as she reached to touch her.

Natalie jerked away, as if terrified. Then she turned her head slowly to meet Mia's gaze. Her eyes, the light was gone, and she stared at Mia as if she didn't know her. As if she didn't know herself.

Mia saw the red dress was ripped, Natalie's neck was bruised, and her lips were swollen and caked with dried blood. "Are you okay?" Mia asked, unable to stop her own tears from coming.

Natalie shook her head once, then returned her gaze to the ocean.

CHAPTER 69

*W*hen Holly reached the end of the hall on the third floor, she saw the door was wide open. The broken lock and a sledgehammer lay discarded on the floor.

Holly rushed through the door and took the stairs two at a time. When she reached the top, she saw her. Mia stood in the center of her old bedroom, blank-faced and staring into the eyes of the portraits she had created years ago.

"Mia?" Holly asked.

"It was my fault."

Holly hesitated for a second, still hoping that maybe Mia hadn't really remembered everything. There may still be a chance to avoid all the truth in this room. But the look in Mia's eyes told Holly it was far too late. Holly saw the same fear and guilt—the anguish Mia had carried in those months leading up to Raphael's death.

"It was not your fault," Holly said.

"I should have told her. I could have saved her. I knew. I knew, and I didn't say anything."

"You were a child, Mia. You cannot blame a child for what happened."

Mia closed her eyes and shook her head. "Do you remember when he made me move to this room?" Mia asked.

"Of course, I remember," Holly whispered. "It was the day after our twelfth birthday."

Mia turned and faced Holly. "He said we were too old to still share a bedroom and that *young women* needed their own space. And then, even though this house was full of bedrooms, he made me move into the attic."

Holly watched her sister. She couldn't imagine what it must feel like to have it all come rushing back at once.

"That first night, I was scared to sleep up here alone. And then, when he started…when he would come, late at night… I was terrified. All the time. I never wanted to come home from school. I would have lived there all year if they had let me." Mia clenched and unclenched her fists. "Over holidays, I prayed he'd be away on location. I used to wish he would have a terrible accident and die. Sometimes, I would lie there and wonder why me." Mia looked Holly in the eye. "We were identical. Why me and not you?"

Holly shook her head. "I don't know. I think…you were so much like Sasha back then. So bold and outspoken. I was always more like Everly. Quiet, reserved, never wanting to rock the boat. I think, maybe, he wanted to break you. It was always about power, and he was the only one allowed to have any."

"Why didn't you tell me we were twins? Why hide that from me?"

Holly closed her eyes. Of all the truths, this was the hardest for her to admit to her sister. "We were so close. Do you remember that? Before Raphael…. Sometimes it's hard to watch Sasha and Everly together. They remind me so much of us." Holly took a deep breath and looked her sister in the eye. "When he separated us, I was devastated. I couldn't understand it. I didn't know how to be away from you. A few nights after you had moved, I couldn't sleep. So, I snuck out of bed. I was going to sleep with you anyway."

Mia now closed her own eyes. "You saw him."

Holly nodded. "I saw. And instead of doing anything, saying anything…I turned away. For years, I would hear him pass by my room on his way to yours." Holly shook her head and tried to swallow back the grief and guilt she had carried her whole life. "I knew what was happening to you and did nothing to help you. And still, even though I was never there for you when you needed me the most, you protected me." Holly wiped the tears from her face. "Those first weeks and months, when you were still in the hospital, the guilt I felt. I didn't think I could ever forgive myself. But you needed me, a better me, a stronger me. As your twin, I failed you in the worst way imaginable. I guess I thought if I could be your older sister now, your protector… I couldn't change the past, but I could try and right your future."

Mia nodded, then strode toward the portraits. She scanned each one as if looking for something or someone. Halfway through a stack propped against the far wall, she stopped. Holly watched as she pulled out a painting of a girl in a red dress sitting on a beach, facing the ocean. Mia looked at it for several seconds before she turned the picture around.

All the other paintings had unfinished canvas backings, but this one, Holly noticed, had paper stapled to its back.

Mia took hold of a loose end near the top and ripped a large tear. She then reached into the painting and pulled out an envelope hidden inside.

She placed the painting back on the floor and held the yellowed envelope in both hands. "She never came back to school." Mia looked into Holly's eyes. "After what happened at that party, Natalie never returned to Riverside."

"I know," Holly whispered.

"She sent me this letter in July." Mia walked across the floor and held the envelope out for Holly to take. "Right before..."

Holly took the envelope from her sister but didn't open it.

"She was so bright and talented and kind. And he *took* all of that from her. He preyed on her and used her. The way he preyed on and used all of them." Mia said, her voice breaking.

Holly watched the tears roll down her sister's face.

"And me," she whispered. "He *took* everything from me. He stole my body, my innocence, my childhood. And then, when I ended up pregnant, at fifteen, they sent me away to a home for girls to give birth to a baby that he—and they lied." Mia cried and shook her head as she finally spoke out loud every horrible detail. "He lied. And Pixlie—" Mia gasped at these words. "She said she didn't believe me. She said...she said it was *my* fault. Blamed me. Called me a whore. But she *knew* what was going on. She *knew* what he was. It's why she never came up those fucking stairs. It's why she still doesn't come up those stairs. She turned a blind eye...to her own daughter. I was twelve years old."

Mia's anguish was too much to bear. Holly couldn't stop her own tears now. "Oh, Mia. I've tried so hard to keep all this from you. I never wanted you to remember."

Mia stared at Holly for several seconds, then wiped her tears away. "Open the letter," she said.

Holly stared down at the envelope. There was no return address, but Mia's name and the Beaumar address were written in a neat, looping script. Holly pulled up the torn flap and pulled out a piece of paper folded into thirds. When she unfolded it, she saw the page contained only three hand-written words.

It was Raphael.

Holly looked up and met her sister's eyes.

"Natalie sent me that letter…and then hung herself in her bedroom closet. If I had told her the truth about what had happened to me. Or never brought her here in the first place…."

"Mia—"

"And even after that. After all he had done to me, Natalie, and all those other girls, I couldn't *say* anything. I couldn't *do* anything." She shook her head. "Not until I saw him…not until that night, and I saw him in your room," Mia finished in a whisper. "And I knew…I just couldn't. I *wouldn't* let him hurt you, too. I went to the library, took a gun from the desk drawer, came back upstairs, and I shot him, Holly. I killed him. For what he did to Natalie. And me. And every other woman and girl that he hurt over the years. I killed him, and then I tried to kill myself. I wasn't pushed. There was never any attack. I *jumped* from that banister."

Holly refolded the letter, placed it inside the envelope, and looked directly into her sister's eyes. "I know, Mia. I have always known. And now," Holly whispered. "I want you to promise me you will never, ever say those words out loud to another person for the rest of your life."

CHAPTER 70

*E*ight Months Later

Mia stretched her bare legs out across her pool lounger and felt the warmth of the mid-June sun on her face.

"I love your suit," Dominique said. "Is it new?"

"Yes," Mia smiled. "It's the first bathing suit I've bought in years."

"Well, it's beautiful and completely suits you."

"Thank you," Mia said as she pulled the bottle of Chardonnay from the ice bucket between them and refilled their glasses. All three kids laughed in the pool as they took turns crawling onto the floating loungers and jumping into the pool.

Dominique took a sip of her wine and turned a page of the manuscript she was reading. It was the latest draft of Mia's book, *Once Upon a Lie: Growing Up in the Renaud Family.*

Dominique gasped. "Mia."

"Yes?"

"This is...raw."

"I know."

"And honestly, kind of hard to read," Dominique added.

"I know. But it was also hard to live, so I don't feel I should sugarcoat it."

Dominique nodded. "This is going to change everything. His legacy will be destroyed. And Pixlie." Dominique shook her head with disdain. "I don't understand how, as a mother, you don't do anything about this. I mean...it was happening right under her nose. How could she not have known?"

"She didn't want to know. Knowing would mean having to do something about it. Change everything. Her way of life. Her place in society. She was completely dependent on him in so many ways. I'm not saying I forgive her because I don't, and I don't think I ever will. But writing that, and trying to understand, at least got me to a place of wrapping my head around why she didn't help me. Or any of those women."

"Have you spoken to her since your memory came back?"

"No."

"Does she know this is happening?" Dominique asked as she raised the manuscript.

"I don't know for sure. But I doubt it."

"Well, it's going to blindside her," Dominique said.

"Maybe. But between living in the past, the drinking, and the pills, she's so out of it most of the time it's hard to know how present she ever is, really."

Dominique flipped through the pages she had left. "Caleb and I have to get going. He has karate in an hour. Are you sure I can't take this with me and finish tonight? I promise I won't let another living soul see it. Not even my own husband."

Mia laughed. "Sorry. Strict orders from my publisher. It can't leave my house. I wasn't even supposed to let anyone else read it. But you've been so supportive, such a truly wonderful friend as I have worked through all this." Mia pointed at the book. "Plus, the separation from Alexander, filing for divorce. Honestly, I don't know what I would have done without you. Thank you."

"You know, if you really want to thank me, you could let me take this home tonight and finish it."

Mia laughed and shook her head.

"Okay, well, at least tell me. Do you speculate about who Raphael's killer could have been? Reveal any details about what you remember about that night?"

Mia took a drink from her Chardonnay, returned her glass to the table between them, and looked her friend in the eye. "No, but honestly, I couldn't. I still don't remember what happened the night he died. I do mention in the book that Raphael had hurt enough people throughout his life—any number of people could have wanted him dead."

"True." Dominique handed the manuscript over to Mia. "But you've made so much progress over this past year. I suppose there's always hope you'll remember who your attacker was, and that justice will be served."

Mia nodded. "Maybe someday."

CHAPTER 71

*H*olly came in the front door and up the stairs as Mia finished tucking the girls into bed. "Is it too late to say goodnight," she asked as she peeked around the edge of their bedroom door.

"Aunt Holly!" Both girls yelled and started jumping on their beds.

"Do you have pictures?" Everly asked.

"Yes!" Sasha added. "How is Stevie?"

Holly pulled her phone from her back pocket and scrolled through several recent text messages from Tabatha Pines, the dog trainer who had taken Stevie on and was working to rehabilitate him. "Here," Holly said as she held out her phone. "See for yourself."

It was a short video. In it, Stevie was running and playing with two other dogs. "Tabatha says he's still not completely ready to find his forever home, and he will need to go somewhere where they don't have little kids, and they understand his particular needs, but he's doing really well. He has dog friends now."

Both girls smiled at this and flopped into their respective beds. "I always knew he was a good dog," Everly said, despite still having a small scar on her hand from when he'd tried to bite her.

Mia and Holly kissed both the girls goodnight and closed their door.

"Thank you for coming," Mia said and led the way to the room that had been Alexander's office—and was now hers.

"Of course, it's no problem. How are they doing, by the way? With the separation and everything?"

"Pretty okay, I think. Sometimes there are still tears. Or they'll ask if we've changed our minds and are going to live together again. But I think, as time passes, they're adjusting to spending time with Alexander at his place in the city and starting to enjoy it. He takes them to all their favorite restaurants and parks, and they always come home stained in ice cream." Mia shrugged. "He's still adjusting, too...we all are."

Holly nodded. "And have you told them about Abigail yet? That she's your daughter too?"

"Not yet. Both Abigail and I are still getting to know each other. Adjusting to even being in each other's lives. The girls met her. We all went for lunch in the city together. But we told them we were just friends. Which is true enough for now. We decided to take it slow, for everyone's sake."

"That's smart."

Mia flicked on the lights and illuminated the office. "I asked you to come because there's something I need you to know."

Mia removed the painting she had hung on the wall. It

was Natalie on the beach, in her red dress, facing the ocean. Behind it, Mia had a wall safe installed. She spun the dial through the combination and opened the door. She reached in, pulled out a slim stack of pages, and faced her sister.

Mia handed Holly the pages. "My book is being released in six months. I know you're not thrilled and think I should let the past stay in the past. But this is important to me. The world needs to know who Raphael Renaud really was. The damage he did. The people he hurt and the lives he traumatized. He doesn't deserve to keep the legacy he has."

Holly held the pages and sighed. "I know. And I realize this is important to you. I just worry about the *whole* truth coming out. I'm worried about you, Mia, not him or the family name."

Mia nodded. "That is what those pages are."

Holly looked down at what she held.

"That is the whole truth. The final chapter of my book details the extent of my personal abuse, the existence of Abigail Byron, and the fact that I'm the one that shot and killed Raphael before attempting to take my own life nineteen years ago."

"Mia," Holly breathed and shook her head. "What are you thinking?" She shook the pages. "The fact that this even exists—it's a confession. This could ruin—"

"I'm not publishing this part." Mia pulled the pages from Holly's hands and returned them to the safe. "At least, not yet. The book discloses the fact that Raphael abused and raped me, along with other girls and women. But the pregnancy and Abigail...the murder." Mia closed the safe and locked it. "That chapter will only be released and added to an edition of the book to be published after my death. And on the condition that Sasha, Everly, and Abigail agree."

Holly still looked concerned. "It still seems dangerous to me. The fact it even exists."

Mia replaced the painting over the safe. "The truth can be dangerous. It can hurt us and twist us and completely upend our lives. But without it, it's impossible to make sense of who we really are. I don't want to pretend or hide who or what I am anymore. I want to learn to live with the woman I have become—make peace with the events that shaped me. Even if that means taking responsibility for the acts I have committed."

"He deserved what happened to him, Mia. You know that, right?"

Mia shrugged. "Maybe. I think some might argue that rotting in a jail cell might have been justice better served."

"Like that would have ever happened to someone like him. Especially back then."

"Who can say," Mia whispered. "But in my heart, I know I did what I thought I needed to at the time. And I also know…the only thing I regret is keeping silent for as long as I did."

THANK YOU READER

If you enjoyed reading *Once Upon a Lie*, please leave a review. Reader reviews and recommendations are the #1 most effective resource authors have to help reach more readers.

I hope you'll also join my Facebook group: Rebecca Taylor's Reading Room. It's a place for you and fellow readers to gather and discuss my books.

And speaking of my other books, you can find a complete list of titles by me on my website along with links to your favorite store. Please visit rebeccataylorbooks.com.

Would you like to receive my monthly newsletter with updates about my current projects, travels, and life in general? If so, use the QR code below and please sign up today! I value my reader's trust and NEVER share your personal email information with anyone.

And finally, if you'd like to drop me an email, or share a picture of yourself and/or your pet reading one of my books, feel free to email me directly at readers@rrtaylor.com If you give me your permission, I may feature your photo either in my newsletter or on my social media sites.

Facebook: RebeccaTaylorPage
Instagram: RebeccaTaylorBooks
www.rebeccataylorbooks.com

I would also like to give a very special thank you to my dear friend, Jill Arnhold, who was the first to read this book. Thank you for your time, your attention to detail, and for being such an amazing friend.

www.ingramcontent.com/pod-product-compliance
Lightning Source LLC
Chambersburg PA
CBHW050108120726
47904CB00004B/1269